Seven Tears in the Sea

Seven Tears in the Sea

Adrienne Moore

Published by Adrienne Moore / Aquarian Answers
Hillsborough, North Carolina, United States of America
http://aquariananswers.com

Seven Tears in the Sea / Adrienne Moore
ISBN (print): 979-8-9880755-9-2
ISBN (e-book): 979-8-9880755-8-5

Library of Congress Control Number: 2023905578

For my grandmother,

Ella Murdoch Miller Moore,

with deepest gratitude.

Chapter 1: Silas

October 1969 - Kearny, New Jersey

Silas's mother had told him the story every night when he was a child. After he was too old for bedtime stories, after his mother became ill and Silas was the one who came into her room and sat on the side of her bed to say good night instead of the other way around, she would sometimes ask him to tell it to her, as if asking him to recite a catechism. Like a song or a prayer whose words he had learned by rote before he could understand them, the importance of the story lay in its repetition, while its meaning often skated beneath the level of his consciousness. If anyone had asked him whether he liked it, he could not have answered. The fable was as regular and unremarkable a part of him as the decaying rubber smell of the stairwell in their run-down tenement apartment, or the act of opening a can of tuna and peeling back the sharp metal top without ever cutting himself, or his mother's tired smile and the clinging scent of lemon Pledge that he always associated with her, even long after she was too ill to go to work cleaning houses.

Once upon a time, there lived a selkie boy. His father was a great gray seal who swam the seas. His mother was a selkie too, but one without a sealskin, forever trapped on land. Without her sealskin, the boy's mother sickened and died while he was still young. She left her son a key, which opened a secret door in her closet. Inside, the boy found his sealskin. He put it on and became a great gray seal like his father. For years, he swam the seas with joyous freedom. But inside his seal's body beat a human heart, which still longed for a home on land. One day, a girl on the shore called out to his human heart. He shed his sealskin and married her, and soon she gave birth to a selkie son. The selkie loved his wife and son with all his heart, but the seal in him longed for the sea. One night, when his wife and son were sleeping, he carried his sealskin to the shore. The sea called too strongly, and he could no longer resist. But a ghostly seal spoke to him from the waves in his mother's voice, saying, "Your father made you a seal, but I raised you to be a man. Go home to your son and teach him how to be both." Released from the ocean's spell, the selkie did as his mother told him. He went home and loved his wife and raised his son to be both seal and man. In so doing, he became fully both himself, and lived a long and happy life.

*   *   *

Silas was fourteen the chilly October morning that he came back, flushed and tingling from delivering newspapers in the brisk air, and found the small, brass key at his place on the kitchen table.

The key lay at an ominously formal and deliberate angle.

Except for the key, the kitchen looked just as he'd left it the night before, the worn linoleum swept, the faded formica counters wiped clean. The kitchen was Silas's job, though it wasn't much of one these days. When his mother worked, she had come home too tired from cleaning other people's houses to clean her own. Now she hardly seemed to eat, and Silas, left to his own devices, subsisted on tuna forked straight from the can, bought with money he earned delivering papers and tutoring at school.

At the sight of the key, an icy lump of dread formed in his stomach. The fear that his mother was dying never lurked far from the surface of his thoughts, and his anxiety was made worse by the fact that she always gently refused to discuss her health. The sight of the key blew up his fear like a giant balloon, making his heart pound and sharpening all his senses. He didn't think of the story. The appearance of a mysterious key and a mother's death were associated for him in a place far deeper than reason.

How long had the key been there? Since last night? He hadn't come into the kitchen before leaving on his route.

This was foolishness. His mother was asleep in her room—of course she was.

He barged through her door with none of his usual care to avoid disturbing her, ready to hold up the key to her startled expression and demand to know why she would scare him like that.

His heart seemed to stop. She was gone, the bed empty, the covers pushed back as if she'd only just slipped out of bed for a moment.

"Mom?" he called, panicked, knowing it was futile. If she wasn't in this room, she was nowhere in the apartment.

He could not imagine her leaving. She had barely left her bed in weeks.

What if she were lying, dead or unconscious, on the far side of the bed, out of his sight?

He skirted the footboard, unable to breathe.

The floor on the far side of the bed was blameless, empty of everything but the worn, pink rug. Nothing else about the room was different. The wind-up clock on the nightstand ticked as usual. The bottle of cod-liver oil—the only medicine he'd ever seen her take—stood beside it, along with a spoon. Artwork he'd made in school, embarrassing scribbles only a mother would save, clung to the walls by means of yellowing tape and thumbtacks.

She could not have gone far.

Still clutching the key, he left the apartment to search for her. For a moment, the task steadied him. If she'd left her bed she must be feeling better? But even as he rushed down the hallway, dodging the bag of trash set out by his neighbor, Mr. Cartwright, anxiously scanning the stairwell on the three flights down, his fear rose again. He'd just been out here. He'd crisscrossed the entire neighborhood. Why hadn't he seen her? Had she crept out in the middle of the night?

He hesitated on the concrete steps of the building, looking up the street and down, shivering with anxiety more than cold. To the right were only some derelict warehouses and the marsh beyond. In spring, the marsh was pretty, all swaying green grass tips and humming insects competing with the traffic's roar, but the sulfurous smell repelled exploration. In the autumn cold, the smell subsided but the marsh stood bleak and gray, veiled in a grimy mist, a no man's land spanning the intervals between the highways that crisscrossed on concrete causeways. Silas's mother would not have gone to the marsh, he was sure, but a quiet collection of police cars and an ambulance bunched up at the corner of one of the warehouses made his breath stick in his throat.

Slowly, trembling, he walked toward the vehicles. Their numbers spoke of importance, the absence of flashing lights and sirens indicated a lack of urgency. Men in waders made a small cluster, some distance into the marsh. As Silas watched, they organized themselves around a stretcher and began to carry it toward the ambulance and solid ground. They were in no hurry. Their shoulders spoke of defeat, endurance of a demoralizing task.

As Silas approached them, he took in details of what they carried. A person, horribly still. A woman in a soaked pink dress. A tangle of long, black hair.

Not a dress. A nightgown. His mother's pink nightgown. His mother's long black hair.

Silas turned and fled. It could not be true. That could not have been his mother's bare arm, pallid and waterlogged, lying along the stretcher.

He had not seen the woman's face. He had to get away, had to hide somewhere this news could never find him. As long as he hadn't seen for sure, as long as no one came to tell him, it wasn't true—it could not be.

His feet took him blindly back inside, up the stairs, back into the silent apartment. His breath came in gasps. He wasn't crying. He knew better than to cry. He was the smallest boy in the ninth grade and he never, ever cried.

Something hurt his hand.

The key, clutched tightly in his fist.

Operating purely on myth and instinct and denial, he threw open the door to his mother's closet. Only a few worn dresses and a coat hung on the rod. He gathered them in an armful and threw them onto the bed. Behind them was nothing, only blank, scuffed wall. He knelt to clear some worn-out shoes and pocketbooks from the floor. A sheet-rocked box had been built into the wall to cover ductwork, perhaps three feet high and two feet deep. A tangle of scarves and belts covered its top. He cleared those, too, and beneath them found a heavy wooden board. He'd played in this closet many times as a kid, and had never questioned the board, which only seemed a shelf to protect the sheetrock. This time, desperate as he was for any crack, any opening in the fabric of unbearable reality, its wobble caught his attention. He pried at the board, and it lifted free.

Beneath was more wood, a kind of lid, with a keyhole in it.

Shaking, he fumbled the key into place. It fit. He had to jiggle and shake the key to turn the stiff lock. When it did turn, with a reluctant click, nothing else happened. The lid didn't lift. But when he pulled the key toward him, the lid slid with it, and an opening gaped against the wall.

Silas peered in, but his shadow blocked the light from the doorway and he could see nothing but darkness. Gingerly, he reached in, and his fingers brushed something sleek and soft.

The sensation of fur against his fingertips before he snatched them reflexively back was brief, but with it, a huge and unexpected sensation surged through him. He gasped. The feeling was—pleasure, expectation, wanting. A physical greed.

Frenzied, he plunged his hands into the soft folds and drew out

—

His sealskin.

The pelt was very heavy, its short, gray fur mottled with black. In one swift, gulping impression he registered a head and clawless flippers—something not creepily empty, as the pelt of any dead thing must be, but a beautiful secret waiting dreamily, peacefully, to be known.

A leaping exultation filled him. The current rushing through him left no room for anything but certainty, but rightness, but a promise—at long last—of wholeness. No part of Silas stood aside from the instinct that compelled him. He gathered the fur in his arms and left the apartment, not even shutting the door behind him, careening down the three flights. He leaped over all the front steps, staggered slightly under the unbalancing weight of his skin as he landed at the bottom, and took off running. He never even glanced toward the marsh. Instinct compelled him in the direction he chose, but whether he ran from the horror and grief of his mother's death, or only ran toward the sea, he never knew. The marsh, with its crisscross of highways, offered no route to the ocean, but the Passaic River, fifteen blocks away, did.

He ran, taking reckless risks at the cross streets, oblivious to the stares of morning commuters wondering at his headlong speed and the animal he seemed to be carrying. He didn't notice several cars that nearly hit him, backing out of the driveways of houses that grew bigger and finer as he crossed town. Beyond the last busy street, which he crossed through a narrow gap in traffic, ignoring the horns, lay a park. He didn't notice the maple leaves flaming in the clear, autumn morning. He didn't give a thought to the freezing temperature of the water as he reached the river at last. His hot breath steaming the cold air, he dropped his pelt briefly on the muddy bank as he shed his jeans and sweatshirt. Bending, naked, he lifted his sealskin and wrapped it around himself with movements as certain as if he'd practiced a thousand times—over his shoulders like a coat where the pelt parted down its belly, then stepping inside with one foot and the other, drawing the head over his own like a hood.

His skin tingled over his whole body as if he'd bathed in peppermint, but with all the ecstasy and none of the pain. In a beautiful blaze, he sank and dissolved, his consciousness narrowing, concentrating, all of him reaching—*reaching*—

When his awareness expanded outward once again, he lay on his belly with the water shining before him. No memory of the moments leading to this one remained. He existed entirely in his present senses. His whiskers twitched. The scent off the river warned him, even before he'd rippled and flopped his way through the rocky shallows and made a straight line of himself, rear flippers to nose, in the swiftly-moving current, how the fresh water would sting his eyes. He craved depth and darkness, the freedom of infinite space, salt and soft buoyancy. This river was meager and ungenerous, making his body heavy.

But none of that mattered. He was on his way. His nose and his powerful body working with the current would take him to the sea.

Chapter 2: Silas

July 1974 - Ocean City, New Jersey

When the fine, whole-body trembling ceased, Silas lay in total darkness, folded inside a sealskin which had separated from him.

He was human again.

He had entirely forgotten about being human. It had been a long time, he thought, casting back though his seal memories—the only ones he had possessed until a moment ago. Four winters? Five? The last time he'd been human was by the Passaic River where, driven by an all-consuming ecstatic instinct, he'd carried the pelt he'd found in his mother's closet, and put it on…

The thought of his mother landed like a blow. His grief was a predator lying in wait. He'd put on his skin and swum away from it before, safe in the blithe consciousness of a seal. But the moment he came back, it ambushed him.

Why was he back? He didn't want to be here!

He dragged the edges of his pelt closely around him, willing it to reabsorb him. His mother was dead. There was nothing and no one here for him, wherever *here* was. On land. He had no home, and no one waiting for him. He felt trapped in the worst kind of nightmare.

Seals didn't have nightmares.

His sealskin was doing nothing but smothering him. The night, like the hide enclosing him, was close and hot. He prickled with sweat. And this human body ran out of breath much too quickly.

Despairing, he threw back his pelt and rolled onto the sand. A faint stirring of air licked his damp skin. He remembered his mother's pale arm, her sodden pink nightgown, the wet tendrils of her long, black hair.

Tears gathered at the corners of his eyes and rolled down his face into his ears. He hadn't cried for her before. He'd never cried in those days, but now he did. His mother was the mother in her story, a selkie without her skin. He knew what that meant, now. She had stayed with him as long as she could, and when she got too sick, she had drowned herself in the marsh.

He opened his eyes, trying to see something—anything—other than that still, wet form on the stretcher.

The black planks of the boardwalk high above him were outlined with light cast by the security lamps that shone hazy green at intervals down the long causeway.

When he was very young, before his mother got sick, they had made the long drive from Kearny to Ocean City and spent the day on the beach. There had been a boardwalk like this one. Maybe it had *been* this one?

He sat up, taking in the same view he'd seen earlier through seal eyes. A wide expanse of beach, punctuated by life-guard stands and flocks of hotel deck chairs. The ocean beyond. The boardwalk raised high on stilt-like pillars. A street behind him, and the glowing neon lights of otherwise dark hotels and restaurants, all facing the water.

But sitting up drew his attention to the body he wore, which was not like the body he remembered. He took inventory, swiftly discovering unfamiliar quantities of wiry hair in various places it hadn't been before, and distinctly more of himself in all his dimensions—most compellingly at his crotch—than he'd possessed when he left. He'd been fourteen. At a loose guess, he was now nineteen or twenty. As a seal, he was in his prime, and had the memories of victories and conquests on the icy winter breeding grounds to show for it. As a man, he felt large and hard-muscled and well-formed, but his experience was still that of a boy who had never so much as held hands with a girl.

Now that his focus was on his bodily present, rather than the ache of his past, he was aware that the feeling that had provoked his seal self into coming here—to this hot, unappealing southern beach glaring with lights and crawling with people—had been very similar to the feeling that took him to the ice fields every winter: A belligerent urgency to rut, and to fight anything that stood in his way.

That feeling hadn't left him, but drew his hands to more exploration and a mounting sense of potential. He didn't want his hands, though. He wanted a woman.

*   *   *

By midmorning, Silas was hot, demoralized, and very, very hungry. He had filled the remaining hours of darkness burying his sealskin in the loose sand beneath some boardwalk steps, a location he was sure he could find again. He'd spotted a pair of swim trunks hanging from the second story railing of a hotel balcony, and had used a flagpole from a nearby lifeguard stand to knock them down. Close up, they'd turned out to be a hideous magenta madras in a size perilously too large for his hips, but traffic on the street had been picking up while the hotels showed increasing signs of life, and he'd been stark naked. He'd made do.

As the morning progressed and the beach and boardwalk became more crowded, Silas's preoccupation divided itself between food and women. Superficially, the humans crowding the beach and boardwalk were not so different from the seals crowding the ice field. The women here—a full variety of shapes and sizes and ages on display beneath scant coverings of swimsuits, shorts, and tank tops—were to a large degree occupied with children and guarded by other males. But Silas knew perfectly well that, human, he couldn't simply attack a smaller man and claim his woman, as a seal would do. And he remained bitterly aware that even the unclaimed girls, the bronze-skinned blonde in the string bikini sauntering down the boardwalk with two plainer girls in tow, the black-haired beauty displaying herself on a towel near a lifeguard stand, would not simply signal him with a look or a restless movement or some imperious call to come over and take what he wanted from her. At least, nothing he remembered from the teasing and abuse and even blatant necking he'd observed in the locker-lined halls at school suggested that human mating rituals were so straightforward.

The twin frustrations of lust and hunger made him reckless. With only the outlines of a plan in mind—he'd grown up poor in a rough neighborhood and knew a con or two—he walked up to a hotdog stand that had no line at this hour of the morning and ordered three dogs with everything. He didn't even like hotdogs, but his mouth watered painfully as the gray-haired vendor lined them up in front of him. It was all he could do not to grab them and run—the strategy of last resort. First, he made a show of reaching into his pocket, then searching the non-existent other pockets with mounting urgency.

"My money's missing," he informed the hotdog seller apologetically. "I had it a moment ago."

The man's face darkened. Silas turned and surveyed the boardwalk behind him, as if expecting the bills to be lying on the ground somewhere in the direction he'd come.

"I'm sorry," he said. "I hope they won't go to waste." His real hope was that the guy would give him at least one of the dogs, since with no one lined up behind him, they likely *would* go to waste.

"Oh, they will," the man growled. "Do you see anyone else ready to pay for them?"

Maybe it was just as well the guy was a jerk. Silas wouldn't have to feel as guilty about stealing from him. He glanced around one more time, plotting his escape route.

"I've got it!" a woman's voice called, and Silas turned in surprised relief.

Across the boardwalk from the hotdog stand, a girl sat at an easel, her pen suspended, her eyes fixed on Silas. She was slim and tawny with summer tan; her curly, golden-brown hair fell around her face; her long, pretty legs stretched between short shorts and sandals. In her eyes, something leaped and reached toward him, forging an instant connection with his crotch. Almost as strong as the desire crashing through him was relieved recognition. It *was* the same with humans, after all.

The next moment her face changed and she shook her head, gesturing toward another woman coming toward him with some bills in her hand. "Let me get it," the other woman said, dividing her words between Silas and the hotdog seller. She was lumpy and matronly, her brown ponytail gathered low beneath the band of her sun visor.

Silas's face felt stiff, and he feared that even his very roomy stolen shorts could not hide the situation mounting almost painfully within them. But he forced himself to smile at the older woman, and as she paid for all three hotdogs, sharing sympathetic remarks equally between Silas and the hotdog man in a steady stream of kindness, Silas's hunger and his gratitude took shape in him again. He thanked his benefactor, his growling stomach adding its own remarks, and, awkwardly gathering all three hotdogs, strode swiftly away down the boardwalk without daring to look toward the girl again. He took the first set of steps he came to down to the beach, and doubled back beneath the boardwalk, wolfing hot dogs as he went. His hunger had become a kind of desperation, and he barely tasted the food in his rush to get it to his belly.

He finished the last dog just as he found the girl. He stopped below her on the beach, keeping out of her line of sight, and studied her through the wooden railing. She was a portrait artist. Earlier he'd noticed a guy sketching caricatures, his subjects rendered as big-headed cartoon figures, but this girl was sketching likenesses in black pen. He couldn't see her easel well enough to judge whether she was good. Her current subject was an old man in a faded ball cap, and the woman who had paid for the hotdogs leaned on the railing beside his chair.

The girl glowed in the sun. Her hair glinted with golden sparks and her tan shone evenly on her long, bare arms and legs. She was graceful even sitting still. She was beautiful, but beyond that, she was *right*. She was like a puzzle piece locking into place.

He glanced down at himself for perhaps the fiftieth time since daylight had made vision possible. He stood much higher from the ground than he had last time he was human—perhaps more than a foot higher. His chest was broad and free of hair, but a black stripe of straight, dark fur began in a point just below his sternum and dove in a neat line behind the waistband of the terrible shorts. He had narrow hips, arms visibly bulked by muscle, and more straight, black fur on the backs of his forearms. The skin of his face felt thicker, and when he ran his palm along his jaw, he felt the first prickling of stubble. His hair felt about the same— thick and curly. As for his face, he would have to hope for the best. He'd been pretty as a kid, with long, thick lashes and deep-set chocolate-brown eyes. His prettiness had been a liability to an under-sized boy, but couldn't hurt this tall, broad body. Maybe it was even the reason the girl had looked at him that way.

With new confidence, he returned along the boardwalk, suspense yielding to relief as he glimpsed the girl again just where he'd left her. She had new subjects now, two little blonde girls squirming in the chair they shared while their mother admonished them to sit still. Silas approached from behind and was impressed at how well the girl had captured her models in only a few swift lines. Fascinated, he came closer than he'd intended and his shadow fell on her paper. She turned her head and saw him.

Again, that leap as her eyes met his. Again, that swift jolt of arousal.

She looked back to her sketch and continued without a word. He stepped closer to the back of her chair, hoping to hide the stirring in his pants. The little girls started pushing each other and tumbled onto the boardwalk. The smiling mother handed over a five dollar bill for the sketch finished just in time, and the trio left Silas and the girl alone together.

Neither of them spoke. Silas continued to stand behind her. Self-consciously, she rearranged her pens, and adjusted the elastic band anchoring her drawing sheet against the breeze.

They spotted the scowling woman dragging a whining three-year-old boy toward them at the same time, her progress further hampered by the toddler settled on her hip. The girl gestured quickly to the chair and said, "Sit down," with an urgency that Silas was already moving to obey before he thought to say, "I can't pay you."

"I know. But that won't go well." She flicked her eyes discreetly toward the woman, who stopped short as Silas settled into the canvas director's chair. The woman didn't bother keeping her voice down as she complained to the struggling boy, "Now, look! You made us miss our chance."

"Do you mind?" the girl asked, her pen poised at the easel, and Silas shook his head. She began to draw, her eyes flicking from Silas to her page and back again.

"What's your name?" she asked, and when he told her she answered, "I'm Sandra."

She drew in silence for a while, with an impersonal, steady concentration that Silas quickly welcomed as it let him watch her as fully as he liked.

She was so beautiful. Her lips were full and pink, and her eyes were a hazy shade of green. A constellation of freckles dotted the bridge of her nose. He hungered to touch every part of her—the curving shell of her ear, the graceful angle where her neck met her shoulder, the perfect twin mounds of her breasts under her T-shirt, the plane of her hip through the crinkled seersucker of her shorts.

All of that beauty made him want to—*touch* didn't really capture it. *Taste* was closer. Or *consume*.

Her skin grew flushed under his gaze in a way that seemed to have nothing to do with the sun, mitigated now by a steady breeze off the ocean. He understood, with a fascination that was not quite surprise, that she was as tense and heated by his presence as he was by hers.

His stomach growled so loudly that it startled them both. He put his hand over it.

"Are you okay?" she asked. "Too many hot dogs?"

Her concern touched him. "Too few," he answered, dismayed to discover this truth. "I'm still starving."

She gave him a worried frown. "If I give you lunch, will you let me finish my drawing?"

Silas was nearly as desperate with hunger as he was with lust, but he hesitated. "I shouldn't take your lunch."

"I have enough to share. Not here. Back at my place."

Silas could only nod, astonished and gratified. Already, the girl was taking him home.

She folded her easel into a carrying case that held her pens at the center. Silas offered to carry the chairs, but she glanced over at the hotdog stand and said, "Clyde will keep an eye on them until I get back."

"He's a friend of yours?" Silas eyed the grumpy old guy dubiously.

Sandra smiled. "He looks out for me."

Silas carried the easel and walked beside her as they left the boardwalk, passed between a restaurant and a movie theater, and continued down several residential blocks that grew progressively shabbier with distance from the beach. Sandra seemed tiny beside him. He shortened his stride so he wouldn't outpace her and glanced down at the top of her head, noticing the haphazard parting of her wavy hair. The novelty of being large, the knowledge of his own physical power, the desire to protect her in her smallness—all mingled with an urgent physical longing that muddled his thoughts. Of course he knew how seals managed this feeling, but surely human, he could not just flatten her beneath him and satisfy himself. He hoped to goodness she knew how it was done, and would show him.

She stopped at a flaking, mustard-yellow door. He noticed that her hands shook a little as she unlocked it with a key from her pocket. She opened the door and gestured him in ahead of her. Stairs led upward. He took them two at a time. The stairwell smelled musty.

She unlocked another door at the first landing—two deadbolts, this time—and again gestured him inside. They stood in a small entryway. The apartment was small and sparsely furnished. She took the easel from him and their hands brushed.

The contact with her skin, warm and brief, made his wanting rear up like a forest fire. His sight went dark with a vision of wrapping her in his arms and shucking off her shorts and sinking into her like a man in flames plunging into a lake.

When he could see again, he found that she had moved past him with the easel and gone into the kitchen. He followed her.

"I hope you like tuna?" she asked, pointing him to a chair at a spindly table.

"I love tuna," he said. Once his mother got too sick to cook, he had practically lived on it.

Very few more words passed between them. She moved around the clean, shabby kitchen, which, with its peeling linoleum and the pattern wearing off its formica counters, reminded Silas with an odd combination of comfort and distress of his old kitchen at home. She put a bowl of tuna salad and a roll of Ritz crackers and a plate of orange slices in front of him, followed by a glass and a plastic pitcher of ice water. Then she pulled a second chair away from the table and unfolded her easel, not setting it up but settling with her drawing board on her lap and beginning with a fresh sheet.

He ate steadily and silently, the tuna finally seeming to touch his hunger in a way the hotdogs hadn't. Made into salad, the familiar staple was a luxury to him. Sandra's pen made small, scraping noises in the quiet room, and this time he was aware of her eyes, her hand tracing the details of his body onto the page as if each glance, each pen stroke were her touch. He ate until everything in front of him was gone, and he didn't look at her, but he was as minutely aware of her body, her presence, her breath, as if he lay with his eyes closed while she ran her fingers over him. He couldn't see her drawing, didn't know if she had chosen to sketch the way his dick was mounding his trunks. He didn't try to hide himself from her. Why should he? All of him was hers.

At last she said, "You're finished," putting down her drawing pad and standing. "Do you need— I could—"

He shook his head, standing, too.

Their eyes met. Whatever she had been about to say evaporated. She took a few dreamlike steps toward him and, reaching out, unsnapped his trunks. When she let go, they fell to the floor.

For a moment they both stood, not touching, looking down at his erection, which was thick and veined, its tip a sculpted, dusky rose—a great deal larger and more serious than he remembered it. She extended elegant fingers and took it in her hand.

He made no conscious choice in freeing her somehow from her clothes, in how to touch and taste her lips, her tongue, her white breasts skirted by her tan, her tight pink nipples, the warm planes of her body and the heated, silken place he found beneath her panties. She pressed herself into his hands, trembling and shuddering and giving gasping little cries as he touched her. He lifted her to the counter, parted her legs, and found his place in her. With that rightness he became entirely lost to motion. The glory that built and gathered in his thighs, his back, his butt, soon exploded in ecstasy deep inside her.

He put his arms around her and drew her close, his eyes closed, his mind blank with arrival, astonishment, completion. The release and satisfaction this moment had always brought him as a seal had not prepared him on any level for the gorgeousness he'd just experienced. The difference was that of bread from chocolate.

He felt that she had stiffened and gone still at some point, and feared he must have hurt her after all. He moved gently now, against and in her, a sort of query. Words were entirely beyond him. She softened and then tensed against him in a new way. Encouraged, he drew her closer, his position in her precarious now, and tasted the salt of her bare shoulder with his tongue. She seemed to turn a corner in his arms, and again her breath came in a series of crying gasps. A rippling spasm drove him out of her. He looked at her face.

Her eyes were closed. A softness at the edges of her mouth might have been the ghost of a smile.

"Are you okay?" he whispered.

"Oh..." She sighed. "Yes..."

Tenderly, he gathered her off the counter and held her. She was heavy, but not too heavy for him to carry, and suddenly all he wanted was to rest with her in his arms. He carried her through the living room toward an open bedroom door, but she said, "The other one," and pointed him toward a second, closed door that he hadn't noticed.

Her room was small and makeshift, her bed a neatly-made mattress on the floor, her clothes in stacked egg crates, some books and drawing pads on shelves made of boards and bricks. But the walls were covered in beauty—a patchwork of drawings and paintings and collages in many styles and mediums, held with thumbtacks. He didn't take time to study them, just tumbled awkwardly with her onto the bed. She didn't protest when he settled on his side and drew her close. Their bodies were a little sticky in the hot, still air of the apartment, but her skin was so smooth and her hair smelled so good—the same flowery smell as her pillow—and he felt dazed and stupefied with contentment.

In his mother's story, a human girl had called to the selkie boy as he swam as a seal, and he'd come ashore and put off his selkie skin to marry her. They'd had a son. Was this happening now? Was the rest of his mother's story coming true?

He wasn't aware of giving in to sleep, only of the blissful state of relaxation, the hopeful flicker of belonging on which he drifted off. He woke when she moved out of his arms. His eyes opened to the sight of her back, which gave a quiver as she sat facing away from him on the edge of the mattress. She sniffed, and he realized with pity and alarm that she was crying.

"What's wrong?" he asked.

She sobbed quietly a couple of times before she answered, and when she did, her voice was thin and small. "I have a boyfriend. I was waiting to—with him. I don't know why I did that with you. I love him."

Silas sat up, struggling to take in her words. "But—*I* would marry you," he said.

Sandra looked over her shoulder at him with a combination of surprise and scorn. "You can't. Rick has the ring and everything. I saw it in his drawer last week. We don't even *know* each other!"

"But," Silas said, and stopped, unable to explain. They'd been as close as any two people could be. Surely that was more important than the kind of knowing she'd meant. She'd said herself that she'd been waiting…

Not meeting his eyes, she said, "I want you to go."

A kind of stillness took up sudden residence in him. He had learned from the bullies at school to hide any sign of pain or weakness. He couldn't afford to feel right now. Instead, he stood without a word, put on his pants in the kitchen, and left the apartment. He imagined her still sitting on the bed, an unmoving statue, as he thudded down the musty stairs.

The mustard-yellow door slammed behind him and he stood, smarting and dismayed, in heat and sunshine. The street looked unfamiliar to him—he had registered no landmarks on his way here. But as he hesitated, he became aware of a threadlike tug that told him the way back to his pelt, and to the sea. That was useful. He began to follow it, the sidewalk burning the soles of his bare feet. He didn't hurry. An instinctive certainty told him that his pelt would have him back now, but he had many hours to endure until dark when he could change unseen. Whatever had stood in the way before was gone. Maybe it was what he'd done with Sandra. Maybe he'd just needed to eat before he could change again. Whatever it was, it was done.

He wondered fleetingly if his mother's ghost would appear to stop him. That's what had happened in the story, when the sea had called too strongly to the selkie and he'd tried to leave his wife and son. Maybe his mother's ghost would try to send him back to Sandra. He hoped so. He longed to see his mother again. He had a lot of questions for her.

But he knew the story wasn't real after all. He'd been an idiot, believing in a fairy tale like that, even for a moment. There was no plan, no set of rules, no person in the world who needed anything from him or cared what happened to him.

He was all alone.

Chapter 3: Silas

March 1975 - Ocracoke Island, North Carolina

When Silas found himself once again human, shaken loose inside his sealskin, in broad daylight on a beach that he felt certain, from the remembered uneasiness he'd experienced as a seal, was well out of normal range for a creature like him, his feelings could only be expressed in curse words. He threw back his pelt and faced the inland side of a high, white barrier dune, where he lay screened by a surrounding patch of sea oats and flanked by a dense tangle of low, waxy-leaved bushes. Having made sure he was unseen, he pounded his fist in the sand and said the ugliest words he could think of.

He had no idea what he was doing here. He'd been compelled by no instinct he recognized, one that ran counter to all his usual seal habits. He wondered how far south he was. Virginia? Florida? The temperature here was balmy enough, the breeze blocked by the dunes. It was morning, the sun still fairly low over the ocean. The pale, thin green of the sea oats and dune grasses told him the season was early spring.

Not much time had gone by since his last human appearance. Only one season at the ice fields. He'd molted his winter coat on the way here, forced to haul out and endure the miserable itchy-skinned, hungry time alone on some strange beach, far from the usual spot and the companionable gathering of bulls that he was used to.

Human again, only bad experiences flooded his memories. His mother's death returned to him with all the sharpness of fresh grief. His bewildered pain at Sandra's dismissal far outweighed his memory of the pleasure he'd—shared?—with her.

He was a bit hungry, but felt certain he was miles from any sort of town. With no civilization in sight, both food and clothing would be damned hard to come by.

Hiding his sealskin was a simple matter of thrusting it against the steep side of the dune and letting the loose, dry sand tumble down to cover it. He couldn't leave it here, of course. His seal tracks led straight to it, and no other landmarks set the spot apart. But he needed to scope out the beach on the other side of the dunes, and he didn't want to carry his skin or leave it unhidden while he looked around.

He scrambled up the saddle between two dunes. The sight that met him as he overlooked the otherwise empty expanse of shining beige sand edging a fractious sea, shocked him like a blow to the chest.

A woman just below him on the beach, facing him as if she were following the tracks he'd made, dropped forward onto her hands and knees with a gasp, just as he spotted her. Her curly gold-brown hair fell to obscure her face, but not before he'd recognized her. It was Sandra. And she was hugely pregnant.

The coincidence was too great. This had to be a second chance, fate insisting that they were truly meant for one another. This time, she would have to see it.

Especially if she were pregnant with his selkie son.

She crouched on the sand, moaning. She hadn't even noticed him.

He scrambled down to her, feeling oddly calm and focused, even though every rational thought in his mind told him he could be of no help to her except by running—*away* from her—to get help. Because she was either very ill, or she was about to give birth, and either way, he had no idea what to do for her.

He knelt in front of her and put his hands on her shoulders. She was groaning loud, rhythmic groans—sounding not so much helpless with pain as purposeful. Her voice seemed to give wordless shape to the effort within her. He'd watched quite a few seal births, and had no doubt that he was now witnessing a human one.

She looked at him when he touched her, but seemed to have to come back a long way behind her eyes before she said, "What are *you* doing here? I need Rick."

Immediately she curled in on herself, forehead nearly touching the sand, and yelled at the top of her lungs.

Her husband? She had married *the boyfriend? Why did she have to keep making this so difficult? His mother's story had been so simple.*

He had no desire to meet the husband. Perhaps that's why he felt unable to leave her side.

"Go get Rick!" she begged him again, when she could speak.

The feeling that gripped him was like stubbornness, only it seemed to come from outside him rather than from within—or at least, from somewhere impossible to argue with. He couldn't explain to Sandra and didn't try. Anyway, she was yelling again.

Silas pulled up her skirt, not for any reason except that it needed to be done. Her thighs were streaked with blood, but only a little. Her panties were soaked and he started to remove them. Unexpectedly, she struggled to help him, working them under her knees and pulling the dress over her head. Now she was as naked as he was.

Appalled and fascinated, Silas studied her as she crouched on the sand. Her belly was a huge, tight ball. Her breasts were fully twice as large as he remembered them.

"Help me up," she panted. Her breath came in odd, animal grunts now.

Silas had no idea what she meant, but she put her arms around his neck and hung on with a vise grip, and somehow he ended up standing with his legs planted wide and firm in the sand while she hung between them from his neck, making guttural growling sounds against his chest. He reached between their thighs and under her to check for the baby. At first, all he felt was heat and slime, but with the next growl something smooth and firm moved unmistakably against his palm.

Holy shit. That was the baby's head.

He thought he should hold onto Sandra, but if he moved his hands the baby would just fall onto the ground. And Sandra was doing a good job of holding on. Her whole weight seemed to hang from his neck. He planted his feet even more determinedly and kept his hands where they were.

She grew quieter, the effort seeming to take all her breath. He felt the head move into his hands as she bore down, then retreat as she sucked in air. He cheered for her, excited, encouraging her.

Another surge and he held a hemisphere. Another and he felt an ear.

"Come on, you can do it," he told her, as if she were a baseball team, and the next moment a hot, slick bundle slid into his hands.

With a startled cry, Sandra let go of his neck and fell backward onto the sand. Not dropping the baby took all of Silas's determination. It was so slippery! But he held on, and a moment later, Sandra reached out and took it from him, just as it gave a loud wail.

The baby had a shock of black hair, was streaked with blood and white, waxy stuff, and after the first, indignant cry, quieted and seemed to look around with grave startlement through wide, hazy-colored eyes.

"It's a girl," Silas noted, somewhat dazed.

Was this yet another mistake? The story had promised him a son.

But then again, he was starting to wonder if this was his story after all. Or rather, he was starting to hope it wasn't.

The umbilicus snaked from the baby's belly into Sandra. The sight of it disturbed him, and he looked away. Wasn't there something about cutting it? But with what?

Teeth, an unwelcome thought nudged. He decided to ignore it.

"Hello, little one," Sandra cooed to the baby. She looked at Silas with a shining face. "This is Alise!"

"Alise," Silas repeated, bending close, entranced the longer he looked by her tiny feet and miniature toes, her little curled fingers with their shell-like nails. "She's perfect," he murmured.

"I need Rick," Sandra said plaintively. "He's back at the hotel." She cast about her and found her dress, extracting a bundle of keys with some effort from a pocket and handing them to Silas before wrapping the dress very carefully around the baby. "The car is that way," gesturing down the beach. "Could you go get him? Please?"

She was much more polite now that she was not giving birth. He wished he could help her.

"I can't drive," he said. That was a convenient excuse. It was true that he'd never taken the class or learned how, but he could have driven a car far more readily in that moment than he could have left Sandra's side. Was it because of the baby? *Was* the baby his?

She didn't look like him, as far as he could see. She was small and red and looked like a baby.

"Could you go find someone who can, then?" Sandra was exasperated. "And don't you have any clothes? Don't you *ever* have any clothes?"

Sandra wasn't wearing any either, but Silas decided not to point this out. Instead he asked, "When did you get married?"

She tossed her head. "Last fall."

Silas could tell he was irritating her. "I'll go get help soon," he promised. "I just need to look at her a little longer."

Sandra softened, tilting the baby toward him a little. "Isn't she amazing?"

Silas nodded, smiling, stroking the baby's impossibly soft red cheek with one gentle finger. "She's a miracle."

Suddenly Sandra shifted and gasped, and then started to cry. "Oh, what happened? I need help. I asked you to go!"

"What's wrong?" Silas asked, looking at her anxiously, and saw that a shockingly large, bloody mass had emerged from her onto the sand between her thighs. The umbilicus was attached to it. Also, a small tuft of pale fur poked out from between its bloody, fleshy folds.

Silas reached out and snatched at the fur before he'd consciously considered the matter. Somehow, he was not surprised to discover that he held a miniature sealskin—pure white, damp, and blood-streaked.

That settled it, didn't it? If the baby was a selkie, she *was* his. She had to be.

Sandra hadn't noticed him take it. She was hunched around the baby, still crying.

"It's okay," Silas said gently. "I'm pretty sure that's supposed to happen. I'll go get help now, okay? Don't cry…"

He patted her shoulder a little helplessly.

Sandra drew a shaky breath. "Rick Miller," she said. "The White Sands Hotel. He's going to kill me."

"Why?" Silas asked, suddenly anxious.

She said, "He didn't want me walking on the beach by myself. I *swore* this wasn't going to happen."

Silas surprised himself by laughing. "Oops…"

"Please go. You really can't drive?"

"I'll find someone," Silas promised. Impulsively, he bent close to Sandra's breasts and kissed tiny Alise, who was making smacking motions with her little rosebud lips, on the forehead. "Bye, kiddo," he said, swept with tenderness. "Be good."

He set off down the beach at a lope and had not gone far at all when he spotted a silver-haired couple, a man and a woman, coming toward him. Holding the little sealskin in front of his groin with one hand and waving them down with the other, he pointed down the beach at Sandra, small in the distance but visible. They stood their ground warily and allowed him to get close enough to shout, "She had a baby! Just now!"

After that they were all swift action. "Give me your jacket," the woman said to her husband. "I'll go sit with her while you take this young man into town. Give him your swim trunks that are in the car. Bless him, he left his clothes for the baby."

Silas hurried with the man further along the beach until they reached some wooden steps leading over the dunes to a nearly empty parking area beyond, attempting to answer the man's questions as they went.

"You the husband?" the man asked.

"No, just happened along by chance." Silas wasn't sure this was true. Twice, now, he'd returned from being a seal and found Sandra. Even if she hadn't married him, that didn't seem like chance.

"You're a brave fellow," the man said. "I've got three kids of my own and have never seen that. They made me wait outside, at the hospital. How did you know what to do?"

"I...well, she was the one doing it," Silas said. "I just went along."

The man laughed hard at that, shaking his head and repeating, "Just went along. Ain't that how it always is with women?"

The swim trunks he offered Silas, retrieved from the back seat of a beige Oldsmobile sedan, were a merciful plain black, and fit better than a glance at the man's generous belly had predicted. "I'm Ed, by the way," he said, when Silas was dressed. Silas put out his hand as he gave his own name, but the man hesitated, then handed him the towel the trunks had been wrapped in. "No offense, but—"

Silas glanced down at his gore-streaked forearm and took the towel with a rueful grin. "Thanks."

He'd been struggling with the question of whether he should go into town with the man, leaving his sealskin behind—something he was very reluctant to do. But after all, with Sandra and Alise there to distract people, no one was going to go looking behind the dunes for his sealskin. And he had another issue to address, which worried him considerably.

What was he supposed to do with Alise's sealskin? She was going to need it someday. He couldn't keep it with him as a seal. He needed a safe place to hide it, and he needed to find out where he *was,* so he'd know where he'd hidden it.

He couldn't begin to imagine how he would get the pelt back to Alise when she was older. He'd have to worry about that later.

He slid into the front passenger seat of the Oldsmobile, which had a bumpy plastic cover on the seats and smelled of cigarette smoke. At first, the road was completely featureless, just a nearly empty two-lane through maritime woods, without a house or a landmark in sight. But then they passed a sign and the entrance to the Ocracoke Island Airport, and another sign announcing Ocracoke in one mile.

Silas had no idea where Ocracoke was, but with his mind at ease that he could walk back to his sealskin from town, he made up his mind to stay there and look for a hiding place. And maybe some food.

"The husband's going to need a ride," Silas said, holding up the keys Sandra had given him. "Because these are his, but his car's somewhere back there, with his wife."

"Sure, I figured I'd help you find him and give you both a ride back," Ed said.

"Maybe just him," Silas said. A piece of truth presented itself as a plausible excuse for staying behind. "I don't care to stick around once he realizes I've been handling his naked wife."

Ed laughed hard at that, too. "Okay, buddy. I take your point. Though he'd have to be a real bastard not to allow for the circumstances!"

Silas thought, with regard to the circumstances, *You have no idea*.

Ocracoke proved to be an adorable village on a harbor, with a pure white lighthouse and lots of hotels and restaurants. Pulling into the shell lot in front of the White Sands Hotel, the man told him, "Keep the trunks. They haven't fit in years. My wife just likes to pretend she's going to make me swim one of these times."

Ed's eyes lingered curiously on the little sealskin, and Silas swiftly opened the car door and stepped out.

The thin, older lady with blue eyeshadow and a fake blond perm at the front desk did not let her excitement hamper her efficiency in the slightest. She dialed the rescue squad on one line, and handed the phone over the counter to Ed for directions to Sandra and the baby. She paged Rick Miller's room on a second phone. "Your wife just gave birth down the beach. There's a fellow here in the lobby ready to give you a ride to her."

Ed was still on the phone with the rescue squad. "That's right. The first access point, about two miles up."

Silas took the opportunity to slip away down the nearest hallway. He was prepared to say he was looking for the men's room if anyone asked, but no one called after him.

He followed the exit signs and went out a side door leading to the pool, which was empty of water this time of year. He let himself out of the pool enclosure and hurried around the side of the building just in time to see Ed come out the front entrance with a young man who had to be Rick. He was sort of a medium-looking guy. Medium tall, medium blond hair, medium good-looking, wearing jeans and a long-sleeved T-shirt and scuffed leather loafers. It was impossible to tell anything about his character, watching him cross from the entrance and get into Ed's car, except that he looked upset and in a hurry.

Bafflement and resentment warred in Silas as he watched Ed's car back hastily out of the lot and speed away. How had Rick ended up with Silas's wife *and* his daughter? Was Silas doing something wrong? Should he be fighting harder? But Sandra kept telling him to go away, and she seemed to mean it.

Sandra must really love Rick. And Rick probably loved her back.

Did *Silas* love Sandra?

He didn't think he did. He hardly knew her. But he *would* love her—he was pretty sure he would—if she'd give him a chance.

A couple of people passing through the parking lot snuck second glances at the little pelt as Silas stood mulling. No wonder

—it looked like a small, cute animal. He needed to get it out of sight before someone came over and tried to pet it.

He was very hungry now, too. Maybe he'd just find a quick, temporary spot to stash the sealskin and then look for a better one after he'd eaten.

He began to wander the little town, keeping an eye out for deposit bottles he could return for lunch money. A map outside the visitor's center answered the question of where Ocracoke was. It was a barrier island off the coast of North Carolina.

He wished he'd asked Sandra what she was doing here. She and Rick were on vacation, obviously, since they were staying in a hotel. Did they still live in New Jersey?

In the story, the mother had died because she was a selkie who didn't have her sealskin. In the real world, Silas didn't have a better explanation for his mother's death. She had been very ill for a long time, and she had never told Silas what was wrong with her.

Silas needed to make sure the same thing didn't happen to Alise. And that was going to be quite difficult if he didn't even know where she lived! But luckily, he had a long time to solve the problem. His mother had lived to be thirty-one, and she hadn't been sick when he was little. As long as Alise got her sealskin by the time she was twenty, she'd probably be fine.

But where on earth was he supposed to hide her pelt for twenty years where no one could find or bother it?

The town of Ocracoke was full of cemeteries. They were tucked away everywhere among the live oaks and between the clapboard-sided bungalows. Most of the cemeteries were just small squares of mowed grass with plain slabs, either flat or upright, marking the graves. But the mausoleum he spotted struck him as promising. It was tucked away at the end of a dirt path between two large, old houses. The vines and branches half-obscuring the marble walls and cast-iron bars at the entrance gave the place an abandoned air.

He padded down the path on silent bare feet.

The most recent of the dates carved beside the tomb's gate was 1918. The gate was latched but not locked, and Silas worked it open, wincing at the screech of the hinges. Inside, lit by daylight coming through the entrance and the matching gate on the other end, were four sepulchers—two on each side, in alcoves set one above the other. Judging by inscriptions carved on each lid, they contained two parents, who had lived to ripe old ages, and two sons, who had not. The sepulchers weren't built into the side of the mausoleum. They were separate, and between each and the wall was a gap about six inches wide.

Muttering, "Sorry buddy," to the youngest son, who was ensconced in one of the lower alcoves, Silas stepped on the lid of his stone box to peer into the upper alcove belonging to the older brother. The granite lid was horribly cold against his bare chest when he lay across it to peer into the crack behind the coffin. Nothing. Just enough dirt, leaves, and spiderwebs to suggest that no one ever cleaned back there.

Of course he wouldn't leave Alise's pelt in a grave for twenty years! But it would do for a hiding place while he looked for food. Once he'd eaten, he was sure to think of a better idea. He tucked the little skin into the space. The slip of fur looked lonely to him, tucked down in that grim marble crevice. "Don't worry," he assured it guiltily. "I'll be right back."

A few paces down the dirt path, the screeching gate shut behind him again, a horrible feeling came over him—a whirling vertigo, a nausea that doubled him over, gagging fruitlessly. At the same time, an almost radar-like instinct told him exactly what was wrong, and where.

His sealskin. Someone was handling it.

Silas took off running. He went in a straight line, crossing yards, leaping fences, crashing through gaps in hedges, oblivious to the sand burrs sticking in his bare feet, barely registering the people in yards and on sidewalks staring at him with startled faces. A bicycle standing unattended outside a kite store caught his eye, and a moment later he straddled it, peddling like the wind, deaf to the outraged shout behind him.

On the bike, he flew down the main road. Only one road ran the length of the island, but out of a hundred roads he would have known exactly which one to take. The sick feeling in his gut had resolved into a sensation that compelled him as unerringly as if he were drawn by an invisible umbilicus connected to his sealskin. He felt as if he were being turned inside out, but he couldn't spare the time even to retch. The only possible relief lay in getting to his skin, and taking it back from whoever had it.

The asphalt lay in a flat ribbon ahead of him, straight and glaring, nearly white with salt and sun and sand. A few cars passed him, coming from town, but none came in the other direction. The entrance to the airport flashed by. The sign for the beach access where he'd left Sandra and his pelt materialized, tiny with distance. He pedaled with all his strength and fury, his breath coming in gasps. He must have made the two miles in record time, yet he despaired that the turnoff was getting no closer, that he would never reach his pelt in time. His survival was at stake, and he could not get there any faster. Careening into the parking lot, he immediately spotted his pelt spread across the hood of Ed's Oldsmobile. Less distinctly, he was aware of Ed himself, and his wife and a couple of strangers clustered around it, staring and discussing. Someone reached out to stroke it, and Silas's nausea surged to a fresh peak. He didn't reason or plan. Ed turned and spotted Silas, but Silas didn't wait for his greeting. He braked hard, shoving Ed with assistance from the bike's momentum as he hurtled off it. Ed crashed into one of the strangers and both men sprawled on the ground. In the confusion came swearing and shouts, but no one actually tried to stop Silas as he snatched up his pelt and continued running full tilt for the steps and the walkway over the dunes. He didn't look behind him to see who watched or followed. He freed himself from Ed's swimming trunks without slowing down, running out of them and leaving them on the sand. At the surf's edge, he flung his pelt around him and launched into the waves.

Somewhere amid the churning breakers, his pelt knitted around him. The seal he became surged out to sea as if chased by the fiercest of sharks, fleeing a danger he no longer remembered except as adrenaline-fueled determination to get *away*.

Chapter 4: Alise

June 1993 - Blounts Creek, North Carolina

The dream was pure anticipation with no story to go with it, as if the feeling itself were so new that Alise's dreaming imagination could supply no explanation. It gathered and built and finally reached a culminating certainty that woke her abruptly: *It's here!*

Without opening her eyes, she took stock, listening intently for what had woken her. A camper out of bed? Some mischief or distress? Somehow, she had not foreseen how often, as a camp counselor, she would be roused from a sound sleep to deal with barfed-in beds.

This time, blessedly, all was quiet, or at least as quiet as a cabin full of sleeping third graders ever got—all heavy breathing and unconscious snores.

She turned over, seeking a cooler section of pillow and mattress from a bed already stripped of all but its bottom sheet against the sweltering, eastern North Carolina summer heat. As much as she sweated at night, the bed could have had the decency to feel cool with dampness, but it never did.

She felt very odd. Not odd in a bad way—always a concern, given the barfed-in beds—but odd enough to have woken up, despite how very tired she was after six weeks of long, hot days full of keyed-up kids, and short, hot nights full of interruptions. She buzzed inside, not with anxiety but with a keen excitement. She could not for the life of her think why. The day ahead held nothing unusual—just canoeing and tie-dying and burger day at the dining hall, which was definitely nothing to get worked up about.

And Alise wasn't the type to get worked up, even about huge, exciting things, like her first real job at the camp she had loved since she was a kid, or her first semester in college that would begin in just over a month. Sometimes she worried that feeling so little might indicate something wrong with her. She had read that depression could be like this—not a pit of pain and misery but a flat sea of nothingness that no storm could excite.

But if depression was her natural state, she was currently experiencing the opposite. Once, a small visiting cousin—Alise was an only child—had woken her up at 4 a.m. on Christmas morning, bouncing on the bed and squealing because Santa Claus had come and all the stockings were filled. Alise had been both baffled and amused. She had never in her life been excited enough about Santa—or anything else—to wake up at 4 a.m. But she was precisely that excited, now. And it really was a Christmas-y kind of feeling, right down to the certainty that something wonderful was waiting for her to get out of bed and come claim it.

She'd been a camper here for so many years that the impulse to wake a buddy if she needed to leave the cabin at night was deeply ingrained. She still felt a little lifting sense of freedom every time she realized that, as a counselor, she was allowed to go to the bathroom—or anywhere else—all by herself. She slipped on her shower flip-flops and let herself out of the cabin, dragging down on the screen door to quell the squeak that was never oiled since it warned, usefully, of campers escaping in the middle of the night.

The cabins had no windows but screens, with canvas flaps to tie down when it rained, so the incessant katydids of summer were no louder outside than in. A welcome breath came off the river, though. She turned her face toward it, and perhaps the hint of coolness led her to the dock. Or maybe instinct: The Pamlico River was over a mile wide here, close enough to the sea that its level rose and fell with the tides, and its water ran fresh and salty by turns. The river had drawn her back to this camp, year after year, because the sweet-salt tide was the closest taste of the sea she could manage on her own. Alise had often heard the story of her unexpected birth on an Ocracoke Island beach, as her parents were attempting to get in one last vacation before her arrival. Her parents dated Alise's affinity with the ocean from that beginning, and yet—bafflingly, infuriatingly to Alise—remained content to live in Asheville, many hours' drive inland. They rented a house at Holden Beach for a week every summer (not Ocracoke, which was almost half again as far when you counted the ferry ride). For Alise, that week was always cruelly short, and camp was a much-needed supplement.

Her parents would have said that going to the beach was the one thing Alise did get worked up about, but worked up was not how she felt about it. Being by the sea was simply a relief from the faint but persistent sense of wrongness that she felt everywhere else. The ocean was the only place in the world where she felt completely herself.

The force that drew her toward the river now was stronger than breeze or habit. The summoning felt like certainty, like fate, like destiny. It felt as right as anything ever had.

She didn't need a flashlight. The moon, worn away on one side like a water-smoothed stone, hung bright overhead, and she could have made her way along all the paths of this tiny camp with her eyes shut, as often as she'd walked them. No one else stirred. All the cabins stayed dark and quiet.

The moon lit a bright path on the water. She noticed that first, before she took in the expanse of dock, its weathered boards featureless except for a mounded shadow rising at the edge, as if poised to slip over the side.

Her first thought, accompanied by a surge of delight, was that she was finally seeing the seal. North Carolina in summer was no reasonable place for a seal, especially this far inland, and yet, for several years now, sightings had been reported. The seals— though according to camp tradition it was the same one every time—always seemed to miss Alise by a few days, a week, two at the most. She'd been here various weeks of the summer, and yet, whether she came the first week of June or the last week of July, the seal always came later than she did. Each near miss increased her determination to see it, and she took each failure personally. Her obsession had become a running joke at camp, so much so that her camp name—self-chosen names all the counselors went by instead of their real names—was Seal. She could not miss the seal this summer because she was here the entire time. Leprechaun claimed to have seen it two weeks ago, but Alise was determined not to believe her. Camp names tended to have some logic behind them: Leprechaun, in addition to having flaming red curls and an Irish grandmother, was a known practical joker.

Alise held her breath and peered hard at the mound on the dock. It didn't look quite right for a seal. It was too flat, and not big enough. Everyone who'd seen the seal said it was huge. Someone had taken a photo, clear enough to identify a Western Atlantic gray seal—a bull. The camp administration had not encouraged that photo, parents being understandably squeamish about a wild animal that *large* around their children. But copies had circulated and Alise had kept one. The lump on the dock was definitely not that seal.

Her real disappointment somehow didn't affect the excitement drawing on her. Reasonable caution would have prevented her from going onto the dock without a better idea of what was there. It was almost certainly an animal, and if too small to be the seal, it might be a largish dog, lying down. Alise was incapable of reasonable caution. She experienced something closely akin to a magnetic force, which propelled her across the dock to kneel beside the mound. She reached for it with both hands.

The soft fur was sleek and short and very dense. It was not an animal but the hide of one, and this didn't worry her either. No bad smell indicated carrion, a carcass. It smelled faintly of mineral and musk, like the scent of the river. She gathered the entire thing in her arms, hugging it close and stroking it and burying her face.

She was eighteen and had never wanted a boyfriend, let alone a lover, but her sheer physical hunger for this pelt felt like lust as she'd imagined it. In another moment she had spread it on the dock and begun purely wallowing against it. Unable to get enough of her skin in contact, she shed the T-shirt and nylon soccer shorts she slept in, and, after the briefest of hesitations, even her underwear. Now she was naked, nearly swimming in this fur, rolling and writhing against it until she encountered a place where it parted. She wriggled inside. The smooth interior felt even more miraculous against her than the fur had. Every fiber of her body grew taut with longing. Some force gathered, gathered inside her, and she drew the skin over her head.

On every surface of her body she caught, kindled, went molten and began to flow. She became a slow and silent explosion, combusting in pure ecstasy, expanding to fill every crevice of the hide. Time stopped. She had no sense of how long she soared on glorious sensation before there was a final knitting up—a sense of closing, finishing—that left her lying on the dock alert, at peace, and filled with wordless wonder.

The water stretched before her, a luminous invitation. She wriggled and bounced on her belly across the boards of the dock. At the end, she didn't hesitate, but launched herself. She plunged through the surface, head first. With an easy swoop she swung above the river bottom. Then she soared through a buoying darkness that wasn't dark to her, all her senses reaching to tell her, *This way to the sea.*

Chapter 5: Alise

August 1993 - Blounts Creek, North Carolina

This is a really long detour," Elliot complained.

"I know," Alise soothed him. "I really, really appreciate it." The drive from Asheville to Wilmington took five hours, and the extra jog north so Alise could swing by camp on the Pamlico River added two more.

"I don't see why they couldn't mail it to you," Elliot grumbled.

"I told you, it's too big. It would cost a fortune." Alise had been over the story with Elliot before, but she kept her patience because she needed his help. She was desperate to get her skin back. She hoped and prayed the pelt was still under cabin three where she had hidden it a month ago on the dark early morning of her return. Her magical stint of underwater freedom had come to an abrupt and unwelcome end only two days after it began, when some ineluctable impulse had compelled her back up the river, the freshening water stinging her eyes the whole way, and ejected her from her pelt, leaving her trembling, naked, and bereft beneath the dock in the middle of the night. She suspected that her parents, who had made a terrible scene when they arrived at camp after her disappearance, had had something to do with her return, but she couldn't figure out what. She'd hidden her pelt while it was still dark, quietly pulling aside a loose piece of corrugated siding beneath the cabin full of sleeping campers, and stuffing the unwieldy bundle of fur through a vent hole in the cinder block foundation. Hopefully nothing but a few spiders had bothered it since. She prayed no cabin repairers or curious campers or exterminators had found it, despite a completely irrational feeling that if anything had happened to it, she would somehow know. Still, her anxiety to have her skin near, safe, *with her*, had been a constant, unceasing uneasiness ever since she'd been forced to leave it behind. Her need to keep it secret had been too strong, her traumatized parents too vigilant, to permit any opportunity for sneaking it home unnoticed.

"I still don't understand why you took an heirloom like your grandfather's coat from the war to camp. In the summer. It's frickin' hot down here." Elliot had been in an increasingly bad mood ever since they'd turned off I-40, fully committing to this side trip.

Alise didn't care how much soothing she had to do, as long as he kept driving in the right direction. "I told you. I needed it for a costume."

"But how are you going to get it now that camp is closed? Won't it be locked up?"

"I know a way to get in."

"We could get in so much trouble for this," he groaned.

"That's why you're going to wait in the car," she reminded him. "If I get caught, no one will know you had anything to do with it."

She and Elliot had already had this conversation several times, but she waited anxiously for his irritated sigh that meant he still agreed—reluctantly—to her plan. Every instinct she possessed told her to keep her pelt out of Elliot's sight. She had already made up her mind to some extreme measures for distracting him once she had her skin back in her possession. The thought of those measures made her stomach knot, but it didn't matter. On some nearly molecular level, she knew that *nothing* was more important than keeping her pelt out of Elliot's—and anyone else's —hands.

Alise still wasn't sure how she had ended up with Elliot. He'd chosen her, she supposed, and she'd accepted? Or at least she hadn't refused, and now he was a fixture in her life, useful and annoying by turns, always around. His name was probably to blame. A long time ago she'd discovered Eleanor of Aquitaine in a book selected from the limited shelves of the bookmobile that visited her house in the summers. The bold and adventurous queen had lodged in her imagination. The name *Eleanor* struck her as a little too severe for modern times, but when she had a daughter of her own, Alise planned to name her Ellie. So the new kid in her homeroom the first day of 7th grade—pale-skinned and nerdy, thick-lipped, blue-eyed, scruffy-haired, nose buried in a Piers Anthony novel—got more of her attention than he otherwise would have, once roll-call revealed his name: Elliot Thorne. She'd kept sneaking glances at him, wondering at how poorly his appearance matched his marvelous name, and hoping he was secretly more wonderful than he appeared on the outside.

Her attention and curiosity, neither of which were offered to him by other members of their class, were the crack he got in by, like an open sliver of doorway yielding to the determined nose of a stray dog. Elliot had accepted her scraps and curled up under her kitchen table—so to speak—and she'd been stuck with him ever since. He was fine, but not noticeably wonderful. He was morose and talkative by turns, insecure and moody but never indifferent, capable of hours-long monologues on the plot of whatever mythology or fantasy he was currently reading if she introduced no subject of her own. Despite the terrible poems and mix tapes with which he'd courted her in the half-dozen years since they'd met, he had never quite become her boyfriend. This disappointed him, she knew, but as long as no one else filled the role, he contented himself with an identity somewhere between a pet and a best friend. At her house, he claimed a spot at the dinner table and a beanbag in her room. He came along for things, even errands she believed no normal boy would have joined, like haircuts and clothes shopping. Whatever Alise was doing, Elliot did, too. She didn't believe he had ever considered a college besides UNC-Wilmington, because she herself hadn't—the in-state tuition and beach location combined to make it her first and only choice.

So, of course, Elliot was coming along to retrieve her sealskin. In this case, though, she couldn't have done it without him. Her parents were still too freaked out and furious about her disappearance to lend her the car, and she wouldn't have one at college. That had left manufacturing a false interest in the optional pre-orientation weekend at UNC-W, so Elliot—who did have a car—would drive her to it. He'd been unusually resistant to the idea. She knew he wasn't eager to meet new people, or for her to meet any, either. He was always a little insecure and jealous of her attention. But the road trip, just the two of them, should have outweighed that reluctance, and she thought his reservations went further this time.

Ever since she'd returned from camp with that improbable story about falling off the dock in the middle of the night and getting swept downriver, Elliot had been treating her with mistrust, as if she might be a counterfeit copy of the girl he knew. She couldn't blame him. She *was* different, though she couldn't put her finger on exactly what had changed. Her depression, or whatever it had been, had lifted like mist burning off the river. She *cared*. Things *mattered*. She was awake in a way she hadn't been before.

She thought the change was a vast improvement, but apparently Elliot had preferred the old Alise.

When Elliot pulled into the camp's gravel parking lot, late in the afternoon, Alise was relieved to find it completely empty. The last session had ended a week before, and fall camp-outs would not begin for another two months, but she had feared that a caretaker might remain in the off season. "I'll only take a few minutes. Wait here in case we need to make a quick getaway, okay?" she told Elliot.

Elliot opened his door. "There's no one here."

She panicked. He was going to tag along, the way he always, *always* tagged along, and this time he *couldn't*.

But it was impossible to say no to Elliot. He never listened.

"I'll be right back," she said. "The caretaker might show up, and I need you to cover for me."

He hesitated, frowning. "What am I supposed to say?"

"Say you're lost. Ask for directions. Just keep her talking until you see me." *Oh, this was never going to work. Elliot hated talking to strangers. That was her job.*

He groaned. "Hurry."

Rushing so Elliot wouldn't change his mind, she retrieved her dad's old green suitcase from the back of Elliot's Subaru. The suitcase had a combination lock so Elliot wouldn't be able to steal a peek inside.

She hurried past the empty cabins, the dining hall, the trading post. The plywood and aluminum structures looked strangely dismal. Closed and deserted, the life gone out of it, camp was like an empty pelt with no one inside.

Cabin three stood right on the riverbank, but she could spare no time to meditate over the dramatic expanse and dreamy peacefulness of the view. Some industrious person had screwed down the loose piece of siding, but she had tucked her Swiss army knife, equipped with both kinds of screwdrivers, into her pocket, just in case. She felt a tingling sense of anticipation that seemed more than suspense over whether the pelt was still here. The feeling was closer to certainty, a fainter but still noticeable version of the magnetic pull the pelt had exerted on her the night she'd found it on the dock. (*Where* had the skin come from? Had someone brought it? Had it swum there by itself? The mystery nagged at her.)

She knelt, thanked her lucky stars when the Philips-head screwdriver fit, and loosened the screws. There were only three. After she got the last one out and tested the siding to see if it pulled free—it did—she peeked around the corner of the cabin to make sure Elliot hadn't come looking for her. Several other cabins blocked her view of the parking lot, and she saw no sign of him.

Satisfied, she hurried back around the cabin, dragged the siding away, and reached anxiously through the vent hole. For a brief moment she couldn't feel anything but dirt, and groped frantically in the dark. Then her fingers touched fur, sleek and almost electric, and with immeasurable relief she pulled out her pelt.

In the late afternoon shadows, she spread the skin on the dry grass and took her first true look. The short, hard fur was greyish-white, covered with dark speckles. She studied the sleek shape of the head, the flippers at each side, the other paired set of flippers at the tail end. The eyes, a little like buttonholes, were empty, and so were the openings in the flippers where claws went. The pelt should have been grotesque, as dead skins of once-living things are. But this was the live skin of a still-living thing, and it was beautiful.

The creature she had been had never seen its own reflection and had not been curious. She had found the pelt in the dark and returned in the dark. She had been fairly sure she'd been a seal, once she'd gotten back and had a chance to reflect on the way she had moved, stayed long underwater but come up for air, eaten every kind of fish. Now she was certain.

She was a selkie. That's what it was called when a human could turn into a seal and back again. Remembering the obscure legend from her childhood reading, she'd hunted down all the stories she could find about the shapeshifting seals after her return, raiding the fairy tale and mythology shelf in the children's section of the library. The legend seemed to fit—not fully, but close enough.

Selkie.

She drew a long, trembling breath, stroking her hand over the slippery fur. The urge to put it on was very strong, but nothing like the compulsion she'd felt the first time. She could resist the tingling in her human skin this time, and that was fortunate. What a terrible thing to do to Elliot, stranding him here while she took off again, leaving him to face her parents' grief and wrath.

Elliot. She quickly rolled up the skin and stuffed it into the suitcase. She had just finished tucking in the last errant edges of fur and was pressing down the lid when she heard a step behind her in the grass and Elliot's voice. "That's not a coat."

Deliberately, she snapped the lock and closed the other two latches, trying hard to maintain an appearance of calm. An irrational panic filled her, a looming horror at the idea of Elliot touching her sealskin. She didn't know whether the stories were true—whether someone who stole her skin would hold her in his power. All she knew was that she would do anything—*anything*—to keep her pelt away from Elliot.

"It's a *fur* coat," she told him.

"It's not a fur coat," he said. "It's a sealskin. I saw its flipper."

She stood and turned to face him. Walking away from her pelt toward Elliot was the hardest thing she'd ever done. She wanted to snatch up her skin and run—or fight him—anything but what she actually did, which was to leave her sealskin vulnerable behind her while she twined her arms around Elliot's neck. His pale blue eyes met hers with a look of mingled disbelief and hope and wariness.

"What are you doing?" he asked.

"Thanking you," she said, and put her lips on his. For what seemed a very long time he stood stock still. She was about to draw back and face the excruciating awkwardness that was bound to follow when he suddenly put his arms around her and began to kiss her back.

Kissing him was just as bad as she'd always imagined it would be. She wanted to shrug him away, jerk her mouth from his, wipe him off her and run. But she didn't. She stood still in his arms and let him press his rubbery lips against hers, probe her mouth with his thick, slimy tongue, run his hands up and down her back. She stood there while his breath grew shaky, while he dragged her closer, putting his hand down the back of her shorts and pressing the hard bulge at his crotch into her stomach. She stood there while he ran his hands up under her T-shirt and then pulled it over her head, while he fumbled interminably with her bra before finally getting that off, too. And she kept standing there as, in a kind of frenzy, he yanked her shorts down and unzipped his own pants. Bearing her down onto the dry grass, he knelt between her legs and shoved his way into her. It hurt. But she tried not to let him see her pain as he labored over and in her, a wild light in his face. She was distracting him. This was the one and only thing she had been sure would work, and she'd been right.

It was worth it.

"Alise!" he gasped. "I love you."

Chapter 6: Alise

November 1993 - Wilmington, North Carolina

Alise crouched beneath the camellia hedge outside her dorm. A week before Thanksgiving, the bushes were blooming with beautiful crimson flowers. At first she'd thought flowers in November an aberration—the El Nino effect?—but a woman from the grounds crew had explained that camellias were winter flowers. Alise had found the little hollow in the hedge a few weeks ago, just big enough to hold her when she curled up with her arms wrapped around her knees. Here, she was hidden behind the glossy evergreen leaves, and she could watch the entrance to her dorm without being observed.

Elliot was waiting for her in the lobby. She had managed to elude him at dinnertime, grabbing a sandwich from the snack bar in the student center after class, and eating on her way to the library. It had closed early on Friday night, though, and she had hoped she could slip up to her room without Elliot seeing her. It was a slim hope. "Your boyfriend's waiting for you," one of her hallmates had warned her on the sidewalk.

"Thanks," Alise said briefly, and the girl had nodded. Mere acquaintances knew Alise was avoiding Elliot, but he couldn't take a hint and leave her alone. The more she hid from him, the harder he pursued her.

He had become a nightmare. That first time at camp, when she had let him—she didn't form words in her head beyond this: She had let him. That's all. The distraction had worked. He hadn't said another word about her grandfather's coat. They had skipped most of orientation weekend to find a Planned Parenthood clinic. There she'd received a prescription for the pill, and instructions to take two at once for the first few days so she wouldn't get pregnant. The double dose had made her horribly nauseated. She had thrown up twice into grocery bags on the way home while Elliot drove—he wasn't confident enough at the wheel to pull over in time—and she had wanly hoped that he'd be too repulsed to ever want to—that—again.

No such luck. Once they were home in Asheville he was there as constantly as always, with the difference that whenever they were alone he tried to touch her—kiss her. Of course he did. What had she expected?

"You're allowed to tell him no," her mother told her once. Sandra had come into the kitchen just in time to see Alise sigh with relief and lean against the door after closing it behind Elliot, having fended off his inevitable attempt at a goodbye kiss. "I know he's your friend, but what you want matters, too."

Alise scowled. "Easy for you to say." As far as she could see, her mother always knew exactly what she wanted, and never felt the slightest remorse in turning down everything else.

"I haven't always said no when I should have," her mom told her quietly.

Alise waited to hear more, curious despite herself, but her mother only poured herself another glass of wine and rejoined Alise's dad in the living room.

Alise didn't say *no* to Elliot. She didn't even understand why she couldn't, except it seemed to her that it was too late. The time to tell Elliot *no* would have been the first day of 7th grade, when he'd asked if he could sit with her at lunch. She hadn't even said yes. She'd said nothing at all, and he'd taken her silence for permission. He'd chosen her, and if she'd ever had a choice, she no longer did. For six years, she had allowed herself to be his only person. He had no other friends. Thanks to Elliot's constant presence, she didn't either. She and Elliot were a closed system. If she cut him loose now, he would probably shrivel up and die. She had let him need her for too long.

What you want matters, too, her mother had said, but that was the rest of the problem. Alise was not sure she had ever, in her whole life, wanted anything except to be near the sea, and now, to put on her sealskin. She'd accepted Elliot because he wanted her, and she didn't want anything else. And now see what wanting did? If it weren't for her sealskin, she would never have let Elliot — She would never have let him.

She did try to put him off. She told him, "It was kind of a bad experience, with the clinic and the pill and the sickness. I wasn't ready after all."

He argued. "But you're on the pill now. It'll be better the next time. *I'll* be better."

"I don't want to," she said, as baldly as she knew how. "I just want to be friends."

The next time he came over her house, he brought up the coat. He'd looked up army-issue coats at the library, but none of them looked like her grandfather's coat. "I know it's not a coat," he said. "It's a sealskin. Just let me see it." He'd begun prowling around her room, opening her closet, bending to look under the bed. Her sealskin wasn't in her bedroom. She'd hidden it in the downstairs closet with her parents' moldering camping gear, which they hadn't used since her birth. But she couldn't bear him even thinking about it, and she knew how to stop him. When she stood in front of him, he reached immediately for her breast.

She'd thought at least it wouldn't hurt the second time, but it did. She closed her eyes and tried not to grimace, hoping like hell he'd finish quickly. He did. *You chose this*, she told herself silently. No matter how wrong she felt, this wasn't Elliot's fault. She was the one who was letting him.

But after he left, she cried. She didn't want to be his girlfriend.

She wanted him to disappear.

She had checked all the selkie books out of the library another time and read them even more carefully, now that she was sure she was a selkie. Although the stories varied—imprisoned selkie wives, lordly selkie princes who loved human girls, angry selkies avenging the theft of their pelts, selkie men taking their sons away from human mothers and teaching them to be seals—the one thing the tales agreed on was that a person who stole a selkie's pelt gained power over her. Mostly men used it to force selkie women to marry them—to get, in other words, the same thing Elliot wanted from her.

In Wilmington, once school started, she rented a storage locker off campus for her sealskin. The rental took most of the small allowance her parents gave her for incidentals, but the relief she felt knowing Elliot couldn't get her pelt was worth the poverty.

At school she managed to avoid him for a while. His dorm wasn't near hers and they had no classes together. She kept a sharp eye out for him and adjusted her routine every time she caught a glimpse of him. She let the answering machine screen phone calls to her room, and her roommate sympathetically agreed to tell Elliot Alise was out whenever he called.

But a few weeks into the semester, he was leaning against the wall when she left her biology lab. He walked her to her next class, and the next day he was waiting on the steps of the art building after her painting class. She lied that she was late for a meeting with her advisor, and he walked her to that, too. She shed him with difficulty at the entrance to the building, then snuck out a side door in case he was waiting for her. She felt no victory in the escape. He knew her schedule: He could find her now whenever he wanted.

That Saturday, when Alise passed through her dorm lobby on her way to a very late breakfast, he jumped up from a couch, calling her name. She snapped. "For god's sake, Elliot, what are you doing here?"

He'd been smiling eagerly at her, but his face changed very suddenly, as if she had punched him. A moment later she saw with horror that he had tears in his eyes. "Why are you mad at me?" he asked in a choked voice.

"I'm sorry," she said, unable to look at him. "I don't know what's wrong with me. I'm in a horrible mood—I think I'm just really hungry."

"I was going to see if you wanted to go to the Pancake Barn for breakfast," he said tentatively.

The Pancake Barn was off campus. He had a car to get there, and she didn't. She said, "I've been wanting to go. But I can't afford it."

His face fell. What she'd said was only the truth, but he thought she was blowing him off again. Her conscience wouldn't let her get away with that. "Let's just eat at the caf."

He lit up with hope. He looked better when he was happy, with his bright blue eyes and his wide smile. *God*, what had she done? He was her only friend, and she had used him, lied to him, treated him meanly. Every item in the catalog of evil things girls do to boys, she had done to him. That's not who she wanted to be.

She didn't want to be anyone at all. She wanted to put on her sealskin and be *gone,* the way she'd been before.

"Let me treat you," he said. "C'mon, please, Alise?"

"I'll pay you back," she promised, resigned. When he took her hand outside the dorm, she forced herself to let him hold it, even though his palm was clammy.

Over breakfast he was pathetically happy to have her attention, pouring out all the stories he'd been saving to tell her these last few weeks. His roommate was an asshole. He was struggling in his classes. He was lonely. He had missed her like crazy. He hadn't even been to Wrightsville Beach yet, when that was practically the entire reason for coming to school here. Did she want to walk the beach with him, after breakfast?

Alise agreed. She had been to the beach every chance she got, which was not as often as she would have liked. Without a car, getting there took two buses and a fair amount of walking.

The beach put her in a good mood, as always—the restless water with its long reach to the sky, the wind, the clownish pelicans. She let Elliot hold her hand some more. It wasn't so bad. He wasn't so bad. She was lonely, too. What had changed, really? Elliot adored her, and she liked to be adored, and there were no other boys she wanted.

When they returned to his car, she let him press her against the door and kiss her. She didn't enjoy it any more than normal, but the hard ridge he shoved against her stomach made it clear that he did. "Is your roommate around this weekend?" he asked breathlessly, hopefully.

Her roommate was never around on the weekends. She went to Raleigh to visit her boyfriend at NC State.

If you only let him when he brings up the coat, a pragmatic, treacherous voice whispered in her mind, *he'll learn to associate those things.*

He drove them back to campus and she took him up to her room and let him for the third time. This time didn't hurt, or feel like much of anything. *I guess this is all right,* she tried to convince herself, as he humped away at her with his eyes screwed shut and a silly-looking expression of depraved bliss on his face. *I'm on the pill. He's happy. I can live with this.*

Afterward she could tell he was hoping she'd let him stay, but she said she had a paper to write. As he was putting on his pants, he noticed the stack of library books on her desk. "So you're the one who checked them all out!" he said.

She froze inside. She hadn't thought about him seeing the selkie books until that moment—Norse and Celtic mythologies from the campus library, plus a couple of scientific books about seals.

"For my paper," she said weakly. "Why were *you* looking for them?"

"Your grandfather's coat got me thinking crazy things. Because it's not a coat—it's a sealskin. I started thinking, *What if your grandfather was a selkie?* What if you put on his coat and turned into a seal, and that's why you disappeared this summer?"

Panic squeezed the air out of her lungs. She gasped a little as she replied, "That's pretty crazy, all right."

Only Elliot—of all the people in the world, *only Elliot* would have come to this conclusion. No one else even knew what a selkie was!

"I know," he said cheerfully. "But once I started thinking, I got a little obsessed. It would make *so much sense* if you were a selkie. It would explain everything about you!"

"Like what?" Her voice seemed to be coming from too far away.

"Like how you love the beach more than anything, and you'd eat fish for every single meal if you could, and—"

"No, I wouldn't!"

"Alise," he said gently. "I took you to a pancake house. For breakfast. And you ordered the catfish."

"Whatever," she said, rallying. "What about the fact that I hate swimming?"

"Yeah… But what if selkies can't swim when they're not seals? You know, like the little mermaid having to give up her voice when she gets legs?"

She tried to laugh, knowing the effort sounded forced. "You've spent *way* too much time thinking about this."

He shrugged, unoffended. "I just like thinking about you. I've always thought there was something magical about you. And the more I look, the more it fits—you even checked out the books!"

"The topic was assigned. I didn't choose it." She made herself go close and kiss his cheek. He turned at the last second so her lips landed on his. She couldn't help flinching slightly, but he didn't seem to notice. "Now go away so I can write my paper."

"Tell me when you turn those books back in," he said from the door. "I want to read them when you're done."

When he was gone, she threw herself on the bed, nearly hyperventilating, saying all the worst words she could think of into her pillow. When she had worn the first edge off her panic, she got up and began to pace, trying to reason with herself. He was just playing a game with the selkie stuff. That was Elliot— always disappearing into some fantasy novel, always making up stories. All she had to do was play along. In a sane world in which she was *not* a selkie, that's what she'd do: She'd probably even enjoy pretending.

As for being his girlfriend…the fact is, there was probably something wrong with her. Other girls seemed to like boys kissing them and touching them and—that other thing. Maybe if she practiced she'd learn to like it, too.

*   *   *

Shivering under the camellia bush for the third time that week, listening to the volume cranking up all over the dorm as the Friday night celebration got underway, she knew she had reached the end.

Playing along with Elliot's selkie game had proved the easy part. He'd even come up with some useful theories. "If I was off swimming around in my grandfather's coat this summer," she'd asked him mock-playfully, actually posing a question that had been bothering her, "why did I come back? Why didn't I just stay a seal?"

"I think your mom called you back," he said, so readily he'd clearly thought about it before. He really did have an obsessive streak. "When you disappeared, there was a picture in the paper of your mom standing in the water, crying. And that's how you call a selkie back to land, you know. Drop seven tears in the sea and call her name."

Alise had not known that. Apparently Elliot had gotten his hands on some book she had missed. But his theory made perfect sense. Her return had felt like a compulsion—not her own choice. And she'd been sure all along that her parents had somehow been to blame.

But being Elliot's girlfriend was a disaster. It had not gotten easier with practice. No matter how much she told herself there was nothing wrong with him—he was nice, he cared about her, he wasn't ugly—the more he touched her, the more he repelled her. From flinching away from him, she had progressed to an instinct to hit his hand away every time he reached for her. She usually managed not to, but a few times he had caught her off guard. She'd hurt his feelings, but he always forgave her instantly when she apologized. She tried to convince herself this was generosity on his part, but his easy forgiveness felt more like blindness, as if the possibility of her feelings never occurred to him.

That other thing, she avoided as much as she could. She had managed to convince him that her period lasted two weeks. Then she'd played up a minor—but real and ongoing—nausea. She blamed the pill, but she was pretty sure it was her diet. She'd stopped eating fish when Elliot was around (which seemed like always) in order to take some credibility away from his selkie theory, and had felt increasingly queasy and listless. She had finally used her last two dollars to buy some on-sale tuna at the grocery store, taking the bus when she was sure Elliot had class and eating it secretly, and had felt much better for a couple of days. She'd ended up taking a work-study job maintaining supplies and cleaning up the art studio, just so she'd have money to keep herself in sardines and tuna. Plus, having a job meant more time away from Elliot.

Lately she had figured out that she could deal with Elliot by hand and avoid having him shove himself inside her. This worked a few times. She did her best to keep her impatience and disgust hidden behind her face. But two days ago he'd asked her to use her mouth, and when she declined he'd pressed her head toward his protuberant crotch. She'd shaken him off and appeased him with intercourse instead, on hands and knees with him behind her so he couldn't see her expression. She'd fled to the shower down the hall as soon as it was over and cried so hard, with so much revulsion over the way he'd tried to force himself into her mouth, that she retched and vomited into the shower drain, and afterward crouched in a corner of the stall, head bent against the wall, and let the dorm's limitless hot water run over her for nearly an hour.

She could not will herself to love Elliot, or want him. By trying, she had turned a friend into someone she all but hated—someone who repulsed her, someone who literally made her sick. She had turned a perfectly nice boy into a source of horror. Under the camellia bush, her coat unzipped and held around her tucked up knees, damp ground soaking through her jeans, the minutes stretching out and out, she was too miserable even to cry.

How had she come to this? How had no one warned her that being nice could make her so mean?

The thought of her sealskin tucked away in its expensive storage locker was as constant and tantalizing as forbidden true love—or maybe an addiction. Her parents would be sad but she could write a letter to them this time, telling them she loved them and she was safe and happy and alive and not to worry about her.

What stopped her was this: *What if Elliot was right about the seven tears?* She would bet her life that if she vanished again without a trace, calling her back was the first thing he'd try. She could picture him all too easily, standing in the surf, dripping stupid, hurt-puppy tears. What if it worked? What if she swam right back to him where he was waiting for her, and he snatched her sealskin away while she was still confused from the change?

He would keep her prisoner forever, just like the fishermen in the stories.

Chapter 7: Alise

November 1993 - Wilmington, North Carolina

A man came down the sidewalk toward the dorm, drawing Alise's attention from her hiding place beneath the camellia bushes. His tucked-in, buttoned shirt, thick shoulders and loafers set him apart from the lanky college boys, who wore hiking boots and unbuttoned flannel over T-shirts. To Alise's eyes, he possessed an unutterable perfection. She couldn't look away. Every moment he approached she was certain some flaw would break his hold on her, but it didn't. He wasn't flashy, showy, theatrical. He was just a man walking down a sidewalk on a Friday evening, leaving work late and not, by his sober expression, looking forward to a thrilling weekend. Yet she couldn't take her eyes off his sheer, physical perfection. He was tall, dark-haired, broad-shouldered, narrow-waisted, long-legged. The shape of his face, his features, the assured way he walked, the fit of his clothes—all seemed to strike a chord in her. She might have carried his image all her life and never known she was looking for him, until this moment when she saw him for the first time and recognized him.

His rightness filled her with an urgency she couldn't contain. She was propelled from beneath the camellia bushes and onto the sidewalk with no plan in her head for what to do next.

He glanced at her but quickly averted his eyes, as if politely ignoring the odd girl in the shrubbery. His glance returned to her again, seemingly against his will, but he didn't stop walking.

"Wait," she said, as he passed her.

He turned as if grateful for the excuse. He had navy blue eyes and long, black lashes—devastatingly delicate in an otherwise masculine face.

A sensation seized her, not unlike terror but somehow hot where terror was cold. "I think you dropped something," she said.

He glanced skeptically back along the sidewalk. She knelt and picked up the first thing she found: a round, gold pebble the size of a small grape, one of the landscaping stones from the camellia border. He held out his hand, and she dropped it into his palm.

He laughed. "What were you doing under there?"

Her heart stuttered at his voice, which was low and pleasant, and his accent, which was definitely not American. "Hiding. Where are you from?"

"Scotland. Hiding from whom?" He hadn't missed a beat.

The smile she saw him holding back transfixed her. She wanted —she wanted to *taste* it. What was wrong with her?

"Elliot," she said. She understood something in a blinding flash. This riot, this revolution happening inside her was what Elliot felt about her. She would do anything for these eyes, this face, this perfect being—*anything* to make him reach out and touch her. This was how Elliot felt, and she would never, never feel this way about him. The freedom in this understanding was like a flock of birds taking off from her chest. She trembled.

He saw her shiver and his expression darkened. "Are you in danger?"

She shook her head. But they were standing in full sight of the dorm. At any moment, Elliot might notice her through the window. "I don't want him to see me. Can I walk with you?"

He hesitated, so she slipped her hand around his arm above his elbow and began walking in the direction he'd been headed. He came along as if hypnotized. She, too, felt drifty and unreal. Beneath his jacket sleeve his arm was solid, with no give to it. In contrast, her whole body felt like butter melting in summer heat, though the sun had just slipped behind the horizon and the November dusk was cold.

"Where are you going?" she asked.

"Home."

"Where's home?"

"Just—" He gestured vaguely ahead of them toward the cluster of apartment complexes that crowded just beyond the edge of campus. "Look..." He sounded unhappy. "I don't know your name."

"Alise. What's yours?"

"Douglas."

"Douglas," she repeated, savoring the feel of his name in her mouth.

"Alise." He stopped walking and turned to face her on the sidewalk, removing his arm gently from her grip. They were out of sight of the dorm, approaching the busy road at the border of campus. A steady stream of cars passed in the dusk, but no other pedestrians approached.

"You should go," he said. "You're having a very peculiar effect on me, and you seem to have enough troubles—with Elliot?—as it is."

She didn't hear him trying to send her away. What she heard was a slight breathlessness in his voice that confessed as much as his words. She felt a victorious rush and scanned him up and down for signs of her effect.

A solid ridge pressed out the fabric just beside his fly. She felt no desire to avert her eyes, no dread or resignation or disgust as she had with Elliot. She only felt compelled.

She stepped quite close to him and looked into his face. "It *is* peculiar, isn't it?"

He closed his eyes but didn't move away from her. "Christ, how old are you?" he asked, like someone in pain.

Instead of answering, she stood on tiptoe and pressed her lips to his. It was one long chain of combustion. He kissed her, but not because she let him—she kissed him first and hard and hungry, and he met her with nothing held back. She could not get him close enough, crushing herself hard against him, as if trying with all her might to push him down, glorying that she couldn't budge him. Her need for him drew every muscle in her body tight and seemed to expand her from the inside out.

She felt between them for his belt.

He grabbed her hand, freeing his mouth from hers abruptly. "Not here!"

"Where?" She looked around. Their surroundings were all very unpromising—a few parked cars, a stretch of sidewalk, open ground. Nothing so accommodating as a camellia bush, even.

"Bloody hell." He grabbed her hand and started walking fast toward the main road. She quickened her stride to match his, and soon they were both running toward the intersection. A red light and four lanes of streaming traffic barred their way. He drew her around and put his hand down the back of her jeans. She dragged him closer by his belt and pressed her face into the curve of his neck, feeling the prickle of his five-o-clock shadow. A tide swelled inside her, gathering all her particles.

A horn blared just beside them. The light had changed and the crosswalk light counted down. They hurried across the intersection, hand in hand again. Distantly, she felt that the situation was funny, but her body was too full, too taut, too preoccupied for laughter.

They picked up speed for another block, fully running again by the time he turned them into the stairwell of an apartment building. She kept pace with him up one flight of stairs and then another, neither of them speaking as they sped along a third floor hallway. He dragged keys from his pocket, letting go of her hand to unlock a door while she leaned against the wall. He shoved the door open and began to kiss her again. She circled his neck with her arms, giving herself fully over to him, and he lifted her inside and kicked the door closed behind them.

When she reached for his belt this time he didn't stop her but shucked her jeans as she dropped his. In an awkward flurry, they kicked away shoes and tugged off coats and shirts. He got her bra off with a miracle of ease compared to Elliot's fumbling ineptitude. She was in his arms, needing him, begging, "Please, please—" A moment later her back was against carpet and he was over her and she lifted her hips to him. He fit her like a miracle. He was as right, as necessary, as her sealskin remaking her, but this time she wasn't alone. They struggled together toward some new kind of completion. She rose and rose to him, drawing tighter and tighter and more and more frantic until—at last—she blossomed, petals of ecstasy unfurling all around his motion.

She came back to herself languorously as he stilled against her, opening her eyes. The room was nearly dark, but she had always seen well in dim light. They lay on the floor, a couch covered with books beside them. He held himself above her, looking down with an expression both stunned and wonderstruck. She opened her mouth to say something—she had no idea what.

"Sshh," he whispered. "Don't break the spell."

She smiled. He let himself down beside her and drew her close. She rested her head in the hollow of his shoulder and closed her eyes again, peace lapping over her. She loved the way he smelled—animal and male and yet fresh as winter air after a snowfall.

She was almost asleep when she felt his touch moving over her skin, slow and warm and hypnotic. She stretched and turned in his hands so he could run them over her hips, her bottom, her sides, her breasts. A drowsy warmth spread through her, building quickly to an ache. She twisted belly to belly with him and felt him stiff and ready between her thighs. Finding his mouth with hers, she kissed him long and slow and deep until their bodies merged once more, and their motion carried her away.

*   *   *

Eventually, their stomachs began to growl in turns, and, laughing, they got up and dressed. He searched the tiny kitchen for food, but there wasn't any so he ordered pizza, not even blinking when she asked for anchovies on her half.

His apartment had the generic furniture of a place furnished by the landlord. Only the books everywhere were clearly his, thick marine biology texts and obscure, academic-looking titles. "Are you a professor?" She picked up a stack of books from the couch and looked for a place to set it down, trying to clear room to sit while they waited for the pizza.

He took the books from her and set them on the floor beneath the window that looked out on the street. "No. Fortunately, since I think you're an undergrad?"

She nodded briefly.

"I'm a post-doc at the marine science center."

"I'm an art major," she said. It was almost true. She hadn't declared yet, but if she admitted that, he'd know she was a freshman. She didn't know exactly how old he was and didn't want to draw attention to an issue that clearly concerned him. She doubted he was thirty, but he was nearer that than twenty.

Together they removed the rest of the books from the couch and stacked them beneath the window with the others.

"Is the art program here a good one?" he asked.

"Yes…but that's my good luck. I didn't know my major; I came here to be near the ocean."

He smiled at her as they settled on opposite ends of the couch, facing each other. "That's why I went into marine biology. To be near the sea."

Their eyes caught and held. It was a relief to have something else in common, besides a bodily attraction so profound that an hour ago she simply wouldn't have believed it was possible. Even now, his smile lodged in her as if she were wet clay and everything he did left a mark on her.

"I don't want you to think…" Her courage nearly failed. She didn't want to make confessions to him—to make him think she'd completely lost her head over him, although she was afraid she had. She just didn't want him to think she was a slut. "I've never done anything like this before."

He looked at her curiously. "Anything like what?"

She felt her face heating up. "Like seeing you and—" she gestured toward the rug.

"But—" He pointed at the rug. "You've done that before."

She nodded, actually relieved to present more evidence that she wasn't just a little kid. "I never liked it before, though."

"With Elliot?"

"Right."

"Just to be clear," he said, "you *did* like—" pointing once more at the rug.

She couldn't tell if he was checking his own understanding of the situation or whether he wanted her to praise him as a lover. She smiled. "Couldn't you tell?"

He looked very slightly sheepish. "I was a bit distracted."

"You liked it, too." She absolutely wanted him to praise her.

"Aye," he said.

It killed her—the impossible appeal of his accent, his unembarrassed admission, the fearless way he met her eyes and the understanding passing between them that whatever they were doing here together was far from over.

The pizza arrived. They put the box between them on the couch, his side loaded with all the toppings and hers with only cheese and anchovies. They ate and made each other laugh over nothing at all. At some point the box moved to the floor. They became more and more entangled and less and less dressed. She lost all understanding of the passage of time. At some point he drew her by her hand from the couch and led her to his bed. Much later—or maybe by then it was early—she rolled a little apart from him and drew a pillow under her cheek and fell profoundly asleep.

When she woke, the covers lay neatly over her. The absence of the snarl of blankets in which she usually awoke alerted her before she opened her eyes to something unusual. By the time she did open them, she knew where she was. The blinds were closed, but the light at their edges showed that morning was well underway. The covers were as neat as though Douglas had made up the bed with her in it, but he was gone.

She sat up and listened. Although the sounds of people running water and moving about came very faintly from around her, they issued from other apartments. Nearby was only empty silence.

A note lay on the other pillow. Her heart thumped painfully as she picked it up. It made no sense that his absence hurt her. She should have been glad of the privacy, aware as she already was of her sour mouth and frowsy hair and the smell of old sex that clung to her as it never had with Elliot because she always washed him off the first moment she could.

Alise—had to go to the lab to check some samples. I wish I had something to offer you for breakfast, but the larder is bare. Here is my phone number, and you know where to find me. Thank you for last night. —Douglas

Oh, she felt unreasonably forlorn. There was nothing wrong with the note. He'd remembered her name. She should be grateful for that. He seemed to want—or at least be willing—to see her again.

Her clothes were in a little pile beside the bed—Douglas must have brought them from the living room and folded them. She picked them up and held them on her lap without putting them on. *What did you want?* she asked herself irritably. *What did you think would happen?* Had some part of her honestly thought he would be here when she woke up, that they'd just carry on indefinitely as they had the night before, always together, always touching, making love whenever they felt like it, from now on? Had she really thought it could be that simple? She didn't know the first thing about him.

But she *did*. She knew everything about him. She knew his name, and the deep, lovely sound of his voice, his gorgeous accent. She knew he loved the ocean as much as she did and ate everything except anchovies on his pizza and wouldn't make fun of her for eating fish. She knew how his eyes crinkled when he smiled, how his tongue felt in places she had never imagined anyone would want to taste her, how he smelled like home to her. She knew that he met her eyes as if he didn't mind at all, in fact he *wanted* her to look all the way inside him and learn every one of his secrets.

Alise walked naked into his bathroom, which was as spartan as the rest of his apartment. She showered, making up for washing him off her body by using his soap, his shampoo. Clean, she would still smell of him.

She tore away the note he'd left her and wrote her number on the remaining part, which she returned to his pillow. She made up the bed smoothly, leaving no trace of herself. But then she buried her face in his pillow for one last, exquisite whiff of him, and wondered if he would search his sheets with his nose for similar evidence of her.

When she let herself out, the door locked behind her.

She walked swiftly back to campus, going straight to the dining hall and bypassing her dorm. The caf was serving the usual weekend hodgepodge of breakfast and lunch. Before noon on a Saturday, empty tables abounded and she saw no sign of Elliot. She heaped her plate high with tuna from the salad bar and ate it all, then went back for seconds. She didn't feel the least bit queasy. She felt—peaceful, powerful, resolved.

When she walked into the lobby of her dorm, Elliot stood from the couch where she had known he'd be waiting for her. From his disheveled appearance and the haunted look on his face, she suspected he'd been there all night, but she didn't ask.

"I'm breaking up with you," she said calmly, gently, looking in his eyes and watching them fill instantly with tears. "I was wrong that I could be your girlfriend. I'm sorry. I tried, but I can't do it."

"Why not?" he whispered.

She could see him crumpling inside as she had dreaded. She'd thought she couldn't bear to hurt him, believed she had no right to inflict pain. Now she watched him with compassion, without looking away. This was a tragedy, but it was not her fault. She would bear witness, but she wouldn't carry the guilt.

"I met someone I want," she told him softly.

*   *   *

Later that afternoon, when her phone rang, a prophetic happiness stole over her even before she answered.

"Alise?"

She loved the lilt of her name on his tongue. "Douglas. How were the samples?"

"Time-consuming," he said ruefully. "They don't understand about weekends and lying in."

"Are you home now?"

"Aye."

"Want me to come over?"

"I'd like that."

Chapter 8: Alise

August 1994 - Beaufort, North Carolina

Alise was caught in a net. She thrashed and twisted, but she couldn't get free. The more she struggled, the tighter it became, wrapped around her middle and squeezing, *squeezing*. She whimpered, but the constriction only drew tighter. It crushed the life from her; it was going to cut her in half, and *what would happen to the baby?*

This thought was so terrible that she woke with a cry. Her eyes flew open, and for the briefest moment she was reassured by her surroundings—the soft blue sheets of the bed she and Douglas had bought only a few months before, the sunlight streaming in between the curtains she'd found at Goodwill and bleached, then painted in intricate patterns and swirls, blue against the white background. Douglas had started work at the Duke marine lab just after Christmas, and she had dropped out of school to come to Beaufort with him. She'd felt like Cinderella going to the ball, simply sloughing off the life she'd longed to escape and emerging into a bright, new, shining one, full of everything she wanted.

She was alone in bed. Douglas must have left for work without waking her. Late now in her pregnancy, she slept so badly that when she actually achieved unconsciousness he wouldn't disturb her for anything short of the house burning down.

The house was not burning down, but the net of her dream had not vanished with her sleep, either. Pain seized her again, tighter than ever, the agony a ring around her huge, hard belly, and even worse around her back. She curled up, her hands protecting the baby, cradling it through the shell of her body. She was wet. Her nightgown, the bed—everything was soaked.

This was no net. She was in labor.

Once she understood the pain, some small, calm corner of her mind could stand aside. Her body was opening to let the baby out. She'd taken the class and read the books. She wasn't supposed to struggle against the pain. She was supposed to be a flower unfurling its petals. She was supposed to relax and let the pain do its work.

She breathed in, slow and deep. In fact, the pain was very slightly better if she didn't fight. The wet constriction of her clothes, however, was unbearable. She wrestled out of her nightgown and underwear.

The pain, when she was distracted by undressing, came back and tried to crush her.

Naked now, she took gasping breaths and tried to collect herself. *She was a flower. All she had to do was open.*

But this time the pain went on and on and on.

She needed to time the contractions so she could call Douglas. How could she do that if the contraction didn't stop? It was supposed to stop!

Fear surged through her, worse than before because she couldn't wake this time. She needed Douglas and he wasn't here. She had to call him, but the phone was all the way downstairs. They didn't even have a cordless—just the old-fashioned kind attached to the kitchen wall. It had seemed like a blessing when they'd moved into this house a few months ago. The telephone was nothing but a tyranny to them, and half the time they kept the ringer off rather than talk to her angry parents, Douglas's bewildered mum, or Elliot who *could not leave her alone*. She was a nineteen-year-old college dropout, a pregnant teenage bride. But she and Douglas were soaring, swooning, giddy in love, and as long as they didn't answer the phone, nothing dented their happiness.

Except this. This was a rather sizable dent, waking up alone, deep in labor. *How had she not had more warning?*

She had to get downstairs somehow. Once more, she breathed in, deep and slow, and once again the pain eased very slightly. Not the pressure, which was relentless, but the agony. She had to *open*.

No, first she had to get out of bed.

She struggled to her hands and knees. She could imagine the next steps. Extend one leg to the floor and then the other. Push off with her hands. Stand up. She imagined it again, willed her weight to shift and her leg to move. Nothing happened.

The pain wanted her knees where they were. If she moved them, it would kill her.

She clutched the top of the low headboard, clinging with her whole strength, as if it were a pillar in a hurricane sea. Dimly, she was aware of yelling—not screaming, but some loud, focused cry. Drag in breath, then yell it out. It felt—effective.

Time vanished. Even the pain was no longer pain. It was a force, an effort, a cataclysm. It was all-encompassing. Her feet somehow moved beneath her. Her hands clutched the headboard. Her breath no longer yelled out of her, but bore down with growling sounds.

With a rush and a spill and a slither, a baby slid onto the mattress.

She looked down at the infant dumbly. She seemed to have forgotten this would be the end result. She took in the wet, dark hair; waxy closed eyelids; smooth, red skin flecked all over with what might have been white sea foam; perfect rosebud of a mouth; miniature, curled fingers and flawless little feet, soles lifted to her. For a moment, the shocking purple rope confused her, because they'd said the baby would be a girl, but then she made sense of the umbilicus.

The baby's eyelids fluttered open, and fathomless, no-colored eyes looked up at Alise.

"Hello, Ellie," she breathed.

How can you want to name her something that sounds so much like Elliot? Douglas had demanded. But she'd chosen the name long ago, and as she looked down at this little being, at the dark eyes that were making heavens-knew-what of this shocking new world, her certainty didn't waver. *It was my name first,* she'd told him. *I won't let him ruin it for me.*

As Ellie gave a tiny shudder, her pink lips opened, trembled. Her little face crumpled up, her eyes closing, and she wailed, the sound unexpectedly deep for such a small creature.

That voice! Alise thought, at the same time that she fought panic at this evidence of unhappiness. But another part of her thought, *That means she's breathing!*

She settled awkwardly against the headboard and scooped Ellie into her arms. There was a lot of blood and slime, and the freakish umbilical cord, but she didn't let herself worry. She found a corner of sheet and used it to wipe away the blood and wax, cradling Ellie against her breasts and cooing at her. "It's okay. It's okay, little one."

Ellie stopped crying and smacked her lips like a little guppy. Alise was so grateful and charmed she was able to push down for a few more moments her growing, uncomfortable awareness that she had no idea what she was doing, and that she was all alone. How on earth was she going to get help now? The phone was as far away as ever. Could she walk?

Miraculously, she heard footsteps on the front porch, which was just below the bedroom window. Someone tried the locked door, paused, opened it with a key.

"Douglas!" she called, nearly dissolving in a rush of gratitude and relief. Ellie's little face crumpled in protest at her loud voice.

"Alise!"

Her whole being seized with shock. The voice wasn't Douglas's. It was Elliot's.

He pounded up the stairs and appeared a moment later in the doorway. He was white-faced, panting, his eyes huge. "Alise! Thank *god*. I thought you were dead!"

"What are you doing here?" she asked blankly. His presence here made no sense at all—not even as much sense as a net in a nightmare. Elliot was supposed to be a hundred miles away in Wilmington, in class. Not here in Beaufort.

"I heard you screaming. I ran down the street to call 911. They're coming—" A siren's wail had started up very close by. "But when I got back you were quiet and I thought..."

"How did you get *in*?" she demanded.

"Your spare key was under the mat. Can I see?"

"You're stalking me!" she accused him, appalled. *He'd been outside her house. Listening to her scream. He'd helped, but only by running away.*

"Not stalking. I just check on you sometimes."

A four-hour round trip to check on her.

She shrank away from his tentative approach, putting her shoulder between him and Ellie, drawing herself protectively around her infant. "Goddamn it, Elliot, don't look at the baby. *Go call my husband!*"

"You're lucky I was here." He didn't retreat, and she felt frantically vulnerable—holding a being she would protect with her life, but naked, lying in a pool of gore, with a slimy cord still roping out of her.

"*Go,*" she spat furiously. "Get away from us!"

Us! She and Ellie were an us! All through her pregnancy she had remained *I*, but now, suddenly, there were two of them.

She felt another very sudden gush and slither between her thighs, and a huge bloody mass emerged onto the mattress. She screamed. All she could think was that this was another baby, an unexpected twin, and there was something very, very wrong with it. It had no features.

"*What's that?*" Elliot yelled.

His panic was like a slap in the face, infuriating her so much that she was suddenly icy calm. The *very last thing she needed* was Elliot freaking out. "It's the placenta," she announced coldly, as if this hadn't just occurred to her. She studied the gruesome thing with new interest, hoping Elliot was too grossed out to come near her now.

Outside, the now deafening shriek of the siren suddenly cut off. Vehicle doors slammed, more feet thudded on the porch, and someone pounded on the door.

A small tuft of something that looked like fur stuck out of a crease in the placenta. That didn't make sense. Heart in her throat, terrified all over again that a second baby was mixed up in this somehow, she reached out and tugged at it.

"Up here!" Elliot answered the voices calling downstairs.

A piece of hide slid free and dangled between her fingers. It appeared to be a small, flat, bloody creature. She squeezed her eyes shut, aware of Ellie, warm and flawless and nuzzling her breast, and at the same time breathless with terror that this was some new tragedy.

A small army tromped up the stairs.

The thing was plucked from her grip. Her eyes flew open.

Elliot held it now, staring, fascinated. "Your baby's a selkie, too," he said.

She had no time to respond, to snatch the tiny pelt back from Elliot. The room filled with men. They swarmed around her with a businesslike efficiency that quickly turned to smiles and warmth and incredulous congratulations. Someone took Ellie from her briefly and then handed her back, declaring her perfect. Someone produced a pair of scissors and a clamp and snipped the umbilicus.

"Please call my husband," she begged them.

"Wasn't he just here? Where did he go?"

"No…" She gave them the number for Douglas's lab, reciting the digits automatically as her heart became a frozen lump inside her.

Elliot was gone. And he had taken Ellie's sealskin.

Chapter 9: Alise

April 1995 - Beaufort, North Carolina

Alise turned off Highway 70 at the graveled pull-out overlooking Core Sound. In the summer, the place was an unofficial boat launch area, but in April, in the middle of a pouring rainstorm, no one else was here, and cars passing on the road were rare. Alise had chosen the remote spot on purpose. She knew what Elliot wanted, and she refused with everything in her to invite him into the home she shared with Douglas for it. She had expected Elliot to protest—they both drove small cars with cramped back seats—but he had not.

She had arrived first. Rain obscured her view of the sound the instant she turned off the windshield wipers. The rain and the water and the sky all merged into one bleak, colorless expanse, relieved only by a blurred green stripe that was the marsh grass along the shore. The downpour suited her mood, though if she had to throw up—the dread and anxiety churning her stomach made this possibility more distinct every moment—she was going to get drenched leaning out her door. She unbuckled her seatbelt but left the engine running and turned the fan to high, directing the vents onto herself in an attempt to dispel the prickly heat of her nausea.

The suitcase containing her sealskin had slid across the back seat during the drive and now huddled against Ellie's empty car seat, as if for comfort. Alise had retrieved it on the way here, from the storage unit in Morehead City where she'd been keeping it since the move to Beaufort. Ellie was with the neighbor for a few hours so Alise could "run some errands." Douglas was at work. He didn't know a thing about this and he never, never could.

The whole situation seemed so inevitable. Didn't it always come down to this with Elliot—sex in exchange for the safety of her sealskin, or in this case, Ellie's sealskin? *It's nothing you haven't done before*, she told herself, swallowing hard. *You can do it one more time for Ellie's sake.*

And never again.

*   *   *

She had called Elliot repeatedly in the weeks after Ellie was born to beg for the sealskin. He always kept her on the phone as long as possible, but refused even to talk about the sealskin. She understood that she was giving him exactly what he wanted—her attention—and he wasn't likely to give the pelt back when keeping it was working so well for him. She couldn't figure out what to do. She had a newborn. She was so exhausted her brain barely worked half the time. And she was frantic to get back her daughter's missing piece.

When Ellie was two months old, Alise drove to Wilmington while Douglas was at work, without telling him. The campus felt surreal to her when she arrived, belonging to a world she'd left behind so completely she was almost surprised it still existed. She didn't know which dorm Elliot was in now, but she arrived just before lunch time and knew she could catch him at the caf. Not wanting to wake Ellie, who had miraculously slept the entire drive, she removed the car seat from its snap-off base and carried the whole heavy basket with her across the quad. Of course, Ellie woke the moment Alise set the car seat down at the entrance to the cafeteria, which was still a few minutes from opening. Alise scooped her out and bounced her gently in her arms while she waited, avoiding the eyes of a couple of students milling around, hoping not to see anyone she knew and worrying because Ellie needed to nurse.

Elliot hadn't changed his habit of showing up for meals the minute the caf doors opened. When he saw her, he broke into a delighted smile. She felt a vicious impulse to slap it off his face, but her hands were full of Ellie. Elliot barely glanced at the baby. "You came!" he said.

"You do understand that the longer you drag this out, the more I hate you, right?" she snapped. "What's it going to take, Elliot?"

They stood to one side of the cafeteria doors, attracting curious glances as people drifted in. Alise didn't care much what they thought of her, anyone who might recognize the girl who'd dropped out halfway through her freshman year and now held the obvious explanation, who was starting to fuss in earnest. But Elliot looked uncomfortable. "Let's go outside," he said.

He stood awkwardly, not offering to help as she strapped Ellie back into the car seat. Ellie—sensing the opportunity to nurse retreating—let out an indignant wail. "Just a minute, sweetheart

—only a minute," Alise told her futilely, slinging the diaper bag over her shoulder and lumbering beneath her burdens toward the door. She would have died before she handed Ellie over to Elliot, but he could have offered to take the diaper bag. His passive helplessness infuriated her. He was such a worthless, ineffective *kid*.

So her first impulse, when they got outside and he said, "Leave Douglas and come back to me," was to laugh derisively.

But he was serious. Her laughter died a swift death.

She hefted a still howling Ellie and left him without another word. The weight of the one-handled carseat made her list to one side and walk with a hitch. He followed her, of course, calling her name, protesting, even walking in front of her to try to stop her. She kicked his ankle. He stopped, swearing, clearly expecting her to turn around and apologize. She did neither. She snapped Ellie's seat into the car and drove away, the baby's furious, despairing sobs expressing the state of her own soul. Elliot's pale, stupid face stared after her in the rearview mirror. She pulled the car over as soon as she was out of sight and nursed Ellie in the back seat, her tears dripping onto the baby's head.

She cried out of fury—with Elliot, but even more, with herself. What on earth was wrong with her, that even now—a whole new person in a whole new life—she still couldn't say *no* to Elliot? She had only walked away, and that wasn't good enough.

A few days later, Elliot called, and for once got straight to the point. "Get a paternity test. Ellie's my kid. Prove it and I'll give back the sealskin."

"Go to *hell*, Elliot," she snapped, and hung up the phone.

The fear that Ellie *was* Elliot's had knotted inside her since she'd first discovered she was pregnant. This had happened on Christmas Eve, a month after she met Douglas. Alise had defied her parents by staying in Wilmington to spend the holiday with Douglas instead of riding home with Elliot. Her parents had been devastated. "What's wrong with Elliot?" they'd wanted to know. Elliot was familiar, safe, a known quantity. Elliot would bring her home, not steal her away, as a much older, foreign man would surely do. They had reluctantly invited Douglas for Christmas, but made it clear that he would sleep in the guest room and be reminded at every opportunity that Alise—who was eighteen to his twenty-seven—was still a child. Alise had snapped. Of course her parents were only acting like parents, according to the rules they knew. But their anxious hovering had dragged her back from being a seal and delivered her into Elliot's clutches, and she'd felt she would rather cut off her own foot than let them hold her back from Douglas.

On Christmas Eve, she and Douglas were in his tiny apartment kitchen, attempting to make dressing. They'd been teaching themselves to cook and were having a wonderful time pretending to disagree over the recipe and getting in each other's way on purpose. But the smell of onions sautéing made her increasingly uneasy in a way she only identified as nausea when she threw up into the kitchen sink. Douglas rushed out to the pharmacy, which was closing early, and returned with Pepto-Bismol and a pregnancy test. Four weeks to the day had passed since she'd crawled out from under the camellia bush and stopped him in his tracks. He stood behind her in the little bathroom where she'd showered the morning after they met, holding her tightly, watching over her shoulder as the test revealed its result. They looked at the pink cross in shared silence for a moment, then he turned her around and bent to look in her eyes. "Marry me," he said. "I know it's happening fast, but you're all I want. You're the only one I'll ever want."

Douglas was all she wanted, too. She clung to him, the need to make him part of her communicating so fully that in moments they were making love with all the urgency of their first meeting, her bottom parked on the edge of the sink. Her *yes* was understood so clearly between them that she'd never even spoken it out loud.

But in the coldest, darkest part of her lodged the knowledge that two days before Douglas appeared to redeem her life, she'd been huddled, sick, in a different bathroom after sex with Elliot. She had been sloppy and forgetful about her pill since meeting Douglas, as she had been with all her responsibilities, as if she hadn't even tried to avoid this outcome—almost as if she had courted it. But how much of that recklessness had been driven by fear, knowing that she often forgot her pill, that she had done so twice in the week before that last time with Elliot? She had no idea whose child she carried.

Pregnant with Ellie, she had been certain she couldn't live without Douglas. The thought of losing him had been like the thought of being ripped in half. But that fear was nothing compared to what she felt now. Since she'd been an infant herself, she had never been so dependent on another human being. Without Douglas, it seemed to Alise that she and Ellie would starve, would die of exposure. She would die from simple lack of sleep. Before, she had needed him for her soul. Now, she and Ellie needed him for the most basic facts of bodily survival. Elliot couldn't take care of her, body *or* soul. The thought of proving him Ellie's father was like staring down the barrel of a gun at her own death—and Ellie's.

She didn't speak to Elliot again until December, when he called her at 2 a.m. His parents' car had struck a patch of ice and skidded into a storm-swollen river. His mom had died instantly. His dad lingered on a respirator, brain-dead from lack of oxygen. In a couple of days, he, too, was gone.

Alise drove home to Asheville for the joint memorial service because Elliot begged her. Her responsibilities in the situation confused her. She had barely known Elliot's parents—Elliot had always come to her house, not the other way around—but the scope of his tragedy seemed to give him rights that trumped her own need to avoid him. And until she recovered Ellie's sealskin, she was tied to him. The fact that he knew this and exploited his hold over her didn't loosen the knot. And his parents were *dead*.

Douglas came with her—his first visit to her parents' house. Alise was relieved, under the circumstances, to lay eyes on her parents and reassure herself that they still existed. Her mom seemed to feel the same way. "Life is too short to keep fighting," Sandra had said first thing, coming out to meet them in the driveway. "Hello, Douglas. Hand me that sweet grandbaby."

At the service, which Alise attended by herself, Elliot was pale, glittery-eyed, jerky in his movements. She had never known Elliot to drink or use any kind of drug, but she wondered, suddenly. The almost visible shroud of isolation that hung around him shocked her—not for its newness, but for its familiarity. *Elliot has always been alone*, she thought. She had always seen this, and pitied him.

Loneliness did not describe Elliot—it defined him. She'd thought it was her job to fill that loneliness because he'd asked her to, but nothing could. Even she had never come close.

"What will I do now?" he asked, when she spoke to him afterward.

She shook her head. "I'm so sorry, Elliot." She couldn't help him. Even if she wanted to, she'd never be enough.

She said no word about the sealskin, that day or for several months. Elliot dropped out of school, where he'd been failing anyway, and stayed in Asheville to deal with his parents' estate.

The first week of April, he called her. "I'll trade her sealskin for yours."

She almost hung up on him again. She'd never flat-out admitted being a selkie—to Elliot or to anyone else. And giving him her sealskin was utterly out of the question.

"Wait—not forever. Just for, like, an hour."

She'd felt a devastating mixture of despair and hope. Despair at what he asked, which seemed instantly inevitable, something that had been coming at her forever. Hope because that probably meant it was the answer.

"How do I know you'd give it back?" She spoke quietly. She had managed to put Ellie down in her crib without waking her, and she hoped the nap would last.

He hesitated. "My dad had a gun. I could give it to you. If I didn't give it back when you asked me…"

"God, Elliot! If I were willing to shoot you, I'd have done it by now, wouldn't I? That would be a nice, simple way to get what I need. No consequences *there*!" She took the new cordless phone into the pantry and shut the door. Hopefully her voice wouldn't wake Ellie.

"Well, what do you propose? I swear—after an hour I'll give it back. I'll do whatever you ask."

The best thing would be for Douglas to come home. He was a lot bigger than Elliot, and Elliot couldn't be sure Douglas wouldn't shoot him. But what if Douglas *did* shoot him? And even if he didn't, he would find out she was a selkie. She hadn't told him. She couldn't stand to tell him. What if he was angry she had kept her secret from him? What if he didn't love her anymore once he found out she wasn't completely human, and neither was Ellie? And—she was pretty sure she knew what Elliot planned for the hour with her sealskin, and if Douglas found out about *that* he really would shoot Elliot. Elliot wouldn't wait around for that to happen, though. He'd simply leave, without returning Ellie's pelt. She might never get it back.

She couldn't tell Douglas.

"What happens during the hour?"

"Probably nothing," he said. "It probably doesn't work."

"*What* probably doesn't work?"

"Anything," he said uncomfortably. "You know. It doesn't work on Ellie."

"What the *hell* do you mean, it doesn't work on Ellie?" She'd read the same selkie stories he had. She knew he hoped that holding her pelt would somehow put her in his power.

"When she was crying a few times, when we talked on the phone, I held her sealskin and told her to stop. But she didn't."

"Fuck you, Elliot!" The idea of Elliot performing mind control on Ellie, even for a reason Alise might have been tempted to try herself, made her want to shoot him after all.

"It didn't work!" he protested. "I wasn't going to hurt her."

She fought for reason, but her tone had a lethal edge. "If it doesn't work, what's the point of taking mine?"

"I just want to know. I can't stop thinking about it. I just want to know if that part of the myth is true. Ellie's just a baby. I was far away. Maybe that's why it didn't work."

She forced her words through tense jaws. "Elliot. I will have sex with you in order to get Ellie's sealskin back. I will do it willingly. You don't need my sealskin to force me."

His voice rose suddenly. "You *won't* do it willingly. You never have. You'll do it because you have to get Ellie's skin back!" He sounded shaky and she thought he was crying. "Just once, Alise, I want you to want me. *Just once.* That's all I ask."

Now she was crying, too. "I *don't* want you. I never have!"

"Goddamnit, Alise, *do you think I don't know that?* That's why it's your sealskin. One hour with your sealskin. Or I will keep Ellie's until I *die*."

She hung up on him. The minute she did, she heard Ellie wailing from the bedroom. She raced for the stairs. Her life was crumbling, was going to fall and crush her. She was a terrible mother, a terrible wife, a murderer in her heart. She wanted to ask Elliot for that gun after all and shoot him first, instead of waiting an hour. The fact that she would never, never do this didn't alter her sick sense that it would be the safer plan.

Later, she called him back. "One hour." A hard, bitter resolve sat in her chest like a tumor. "Give me her sealskin back first, and you can have one hour. And then I *never* want to see you again. Is that clear?"

"Clear," he said. He had the gall to sound *hopeful*, as if he thought her undying hatred of him might prove reversible.

"There is no magic in the world that will make me want you." She was as sure of that as she had ever been of anything.

*   *   *

Tires crunched gravel. A car door opened and slammed again.

Elliot was here.

Anxiety seized Alise so tightly that she seemed to drift a little above herself, as if the fear had crowded her out of her own body. Then her own passenger-side door opened and Elliot intruded, shoving a black backpack ahead of him and slamming the door quickly against the rain.

Elliot looked the same as always, except wetter. Tall and gangly, pale blue eyes blinking nervously beneath dripping bangs, damp T-shirt tucked into his pleated-front khaki pants. Muddy white tennis shoes. Backpack on his lap: The pack must contain Ellie's pelt.

She felt the usual disconnect. She made him an object of so much oppression and horror, but when she saw him again he was just—Elliot. Dorky, annoying—not sinister.

"How are you doing?" she asked. It was the first time she'd seen him since the memorial service. The villainous Elliot in her head didn't deserve pleasantries, but hapless Elliot in the flesh elicited them from her despite herself.

He shrugged. "Okay, I guess. I'm selling the Asheville house."

She was startled. "Where will you go?"

He hesitated. "My folks had a place in Maine. It's mine now."

"Wow." This was the worst idea she'd ever heard, going to a lonely place where he knew no one, to grieve by himself. She felt guilty about how glad she was.

"No one ever goes there. You'll never see me again, just like you wanted." His voice shook.

"Stop." She couldn't locate the compassion to lie and say she didn't want it. "Could we just get this over with?"

He twisted to look into the back seat. "That's your sealskin?"

"Ellie's first. You promised."

"Yes, but show me first, that yours is really in there."

She glared at him.

"I won't touch it. I just need to know you're being straight with me."

She released her seat lever and slammed her seat back down as far as it would go, venting her feelings with the violence and also avoiding leaning any closer to Elliot than she had to. Half-lying across the back seat, she unlatched the suitcase, flipped back the lid briefly to reveal the pale fur, then slapped it shut again. "There." She shoved the suitcase as fully behind Elliot's seat as it would go, so he couldn't reach it without turning around on his knees or getting out and opening the door to the back seat. She returned to upright and glared at him. She pulsed inside with the impulse to fight him, but held herself in check. She needed Ellie's sealskin. She was not strong enough to take it from him by force.

"Okay." He unzipped the backpack on his lap and lifted out a tiny, snow-white pelt.

Alise snatched it from him. He sat quietly in his seat as she examined it. The pelt was perfect—soft and sleek, tiny flippers, tiny nose, little whiskers, somehow alive despite the quiet holes where eyes would be—alive, yet dormant. She ran it through her hands, consumed with wonder.

"Beautiful, isn't it?" he asked.

"It's not yours!" she snapped, hating how proprietary he sounded, hating that he had possessed this part of her daughter while she had not.

Instead of answering, he opened his door and stood into the downpour. Anticipating his next move, she threw herself between the seats to protect her sealskin, her body stretched between the front seat and the back, clinging to the suitcase with both hands and trying to shield it with her chest. Rain swept in as Elliot opened the back door. He made no move to get in, apparently not caring that he was getting drenched. She clenched herself so tightly around the suitcase that she squeezed even her eyes shut, prepared for him to wrestle it away from her and determined to use every ounce of her strength to prevent him.

"We had a deal," Elliot reminded her. He sounded unusually calm, as if certain the deal still had power.

It didn't. She understood that now. She could no more hand him her sealskin than she could calmly allow him to murder her. On some molecular level of her being, the two were the same thing.

"Well," he said, and she felt him lean over her into the car. She braced for his attack, remembering too late Ellie's pelt lying undefended on her lap. As he seized it she twisted, grabbing at him, raking at him with her fingernails, trying to get her teeth into him, a panicked wild thing fighting for her life. But her position was too awkward, and he was much stronger than she was, and she had committed the fatal mistake of letting go of the suitcase.

In moments, the struggle was over. She felt the suitcase wrenched from beneath her, and she was left twisted between the seats, grabbing frantically at raindrops, as Elliot retreated out of reach.

She began to scream. It was not a reasoned attempt to summon help. There was no one in that pitiless expanse of marsh and sound and sky and empty highway to hear her, except Elliot. It was simply a protest from the bottoms of her lungs and the depths of her soul. Her screams were horrible, tearing things that seared her throat.

Somewhere very far away Elliot was shouting something, too. In an instant, the nightmare plunged to an entirely new depth of horror. She was strangled to silence, the compulsion to scream denied as completely as a candle flame snuffed by a gust of wind. She felt Elliot's violation of her in every cell. A fainting horror seized her, a blackness in which she didn't fall but felt herself receding very swiftly, her soul escaping from unbearable reality.

With the last shreds of her being, knowing she had only moments to act before Elliot used his awful power to stop her, she wrenched herself back into the driver's seat. She threw the parking break, ground the car into gear and stomped down hard on the accelerator. Her muscles went slack along with her will as Elliot shouted after her, but by then the car was already launched over the embankment, and no force on earth could have kept it from crashing and tumbling the rest of the way, glancing off a pillar by the boat ramp and shattering the windshield just before it struck the water.

Chapter 10: Silas

May 1996 - Camden, Maine

*B*y late spring, fish were shoaling and food was so plentiful that the seals had no need to spread out and hunt singly. They congregated on the rocks, soaking up the sun. The belligerent urgency of the winter ice fields didn't trouble them now, though they mostly minded their boundaries and enforced a bit of distance with their neighbors as they sunned, biting out and honking if anyone came too close. The exception was a bit of play between the little females and the bulls. So it was nothing out of the ordinary when the graceful, buff-colored female with the speckled face teased the big, gray bull with black splotches merging to a solid stripe along his back. She nudged her way into his space, and when he lunged at her she rolled onto her back without retreating and seemed to laugh at him. When she'd provoked him a few more times he chased her off the rock into the water. She twined her body around his, and he felt a lazy, playful version of the ice field excitement and twined back. That was how it started. Over days, the two stayed near each other. He hunted when she hunted, sunned when she sunned, and mock-

defended her when other bulls came too close. He didn't bite at her when she came near. Sometimes he rolled over on her on purpose.

On the morning she put her nose in the air and sniffed something he couldn't smell, then plunged off the rock in search of it, he came, too. He kept pace with her as she swam steadily south, obeying an instinct he didn't share. His own instinct was to stay with her. They swam for three days, resting a few times in shallow coves where they dozed on the bottom and swam up at half-waking intervals to breathe.

She wriggled ashore in the middle of the morning, though choppy surf that broke far from the beach and left foam on the rocks for the wind to blow in flecks and pieces. She didn't seek an open, sunny rock, but instead headed for a sheltered crevice where she lay still and began to tremble. Troubled, he touched his nose to her flank, and began to tremble, too.

*   *   *

For once, when his sealskin shook him loose and left Silas a man again, he didn't rage and swear. Intensely aware that he was not alone, he lifted his pelt and looked out warily.

Beside him lay familiar buff-colored fur, but the pelt was inert and flattened, and as he watched, it twitched and lifted. A woman's face looked out at him. Her eyes meeting his grew wide and round, and she heaved her sealskin aside and sat up fully. He did the same.

"You're a selkie, too!" she exclaimed.

Speech didn't occur to him at first. He knew her well as a seal, but as a woman she was entirely new to him, and she entranced him fully. She had a sweet face with wide-spaced hazel eyes and a sharp chin. Her hair was long and chestnut-colored, not at all the same as her buff seal's body, but not so far from the color of her speckles. Her skin was creamy smooth, not freckled at all, and her breasts were objects of stunning beauty—full for her slender frame and decorated with wine-colored nipples. She was young. She could not be much older than Alise had been when he'd waited beneath the dock for her to put on her pelt, which made the girl much, much younger than he.

He hoped his age wouldn't trouble her because beneath the fold of sealskin covering his lap she had seized his whole attention, and when he moved there'd be no hope of hiding how he wanted her.

"I'm Nora," she said. Her voice was low-pitched and seemed to hold a tumble of laughter. "Who are you?"

"Silas."

"You came with me!"

"I…did."

She laughed. "I've never heard of that before—two selkies finding each other as seals but changing back in order to…"

"To…?" Silas asked, hopefully.

She smiled. Her lips had looked narrow before, but now they widened bewitchingly. "To…introduce themselves? Have a cup of tea? Go to the movies?"

He looked at her with mute appeal. His erection was so urgent that his palms ached with the force of his need.

"I'm teasing," she said. "The only reason I'm not in your lap right now is the question of what to do with our pelts."

His delight at her astonishing directness was tempered by her point.

He fully remembered the nauseating horror he'd felt when Ed had handled his sealskin all those years ago. But now... Other rules seemed in effect. She was near enough to reach out an arm and touch his pelt, and he could do the same with hers. And he didn't feel frightened at all—only compelled.

"They didn't mind touching when we were seals," he offered.

"That's true..."

She met his eyes, and he could see her desire staring frankly back at him through her wide, dark pupils. She wanted him as badly as he wanted her. Her skin was flushed and her nipples had become hard, tight knots in the center of her areoles.

"Let's try it together on the count of three," she said. "If it's bad, we'll stop."

He nodded mute acceptance.

"Are you scared?" she whispered.

"I'm dying," he said hoarsely, and in response she gave a breathless little gasp and shut her eyes briefly.

"One-two-three," she said all in a rush, and reached for his fur as he did hers.

They made contact at the same moment. The sleek softness of her fur on his fingertips, which was finer than his, was accompanied by an awareness of her so complete and tender and all-encompassing that it felt exactly as if he had joined his body to hers and begun making love to her. Her swift sigh, the yielding in it, told him she felt the same, but more than her sigh, *she* told him. The communion between them had no words, but touching her pelt like this, he *knew* how she felt, as fully as if they inhabited the same skin.

With no need to discuss, they moved their bodies and their sealskins together into a tangle in which everything was touching exactly as it needed to. Their desire had merged and doubled at the contact with one another's sealskins, and the force should have been more than either of them could bear, but instead, their desperation replaced by certainty, they made love with exquisite slowness. When he kissed her, suckled her, stroked her, he felt her pleasure as his own, and when she made good on her intention to sit in his lap, straddling his hips with her knees and sinking him deep inside her, he was astonished by her delight, as well as his own almost painful gratification. He looked into her green-brown eyes as she rocked her hips slowly, stroking his length, and knew he'd never be closer to another being than this. He wanted to go on forever with her, in her, and she wanted that, too. And when they inevitably changed their minds and wanted to rush headlong toward the glorious conclusion, they did that together, too. The moment of detonation was a joy so transparent he could see straight through it to grief on the other side.

"Silas," she sighed afterward, and in her voice his name sounded like the name of god, like an infinite blessing.

I love you, he wanted to say, but forced into words this truth was so improbable that he wept, instead. *She* was the one from his mother's story—the girl who spoke to his heart and pulled him home from the sea.

She caught his tears on her fingertips and put them in her mouth. "You don't need these, silly," she told him tenderly. "I'm right here."

She read in his face that he didn't understand.

"Seven tears of true love. Don't you know that's how you call a selkie home?"

He shook his head slowly. "Since I've been a selkie, I've never had a home."

He felt her compassion—the way she understood his loneliness and was saddened by it—like a current moving through her sealskin, and saw the feelings echoed in her eyes. "Then it's good you came home with me."

He looked around them curiously, but the little hollow of rock they lay in hid his view of their surroundings. "You live here?"

"Right over there!" She stood up and pointed, and he stood, too. The roofs of a neighborhood receded from the edge of a low bluff, just down the shore from where they stood. Wooden steps wound from the top of the bluff to a wide, tide-swept shelf of rock at the bottom. From where they'd lain they might have been the only creatures in an empty world. He was shocked to find civilization so near.

She hoisted her sealskin over her shoulder. "Come on. Mom's expecting me, so there should be plenty to eat."

Silas's grip on this situation seemed to recede further with every revelation. "Wait. Your mom? Are we just going to walk naked through your neighborhood carrying our sealskins? What state is this, even?"

"This is Maine," she informed him, her mouth twitching with amusement. "Just outside Camden. And we're going to sneak in the back." She beckoned him, and instead of leading the way to the steps, she scrambled up the bank behind their hiding place and vanished into bushes at the top. He followed her with his own sealskin and found a narrow path between a tangle of low trees and shrubs. In a few moments they emerged into a backyard that was flanked by high wooden fences screening it from the yards to either side. Silas could hear children's shouts and dogs barking from nearby, but the house in front of them was quiet. For the first time, Nora hesitated. "Mom's probably at work."

"How long have you been gone?" Silas asked.

"A year." She glanced a little doubtfully around the yard as she said it, though.

"I'll be in the way," Silas said. "With your mom, I mean."

"No. Mom will understand about you just fine. And you're hungry, aren't you?"

Silas couldn't deny it. No longer touching her sealskin, he couldn't feel what she felt, but he'd been aware of her hunger down on the beach, as she must have been of his.

Nora said, "Let me just see if she's here." She ran up the back steps and opened the door, which was unlocked. "Mom?" she called, disappearing into the house.

He waited in the little yard, looking around to note the wooden enclosure for an outdoor shower, and all the flowers. Except for the rosebush, he didn't know any of their names, but there were lots of them around the borders of the yard, and a pole with several bird feeders hanging from it centered in front of a picture window.

Nora stuck her head back out. "She's not here. Come in!"

To Silas, comparing the interior of Nora's home to the poverty of his childhood apartment, the little house was a wonderland. Silas and his mother had made do with cast-off furnishings, small rooms, marred wallpaper, and worn linoleum. The rooms of Nora's house were full of warm wood and brightly patterned rugs and cosy furniture. Framed art hung on the walls. In the living room, a coffee table held a huge vase of fresh flowers. Bookshelves stood everywhere. In the kitchen, sunlight spilled and shone on blue and white tile countertops.

"You can put your sealskin in here with mine," Nora said, disappearing into a closet off the kitchen that turned out to be a rather large pantry full of glass jars of canned goods. She tugged at the pegboard on the back wall, and it swung unexpectedly out to reveal another closet behind. Inside were two large, wooden crates. She put her skin in one and left the other to Silas, which, after a moment of gawking, he filled with his pelt. Nora said, "It locks, but I only have one key, and we'd have to fight over it," as she closed it up again. "They'll be hidden enough for now. See, the latch is under here and then you just pull, so you know how to get in if you need to."

"When will your mom be home?" Silas asked, deeply uneasy.

She bit her lower lip. "She'd never touch it, but I see why that's a problem. Here, you wear the key." She reached behind some other items on the shelf and removed a box that contained a brass key on a lanyard.

Her trust took Silas's breath away. But she acted as if it were the most natural thing in the world as she showed him the keyhole concealed, along with the latch, on the underside of a shelf. He turned the lock and tested the latch carefully before slipping the lanyard over his head, not trusting himself to speak.

While he'd been busy with the key, Nora had moved out into the kitchen, and now she said, "Oh my god!" in unmistakable dismay. He turned quickly and saw that she was staring at a calendar on the wall. "May, ninety-six! Silas! I've been gone for three years!"

He came and stood beside her, making his own calculations. "That's bad?" He was forty-one, now. He'd last been human three years ago, too. His trek from Alise's camp to Ocracoke and back with her sealskin had taken place in ninety-three.

"It was supposed to be one! I thought the things growing in the yard looked big…"

He put his hand gently on her shoulder, anxious at her distress, unsure what to ask.

"I got my skin when I graduated high school," she told him. "Mom thought I should spend a year as a seal—kind of a gap year —and then decide about college or whatever when I got back."

"Do you think everything's okay?" Silas asked.

She shrugged unhappily. "The house is fine. The flowers are fresh. I'm sure she's just at work."

"Do you want to call her?"

Nora frowned. "If she's done without me for three years, she can wait a little while longer. And I kind of like having you to myself. Come on."

Silas was terribly relieved. He didn't want to share Nora with her mother, either.

She led the way upstairs, their bare feet muffled further by a runner of soft, beige carpet. At the top was a small landing, a bathroom straight ahead, and doors to either side. The one on the left was open and Silas caught a glimpse of gleaming wooden dressers and a neatly made white bed. The door on the right was closed, and Nora opened it.

"Oh!"

Silas looked over her shoulder for clues to this new dismay. The room was bright and cheerful, a patchwork quilt covering the large wooden bed, a striped, woven rug in many colors on the floor. A small desk and a chair fit neatly into the alcove of a dormer window. The walls were painted pale yellow.

"What's wrong?" he asked, unable to guess.

"She redecorated! I mean—it used to be posters of rock bands everywhere and green—I like green—and all of this is new. The rug, the quilt, the paint. Everything of mine is gone!"

"It's pretty," Silas said tentatively.

"Yes! It's much prettier than I left it. That's not the point."

"Why would she do that?" Silas asked, fully understanding how strange he would have felt if he'd come home to his old bedroom and found everything different. He wondered fleetingly what had happened to his old home. There had been nothing worth keeping, really. The landlord had probably thrown everything away.

The idea of his whole childhood—every remnant and memento of his mother's life—lying torn, ruined, and abandoned in some dumpster made his chest tight and his throat ache.

Nora replied, "Oh—knowing Mom, she did it five minutes after I left. She hated my room." She crossed to a closet and opened it. "At least my clothes are still here! I was beginning to wonder if she'd moved someone else in."

As she found clothes and put them on, he ducked to see himself in the mirror on her dresser. He frowned at his hair, which had gone all salt and pepper. But in other ways he still looked oddly the same as he had twenty years ago, his skin unweathered, his face unlined.

But then—lines and weathering got there with use, didn't they? And he used this body so rarely.

"I don't see anything to frown about," Nora said, coming over to look in the mirror with him. She wore jeans and a plain green T-shirt that set off her eyes, and he was stunned all over again by her prettiness. And her youth.

She stroked the path of hair down his chest and over his belly. "I love this stripe." That fur, at least, was still dark, and his body was strong and fit. Somewhat to his disappointment, she stopped at his navel. He put his hand over hers, and his stomach gurgled with hunger.

"Don't you mind that I'm old?" he asked.

She tilted her head and studied his reflection quizzically. "*Are* you old? You don't seem old."

"I was born in 1955," he said, a little desperately.

She smiled, but her eyebrows went up in surprise. "I was born in 1975, so I'm—jeez, I'm old enough to drink, now."

"I'm twenty years older than you." For some reason, he was determined to make her admit the seriousness of this age difference.

"Okay," she said, "but how old were you when you got your sealskin?"

"Fourteen."

"Whoa, that's young. And how much time have you spent being human since?"

"Um..." He tried to calculate. He'd stayed only a few hours both times with Sandra, but walking and hitchhiking from Alise's camp to Ocracoke and back had taken many days. "Maybe two weeks?"

"Ha!" Her whole face sparkled with fun. "I was *eighteen* when I got my sealskin. So I'm four years older than you!"

He turned away from the mirror to look at her real face, torn between admiration for her cleverness and real discomfort with this view of his age. She laughed up at him and then stood on tiptoe to kiss him. He kissed her ardently back, scooping her closer to him with his hands on her wonderful round bottom, his dick nudging hard against her as she melted to him.

But she wriggled away laughing, and said, "We need to *eat* before we do that again! Come get some clothes."

She dragged him by the hand across the landing to the other bedroom as a novel realization managed to penetrate the fog of his arousal. She wanted to have sex with him *again*. Nothing in his experience, either human or seal, had led him to expect such a wonderful possibility.

From a shelf in the other closet, she handed him a pair of jeans and a gray henley shirt. "See if these fit. I think they'll be close. How do you feel about wearing another man's boxers?"

"This is fine," he said. "I'm out of the habit of underwear."

The jeans fit better than any pants he'd ever stolen. He asked, "Are these your father's?"

She smiled. "They are, actually, but he wore them, like, once. He's a selkie, too."

Silas wasn't sure why her father's being a selkie should surprise him, but it did. He pulled the shirt over his head and marveled at its softness. "So he's gone a lot? Being a seal?"

"He's gone *always*, being a seal. I only met him once, when I was sixteen. He came back because my mom hadn't given me my pelt yet, but no one told me that at the time. She told him she'd give it to me when I was eighteen and sent him away again. He stayed for a day or so. I got to meet him, and Mom got him those clothes."

Silas thought Nora's mom sounded a lot like Sandra. "Did you like him?" he asked.

"I guess. He was nice. But Mom told him not to tell me he was a selkie or anything about it, so you can imagine how weird it was. I didn't know he came back for me. I thought he was just this deadbeat guy who'd been gone my whole life and then just dropped in for an afternoon. We had no idea what to say to each other."

Silas could imagine all too well and painfully. "Maybe you'll get to meet him again someday."

"I hope so," Nora said. She led the way back downstairs. In the kitchen, she opened a cabinet and sighed happily, then began pulling out cans: tuna, sardines, smoked oysters, salmon. "I hope you don't mind eating out of the can," she told him. "I'm much too hungry to *do* anything to it."

"I feel exactly the same," he said gravely, aware that he had never, as a human, faced a meal that suited him better. She handed him a fork and a can opener, and for the next little while, they were too busy eating—perched side by side on bar stools at the counter—to speak.

When they had both slowed down slightly, she said, "What about you? I want to know everything about you."

He looked at her silently, an odd feeling stealing into his chest.

"What?" she said. "Don't you want to tell me?"

"I do," he said, vastly understating the pressure of his desire to pour out the story of his life to her. "It's just—no one's ever asked me that."

"I'm not just being polite," she said. "I feel like I know you completely, but I don't know anything about you. Isn't it strange?"

"I've been feeling that, too," he said, smiling at her.

She pulled back the tab on another tin of sardines. "So talk."

For some time he did, and she listened with few interruptions, though her eyes filled with tears when he told about his mother, which nearly foiled him in his own determination not to cry. He told her about Sandra, and Alise's birth. Then about the inexplicable impulse he'd felt several years in a row to travel to the same far-southern river mouth in the hottest months of the year, which finally made sense the year his sealskin spit him out and he'd spied the girl who could only be his daughter leading a parade of little girls past the stored canoe under which he was hiding. He hadn't doubted that he was there to return her pelt, but he'd despaired that the little thing could have remained in that mausoleum, undisturbed by human, animal, or hurricane, for all the years it had taken Alise to grow into that lovely young woman. A furious self-hatred had gnawed at him, that his carelessness, his feckless seal's instincts, had doomed his daughter to the same horrible fate his mother had faced. Nevertheless, he had begged, stolen, borrowed and hitchhiked his way to Ocracoke, stowing away on a ferry for the last leg. When he'd found the crevice behind the older brother's sepulcher filled with speckled, warm-gray fur—the little tuft grown to a full-sized pelt —he'd experienced a gratitude so intense he could only describe it as grace. He had not dared to hitchhike back to the camp, too afraid of anyone seeing the pelt, of anything at all happening to it in the eleventh hour before he returned it to Alise. He'd walked the hundred miles back, traveling only at night.

"You don't know what happened to her?" Nora asked softly.

"I suppose she's still a seal," Silas said. "And I'm sure she's happy that way. But I feel very bad for Sandra."

"Do you love her?" Nora asked.

"Sandra?" Silas was puzzled.

"Well, I meant Alise. But *do* you love Sandra?"

Silas hesitated. He hadn't told Nora about his mother's story—the selkie boy who gave up the sea to stay with his wife and child. Nora was smiling a friendly half-smile at him, but he felt uneasy. "I don't love Sandra. I thought I was supposed to, though. I thought at first that's why I was human again—that she had called me. I know it sounds silly."

Nora laughed. "She probably did call you—not that she meant to—but only because she had enough selkie in her to have a selkie baby with you. That's how *I* got here. My mom did the same thing to my dad."

He shook his head, unable to make sense of her words.

She said, "Selkies seem to be incredibly sexually attracted to each other. I think it's because we're so rare. If we didn't have sex with each other at every possible opportunity, we'd die out in no time. The sea breeze probably wafted Sandra's selkie pheromones out to you and reeled you right in."

"So that's why I followed you here?" He felt very sad, suddenly. Was that all Nora thought was between them? Animal sex drive?

She seemed to sense his fear and put her hand swiftly on his arm. "I don't know why you followed me here. I've never heard of anything like it. All I know is, now that you're here, you can call me any time you like and I will come straight to you."

"Why?" he whispered, his heart filling.

She looked away, suddenly shy. "It's why I asked if you loved Alise," she said. "If you love her, you can call her back."

Silas was both confused, and very, very happy. "Are you saying I love you?" he asked foolishly.

Her face flashed bright with laughter. She was in his arms, her lips very close to his. "Yes. I'm saying I love you."

She tasted, delectably, of sardines. Once the kiss began it seemed to have no stopping place. She flowed off her bar stool and stood between his legs, and he slid his hands under her shirt against the smooth skin of her waist, her belly. He couldn't believe how perfect she was, how instantly hard and straining she made him, how desperately he needed her naked skin touching his.

She stopped kissing him to pull his shirt over his head, and he stood and returned the favor. "Nora," he whispered, stroking her breasts and tight nipples, thinking again of his mother's story and of what Nora had told him about selkie attraction. He knew he was asking too late. "What if you have a baby?"

She opened his pants and smiled at the way he sprang through the fly. "Don't worry about that. There's a morning-after thing, now." Then she dropped to her knees and took him in her mouth, and for some time after that, he couldn't speak at all.

Chapter 11: Silas

February 1997 - Camden, Maine

When Silas's sealskin shivered him out on the familiar crevice of beach just below Nora's house, he was delighted that, for the first time in his life, he knew where he was, and why, and was glad of both. He was only startled, from the bitter cold and the powdery snow blowing off the drifts of seaweed on the shore, that Nora had waited so many months to call him back.

The day back in May when they had shed their skins together and she'd taken him home, they had spent all afternoon in her bed talking and making love as if those two things were the same activity. They'd decided that he would go back to the sea before her mom got home, to give her time for the reunion and explanations that he felt awkward being a part of. "I need to get my bearings," she'd told him. "I've always assumed I'd go to college, but now I know I need time to be a seal, too, and I need to be with you. I need a different plan than I had when I left. And I'm *old* for college, now." It hadn't felt strange to either of them to be planning a future together. Although they'd left their sealskins in the pantry downstairs, the intimacy of their union on the beach had forged something between them that felt unbreakable. "I can tell you anything," she said with wonder to him as he propped himself over her on the bright quilt, still inside her. "You can touch me anywhere. I never imagined it could be like this. I feel like we have the same soul."

"I love you," he told her with passionate certainty. "I will love you forever, even when I'm dead."

He should wait to call Alise, they decided, until Nora had settled things with her mom and he was back to meet her when she came. "Maybe she'll just want to go back to being a seal," Nora said. "But at least she'll have a chance to tell her mom she's alive if she wants to, and you can stop worrying."

Just before Nora's mother was due home, she'd gone down with him to the beach, and he'd kissed her and kissed her and she'd promised to see him *soon*. He'd subsided into sealhood again with a glancing surprise that changing was no longer the most ecstatic experience he knew. Making love to Nora was even better.

Now, wrapping his sealskin tightly around him against the bitter wind, and noting by the sun over the ocean that it was mid-morning, he thought a little anxiously that sorting everything out must have proved more complicated than Nora had expected. He couldn't believe she had changed her mind about him. The fact that he was here now proved she hadn't, didn't it?

He hurried up the snowy path, his bare feet burning with cold, worrying about whether her mom would be at home, trying to decide whether to risk knocking on the door with his skin wrapped around him. The instinct to keep it out of her mother's sight was very strong. The instinct to avoid freezing to death was also strong. His feet were already numb and white. And Nora's mom was used to selkies. He decided to chance it.

Glancing first through the picture window and seeing no one in the living room, he knocked on the back door. Moments later, it was snatched open. He could not mistake the look of blazing delight on Nora's face. "Silas! Oh, I've missed you! Come in quick!"

An unfamiliar stately sway in the way she stepped back from the door alerted him to something different, and by the time he was inside with the door shut behind him, he'd made sense of a new roundness in Nora's features and the swell of belly beneath her sweater.

"You're pregnant!" he managed through chattering teeth, the sudden relief from cold making him shiver convulsively.

She flung her arms around his neck, and he let his sealskin fall to the floor as he held her tightly, breathing in the flowery scent of her hair, bending himself around the firm curve of her stomach.

"I missed you so much, and I have so much to tell you, and—" Nora's breathless flow of words stopped in a sudden gasp. Silas felt hot fluid soaking his thighs.

"Damnit," Nora said against his shoulder, "I need to talk to you!" and then she tensed all over in his arms and seemed to hold her breath.

"It's okay," he soothed her, tenderness and pride and a rather delightful sense of competence already replacing his shock. "We can talk later." Sitting on a low bench beside him in the entry alcove, he drew her onto his lap. She gave him a look that pulled on his heart with the mix of gratitude and fear in it, and then she doubled over with a wrenching moan.

"Let's get these off," he said, tugging the wide, stretchy waistband of her soaked jeans when the contraction let up, and she assented, but then another pain doubled her over, and she became too rigid to budge. He held her through it. Working in the brief lulls between pain, they wrestled her out of her clothes. Eventually she was naked except for the key to the hidden cupboard behind the pantry, which she wore around her neck.

With Sandra, he'd been too shocked by the changes in her shape, and too overwhelmed by what was happening, to admire her. But Nora's pregnant body, her ripe breasts and spreading nipples, her hips and belly rounded like a Grecian urn, struck him as astonishingly beautiful, even as he ached for her pain.

"Bed. Upstairs?" she suggested in a gasp that immediately gave way to a yell. Her cries had grown steady and focused, rising loudest in the middle and fading at the edges. He felt he could hear the force and shape of her body's opening.

"No, my love," he said, smiling. "You might have this baby on the steps. Here is good." The alcove they were in had a tile floor and held only the bench they occupied, some coats hanging from hooks behind them, some boots beneath the bench, and his sealskin in a pile on the doormat.

She protested, "It won't happen that fast!"

"It might." He said it as reassuringly as he could, kissing her damp temple.

"It hurts so much!" she cried piteously, tears streaming from her closed eyes, her face screwed up in agony.

"I know," he whispered. He felt close to tears himself. He felt it would be easier by far to bear the pain himself than to watch her suffer.

In sudden inspiration, he hooked his sealskin with his foot and dragged it close. Pulling a section of it across his chest, he turned her so she sat facing away from him with her thighs over his, settling her against him so the sealskin lay between his belly and her back.

He'd had the idea that if she rested on his sealskin, he'd be able to comfort her with his strength and reassurance and his confidence in her. Instantly, he realized his mistake. The contact brought *her* pain—not the hurt itself, but the fear of not being able to bear it or escape—so strongly to him that he was overwhelmed. For a moment he could only struggle along with her, gasping to breathe.

But as her pain eased very briefly, he sensed her gratitude for his presence, for his body supporting hers, her confidence that he, at least, knew what they were doing. He rallied, feeling a new fierceness on her behalf. Knowing what she felt was better. This way he could know what helped her.

Her pain did not let up again. He rode it with her, holding her through it, humming reassuringly in her ear. He held her hips, containing her, and when he felt her relief at his pressure there, he increased it. Her cries lost their focus around the relentlessness of the force that gripped her.

As her sounds shifted from formless wails to panting gasps and then deep groans, she and Silas seemed to work together as one body. She braced her feet against the alcove wall and pressed back against him with all her strength. He put one hand between her thighs and one beneath his leg, and soon he felt the miraculous curve of an infant's skull pressing into his palm.

A few more heaves, and the whole child slithered into his grasp.

For a moment there was silence. Then, with a low cry of wonder, she reached down and took the baby from his hands.

He peered around her shoulder. The little red face, Nora's wide-set eyes already perfectly recognizable, worked in a grimace as the baby made adorable, discontented grunting noises. The miniature genitals led Silas to breathe with delight, "He's a boy!"

His mother's story had promised him a son, and here he was.

Nora sighed, her amazement flooding Silas along with his own. "I thought I'd name him Patrick. Do you like that name?"

"I do," he told her gravely, reaching around her to cup her arms with his, embracing her and the infant at the same time. "Hello, Patrick."

Nora reached down for her sweater and used it to wipe some of the wax and gore away before wrapping it around the baby, who protested with a few more grunts. "He's so incredible," Nora said. "Look at these hands and feet, and this adorable nose, and his little ears! And his teeny tiny penis!"

"He'll grow," Silas felt the need to defend him.

"What should we do, now?" Nora asked. "We should cut the cord. Should we go to the hospital? And I have to call Mom. I didn't realize it would happen so fast! I wasn't ready."

Silas kissed her neck, amused by her energy. "Just rest a little. The afterbirth will come soon, and we'll put away his sealskin before we call anyone else."

"Do we know he'll be a selkie?" Nora asked, and then answered herself, "Of course he is. Or you wouldn't be here. Does the afterbirth part hurt?"

"I don't think so," Silas said. "It just looks kind of shocking."

She snuggled against him. "Look how wide awake he is," she said. "He's just looking and looking at us. Oh!" She giggled. "What are you doing, silly?"

Patrick was turning his head against her, nudging her breast with his cheek.

"Is he trying to nurse?" Nora exclaimed. "Oh my gosh, he's doing it! Ow!"

For a little while they both watched Patrick's lips circling Nora's nipple, his little cheek caving in as he sucked.

"Does it hurt?" Silas could feel her tension, both through his sealskin and in her body.

"Kind of. Yeah. I guess I'll have to toughen up."

They sat quietly, listening to the little smacking sounds Patrick was making.

"Nora," Silas asked quietly. "Why did you wait so long to call me? I wish I could have seen you pregnant, watched him growing in you. It must have been amazing."

"It was," she said in a small voice, pressing her cheek against his neck. "I wanted you here, too, but...this is what I wanted to tell you. You know my mom waited three years to call me back?"

Silas nodded, remembering.

"She didn't wait that long. She says she didn't. She says she called me several times and it didn't work. She thought I was dead."

Silas didn't know what to say. "That's awful."

"Yeah...she has all these theories about why it didn't work. She's a reference librarian, she's researched everything about seals and timing and reproductive cycles and says maybe she just called me at times I couldn't come for whatever reason…"

"She must have been so happy to have you back!"

"You'd think," Nora said. "I mean, of course she *said* she was. But I also got the feeling she'd gotten used to my not being here. Like, sometimes I actually wonder if she didn't *miss* me enough to call me back."

"I can't imagine that," Silas said. "I can't imagine anyone not missing you."

She nuzzled her cheek against him. "You're sweet, Silas. Anyway, the point is that things were really weird between me and my mom when I got home. And I knew, basically the second you left, that I wanted our baby if I was pregnant. But that didn't seem like something to tell my mom at first, so I didn't mention you until I knew… Well, I waited a while to tell her."

She shifted on his lap. He expected the placenta, but instead she gave a quiet laugh. "Look at how adorable he is. He's gone to sleep!"

Patrick had, his little mouth slackly open. Silas could hear the quick sighs of his breath.

"He's perfect," Silas said.

"He is," Nora agreed. "She'll be glad of him, now that he's here. But she was so upset. So much worse than I expected. *She* was a single mom. *She* wanted my dad to stay around and he wouldn't. She kind of lost her mind thinking about watching that whole story over again—"

"I *will* stay around," Silas burst out.

"I know," Nora soothed. "I know you will. But she doesn't. And I realized, I couldn't bring you back and make you deal with her craziness. I knew you'd come back when the baby was born—"

"*How* did you know?" Silas asked.

"My father came back when I was born. And you came for Alise."

Silas was touched by her faith, but a knot of anxiety formed in his stomach. "Your mom still doesn't want me here."

"She'll be fine now that you're here and the baby's here," Nora said. "She just needed some time—" She broke off suddenly. "Oh no, I think—"

Something large and hot slithered between their stacked thighs and landed with a rather horrible splat between Silas's feet. "Euugh," she said. "I'm afraid to look."

"It's okay," he said, kissing her and then shifting her over to one thigh. "It's kind of neat."

She peered anxiously over the sleeping infant as he bent and retrieved Patrick's sealskin, then held it up for her to see.

"It's so tiny!" She stroked the wet, white fur with her free hand. "And so soft!"

"I'd forgotten how small," Silas said, moved to see the tiny, unconscious pelt and the tiny, unconscious child together, a matched set in red and white. "Alise's was so big and heavy by the time I had to bring it back to her."

"That's so weird that they grow when no one's even wearing them."

"I know," Silas agreed.

Nora sighed. "I guess we should hide that, and...should we cut the cord? Or just take that thing—" she frowned at the bloody mass of placenta, "with us to the hospital?"

Silas was at a loss. His useful experience ended here. "I could call an ambulance?"

"Oh, that's so dramatic. And probably expensive. We can just drive."

"But—*you* shouldn't drive," Silas pointed out uneasily.

"Oh," Nora said after a pause. "I forgot you're not old enough to drive."

She said it with a smile, but Silas felt his inadequacy very keenly.

"All right," Nora said. "Here's what we do. Bring me the phone from the kitchen and I'll call Mom." She lifted the key on its ribbon over her head and handed it to Silas. "You hide Patrick's sealskin and yours, and then go upstairs and find some clothes. There are some shoes, too..."

Silas couldn't find the phone. He scanned the kitchen up and down, walls and surfaces, assuming that a cord long enough to reach Nora would be easy to spot. By the time Nora's confused directions gave way to laughter and he'd brought her the odd handset from the counter that he'd taken for a radio or a walkie-talkie, he felt too humiliated to share her amusement.

As he put the sealskins away in the pantry and went upstairs for clothes and towels and blankets, he could hear Nora talking to her mom. "Silas came! He was wonderful. Yes, I think we're fine, but we don't know what to do about the cord, and...the blood...I know, but I don't think I should drive. He can't. Mom—he's never had a chance. Look, could you just call the rescue squad and meet us at the hospital? I know. Okay. Okay. Bye."

The harassed note in Nora's voice reminded Silas that he was very anxious about meeting Nora's mom. He didn't even know what to call her.

"Nora, what's your last name?" he asked, as he settled towels under her, hoping anxiously that all the blood was normal, and wrapped blankets from her bed around her shoulders.

"Fisher," she said. "Appropriate, isn't it?"

"So your mom is Mrs. Fisher?"

"Well, Ms. Fisher, since she's not married."

Silas frowned. "Miz? Not Miss?"

Nora gave him an astonished look, then burst out laughing. "Oh, Silas, you're such a Rip Van Winkle! I'm going to have to teach you about feminism!"

The rescue squad arrived very quickly, and the competent efficiency of the three young men whom Silas let in the front door did nothing good for his growing sense of inadequacy. Nora gave such chipper answers to their questions about her pain that one of them laughed. "Oh, you're high as a kite on endorphins! You're not feeling a thing!"

Another one joked, "Think I'll stick to running!"

"Is she okay?" Silas asked anxiously.

"Are you Dad?" Silas sensed them assessing his greying hair, and realized the ambiguity of the question bridged the possibility that he was Patrick's dad—or Nora's.

"He's the dad," Nora said, her slight emphasis telling Silas that she'd picked up on the confusion. "You can tell him anything."

"She looks good. They'll check her out at the hospital and make sure, but she's young and healthy. She's a champ."

Young. All three EMTs were closer to Nora's age than Silas's.

They cut the cord and clamped it. Ordinarily, Silas would have been fascinated by the ride in the ambulance and all the equipment, but he was too focused on Nora and Patrick—and too anxious about meeting Nora's mom—to pay attention to his surroundings.

Nora's mother was waiting in the emergency room when they arrived. She completely ignored Silas in the initial confusion, inspecting Patrick and asking Nora anxious questions and barely glancing at Silas when Nora tried to introduce him. All the while, the hospital staff were asking Nora questions and wheeling her into a room and unbundling Patrick to examine him, which he resented with squawking cries that made Silas want to snatch the baby back from the strangers who were upsetting him. Ms. Fisher was older than Silas had expected—probably around sixty, gray-haired and matronly without being quite plump. She was brisk and sharp with the nurses, fixing them with a disconcerting pale green stare from behind silver-rimmed glasses.

Much too soon, Nora was moved to a room in labor and delivery, Patrick was carried off for a bath, a doctor came to examine Nora, and Silas and Ms. Fisher were banished to the hallway together, Nora calling after them, "Silas, aren't you starving? Mom, Silas needs to eat."

In the hallway, Silas found Ms. Fisher's pale green eyes on him, her gaze full of disfavor. Silas had not been conscious of hunger until Nora mentioned it, but now he was aware of being actually lightheaded. Still, the impossibility of asking this hostile woman to buy him a meal made him say, "I'm fine."

"Nonsense," she said. "You haven't eaten since you got here, have you? You'll be no good to anyone passed out from hunger." She walked off down the hall at a brisk pace, and after a moment Silas hurried to catch up with her, unwilling to trail her through the corridors like a sulky child.

In the hospital cafeteria, crowded at what Silas was surprised to find was still lunchtime, Ms. Fisher secured a quadruple portion of baked fish from the hot food line without consulting him. Sitting across from him at a small formica table she said, "You eat. I'll talk."

Silas ate, too hungry to argue.

Ms. Fisher sighed. "Look, Silas. I don't know if Nora's had a chance to tell you her pie-in-the-sky plan about your moving in and becoming domesticated. I believe her thought is that I will work to support the family, she will go to nursing school, and you will stay home and look after the baby."

Silas looked at her as he chewed, uncertain whether she expected him to respond.

"Well?" she prompted.

"Nora and I haven't had a chance to talk about it," he said carefully, "but that makes sense to me. I don't know how to look after a baby yet, but I'll learn."

Ms. Fisher gave a shrug of impatience. "But you won't *stay*."

"I will stay," Silas contradicted her firmly. "I love Nora. I want to be with her and help her however I can." *I promised my mother,* he wanted to add. Although he hadn't. But he didn't need his mother's ghost to make him stay with Nora and Patrick. It was all he wanted anyway.

Ms. Fisher said, "All right, there are two problems here, Silas. One is that you won't stay. You might think you will, but there's going to come a point when it's too hard, and the way out is too easy. That's how it is for your kind. I'm worried the same is true for Nora, to be honest. But for you, when the only thing you can do with any competence is be out there? No question. You'll leave. She'll be left with no one to depend on but me. I'm being very honest with you, Silas.

"The other problem is, I don't want you here. From my point of view, your staying is like me adopting a teenaged foster son. From what Nora tells me, you've been out—" Silas realized she was speaking in code in case anyone at the surrounding tables was listening, "since you were fourteen. Correct? You don't have a high school diploma. You can't drive. You have no marketable skills, and possibly no legal identity. You can't support yourself, let alone my daughter and my grandson. I'd have to pay to feed you, pay to educate you, pay for the roof over your head—at least until Nora has her degree, and that may not be any time soon, now that she's saddled with a baby. Odds are, with you around, that baby would be followed right up by another one, too. I'm getting old, Silas. I want to retire soon. I have no intention of working into my old age to support my daughter's family."

Silas had stopped eating near the beginning of this speech, a furious resentment swelling in his chest until he knew he was going to explode with killing force all over this hateful woman if he tried to speak. He rose without a word, leaving his plate on the table, and strode blindly from the cafeteria.

His first instinct was to get as far away as possible from Ms. Fisher, and he turned corners and took stairs at random, his pulse pounding in his ears and his breath coming short, until he reached a deserted stretch of hallway in a basement maintenance area. Here he felt safe stopping, and gave into the impulse to pound his fists against the cinderblock wall and kick it with the too-big toes of his borrowed sneakers. He hated wearing clothes that belonged to that woman, and if he'd had anything else to put on, he would have ripped off every stitch and hurled it down the hall.

Gradually, though, his fury ebbed, and left a bleak despair. He put his back to the wall and slid down it until he huddled on the floor, his hands and feet throbbing. He had no answer for the woman. She was right. He could be of no possible help to Nora, or to Patrick, or to anyone. If Nora loved him now, she wouldn't for long—not once the glamor wore off and she saw him plainly. Who was he to offer love? He was a child in the body of a middle-aged man. His love was a burden, not a gift.

In a haze of grief, he got to his feet and started to wander again until he found his way outside. The air was bitter cold, but the sun shone brightly, despite Silas's sense that a great deal of time had passed, that by now it should be darkest, coldest night. He still wore the key to the hiding spot in Nora's pantry, but he had no idea how far it was back to her house. The ambulance had had no windows in the back. The ride had taken ten or fifteen minutes. That would be quite a long walk in the snowy cold with no coat, but Silas was less bothered by the cold than most, and after the journey to Ocracoke and back, this walk would be nothing, really.

In the hospital parking lot, he stood on a grassy median and closed his eyes. Yes, there it was—a sort of tugging when he felt for it, telling him the way back to his sealskin.

He was in danger of sobbing out loud when he thought of Nora, of the hurt and betrayal in her lovely hazel eyes. The only thing he wanted was to run back to her and hold her in his arms and never let her go. He wanted to cradle Patrick and shower his tiny head with a hundred kisses. But the idea of saying goodbye under Ms. Fisher's smug gaze, of being the one to convince Nora of the justice of all her mother's hideous points against him…his stomach galled him like a burning thing. No, better to let her mother explain it. If he went to Nora, it would only seem he wanted her to talk him into staying—and he *did* want her to, more than anything. But there was nothing she could say to change the fact that he was a burden. And he would rather cut out his own heart than rely on that woman—her mother—for anything. *Anything.*

An hour later, striding beside the divided highway with his hands tucked into his armpits against the knife-like wind, a gray sedan pulled over in front of him on the shoulder. When he came even with the passenger door and peered through the lowered window, he saw that the driver was Ms. Fisher. Suppressing rage, he turned his face from her and kept walking without a word.

She drove beside him and called through the window. "Let me give you a ride. It'll be quicker for both of us that way."

He ignored her, and kept walking. He would not get in her car. He would not leave faster just for her convenience.

She kept pace with him. "Silas. I'm only going home to fetch some things for Nora. When I leave, I'm going to lock the doors, and I don't want to wait for you to get there. Get in!"

Silas gritted his teeth and kept walking. If she locked him out, he'd break a window. She'd deserve that.

She inched forward again and this time said, "Silas, don't be an idiot. I have a spare key to the sealskin closet. In five minutes I can get my hands on your pelt and force you to do anything at all. Don't push me."

Feeling murderous, Silas got in the car.

Neither of them spoke a word until she pulled into the driveway. When she removed the keys from the ignition, Silas took them, not hesitating to crush her fingers when she resisted. She turned a little pale but didn't make a sound. He said, "I'm leaving now. But you are going to stay right here in the car until I'm gone. If you come inside while I am there, I will *hurt* you. Do you understand?"

Ms. Fisher nodded mutely, and he felt an ugly surge of satisfaction at the fear in her face.

The front door was unlocked, as Silas had thought—he'd only taken the keys as a precaution. The metallic, oddly dusty smell of blood greeted him as he stepped inside.

He took his sealskin from the hiding place and left the key on the pantry shelf. He felt uneasy that the woman had access to Nora's skin—and Patrick's. But Patrick's, he was nearly certain from his experience with Alise's, would remain inert until the child wore it for the first time. And the woman had apparently never abused her access to Nora's.

He left his clothes in a pile on the kitchen floor, stepped over the birth spatters in the back entry, and let himself naked into the cold. He didn't bother shutting the door behind him. He wasted no time on the path to the shore, not putting it fully past Ms. Fisher to come after him. Bitterness threatened to choke him.

The change was not ecstasy. He seemed to have lost all capacity for delight. He felt only a relief so profound that it was nearly pain.

Chapter 12: Silas

May 2012 - Camden, Maine

After Silas trembled his way back to human form, he lay still inside his sealskin, deeply troubled. Once again, he'd returned to the beach below Nora's house. He remembered with the force of freshness the grief and fury he'd felt leaving here the last time. He had betrayed Nora, abandoning her without a word, and he could not imagine that she'd ever want to see him again.

Yet, he was here.

How much time had passed? A lot of years, he felt grimly. He was, by now, an old seal. He no longer reigned over his own territory on the ice fields at breeding time, but poached from the edges as he'd done when he was young. He was no match for the bulls in their prime, and too canny to challenge them directly and risk injury.

He feared the age his human body must be now. He felt normal enough where he lay, but he hadn't moved yet. He felt no eagerness to finish up whatever human business had brought him here and return to being a seal. He'd *done* it all so many times by now.

Patrick. Was he here to give Patrick his sealskin?

Anxiety seized him suddenly. Why wouldn't Nora have done that, if the time had come? Had something happened to her? He flung aside his sealskin and sat up swiftly.

The rocks were warm from the noonish sun, the sky was hazy blue, and the breeze nibbled a chill against his bare skin. The shades of green on the bank above him were neither the thin transparency of early spring nor the dark shades of summer and fall. The time of year felt very much the same as the day in May when he'd first come here with Nora. The sameness of everything filled him with a sense of fragility and grief, an impression of the world as an indifferent backdrop to the whirling passage of time, decades vanishing in a blink, everything that mattered to him crumbling to dust while the sky and rocks and sea and land pretended nothing had changed.

Nora. His heart felt ready to crack in half at the thought that she might be gone, that he might go up the path and find her house empty of her.

Would Patrick be there? Would horrible Ms. Fisher be there?

He stood. The slight stiffness he felt doing so was not unfamiliar to his seal's body, but new to his human one. The stripe of fur down his chest and stomach was thoroughly frosted with gray, and so was the hair on his arms. He ran his palms over his face and hair, but touch told him little. He still *had* hair, anyway, though it might have grown a little coarser. Beneath the gray, his body seemed okay. He might be a little wirier, but his skin still seemed unweathered and mostly unlined. He didn't seem to sag anywhere.

The beach looked as he remembered it, with the stairs going up the bluff, and the houses overlooking the sea.

He was stalling.

Fear ground away inside him. Nora might be gone—lost at sea. She might be dead. She might be here but hate him now. Something terrible might have happened to Patrick's sealskin. Something involving Ms. Fisher?

His heart pounding, he gathered up his sealskin and scrambled up the bank to the path. Better to find out what he was facing than stand here and worry.

Almost immediately, he stepped on something soft. A pile of clothes.

A new fear electrified him, that some swimmer had left clothes here and was on the beach somewhere—had seen him change.

But he'd looked and seen no one, both before he changed and after. And clothes were useful.

These were folded neatly in the middle of the path. Men's clothes. A soft flannel shirt in a shade of dark burgundy. Jeans, made of a softer, stretchier denim than he'd ever encountered before. A pair of socks, still held together by a plastic thread. And leather moccasins.

No swimmer had left a pair of brand new socks here. These clothes were for him.

He got dressed slowly. Everything fit, the shoes even better than the sneakers he remembered from last time. Belatedly, he noted that the collection included no underwear. *I'm out of the habit of underwear,* he had told Nora.

The clothes meant someone expected him—they had to mean Nora had called him. No one else could. But the formality was unsettling, between two people who'd nearly always been naked together.

He reached the end of the path and stood still, gazing across the yard at the house. The bathhouse still stood, in a considerably more weathered shade of gray. The flower borders seemed wilder and less well tended than he remembered them. A new deck adorned the back of the house, and the bird feeders hung on poles lashed to the deck railing, rather than from their old post in the yard. The house looked different—larger, or a different shape. Looking more closely, he saw that another room had been added, along with the deck.

Before he found the courage to cross the grass and knock on the door, he caught a flicker of movement from beyond the picture window. A moment later, the back door flew open.

"Silas?" Nora's voice sounded thin and anxious.

It was unquestionably Nora who hovered in the doorway before stepping onto the deck, into the sunshine. Her chestnut hair had a single streak of silver where it fell away from her forehead. She was perhaps a little curvier than she'd been when they first met, though slender compared to his memory of her pregnant. She wore a soft green tunic with a scooped neckline, and jeans that flared a little at the ankles. She was barefoot.

"Nora!" He walked to her, his eyes on her face. She had the same pointy chin and wide-set eyes, and he felt the same welling up of admiration for her beauty, the same swell of adoration. But he struggled to read the expression on her face. Was she—crying?

Her face crumpled as he reached her. He dropped his sealskin on the deck and she rushed into his arms. Her warmth, her softness, her whole existence, filled him with wonder. He held her close, close, unable to speak to ask her what was wrong.

She gasped, pressing her damp face against his neck. "I was so afraid you wouldn't come! I can't believe you're here!"

He stroked her hair, breathing in her sweet scent, struggling to assimilate her words. She was glad to see him?

She was. He couldn't be mistaken about the way she felt in his arms, like she'd never stopped belonging here.

He pressed her from him gently so he could look at her. She ducked her face away from him. "Don't look at me. I'm old and dripping."

"You're beautiful," he said. She had fine little lines at the corners of her eyes, which were red with crying, and her nose was running. She *was* beautiful, but his delight in her went so much deeper than that. "No one in the world will ever be as beautiful as you." He stroked the silver streak in her hair. "I love this."

That made her smile, wryly. "I had it done just for you."

"Nora," he asked nervously, "*You're* not old, but—"

"*You* look exactly the same," she reassured him, wiping her nose and looking up at him. "Exactly. Except silver. You have your same young face and shining silver hair. It's unbelievably handsome. You look—" She smiled, still watery, but with her old, irrepressible sparkle showing. "Fey. Like there might be something magical about you."

He had to laugh. "Surely not."

A pause fell between them, an awkwardness. "How long—" he began.

She answered swiftly, but with an air of dread. "Fifteen years. Patrick is fifteen. I'm thirty-six. You're fifty-six."

He took this news in silence. He *was* old. Patrick was fifteen—older now than Silas had been when his mother died.

Nora closed her eyes, her face pained. New tears slipped from under her lids. "I'll explain, but I'm afraid to."

"Why?"

She turned away from him, hiding her face with her hands. "I'm so afraid you'll feel I didn't love you enough!"

"Nora!" He walked around her and pulled her hands away from her face. "I thought you'd hate me for the way I left you."

She shook her head, still avoiding his eyes. "I never hated you." Moving to the door, she said, "Come in. No one's here. Patrick's at school."

Silas hefted his sealskin. "Your mother?"

"She—died. Last month."

She held the door. Silas stopped in front of her. "I'm—sorry..." The words seemed meaningless, but they were the only ones he could find.

The formality seemed to steady her, and she looked him in the face again. "Thank you."

The sight of the bench in the alcove brought back, in a visceral flash, Nora on his thighs birthing Patrick into his hands. The intimacy of the memory nearly overwhelmed him, along with an eroticism he hadn't experienced at the time. The clothes they both wore now imposed so much distance between them. He hungered for the touch of her skin.

Nora followed his gaze to the bench and said, "I know. I think about it every single time. It's like a shrine."

Every single time for fifteen years. He asked, "Is Patrick...?"

"He's wonderful," she answered him simply. "We did a good job when we made him."

He was touched that she gave him credit, even as he ached that his son—like his daughter—was a stranger to him.

The house had shifted in its details, but not in its essence. He glimpsed the new room off the living room, the door half-cracked so he couldn't see in. The rest was still cozy with colorful rugs and warm wood floors, art on the walls and bookshelves everywhere. Nora led the way to the kitchen, lifting the key over her head from beneath her shirt. It was on a chain, now, instead of a ribbon. The kitchen had changed, no longer blue tile, but wood floors like the rest of the house, and counters made of speckled stone.

"At least I can still recognize the phone," he commented, nodding at the base and handset on the counter. It was made of black plastic now instead of beige, and was smaller and sleeker than the old one, but was clearly the same item.

Unexpectedly, Nora burst out laughing. She reached into her back pocket and drew out a small rectangle with a green rubber frame and a plain black surface, that, in her hand, lighted like a jewel. A boy's face appeared on it. "Oh, no. We changed it on you again. I use the landline less and less."

Landline? Wasn't the whole point of the other phone that it had no line—no cord? Silas could make no sense of the thing Nora handed him. It didn't have a single dial or button, just a shallow round indentation at one end. "This is a phone? Do you control it with your mind?"

Nora's laugh bubbled up infectiously. "Oh Silas, please stay this time. I can't wait to teach you everything."

The thing went dark in his hand, and he handed it back to her. *Stay, this time.* He wanted to, more than anything—too much to acknowledge her words, in case she hadn't meant them. "Whose face was that?" he stammered instead. Did the face come with it? Was the thing supposed to have a personality?

Nora seemed puzzled for a moment, then lighted the rectangle in her hand again. "Oh! Patrick! From a year or two ago. I love this picture."

He studied the face, his hand cupped around Nora's. The boy still had the luminous skin of a child, his dark, wavy hair was streaked with blond, and he had Nora's uncanny hazel eyes and vivid smile. He was handsome in a way that tugged Silas's heart. "He looks like both of us," Silas said.

"I know," Nora agreed.

She unlocked the cupboard behind the pantry. "You'll be amazed how Patrick's pelt has grown."

He *was* amazed, even though he knew what to expect. The little white slip had grown into a mass of shining, mostly black fur that filled the box next to Nora's familiar speckled buff. It was at least as large as Nora's, now. "Does he know?" Silas asked.

Nora shook her head. "I wanted so badly to tell him, so he'd grow up knowing who he is. But it's too big a secret for a child to keep. Sometimes it almost feels too big for *me*. So he doesn't know yet. I think eighteen, when my mom told me, is probably right. After he graduates."

Silas nodded. Being a selkie was an easy secret for a seal to keep. But for a boy? A secret so amazing it was practically a superpower? Silas was pretty sure he could not have done it.

He hesitated to pile his pelt on top of Nora's, not because it was too intimate, but because it wasn't intimate enough.

"Remember?" he asked shyly. "Our first day?"

She nodded, but with a shadow entering her face.

"Could we? Now? I want to understand…"

"Oh…" She turned her face away. "I'm afraid."

"Afraid you don't love me enough?" His own fear made him ask the question very gently. Wasn't that what she had said, outside?

"No! Silas, no!" She put her hand on his arm, though she was careful not to touch his pelt. "I'm afraid of knowing how you feel, when I explain… I'm so afraid of hurting you."

He sought her gaze. "I've hurt you, too. I need to know how much."

Tears welled in her eyes again. "Oh, Silas. You're braver than I am." But she leaned into the hiding place and drew her sealskin out. "Come upstairs."

He went first, while she locked the hiding place and followed him. "I have the same room. We added one downstairs for Mom, and Patrick has her old one." The open door to Patrick's room revealed the apparent scene of a recent hurricane, clothes and towels flung on the floor or heaped on furniture, bedclothes trailing onto an orange rug, shells and rocks and pieces of driftwood strewn across desk and dresser, cords and unfamiliar pieces of equipment lying around, something like a TV screen on the desk swirling with a random, moving spiral rainbow. Nora said, "Don't look. It's frightening."

Silas remembered that he'd always left his own clothes all over the floor. But he and his mom had been too poor for his room to be much of a mess. He'd hardly owned anything.

Nora's room was different and the same. The tufted rug in swirling shades of blue and green was new. The white on white embroidered quilt was new. The walls were white. The furniture was the same.

He longed to undress her and lie naked with her between their sealskins on her bed. But she held a distance between them that warned him not to press. Instead he waited while she spread her pelt on the bed. "Put yours here, too, I guess. And we can sit touching them both?"

He spread his pelt beside hers. She waited until he'd settled on the bed to choose her own spot, facing him but with their sealskins making a shining barrier between them. Together, they each gathered up a bit of the other's pelt.

Immediately, as the sense of Nora flowed into him, his uneasiness gave way. Her desire for him was a yearning ache—only fear held her back from him.

He reached for her. "Don't be afraid…"

"Wait," she said. "Let me tell you first."

He nodded.

She spoke swiftly, in a hurry to get the story over with, to have the damage done. "When you left, I was devastated, but Mom told me what she'd said to you. I understood why you left."

"I should have told you, though," Silas said.

"You should have. But I also see why you couldn't. I couldn't have said anything to change it."

Silas remembered his burning, galling sense of uselessness all too clearly. "No. Your mom was right. I had nothing to give you. I couldn't even drive you to the hospital or call the ambulance. I would have been nothing but a burden on your mother, and she needed to take care of you and Patrick."

He felt Nora's grimness flowing through the fur as much as he saw it on her face. "At first, I thought I'd just call you back, as soon as we got home and settled. I thought I'd force her to accept that I wouldn't give you up. But god, Silas—it was so hard. I had trouble nursing, and Patrick lost a lot of weight, and he got sick, and I got sick... I adored Patrick—I never would have given him back—but I saw why my mother was so angry that I'd decided to have the baby. Because she knew how hard it was going to be, and she knew I couldn't take care of myself and Patrick without her. I'd been so focused on you and me and our amazing perfect love and the child we'd made of it. I didn't realize how selfish it was to do that to Mom. *I* was the true burden, not you."

Silas said, "But I would have made it worse."

Nora said softly, "That's what I came to see. So—I realized it was going to take a few years, until Patrick was a little older, and I could get my nursing degree and support us, and we could move out of Mom's house. Then I could call you back."

Now, for the first time, Silas was afraid of what she would say next. "But you changed your mind about wanting me? I would have been a burden on *you*, then, instead of your mom."

"Oh, no! Are you kidding me? Free child care, a burden? But just when I could have—I finished my degree and had a bunch of job options, and Patrick was starting kindergarten—I took some time to be a seal. It was only supposed to be for a few weeks, while Patrick was with my mom. It was the first time I'd been back out, and I missed it so much I thought I would die.

"But while I was gone, Mom had a stroke. It happened while Patrick was at school, and it took hours for anyone to come home and find her. It was really bad. She was in the hospital for weeks, and of course she couldn't call me home, and Patrick was with neighbors… It was horrible. Horrible. It took months before she was well enough and could get someone to take her down to the water to call me."

"Seven tears in the sea," Silas remembered. "It worked that time?"

"Seven tears of true love in the sea, and call my name," Nora clarified. "That's the whole spell."

Spell. Silas found it odd to think of it that way. Being a selkie wasn't magic to him. It was just life.

"It did work," Nora said. "Although the backup plan in case it didn't was to have Patrick be the one to call me. And I kind of think that might have been what happened, though Mom would never admit it."

As always, faced with Ms. Fisher's coldness towards her daughter, Silas was at a loss, uncomprehending.

Nora went on. "Mom couldn't work any more after that. And she couldn't live on her own. I started working, but I needed to take care of her, and pay for the changes to the house since she couldn't go up and down the stairs anymore, and Patrick was getting too old to share my room. And…it just went on like that. She got better for a while, then she had another stroke. I missed you so badly, and I wanted you here, but I also knew…"

"I couldn't have helped you," Silas said. She'd been right that what she had to say would hurt. It made a tight, sad place in his chest. But he felt her sadness, too, so much older than his, and sharper. "You were taking care of everyone else, and you couldn't take care of me, too." Bitterness surged up in him, not at her, but at himself, at fate, for making him so useless, such a child when Nora had needed a man.

"It wasn't that," Nora said. "You could have been a world of help. My god, you can't imagine how much. But it would have been hell on earth for you. Because what I would have needed was you here, looking after Mom and Patrick while I worked. But I worked all the time, and—Mom was so mean those last years. Not just mean in general, but especially mean about selkies. Bitter that all my dad had done was saddle her with me, and she thought you had done the same to me, and she felt she wouldn't have had the stroke if I hadn't gone off and left her alone. You would have been stuck here with her while I was gone all the time, and she would have just *corroded* you. She would have corroded *us*."

She was crying again. This time when Silas reached for her she let him pull her to him. They lay across the sealskins, clutching each other, her tears absorbed by the flannel of his shirt. His body stirred with wanting, but her pain still lay over them like a blanket. "I understand all that," he whispered. "I do. I proved I couldn't deal with her by running away the first time I had to face her. Why are you so sad?"

"Because I spent my whole life trying to get her to love me. And I honestly don't think she did. Not enough to call me back from being a seal. And if my own *mother* couldn't love me, how could I ever, ever expect that anyone else could?"

Now Silas was crying, too. He wanted to speak but his breath was clogged.

Nora said, "What we had seemed too amazing to be true, and she said it wasn't true, and nothing I knew of love made me trust that it could be, and I couldn't bear to call you back and prove her right if we just fell apart."

"She's not right!" Silas didn't have any proof at hand, but that hateful woman was wrong. He knew it in his soul.

"She wasn't right," Nora agreed, sighing. "It took Patrick to show me. Love isn't like that. What she gave me wasn't love."

"I do love you," Silas said, speaking intensely. "I don't know anything about life or how to help you or what it's going to be like. I'll probably mess up a thousand different ways. Every day. But it won't be because I don't love you. That's the one thing I know. The only thing."

Nora sobbed, burrowing into him. "Oh, Silas. You don't think it's too late?"

"Shh," he soothed her into her hair, gathering her even more fully against him. "Why would it be too late?"

"Because I wanted Patrick to have a father, and he's almost grown up, and I might be too old to have another baby, and you might be too old to want one. We're all so fucking old!"

Despite the grief and fury he felt from her, as fully as if they were his own, he couldn't help starting to smile. "Speak for yourself," he said. "Me, I'm still younger than Patrick." A thought struck him. "Does he know how to drive?"

Against him, Nora laughed, her body softening. "He's got driver's ed this afternoon. It gives us two extra hours before I have to pick him up from school."

As eager as Silas was to meet his son, he had increasingly pressing reasons to be glad of the extra time.

Those reasons were not a secret from Nora, who stretched against him, the pressure of her hip seeking out his erection. "Want me to call the school and see if you can join in?" she teased.

He felt how little intention she had of leaving the bed, or letting go of him. Her own desire was building like a long, slow breaker, and he was helpless in the undertow. His eagerness to be rid of their clothes reminded him of another fear, though. "Are you afraid to see my old man's body? Is that why you left the clothes for me?"

She made a noise of dismay. "Of course not! It's the opposite. Men get to stay handsome as they age. But I'm fatter and I have stretch marks and a poochy belly, and I thought, if it were me, I'd jump back in the ocean in my human skin and freeze to death before I would have walked naked up that path to you after all this time..."

He kissed her. He kissed her until he felt all her little spikes of anxiety settle and smooth. He'd forgotten how safe she felt with him, the almost drug-like state of wholly peaceful bliss that descended over her with her certainty of his wanting. When he began to undress her, she helped him, and then, together, they undressed him, too.

He rolled her this way and that on the sealskins, sunlight falling through the window on her creamy skin, her round breasts and tight magenta nipples that he couldn't stop himself from tasting. The tracery of faint, white lines, like long-healed scars, across her belly and her back were new. "Are these the dreaded stretch marks?" he asked.

She grimaced.

"They're lovely, you know. Like spiderwebs. Or tiger stripes."

She couldn't disbelieve him, with his hard dick nearly touching his belly and her sealskin letting her know he couldn't wait for her much longer.

"Come here," she sighed, lifting her thighs toward her stomach and reaching for him. "Oh Silas, please—"

He sank to her, knowing beyond doubt—as his yearning met hers and balanced briefly at the crux between all he'd ever longed for and a driving greed for more—that he had come home.

*   *   *

Silas stayed at the house when Nora went to pick Patrick up from driver's ed. She'd wanted the ride home to prepare him. When Silas heard them at the door, he rose anxiously from a kitchen bar stool where he'd been waiting. A boy as tall as he was—but with the stretched skinniness of swift and recent growth—stepped into the kitchen ahead of Nora, smiled a dazzling smile just like his mother's, crossed the floor in two strides and shook hands with a warm, sure grip. "I hear you're my dad," he said. "And a selkie, too."

Silas sought Nora's face as her expression went suddenly blank with shock. "What do you mean?" she asked, very quietly.

Patrick turned his dazzling smile on her. "Grandma told me a couple of years ago. She said you were afraid I couldn't keep a secret, so I had to show you by keeping it from you." He glanced back to Silas, clearly enjoying himself. "She also said Mom would call you back as soon as she was dead, so I've been expecting you."

Nora sagged against the doorframe, shaking her head. "*Mom!*" Silas couldn't tell if it was a protest or an explanation.

He started to laugh, and Patrick joined, and finally Nora, a little weakly. Nora collared Patrick with an elbow hooked around the back of his neck, forcing him to bend down to her height, and vigorously messed up his hair. "What am I supposed to do with you?" she asked. The face that she turned to Silas, including him in the question, was filled with happiness and dismay.

"Give me my sealskin?" Patrick suggested shamelessly. "Grandma never would tell me where you hid it."

Nora widened her eyes at Silas in wordless protest. "Your dad and I will talk about that. *Later.*"

Patrick grinned and shook his head. "Man, that sounds weird."

Silas thought it sounded wonderful.

*   *   *

That night, when Nora pulled back the white quilt of her bed, revealing blue-green sheets, and said to Silas, "This is your side; is that all right?" he felt an upwelling of emotion that he feared for a moment would overwhelm him. He didn't know if it was grief, or joy—he only knew it was huge.

"What's wrong?" Nora asked him with swift concern, seeing the expression on his face.

Silas was afraid that if he moved or spoke, he would burst into tears, but as he slid between the soft sheets and struggled to answer her, he discovered that what fought for release in him was, in fact, his mother's story.

It was a bedtime story. And tonight was the first time he'd slept in a bed—the first time he'd had anyone to say good night to—since the night his mother died.

He poured it out to Nora, who lay beside him watching his face intently and petting him gently as he spoke.

Once upon a time, there lived a selkie boy. His father was a great, gray seal who swam the seas. His mother was a selkie too, but one without a sealskin, forever trapped on land. Without her sealskin, the boy's mother sickened and died while he was still young. She left her son a key, which opened a secret door in her closet. Inside, the boy found his sealskin. He put it on and became a seal like his father. For years, he swam the seas with joyous freedom. But inside his seal's body beat a human heart, which still longed for a home on land. One day, a girl on the shore called out to his human heart. He shed his sealskin and married her, and soon she gave birth to a selkie son. The selkie loved his wife and son with all his heart, but the seal in him longed for the sea. One night, while his family slept, he carried his sealskin to the shore. The call of the sea was too strong, and he could no longer resist. But a ghostly seal spoke to him from the waves in his mother's voice, saying, "Your father made you a seal, but I raised you to be a man. Go home to your son and teach him to be both." Released from the ocean's spell, the selkie did as his mother told him. He went home and loved his wife and raised his son to be both seal and man. In so doing, he became fully both himself, and lived a long and happy life.

"I hope I never do meet her ghost," he concluded quietly. "She'd be so disappointed in me."

"Oh, Silas." Nora touched his cheek. "Don't you see that the story *is* her ghost? My mother told me the exact same thing my whole life, just not as nicely. *Don't you dare grow up to be like your father.*"

Silas absorbed her interpretation in silence. She was right. Of course she was.

He said, "I did grow up like him, though. I've been off being a seal, just like him, not raising my children."

Nora gripped his shoulder, as if willing her words to make an impression. "The difference is, you wanted to stay, and we didn't let you. I didn't. Sandra didn't. It wasn't up to you. And it wasn't up to your mom."

He looked at her. She lay on her side, propped on her arm, pushing her dark hair with its silver streak away when it tried to fall across her face. Her eyes searched his, her gaze so open to him he couldn't doubt how fully she was with him, how glad she was that he was here. He knew that expression. He had seen it in his mother's eyes, too. It was love.

He asked her softly, "Do you know what I think?"

She shook her head, her eyes never leaving his.

"I think when we first met, we called each other back. That proves it's love, right? That's the thing that calls a selkie home?"

He watched her eyes fill with tears before she kissed him.

"That's beautiful, Silas. I think you're right."

Chapter 13: Torran

June 2014 - Edinburgh, Scotland

Torran MacMara eyed the slim, golden-skinned girl slumped on a bench just beyond the Edinburgh airport customs exit. She had walked past him without reading the name, *Ellie Murdoch*, on the sign he held up, almost as if she were sleepwalking, and settled on that bench. Now she rested with her forearms on her knees, lots of wavy, dark hair with improbable bright gold sun-streaks in it obscuring her face. She appeared dormant.

As the minutes had gone by and the passengers emerging from customs had shifted perceptibly from the large, loose Americans who had accompanied the girl to slender, stylishly dressed Asians speaking Japanese into their cell phones, he became more and more sure that the girl was the Ellie Murdoch he'd been sent to pick up. But he was also increasingly certain that she was a selkie, and that presented a complication.

That's why he hadn't approached her yet.

Torran knew quite a bit about selkies, not only because he was one. Selkies were not exactly common in Scotland—or anywhere else that he knew of—but one certainly ran across them from time to time. His own mother had been one of the sea-born, and had bolted off back to the sea several months short of Torran's second birthday. He didn't remember her at all. Donald MacMara, Torran's da, was a selkie, too, although he was the domesticated kind who held down a job, provided for his family, and spent only his summer holidays as a seal. Donald always said he'd never expected Torran's mum to stick around. Torran figured his mum must have been a phenomenal lay, for his da to have foreseen that long road of single parenthood and launched down it anyway, knob first.

Torran's own experience had informed his notion of his parents' relationship. Once, a dark-eyed girl in a club had dropped her knickers onto the dance floor and taken him right there under the dubious cover of her very short skirt, legs wrapped around his hips, the dense throng of dancers thrusting and grinding around them approximating the act sufficiently that their shameless coupling had—he hoped—gone unnoticed. Another time, the sleek-haired shop girl ringing him up for canned mackerel and milk had engaged him in a galvanizing silent negotiation that had led to her handing him his change, announcing that she was going on break, removing her apron, and leading him out back to a spot behind the bins. They'd done it with her jeans still hooked around one ankle, the other leg freed by kicking her shoe off bent up by his thigh, her back against the brick wall. They'd gone their separate ways with barely a word exchanged, and he'd switched shops after that. Torran didn't date much. Knowing there were lasses who would stand him up by the roots and shag him on the spot made it hard to bother about the ones who didn't. And the ones who did—well, it was difficult to know where to go with them after. Judging by the way they'd so far promptly vanished afterward, they seemed to feel the same.

The lass—Ellie, if it was her—definitely provoked a tingle, despite the way she drooped. She had classic selkie looks—svelte body, a certain grace, a hard shine to her hair, and skin that was likely that same deep, summer tan even in the depths of winter. The mad attraction didn't always indicate a true selkie—only someone with a strain of it running in the family. But her looks told him this one was the genuine article, the kind with a pelt tucked away in some hidey hole. She was his age or a bit younger, about twenty, maybe—old enough to have had her sealskin a few years and been out in it a time or two.

Once he got her attention, odds were they'd be going at it in the back seat of the Skye Tours Ltd. sedan as quickly as they could reach the car park. But he'd been sent to drive her the five hours to Portree, and if they experienced the usual impulse to flee one another's company afterward, that drive was going to be very awkward for them both.

On the other hand, she really didn't seem well. She might not be up for it, and, under the circumstances, that would be for the best.

Otherwise, he was going to have to exert a degree of self-discipline that remained without precedent in his life so far.

What was that phrase about girding one's loins? That was about not flopping around during battle, he thought, but it seemed to apply here, too. He walked over to her. "Ellie Murdoch?" he asked.

Slowly, she lifted her head, moving her hair out of the way. She looked up at him with extraordinary eyes. Most selkies had brown eyes, but hers arrested him—bright somehow despite their deep color, like glass held to the light. They were fringed by long lashes and set above full lips, in a face as delicate as a shell. He wanted her, no question.

She seemed to take a moment to get her bearings, as if she'd forgotten where she was. He showed her the sign. "Are you Ellie?"

"I'm Ellie." There was an unspoken question in her words. *Who are you?*

"Torran MacMara. I'm to drive you to Portree. To the Skye View Inn?"

She studied him in confusion, reading the logo on his turquoise polo shirt, the *Skye Tours Ltd.* uniform. She seemed well enough now that they were talking. What she didn't seem—and he had distinctly mixed feelings about this—was gripped by any urgent need to get him alone and out of his trousers. He was pretty certain the thought hadn't crossed her mind. It was a surprisingly easy thought to read on a woman's face, and hers gave no sign of it.

She said, "My aunt runs it—Maggie MacLeod. I'm coming to stay with her. But—you're from a tour company?"

He made sense of her confusion. "I wasn't sent to give you a tour. I'm headed to Skye and the boss asked me to pick you up and bring you along. I think he's a friend of your aunt. It's the high season now and it's a fair drive—your aunt probably couldn't get away to meet you herself."

"That's okay. She said she might not be able to." She stood, a little wearily. Not as if moving hurt her, exactly—more as if she struggled to see the point.

"Do you feel all right?" he asked, picking up her suitcase for her. He didn't have to carry it. He was getting paid for the trip, not the passenger, and he had no reason to go out of his way for her. But she struck him as needing help, and he couldn't seem to stop himself from offering it.

She gave him a wry smile. "As right as usual, anyway."

She walked beside him out to the car park. He was terribly aware of her. She was like the fish and chips of the person ahead of him in queue when he was starving—right there in reach and utterly enticing, but not his. She, on the other hand, hardly seemed to know he was there.

He offered her the front seat. It was breaking the rules a bit, but he wanted to talk to her, and again, she wasn't a paying passenger. He had to make the offer twice before she pulled her attention back from wherever it had disappeared to and accepted.

Conversation with her did not flow easily. She'd answer questions, but she didn't ask any of her own, and she seemed to drift away in the pauses between. He got out of her that she was from Beaufort, North Carolina, which she said was a small, historic beach town. That made sense for a selkie. "Do you swim?" he asked. It was a bit of code. Selkies generally couldn't bear water when they weren't wearing their sealskins. All their instincts were to head deep and stay a while, and the human body didn't stand up well to that. Most selkies had near-drowning incidents in their childhoods, and lingering trauma to go with them.

The coded answer was, "Under the right conditions," or, "Only when I'm dressed for it." Something like that.

"Ugh, no," she said. "I like boats, though."

Maybe she'd never learned the code. He had the impression there were a lot fewer selkies in the States, so maybe they didn't learn to recognize one another.

"Are you at university?" he asked. How old was she, anyway?

"Yeah. Just finished sophomore year. I don't know if I'll go back in the fall, though."

"Why not?" He'd been right about her age, at least.

She shook her head as if refusing to answer. Then maybe she decided it didn't matter what she told him. "I'm…struggling. I'm just having a lot of trouble focusing lately. I used to be good at school but my grades are crap right now. I'm here because Dad's making me do something besides sit on the beach and watch the waves roll in, which is kind of my default. Aunt Maggie's a single mom and she runs a bed and breakfast all by herself. The idea is, maybe I can help her, and if not, at least, since she's family, she won't be paying me."

"You can watch the waves roll in on Skye, too," Torran said, trying for something neutral. In fact, a dreadful thought had occurred to him.

What if she didn't have her pelt? He'd heard of this happening, a sealskin being lost or destroyed somewhere along the way. Selkies didn't live to grow old without their pelts. They sort of— wound down. That's what his da had told him. Donald'd had a cousin once, before Torran was born, who used to spend all her time on the shore, just staring out to sea. Then one day, she'd walked into the waves and drowned herself.

Bloody hell. If that's what was wrong with Ellie, there wasn't any help for her.

He lapsed into silence for a while, too disheartened to ask any more questions. She didn't seem to care. She leaned her head back and closed her eyes.

The more he thought, the more sure he was of his guess. A missing sealskin would explain her lack of interest in him, too. Selkies seemed to keep their passion in their pelts. Torran had first worn his when he was sixteen, and his interest in the lasses, which had lagged troublingly behind his peers, had caught up to full speed after that.

She probably had no idea. She didn't know she was a selkie, didn't know why she was ill, didn't know she'd be dead in just a few more years.

This was how a doctor must feel, facing a patient with incurable cancer who didn't know, yet.

Except it wasn't Torran's job to tell her.

Was it? What possible good could it do?

Knowing that the girl was dying caused him an almost physical ache somewhere inside his ribcage. He wished to hell he'd never met her. But it was too late now, like witnessing a terrible accident and not being able to unsee the details. Even if he drove her all the way to Skye without waking her or speaking to her again, and dropped her with her aunt and went his merry way, the thought of her was going to bother him. It didn't matter that he hardly knew her, didn't even know if he would like her if they got to know one another. She was one of his kind, and she was broken, and it hurt him. It was going to hurt him every time he thought about it from now on.

Bloody, bloody hell.

There was a way he could help her. It was no cure and probably wouldn't last long, but it would make her feel better and that was something. His da had told him about it, a thing he had done for that cousin of his.

A few miles later, Torran pulled off the highway at the travel plaza with the good fish and chips place. Ellie didn't stir when they stopped, just stayed with her eyes closed and her head back against the headrest. She was asleep, but she seemed farther away than most people do when they're sleeping. *Dormant,* he thought again. He was kind of glad. Maybe he could do it without her even noticing.

He filled his lungs with a slow breath and leaned over to her. This close, he could almost feel the warmth of her skin, and it was impossible not to imagine his hands on her, her body turning eagerly to his.

She wouldn't turn to him, though. In that way, she really was dormant.

Instead, he drew a slow breath and exhaled gently across her shell-like cheek, the bridge of her long, straight nose, her closed eyelids and reposing lashes. His breath stirred the hair at her temple. Then he leaned away again to watch what would happen, uncertain whether any effect would be visible.

She woke abruptly, with a gasp. "Oh!" she said, her hands lifting from her lap in reflexive surprise, her eyes flying open. "What *happened?*"

He didn't answer, waiting to see what she would do. She put her hands against her face and briefly against her lips, as if feeling to see if she were real. She shivered suddenly and hugged herself, turning to him with bewildered amazement, gathering her breath as if she would say something. But then she just shook her head instead, seeming completely overwhelmed.

"All right?" Torran couldn't help smiling at her. This was much more dramatic than he'd expected. Of course, he'd spent all winter as a seal and only come back last month in time to start the job at *Skye Tours*. His breath was probably pretty potent, still.

"Oh my god," she breathed. "I feel *amazing!* Did you *do* something?"

He shook his head, a refusal to answer which, of course, she took as denial.

"Where are we?" she asked, looking around. "Are we eating? Oh my gosh, I'm *starving*."

"Do you like fish and chips?" He already knew the answer.

For reply, she opened the door and all but bounded out of the car. She was an entirely new person.

Torran had reason to regret, over the next few hours, that he had not waited to breathe on her until they got to Skye. Not because Ellie wasn't delightful, but because she was. Knowing her fate had been bad enough when she was nothing more than a fellow-selkie and a stranger. But the more time he spent with the bubbling-over, enthusiastic girl, face no longer like a shell but like a sparkling, twinkling star, the sharper that hurt in his ribcage when he thought of her snuffed out. He tried to avoid the pain by thinking of anything else, which only plunged him straight back into her brightness—bright eyes, bright face, bright laugh, bright wit. She stirred his lust with everything she did, too—every glance and toss of her hair, every movement of her long, elegant fingers, every flash of her warm skin in that selkie shade so difficult to describe—not really brown, but as if a very fair-skinned person had nevertheless managed a very thorough, very even tan. He could hardly sit still around her, the way he kept having to adjust his trousers.

She did not share his affliction. She was as oblivious as a child.

She ordered fish and chips, scarfed down the fish, left the chips completely untouched, and ordered a second round. She made up for her earlier lack of curiosity by asking him a million questions, drawing out of him that he'd finished at university last year with a degree in history and folklore, had traveled all winter (he didn't mention the underwater part, and the thick pelt), and was driving now for Skye Tours, where he hoped to become a tour guide when they had an opening. He told her how it was just his da and his gram when he was growing up, his mum leaving when he was wee, how his da was a secondary school teacher, mostly history and civics, how his gram had died a couple of years ago and he still missed her.

"I never had a mom, either," she told him, and his ears pricked up. Her mum would have been the selkie, then.

"What happened to her?" He fully expected to hear that she had done a bunk. His gram had often made the point that selkie lasses were ill-suited to motherhood, since seal pups required so little of them—just a couple of weeks of suckling and that was it. "No maternal instinct," she would say whenever the subject came up, shaking her head disapprovingly.

Ellie said, "She died in a car crash when I was a baby. Her car skidded off the road into the canal. I'm lucky I wasn't with her—she was out running errands and left me with the neighbor."

Torran was bursting with a question he felt it would be very odd to ask. Luckily, she answered it without his having to. "They never found her body. The windshield was all smashed, and she must have washed out to sea."

"Your poor father," Torran commented, his brain busily spinning scenarios. Faking death was a pretty extreme measure, especially with a selkie child in the picture. It meant Ellie's mum had never intended to come back. Was Ellie's dad a selkie, too? Or was he so much of a monster that Ellie's mum had run away from him like that?

Ellie was too lovely to have been raised by a monster. He could tell just being around her that her da was a good sort.

But if Ellie'd had a sealskin, wouldn't her mum have taken her, too? Was Ellie's skin already missing—destroyed at birth, maybe by Caesarean section?

"It nearly killed him," Ellie said. "The neighbor who was babysitting me when my mom died says that if Dad hadn't had me to look after he would have followed her right into the canal. Apparently they had one of those fairytale love stories, Romeo and Juliet, one look and that was it. *Really* Romeo and Juliet, because Mom was super young. She dropped out of her freshman year of college to marry Dad, and Dad would *kill* me if I pulled something like that. He *teaches* college. Education is a value of his. Also, Mom had to have gotten knocked up on like, their first date. It's crazy imagining Dad being so irresponsible. Dad says no one else has ever held a candle to her. I think it's hard for him that I look like her. He doesn't talk about it much, but I can tell he still misses her like crazy."

Torran didn't have any trouble interpreting this story as being nearly identical to his own parents'—mad selkie passion and a mum who took off, seal-like, the moment the child was weaned. But *was* Ellie's father a selkie, too? Or was he just selkie-compatible, enough seal running through his family tree to make him irresistible to a selkie mate? As a college professor, he'd have the same advantage—so necessary for a selkie—that Torran's da had as a school teacher: Long summer holidays. Torran had spent most of his with his gram, while his dad went off on month-long "fishing trips."

"How'd you spend your summers when you were wee?" he asked.

She tilted her head a little quizzically at the seeming randomness of the question—they were back on the road by then —but answered, "Dad's a marine biologist. I used to spend a lot of time out on the research ship with him. He teaches summer programs for the marine lab where he works."

"That sounds nice," Torran said absently. Not a selkie, most likely. Not if he led the trips and took Ellie along.

"Not really," Ellie said drily. "I spent the whole time dreading the moment when the students would figure out I was scared to swim and try to teach me by throwing me in. It generally happened about once a summer."

"Oh, aye," he said feelingly. "I lived three blocks from the harbor in Oban, and never went near it after some of the lads pulled that stunt—took me out in a dinghy when I was seven or so and tossed me overboard. They told me to swim to shore, but I went straight for the bottom in thirty feet of water. If one of them hadn't been a canny diver, I wouldn't be here to tell about it."

"Oh my gosh, we're twins," Ellie said. "Dad saved my life every summer, diving in and hauling me up. I don't even sink to the bottom. I *swim*, like I've got some kind of death wish. It puts swimming lessons completely out of the question, since the only direction I seem to go is down."

Torran shook his head as if he found this as baffling as she did. But at the same time he was thinking, *Her da's definitely not a selkie, then.* Donald MacMara would never be the slightest use in a rescue attempt—he'd drown right alongside, in the grip of the same perverse instinct.

"It really is crazy how much we have in common. Both of us are from little beach towns. Both of us were raised by single dads. Neither of us can swim. What else? We both love fish and chips. Fish, anyway. You didn't really eat your fries, either. And we look alike. Did you notice that? We have the same eyes and the same kind of hair, except yours is darker, and we have the same color skin. Isn't that weird? Do you think we really are related? My dad is from here, you know. Are you kin to any Murdochs?"

He smiled at her. He couldn't help it. The same feeling was working on him, and the fact that he understood it and she did not didn't make much difference. It was finding someone you matched, someone who could understand you, someone you were safe being yourself with. She'd probably never met another selkie before. And even though he had, he'd never lasted long enough around a selkie girl to feel this—warmth—before sex got in the way. Though sex was part of this, too, since fully half the warmth he felt for this vivid girl was located in his groin.

She wasn't feeling that half. For her, it was all sisterly affection.

Also, she was going to die. She was *dying*. He was *not* getting attached.

"What's wrong?" She'd sensed the darkening of his mood, even though he hadn't said anything.

He forced a renewal of his smile. "I don't think being raised by single dads is a heritable trait."

"Whatever," she said, humorously. "*Do* you have any Murdoch cousins?"

"Bound to," he said, "if you go far enough back. No recent ones that I know of, though."

"Hm," she said, and he wondered if she had deduced his non-platonic interest in her from his lack of enthusiasm for being her relative.

He couldn't help wondering what she thought of him. She didn't desire him. That was clear enough. But she didn't seem averse to him, either. He wondered if she'd warm up, if he...

If he *what*? He'd never had to work to interest a girl before. He didn't have the first idea how to go about it.

And he was *not getting attached*.

He was going to drive her the rest of the way to Skye, drop her with her aunt, and do his very best to forget about her. He pressed down slightly on the accelerator.

But in the remaining hours of the trip, she extracted from him more details about his family, his childhood, his education and his views on life in general than anyone besides his da and gram had ever shown such interest in. What she revealed about herself only made him hungry to know more. By the time he pulled up at the Skye View Inn, he'd fatalistically resigned himself to dropping by from time to time to breathe on her. He was meant to be on Skye for the next few weeks at least, and maybe for the whole summer. The Skye View Inn was one of the spots Skye Tours regularly booked its guests, so he was certain to be back.

The time was nearly nine at night, but so close to midsummer, the tastefully expanded two-story cottage overlooking Loch Portree was fully visible as they turned in. Its white paint glowed rose-gold in the sunset light. Torran watched with dawning astonishment as a slim, golden-skinned woman came down the front steps with eye-catching grace, her chestnut hair wound in a sleek, braided bun at the back of her head, beaming as Ellie stepped from the car to greet her.

Maggie MacLeod was a selkie, too.

Chapter 14: Torran

June 2014 – Isle of Skye, Scotland

Torran got out of the car and watched with close interest as the two selkie women greeted one another. Maggie hugged Ellie warmly but briefly, putting her away by the shoulders to study her. "My goodness, child! Who do you look like? Not Douglas, that's for certain!" Her eyes moved searchingly over Ellie's face, and she fingered Ellie's gold-touched hair. Torran was fairly sure he read shock in Maggie's reaction to her niece.

"I look like my mom," Ellie said.

"My goodness," Maggie said again, a little blankly, as if looking like one's mother was a very surprising thing to do. Torran understood better a moment later when she added, "I'm so glad to finally meet you. It's a perfect disgrace that you've gotten to be, what is it, twenty years old, before I ever laid eyes on you?"

Had the woman not known her niece was a selkie, too? Torran suddenly became very keen to manage a private conversation with Maggie.

Although—the fact that Maggie likely had a good fifteen years on him didn't seem to affect his predictable physiological response to a female selkie. And if Ellie got wind of him and her aunt getting it on in the next guest room or whatever, she might consider it an act of bad faith…

Although, bad faith in *what*? A relationship he was definitely not pursuing with a dying girl?

Might be best to blow off steam with Maggie and put Ellie off him. Then he could give up this bloody, fruitless preoccupation with her because she'd want nothing to do with him herself. Anyway, pretending he had free will in this matter was ridiculous, because after the repeated flarings of arousal he'd endured in the last five hours, his self-control was all used up. One look from Maggie and he'd be beyond helping himself.

Except. This woman was an important business contact for his company, and he'd have to work with her all summer, so shagging her was a far worse idea than shagging Ellie at the airport would have been. Though offending Maggie by not shagging her might be bad, too.

Christ!

Suddenly all he wanted was a bit of privacy so he could beat off in peace. With that taken care of, maybe he could think straight again.

Maggie turned her attention to Torran. "You're the driver for Skye Tours? You must be new."

He stepped forward to shake her hand, and by the time that brief transaction ended, a couple of unspoken points had been established. The first was that Maggie absolutely recognized him for a selkie and was beyond floored—with good reason, because one selkie was rare enough, two together were very uncommon indeed, but *three* thrust together by random chance was almost unprecedented. The second point was, although Maggie's dark brown gaze reflected all sorts of shock, astonishment, and keen interest—and a concern that probably had more to do with Ellie than with him—she showed not a glimmer of response to the frank lust Torran was all too aware he projected with the intensity of his gaze, the pressure on her hand, and the tightening fabric of his trousers.

Or rather, her response was to let go of his hand at precisely the moment any ordinary handshake would end, and to give him a tight smile of rueful apology that made her understanding of his predicament clearer than he preferred.

"You've had a long drive," Maggie said. "Fancy coming in for a pint?"

Despite various reservations, Torran did very much fancy the pint, and the opportunity to gather more information. He got Ellie's suitcase from the boot and followed the two women into a wide entrance hall, carpeted softly with green and cream runners, stairs going up on the left and open doors revealing sitting and breakfast rooms on the right. The hallway ended in a green baize swinging door that indicated a kitchen beyond.

Maggie sorted them deftly according to their needs. "Would *you* like a pint, or a glass of something?" she asked Ellie. "Or the loo, or a moment to freshen up?" She included Torran in the second question.

Ellie yawned hugely, covering her mouth with slim fingers. "Oh, I'm sorry," she said. "I'm just realizing I haven't slept in about twenty hours. I hadn't noticed until I got out of the car."

"Let me take you up to your room, then," Maggie said. "We'll tiptoe, because Cait and Alec are already asleep—or supposed to be. They're very curious to meet their cousin, but I didn't know when you'd be getting in, so I didn't let them wait up. I've put you in the upstairs office—on the family side, with us."

To Torran she said, "I've a blonde, a blaven, or an I.P.A., all local brews."

"I'll wait for you to join me," Torran said.

Ellie gave him a hug, the soft pressure of her breasts, her hair against his neck and the scent of her—a distinctive blend of mineral, musk, and spice that all selkies seemed to share—enflaming him. It took everything in him not to draw her full length against him, to preserve a non-disclosing distance between her body and the erection that was as hopeful and immune to good sense and common decency as a puppy. She pulled away. "Thank you so much for driving me. Will I see you again?"

Torran nodded, and Maggie put in, "I expect nearly daily. Most of our guests book day trips with Skye Tours. Unless you're one of the Edinburgh lads?"

"I'm here for a few weeks, anyway," Torran said. "I'll see you again."

"Good," Ellie said.

Once Maggie and Ellie had vanished through the swinging door—which did reveal a large, gleaming kitchen on its other side —Torran made a beeline for the WC beneath the stairs. It really was a closet, just room enough for the toilet and an almost child-sized sink, its little oval bowl glazed with a pattern of spring flowers. The sink seemed too innocent for the purpose he required of it. "Don't watch," he admonished it, and shut his own eyes, the better to imagine Ellie's enthusiastic participation in relieving a pressure he was certain had rendered his balls a suffering shade of blue.

By the time Maggie came back, Torran was waiting for her in the sitting room, flipping idly through a local sightseeing guide from the coffee table and feeling much more sanguine about his prospects for enjoying a beer and the company of the second wildly sexy woman to show no interest in him that day. He had even had a chance to become curious about Maggie. He was beyond certain that she had recognized both him and Ellie as selkies. At fortyish, she was older than any selkie could live to be without a pelt. Therefore, she'd had a pelt and worn it at some point in her past. Had something happened to her sealskin? Or were the selkies in this family simply possessed of some cruel immunity to his charms?

"Well," Maggie said, standing in the doorway and surveying him with the air of a climber assessing a challenging rock face. Sadly, the wry humor in her expression failed to support the innuendo to which that image lent itself. "Come into the kitchen. It's cozier there, and I expect we have matters to talk about."

Torran stood in agreement, and followed her.

The kitchen had a split personality. One half was all hard counters and stainless steel efficiency, a restaurant kitchen plainly capable of providing an inn full of guests with a full-scale Scottish breakfast. The other side held a large, scarred wooden table and solid wooden chairs that nevertheless looked inviting enough for a long sit. Maggie waved him toward the table. "I believe I'll have a whisky," she said. "Would you care for that, or the pint?"

"I'll stick with the pint," Torran said, with a certain reluctance. He had only a mile or two further to drive the company car, but Maggie was good friends with the boss, after all.

"If you'd rather have the whisky, I won't tell on you," Maggie said, with all the perceptiveness of a good innkeeper.

Torran laughed slightly. "All right, whisky then," he said.

Maggie busied herself with glasses and a bottle of Laprohaig, adding a dash of water to each. She set one glass in front of Torran, the drops of water crinkling the golden liquid into scintillating fractals, and settled across the table from him. "All right, then," she said. "It's clear enough we both fancy a swim when we're dressed for it, and I'd as soon speak plainly, if that suits you?"

"Aye," Torran said, lifting his glass toward her.

"*Slàint*," she said, clinking her glass to his and sipping as he did. The whisky with the water added was more warmth than bite, sweetness and smoke on the back of his tongue.

"You didn't know before that Ellie's a selkie?" Torran asked, since Maggie had given permission for directness.

"I never dreamed of it," Maggie replied. "Her father's my half-brother. Our dad left his mum for mine—mine was the selkie—and there was no love lost between the new wife and the old, as you might imagine. Douglas and I rarely saw each other growing up, and with him in the States the last twenty-five years, the most we've had to do with each other until quite recently was a card at Christmas."

"Your da had enough selkie in him to attract a selkie wife, and so did your half-brother," Torran said, interpreting this story.

"Apparently so," Maggie said. "I had no idea Douglas's wife was a selkie. I never met her."

"Ellie told me about her parents," Torran said. "Do you think her mum is as dead as everyone's been led to believe?"

Maggie frowned and took another sip of whisky. "Maybe not… given the circumstances of her death."

"How did you come to invite Ellie here?" Torran asked. "She said…you do know she's quite ill?"

Maggie sighed deeply. "You breathed on her?"

Torran nodded. "It worked wonders, but she's bad off."

Maggie nodded, tucking in her bottom lip. Torran's lust, slightly appeased but still alive to the tiniest nuance where this woman was concerned, had no trouble imagining a similar lip-tuck provoked by a moment of passion, and got briefly lost in imagining her slim hips rocking against his. When Maggie started speaking again it took him a moment to catch up.

"Douglas and I are closer these days. When my husband left a few years ago, I didn't send a card at Christmas and he called to check on me. We spent a few hours talking and realized we liked each other. We've stayed in touch since then. With Ellie—he said she was going through some depression, thought she could use a change of scenery and something to occupy her, but despaired of her taking any initiative. I thought she might do better here, and if not, at least she'd do no harm."

"So you've no idea what the story is with her sealskin," Torran said grimly.

Maggie shook her head slowly, biting her lip again. Torran turned his gaze deliberately into his glass, which was approaching empty faster than was probably wise. "This is the first I've known to wonder," Maggie said. "I know that...well, I know very little, really. If her mum—Alise was the name—was a selkie, it's reasonable to suppose that Ellie's skin survived her birth. All that tends to go more smoothly when the mum's the selkie."

"Is there a way to call her mum back and ask her?" Torran asked bluntly.

Maggie considered, lips pursed and eyebrows raised. Torran wondered how her ear would taste, if he took the whole thing in his mouth. It was such a smooth, pretty ear.

"Douglas loves her enough to call her home, no question," Maggie said. "It would mean telling him. I'm sure the poor man has no idea..."

"He might love her less if he knew she'd run away and left him to mourn her for dead all these years," Torran pointed out.

"True..." Maggie agreed. "I think that would be the option of last resort. We don't even know if the woman's still alive. But it's hard for me to credit a selkie mother...I mean, faking her own death was a deliberate act. She must have planned it. And I can't imagine she would have left without making sure Ellie's skin was safe. Selkie mothers aren't the most reliable for sticking around, but the instinct to take care of the baby's sealskin is quite strong."

"She should have been called back," Torran realized. "Ellie's suffering should have brought her back if she could come."

"Another reason to think she might not be alive now," Maggie agreed.

They both took unhappy gulps of whisky and finished at the same time. Maggie stood and refilled both their glasses.

"It comes to this," Maggie said, sitting down again. "Alise almost certainly stashed that skin somewhere. And a good, proper search might turn it up."

"Who should do that search, though?" Torran asked. "Ellie or her da?" Maybe Maggie could explain the situation to Douglas and he could find the pelt without Ellie's ever having to know about the death sentence awaiting her without it. Torran didn't know Ellie's father, and the notion of his trauma bothered Torran less than the notion of Ellie's.

"Ellie should," Maggie said, decisively. "Douglas isn't a selkie. He should only learn of us if there's no other option."

Torran grimaced, aware that she was right. His gram had been the rare non-selkie to know of their existence, and the knowledge had been safe enough with her, once she had a son and a grandson to protect. Selkies were too vulnerable to enthrallment by someone unscrupulous enough to steal a sealskin for any selkie to go spreading the secret around without a bloody good reason. And Ellie's mum had apparently not told Douglas. Perhaps she'd known of a reason not to trust him.

"When will you tell her?" Torran asked. "*How* will you tell her?" Better Maggie than him, was all he could think.

Maggie's forehead puckered. "It's really not the kind of thing you *tell*."

"It's better shown," Torran agreed. His own experience, and he had to imagine that of most other selkies, was almost completely nonverbal. His father had taken him down to the shore one dark and early morning, and shoved a duffle containing his sealskin into his arms. As soon as Torran had pulled back the zipper and felt the seduction of fur against his hands, he'd succumbed to blind instinct, out of his clothes and wrapped in that pelt without another word being said, and lost to an ecstasy he despaired of ever experiencing again. Being with a woman was close but not as good, and subsequent times he'd worn his pelt, he hadn't felt the same intensity—though it was a bloody good feeling, changing into a seal, no question.

Thinking about it now, he began to feel downright sorry for himself that Maggie showed no sign of wanting to approximate that feeling with him. Was it *him*? Was something wrong with *him*?

"I can't show her," Maggie said softly.

Torran dragged himself back from his thoughts, registering her reluctance but unsure what she'd said. "*I* wouldn't want to have to break it to her," he said, intending sympathy.

"I *can't* show her," Maggie repeated, more emphatically. "I don't know where my sealskin is, either."

Torran froze, holding the sip of whisky he'd just taken in his mouth while he tried to make sense of this statement. When he drew the logical conclusion, he gasped involuntarily and choked.

Maggie watched him bleakly while he hacked, and finally he managed to get out, "Are you *enthralled*?" She seemed so normal, he couldn't imagine that she was anyone's puppet slave. She was a mother, a competent and successful business owner... If she were enthralled, would she even *know* it? Enthrallment, for Torran, was no more real than the kidnappers who were reported to snatch up unattended children from playgrounds or shopping malls. He'd been warned about the possibility in no uncertain terms, but he'd never come close to it himself, or known of any other selkie who had.

"Only a little," Maggie said, with no hint of joking on her face. In fact, Torran was suddenly afraid she might be going to cry.

If she did, and he comforted her, would she maybe want to…? He kicked himself mentally. *Down boy.* He wasn't at all certain he would want to shag an enthralled woman, anyway.

"It's perfectly humiliating," Maggie said, looking away from him. "But it's worth your knowing the story for the lesson in it, if nothing else. In case you marry a selkie lass someday."

Torran waited, afraid that anything he said would come out wrong.

"My husband, Logan, is a selkie, too. And when we decided to raise a family, knowing our children would be selkies, we neither of us wanted to risk my taking the route that Ellie's mum apparently did, bounding off to sea when the responsibilities of motherhood got too heavy. I didn't think I would, but we wanted to be safe. So we agreed that Logan would hide my pelt, and the children's, until they were old enough to be told. And since that meant I'd be spending a long time ashore, Logan would go out frequently for brief periods so he could breathe on me with his selkie breath and keep me healthy."

Torran nodded cautiously. Maggie had put a huge amount of trust in her husband. It was a crying shame the bastard had proved unworthy.

She said, "We fought about his going out. He'd stay gone too long, and leave me alone with the inn and the infants, and I'd call him back, and he'd get angry. So—one day he went out without telling me, and I couldn't call him back. I thought at first I was in too much of a rage, but gradually I realized that I couldn't cry for any other reason, either. My tears had all dried up. And after that…I tried to look for the sealskins and found I couldn't."

"What happened…when you tried?" Torran was consumed with horrified fascination. The idea that the woman across from him, as mesmerizingly sexy as he found her, had an invisible streak of enthrallment going through her—it was like knowing that she contained hidden veins of insanity. How much more awful must it have been for her to make the same discovery about *herself*?

Maggie said, "You know that feeling when you walk into the next room to get something, and once you get there you can't remember what you're after? Or maybe you're too young to have that happen."

"Not too young," Torran said. "I know what you mean."

"It's a bit like that," Maggie said. "While I'm sitting here talking, I'm aware that the sealskins are missing and I even know why, and I can speak about it sensibly. But the moment I decide to get up and *look* somewhere, I immediately forget what I'm doing. I remember if I sit back down, but the moment I decide to look again, my mind shuts off and I find myself doing anything else instead."

Torran thought about that for a while, unwilling to let Maggie see his instinctive horror. "Could you tell someone else where to look?" he asked. "I mean, while you're sitting here talking, do you know where they are? Could you tell me?"

Maggie shook her head miserably. "I can think of places, and I could tell you. But I pretty much know that they're not going to be there. Wherever they are, it's someplace I can't think about."

Torran crossed his arms over his chest and leaned back in his chair until he was staring, broodingly, at the ceiling. The ceiling was white, and smooth, and as befitted a restaurant kitchen, not a single cobweb could be seen.

No wonder Maggie wasn't attracted to him. Now that he knew she was enthralled, his attraction to her seemed to have shriveled up and died a horrified death. No small part of him wished he'd woken up with a flu this morning and never met either of these wretched selkie women.

Because the truth was, now that he'd met them, he had no choice. If he walked away from either of them now, he'd never be able to look himself in the washroom mirror again.

He sighed heavily and sat up. "I'll demonstrate the change for Ellie, then. And. I'll help you find your sealskins."

It was easier meeting Maggie's brown selkie eyes, accepting the gratitude in them, now that he knew he was at least safe from her tears. Logan, that arsehole, hadn't even stuck around to enjoy this benefit of his own creation, a woman who couldn't cry.

Chapter 15: Ellie

June 2014 - Isle of Skye, Scotland

Ellie had been at Aunt Maggie's for a week, and she loved it. The transforming euphoria that had bloomed over her on the drive from Edinburgh with Torran had buoyed her through a series of days rendered magical less by their details than by her mood. Although she had helped Maggie some with cleaning and making up the pretty guest rooms—each one decorated differently—and lending a hand at breakfast, she had proved most useful as a babysitter. Her cousins Cait and Alec were seven and five, respectively, and out of school for the summer holidays. Maggie generally relied on an elderly neighbor to keep them occupied in the summer, but the neighbor was overly cautious and the kids were not a bit tactful in expressing an immediate preference for Ellie. The neighbor, Ellie gathered, was happy to have a holiday of her own. Ellie found the kids charming, if exhausting. She had played chase with them on the pebbly beach by the inn, poked into tide pools, and walked with them into the little town of Portree to play in the park and get treats. Ellie had expected to buy them ice cream, but they'd proved their kinship to her with a marked preference for the fish-flavored Japanese crackers they could get in one of the little specialty foods shops in town, and a delicacy new to Ellie—canned mackerel in tomato sauce, which they liked to eat straight out of the tin with their fingers. Ellie thought ruefully, with regard to the tomato-stained clothing, that even ice cream cones would have been less messy.

The Isle of Skye spoke to her on a level she could only attribute to ancestral belonging. Its beauty was by turns bleak and empty—wide open spaces and naked rock and bare land rising up to blank sky—and glowing with richness—roses and lobelia twining on trellises or overflowing baskets and rock borders, shop fronts in a bouquet of sherbet colors ringing Portree harbor, the harbor itself bobbing with every type of boat from dinghies to brightly colored sailboats to pleasure yachts. Loch Portree, despite its name, was not a lake, but part of the inlet of sea that separated the Isle of Skye from the Scottish mainland. The sea air was wetter and more intimate here than at home, maybe because the frequent fog and misting rain brought the smell of salt water vividly to Ellie's nose every time she walked outside. The omnipresence of the ocean, even on this sheltered harbor side of the island, soothed Ellie's senses like nothing else.

She'd caught glimpses of Torran a few times behind the wheel of a *Skye Tours* minibus, picking up or dropping off guests, or, once, driving through town. He'd waved to her in a friendly way, but there had been no chance to speak. She was itching to spend more time with him. She didn't think she had a crush, exactly— she never really seemed to get those—but she'd felt such an affinity for him. They were alike in ways she'd never felt *like* anyone before—that odd thing about the swimming!—and she associated him with the astonishing surge in her energy and spirits that had come over her as she slept beside him in the car. Perhaps this was why her impatience to see him rose as she sensed herself starting to fade again. She had not let herself hope that the problem was gone forever, but that bit of mental prudence couldn't insulate her from her disappointment—fear? grief?—when she sensed the old emptiness asserting itself again. She'd been treated in various ways for depression, and maybe that's what it was, even if none of the drugs seemed to touch it. She didn't like to be morbid, but to her the situation felt more like a leaching away of self, a sort of desiccation. She felt, to be blunt, as if she were slowly dying, the vibrant stuff of herself sinking away from her into the sand and leaving an emptying husk behind. Since coming here, she'd felt replenished, topped off. But the essential crack through which the brightness escaped remained unmended, and a week after coming here, she was already depleted again.

Her lagging spirits made matching the energy of the kids difficult, so she was relieved the morning that the neighbor arrived just after breakfast to take them for the day. Three sets of guests checked out that morning, too, and Maggie had just turned to Ellie in the kitchen they had not yet cleaned from breakfast to say, "I've a plan for you today," when a knock sounded at the back door. "Ah, there he is," Maggie said, and Ellie hoped so unreasonably that it was Torran that she couldn't ask, but only followed Maggie out of the kitchen to see who came in through the mudroom full of coats and boots and fishing gear and gardening tools, the back entrance never used by guests.

It *was* Torran, carrying a large, army-style duffle bag slung by its handles over his shoulder. "Hi!" she greeted him, aware that her enthusiasm was showing in a way he might easily misread as the crush she didn't have on him. Ellie was pretty sure she was asexual. The psychologist she'd seen at school seemed to feel her lack of interest might be just another symptom of her depression, but Ellie didn't think so. Her private opinion, too eccentric to discuss with even a woman who treated crazy people, was that she had some flavor of sexuality like being queer but based on a quality, unlike gender, that she hadn't encountered yet. Perhaps she could only be turned on by space aliens, or some very obscure ethnicity or temperament. Her sexuality seemed to her not so much missing as untapped—walled off in her behind something too thick to breach. Torran couldn't breach it either, but she wished that he could. He was so lovely—from a purely aesthetic point of view—all bright smile, bright eyes, shining black hair, and skin a color that looked somehow warm to the touch. He paid her a quality of attention that she was afraid might mean he was attracted to her, and she didn't want to lead him on or disappoint him. But she didn't want him to stop, either.

"Hi yourself!" he said, setting down the duffle bag in a corner of the entry and exchanging a look with Maggie—friendly but with something else, almost like the look teammates might exchange at the start of a big game. He came into the foyer between the kitchen and the living room and gave Ellie a hug before putting her away from him a little and studying her face. "How are you?" he asked with an odd searchingness, as if the answer really mattered to him. He looked at her, still holding her shoulders, as if she were good to eat. She liked that.

She nodded a little equivocally. "I'm good," she said.

He frowned slightly and leaned toward her, opening his mouth as if perhaps he *did* intend to eat her. She closed her eyes, determined to accept whatever strange thing he was doing calmly, so as not to embarrass him.

She felt the warm gust of his breath—which was faintly and appealingly sardine-scented—across her forehead and the bridge of her nose and her closed eyelids. Immediately, she felt that up-welling of self, that glorious sense of being filled to overflowing with her own spirit and enthusiasm. Her eyes flew open. "*You,*" she breathed. "You *did* do it."

He shrugged slightly, looking sheepish.

"What *is* it?" Ellie demanded. "Can you *bottle* that?"

"It's a...sort of a traditional greeting, I guess," he said.

"*Whose* traditional greeting?" Ellie asked. Whoever the people were who had come up with this, she needed them to adopt her.

"Just—" He waved his hand vaguely at their general surroundings, and grinned at her as if he'd answered her question.

"Have you eaten?" Maggie asked Torran, and Ellie suspected her of deliberately changing the subject. "Come into the kitchen while I finish clearing, and then we can go."

"Go where?" Ellie asked, as they all flowed back into the kitchen. The kitchen was the heart and soul of this house. It was the source of all activity. Ellie had worried, initially, about depriving Maggie of the upstairs office, but had soon realized that Maggie naturally managed all her accounts and reservations with a cell phone and a laptop at the kitchen table. The office had probably belonged to Logan the Missing, as Ellie had begun to think of him. Her dad had told her that Maggie's husband had left four years ago—just walked out—but since Ellie had been here, no one had mentioned him directly, not even the kids.

"Seal spotting," Torran answered her, grinning again.

"Really?" Ellie was delighted. "I *love* seals." North Carolina was too far south for seals to live, but they occasionally came down for a visit. Often when they did, they made the news, and once Ellie had tagged along with her dad when the marine lab rescued a stranded spotted seal. The poor thing had had such speaking eyes, Ellie had been sure she could explain that they were trying to help, if only she'd been allowed close enough.

"Where are we headed, exactly?" Torran asked Maggie. "Neist Point?"

"No," Maggie said quickly. "I'm thinking closer by. Loch Snizort Beag."

"Isn't that more populated? Or at least, more exposed?" Torran said doubtfully. "Neist Point, down at the bottom of the cliffs we're completely hidden from the visitors trail—"

"No."

Torran cocked his head at Maggie, clearly waiting for an explanation that didn't come, as Maggie busily filled the dishwasher. After a longish pause, he shrugged. "You're the native."

"I'll finish here," Maggie told Ellie. "Go get ready. You'll want a windbreaker, and trainers or shoes you can hike in."

Soon, Maggie was ushering them to the small blue van with *Skye View Inn* painted on the side. Maggie offered Ellie the front for the best view, while Torran climbed in back, humorously remarking on how good it was to be a passenger for a change.

He'd brought the duffle bag, not tucking it in the back as Ellie expected but hauling it into the van with him and keeping it by his feet. Ellie wanted to ask him about it, but he maintained a private attitude around the bag, not meeting her eye or drawing attention to it, that made her hesitate.

They quickly left the outer fringes of Portree behind. Soon there were no houses, just pasture and fences along the road, grassy fields rising up to distant hills and sky, and every once in a while, a stand of low bushes or pine trees. The landscape was beautiful in its simplicity. The shape of the earth showed clearly through its thin covering of vegetation.

Ellie wished she were alone with Torran. Maggie's presence seemed to make the easy conversation of their earlier car trip impossible, and Torran, quiet in the back seat, apparently felt the same. Eventually, Maggie asked after Torran's boss, who was an old friend, and Ellie's mind wandered as the other two talked about people she didn't know.

After a while, as the road rose and fell and curved, she began to catch glimpses of a large body of water in the distance. Soon, Maggie turned off onto a track so narrow, Ellie wondered what would happen if a car came from the other direction. She was relieved not to find out. The road ended in a slightly wider area of pavement where Maggie parked the van beside two other small cars. When they all got out, a wall of greenery surrounded them— tall grass and ferns, dense shrubs. A narrow trail broke through, and Maggie led the way along it, Torran following with his bag and Ellie bringing up the rear. No one talked except Maggie, who warned about thorns, and they all walked very quickly. Ellie sensed an odd air of urgency and suspense coming off the other two.

"Are we worried the seals are getting away?" Ellie asked.

"No." Torran flashed her a smile over his shoulder. "I believe you'll spot at least one."

Maggie snorted but didn't slow down. Ellie didn't ask any more questions.

They suddenly topped a rise, and the land fell away from them in steep, grassy bluffs to a long inlet, narrow across but curving around a point to the left and widening out to meet the sky on the right-hand side. The view was soaring, the world seemingly spread at their feet.

"It *is* very exposed," Torran said accusingly to Maggie.

It was. They could see for miles and miles. A few white houses dotted the far shore, widely separated and small with distance. A man and a boy were fly-fishing down the shore from them on the right. The loch itself was speckled here and there with boats, a sailboat in the distance and a couple of louder motorboats kicking up a spreading trail of wake waves behind them.

"Tuck down by Seal Rock, there," Maggie said, pointing.

Ellie peered at the wide, flat outcropping Maggie indicated, below them and to the left. Then she looked harder, squinting, and caught her breath. "Oh! There *are* seals!" They blended into the rock at first glance, nearly the same color and revealed mostly by the shadows edging their torpedo shapes as they drowsed in the sun.

"There are also *tourists*," Torran said, sounding close to fury.

"We'll wait for them to leave," Maggie said soothingly, but Torran didn't look soothed.

A lean, long-limbed, athletic-looking couple and their two blonde children stood a little way along the bluff, overlooking seal rock, taking turns with a pair of binoculars. Ellie followed as Maggie and Torran ambled with slow reluctance toward them and paused a pointed distance from them.

"*Gruss Gott*," the woman greeted them softly in what Ellie though was German, obviously not wanting to scare the seals. She gave them a friendly smile and pointed happily at the rock. Ellie smiled back at her, sharing her pleasure, disapproving of Maggie and Torran's attitudes.

Ellie could see now that the rock was actually an island, separated from the shore by a narrow channel, and not nearly as flat as it looked from above. "All right," Torran muttered. "That *might* do."

Ellie watched the seals. There was something so compelling about them—her heart reached out. She understood that to many people, seals were ungainly, wallowing creatures that belched and farted and reeked of fish, but Ellie purely loved them. She always had, out of all proportion to the number of times she had encountered them. They filled her with awe, and a sense of kinship, and—when *nothing* else made her feel this way—something very close to joy. At school, she had declared a marine biology major, following in her dad's footsteps, and did every research project she plausibly could on seals.

A sleek head popped out of the water beside the rock, accompanied by soft gasps and quiet exclamations from the German family. A moment later a female, judging by her pale coat and small size, wriggled onto the rock. The seals already there lifted heads and hooted at her, lunging and biting out in a half-hearted manner as she came too close. Seals didn't like to snuggle, Ellie thought, which was funny to her because they seemed so wriggly and affectionate. Eventually, they all settled down with the requisite few feet of space between them, the new one established in her own spot in the sun, and the heads flopped down on the rock again. Ellie was too far away to hear the sighs she imagined. On the rock were five females and a larger bull with a mostly black coat and a proud, Roman nose. These were grays, not the smaller, speckled common seals Ellie knew were also found on Skye. Ellie wished it were winter so there'd be a chance of seeing the little white pups. "This isn't a rookery, is it?" she asked.

"No," Maggie said.

"It's far too accessible to humans," Torran said. "The rookeries are all much more difficult to reach." He frowned at Maggie, sounding almost accusing.

The German family left, nodding and smiling as they all made room for each other on the track.

"All right," Maggie said the moment they were out of sight. "Go on down, and I'll stand here and let you know if anyone else is coming."

Torran gave a grunt of acknowledgment and started down the bluff toward the rock.

"Go with him," Maggie urged Ellie.

"We'll scare them!" Ellie protested softly, hanging back.

Torran glanced over his shoulder. "Hurry!"

The seals lifted their heads all at once and watched Torran's approach. Then, almost as one, they slithered off the rock, disappearing with a swift scatter of splashes into the water.

Ellie couldn't suppress a noise of annoyed dismay, but she followed him.

A steep, narrow beach of round, ankle-turning rocks rimmed the loch, and Ellie could see by the telltale lines of debris that the tide was out. As the presence of seals made evident, this loch, like Loch Portree, was not a true lake but an inlet. A channel only a few yards wide, but clearly deep, separated the shore from Seal Rock, which rose steeply above their heads. She wished she could climb the rock and lie in the sun as the seals had done, but of course, since it would mean swimming the channel, she couldn't.

She crossed her arms over her chest, annoyed by this adventure, by Maggie and Torran's surly moods, by the scared-away seals.

Torran glanced up the bluff to where Maggie stood, silhouetted against the hazy blue sky. "Go ahead!" she called down quietly. Both motorboats were out of view now, though Ellie could still faintly hear the whine of their engines.

"Watch me," Torran said to Ellie, giving her a glance she couldn't read. "I'm going to show you one more seal."

He didn't wait for her skeptical look but stepped out of his shoes, and, balancing on one foot and then the other, deftly removed both socks without even wobbling. Then, his back to her, he seized his shirt one-handed by its scruff and drew it swiftly over his head.

What was he doing? Torran didn't swim either!

His back was just as beautiful as his face, wide at the shoulders and tapering to his waist, his spine making an elegant channel between his shoulder blades, parting the muscled mounds of his lower back. His golden skin shone in the sunlight. Despite her irritation, Ellie found herself thinking that he belonged in a museum, his lovely shape cast in bronze or carved from marble, preserved for the ages.

He unbuckled his belt and dropped his pants. He wasn't wearing anything underneath them. He had no tan lines. His bottom was as golden as the rest of him.

"Um?" Ellie said.

"Bear with me," Torran said, without turning around.

There was nothing of the strip tease in his manner. He was as matter-of-fact as if he were undressing for bed in a room by himself. Below the muscled curves of his buttocks, his legs were long and beautifully shaped, the golden skin furred with straight, black hair that became denser toward his ankles.

He knelt, which brought his purple scrotum into view, and she couldn't help glancing, shocked, up the bluff toward Maggie, who gestured forcefully for her to keep watching Torran. No one spoke.

Torran opened his bag and drew out something furry and large. He stood in order to lift it fully free, and Ellie saw that it was an animal skin. A…sealskin. She could see its twinned rear flippers and another at the side, the characteristic way the pelt was pale at the edges, with speckles pooling to a dense, solid black where the spine should be. The head hanging down, empty holes instead of eyes, should have looked grotesque, but seemed instead beautiful and majestic, like a ceremonial mask.

Ellie felt a prickling all over her body. She couldn't form coherent thoughts or speak. Her eyes told her that Torran held the remains of a dead seal, which should have been abhorrent, but her heart understood something different, something—wonderful.

He turned around, the sealskin he'd slung over his shoulder doing absolutely nothing to cover his penis reclining casually against his equally casual balls. The look he gave her was—apology? Pity? It made her suddenly afraid. "See you tomorrow morning," he said. "Sunrise."

He faced the water again and stood still for a moment—for concentration or effect, Ellie wasn't sure. Then he drew the skin across his back as if slipping into a heavy cloak, and it parted, open down the belly. He stepped fully into it and drew the head up, hoodlike, over his own.

Everything happened very quickly then. Only afterward, as Ellie replayed it in her mind, did his transformation move in slow motion. The skin, with Torran inside, began to collapse and inflate. It settled to the stones of the beach and yet filled out as it did so until—impossibly but unmistakably—a living, moving, breathing, utterly enormous seal lay where Torran had stood a moment before.

The bull turned his whiskered face to Ellie. She could see nothing of Torran in those dark, liquid eyes, and yet she was convinced that the whole, buff-colored patrician face shone with a deep happiness. He was only a few yards away, but it didn't occur to Ellie to be frightened. Then, nose toward the water, he gave two powerful, rippling heaves and launched into the channel with a tidy splash. A sinuous line moved swiftly beneath the surface, and was gone.

Beneath her, Ellie's knees gave out quite unexpectedly, and she sat down hard on the grassy bank. "Oh," was all she could say. "*Oh.*"

Chapter 16: Ellie

June 2014 - Isle of Skye, Scotland

The next morning, Ellie drove across the island on her own to retrieve Torran at sunrise. She hadn't really slept, but she didn't feel tired. Her whirling thoughts showed no sign of settling, and she welcomed the challenge of piloting an unfamiliar vehicle on the wrong side of the road, in the dark and the mist, for the focus it required. Hardly any other cars broke her solitude. Sunrise came appallingly early this far north, so close to midsummer. Maggie had said that sunrise would prompt Torran's return and he would appear sometime later, once he'd swum back from wherever he'd gone since yesterday. But Ellie wanted to be there in time to watch him change again.

Through some miracle of management, Maggie had cleared the previous day of guests and children, but today all of her regular duties pressed and Ellie was on her own to collect Torran. She suspected that she and Maggie were equally relieved by the separation. Ellie was used to operating at a bit of a remove from her own feelings—her so-called depression had taught her that—

and she was pretty sure yesterday's news had been harder for Maggie to deliver than for her to receive. She'd felt oddly responsible for comforting Maggie about the likelihood of her own death, and now her pleasure at the prospect of having Torran to herself was marred by weariness at the thought of having to do the same for him.

Maggie obviously believed Ellie was in shock and would fall to pieces when full understanding struck. She'd studied Ellie very carefully in the kitchen that morning when giving her last minute directions and handing her the backpack full of food to share with Torran, who she said would be famished from the change. She had apparently decided Ellie was coping well enough to be trusted with the van and the drive, but Ellie could tell she was still waiting for the other shoe to drop. Ellie didn't know if there was going to be another shoe or not, but Maggie's hovering annoyed her. She hoped Torran wouldn't hover. Or, if he did, she hoped she would mind his style of hovering less.

She recognized the turn-off just as it was getting light. She parked, slung on the pack full of food, and hurried through the dew-soaked bushes and ferns towards Seal Rock.

The loch and the lands that sloped into it gave her, once again, the feeling of the world spread at her feet. The sun rising behind her spilled rosy-gold light over bluffs and lake and sky, lending a luster of enchantment. Luminous tendrils of mist rose from the water's surface and lay in the folds of the hillsides, as if the landscape had adorned itself with a collection of shining silver scarves. This was just the place for breakfast with a selkie, she thought, shivering a little with the strangeness of everything. Might as well keep her eyes peeled for fairy rings, water horses, the sinuous necks of monsters, or hands gripping magic swords rising from the loch. None of those things was any stranger than imagining that a stranded seal was killing her slowly from the inside for lack of a pelt to swim away in.

She was relieved when Seal Rock came into sight, the mist not thick enough around it to obscure her view. She surveyed it closely for signs of Torran, but it was deserted. Good—she had arrived in time. Maggie had warned her to keep out of sight, but that was more easily said than done. The whole landscape was so exposed. Eventually, she lay down reluctantly, full length, at the top of the bluff. The long grass was damp with dew, but her windbreaker helped. She'd just have to live with wet jeans. It was not reasonable to expect supernatural adventures involving selkies to be perfectly dry.

Peering through parted grass stems, she watched light spread gradually over the top of the empty rock, darkening the shadows at its base in contrast. Apart from the unpleasant dampness down the front of her legs, nothing seemed real. Her surroundings were a dreamscape. She felt no more substantial herself. She was a figment suspended between two futures. Either she would successfully complete a quest to recover her missing selkie skin, and become a woman who was also a seal, or she would fail, and die. Of these two possibilities, the second was far easier to imagine. She'd been living with the presentiment of death for some time.

She kept her eyes on the empty surface of the water, rendered ghostly in the semi-transparent mist. He might come now. Or now.

The time that seemed long in passing collapsed to a blink when, just as she'd imagined, a dark shape broke the surface beside the rock and glided into the channel. The next moment, shoulders and a huge, bulky body emerged, and a giant seal rippled onto the beach. She longed for binoculars, holding her breath with anxiety that she was too close. What would happen if he sensed her? Would he leave? He scanned his surroundings, sleek head turned alertly toward her, his whiskery nose lifted to the breeze. What if he smelled her?

He must not have, because, just as the seals yesterday had done, he put his head down, chin flat against the pebbles of the beach. She thought she could see his sides heave with his sigh. But no—his subsidence went on too long for a sigh. He seemed to be deflating slowly, trembling. He shrank and flattened and shivered, and soon he was not a seal at all, but a still mound of skin and fur.

Watching, Ellie wasn't filled with the wonder and awe that come of observing a seemingly impossible feat, but with the satisfaction of seeing a familiar task performed well. Nothing about selkies seemed to surprise her, after that first, shocking moment. Knowing that selkies were real and she was one felt both massively illuminating and inevitable—as if she were a puzzle piece stored all this time in the wrong box, now introduced to the puzzle where she belonged.

The pile of fur gave a sudden heave. There was Torran, lifting his sealskin away with one arm, like someone throwing back the covers to get out of bed. He stood from his pelt, stretching long and luxuriously as he looked around him. He still didn't appear to see her. Oh, he was pretty—as perfect and unselfconscious as the wild animal he'd so recently been. She could not avoid taking in the full frontal view of him, but his parts looked normal and harmless, mere anatomy. She wondered if another girl, one who experienced desire or who had viewed enough penises to have a basis for comparison, would feel something else.

He located his bag where Maggie had placed it—tucked away but still visible from the shore in a hollow of the bluff. She heard the whine of the bag's zipper and watched him dress, admiring his grace, his balance, his economy of motion. As soon as he was clothed, he bundled up the sealskin and stuffed it into the bag, zipping it out of sight.

At last she stood up, brushed herself uselessly, slung on the backpack, and started down the bluff, placing her feet sideways against the steep decent. She saw the concern that flashed across his face once he spotted her—worry *for* her, not distress at her presence, she felt sure. She avoided his gaze self-consciously as she picked her way down to him.

"Maggie said you'd be hungry," she said by way of greeting when she was closer, showing him the pack.

"Thanks," he said softly. "How are you?"

"All right." She set down the pack between them. "I hope you don't mind that I watched."

"I hoped you would."

She dared a swift glance at him. He was looking at her with all the pity and concern she had feared.

She didn't know how to account for herself to him. She didn't want to try. She said, "*Are* you hungry? I am." This was the problem with not sleeping. She'd been hungry since around 2 a.m. But if she said she hadn't slept, he'd pity her more.

"Starving," he admitted. "I always am after changing, but twice in twenty-four hours is tough. Uses a lot of calories."

"I think there's a lot of food here. I don't know what, though." She knelt to open the pack. He crouched, too.

At the top was a folded cloth, and he helped her find a spot on the beach smooth enough to spread it. Ceremoniously, she took out each item and handed it to him to arrange on the blanket. A loaf of sliced bread. Butter. Two foil packages of smoked salmon. A jar of pickled herring. Several other types of pickled vegetables, including onions. Chutney. A huge lump of creamy white cheese. A thermos of hot tea. Half a dozen still-warm, boiled eggs.

Torran sighed happily at this assortment. "Ploughman's lunch. She's a queen, Maggie." He settled cross-legged on the ground, his back to the grassy bank, and reached for the bread. Ellie sat opposite him on a beach boulder large enough to keep her off the damp ground.

The duffle bag rested as far away from her as possible while still remaining within Torran's reach. "Does it mind being put away wet?" she asked, nodding toward it.

"Nah. Eventually I'll air it out and let it dry, but for now it's more important it be hidden. The first and last rule of selkie etiquette is, *Don't touch another selkie's pelt.* And the corollary is, *Don't leave your pelt where anyone might be tempted.*"

She gripped her hands together in her lap, a little stung. "I wasn't going to touch it!"

"Not you. Other selkies seem to instinctively avoid it. I meant, if anyone else happens along."

She looked curiously at the duffle bag, wondering if she *did* instinctively shy away from touching it. She certainly didn't feel drawn toward it. She thought of the seals on the rock yesterday, hooting at the newcomer and rearranging themselves to keep the right amount of space between them.

Torran assembled a pile of all the foods onto a single slice of bread, ate it in three bites, and started over again with a second slice.

"How are you, Ellie?" He was careful not to look at her, busy with his sandwich.

She sighed. The small talk they'd been making was a long way from the easy flow of conversation she'd enjoyed with him the first day. She longed to have back that lovely feeling of affinity, but she doubted it was possible. Her sense of kinship to him was fully explained now, but also mostly ruined by her missing sealskin. Without her pelt, they didn't have the truly important things in common at all.

He could swim as a seal. She was dying.

"I'm okay," she said. "It's a lot to process."

He frowned and took a bite. She began to assemble her own sandwich, fearing she had offended him with an answer she knew was a brush-off, but unsure how to apologize.

"I don't mean to pry if you'd rather not talk to me," he said. "I can't imagine what you're going through. But I'm one of the very few you *could* talk to, and if you want to, I'd like to listen."

He met her eyes fearlessly, and something loosened a little inside her. Unlike Maggie, he didn't need her protection and wasn't asking for it. He really wanted to know how she felt. And suddenly, she wanted to tell him.

She said, "I think I've known for a couple of years now that— everyone calls it depression, but I've known it was killing me. Slowly. I couldn't say that to anyone, though. It's a weird relief to have it said out loud. Maggie acts like I'm a bomb with a lit fuse, but I—that part is the easy part, for me."

Torran studied her, then nodded thoughtfully. He took a bite and chewed, waiting for her to go on.

"Maggie says I might have a sealskin somewhere. She says my mother might have hidden it, and if I can find it, I won't die. That's the part I'm having trouble with. When I watched you change, it seemed—*normal*. I don't have any trouble believing that's part of me. But...I...if I believe in my sealskin—in the possibility that I could find it—then I have to hope. Hope is the part that hurts. I've worked very hard to kill off hope."

"I think I understand," he said.

She nodded, looking down at her lap. That was nice of him to say, but she doubted very much that he did.

He said, "You don't want to undo all the accepting you've done, if it turns out your sealskin can't be found and you have to give it all up all over again."

She stared at him, astonished by his insight. "How do you *know* that?"

He tilted his head quizzically. "Isn't that what you just said?"

She smiled at him, amazed and grateful. "I guess. But most people don't listen that well."

He shrugged, seeming embarrassed. After a moment he asked, "But—you *do* mean to look for your sealskin, don't you?"

"Of course I will," she said swiftly. "I'd be crazy not to. I just—don't know how to balance it. Hoping enough to look but not enough to despair if... I mean, it all seems so unlikely! My mother's been dead—or whatever—for more than eighteen years. If she'd left anything, we'd have found it by now."

Or whatever. The possibility that her mother wasn't dead, which Maggie had brought up yesterday, was a thought Ellie kept bumping into and glancing off again, unwilling to fully engage. The idea was the kind that could sink you—imagining your mother swimming away on purpose and leaving you behind—and Ellie had enough dragging her down as it was.

He said, "It would be well-hidden on purpose, though, and you weren't looking for it. Looking makes a difference, when it comes to finding."

The knot inside Ellie loosened further. He was right. Maybe she could hope—a little.

Torran passed her the thermos, and she sipped the sweet, milky tea directly from its brim, as he had done.

"I wish I could help you," he said. He busily scooped a hard-boiled egg from its shell with a spoon, not looking at her again.

"I wish you could, too." She wanted that badly, in fact. He was such good company, even if they didn't find her pelt, she'd still get something pleasurable from the whole thing, before... "You could breathe on me and keep me going longer."

"You'll need that," he said seriously. "Let me think about it. I'm not sure I can afford the ticket, but maybe..."

"You work for a tour company," Ellie said eagerly. "Maybe they could get you a discount. Or maybe Dad—" She broke off suddenly, afraid of pushing too hard.

"We'll see," he said.

His note of reserve had her backpedaling in an instant. "I'm sorry. I got carried away. It would be nice not to be alone. But it's a lot to ask."

He said, awkwardly, "I do want to help. But you have to begin right away, and I have to work…"

"Of course."

"By the time I'm free, you'll have found it yourself and be off swimming in the sea."

His words were kind—and of course he had to work—but she was miserably aware of all the reasons he wouldn't want to get involved with her. Who would want to get too close to a dying girl? It was a recipe for pain. And she couldn't even offer him the consolation of sex—at least, not the kind he'd probably want, the kind with a girl who wanted him back.

The idea that he had any interest in sex with her was probably absurd, anyway. Maybe that was his objection—a fear that she wanted to entangle him in more than a hunt for her missing sealskin. She said, "I'm not coming on to you, you know. I like you a lot and I'd love to have your help but I'm…I think I'm defective in that way. I don't…get attracted to people."

She watched him anxiously, unable to decipher his reaction from his bemused expression. She'd meant to reassure him, but—was he offended?

He said, "Didn't Maggie tell you? When you find your pelt, that will come with it."

When. She liked his optimism. The rest took longer to register. "Being attracted to people? Will come with my pelt?"

"Well, being attracted to other selkies will come with your pelt. Regular humans might not ever interest you much, to be honest."

Ellie was still processing this revelation when he added ruefully, "Other selkies, though, will interest you a great deal."

She eyed him curiously. The way he avoided her gaze seemed to confirm the logical conclusion. "*I* interest you—in that way?"

He protested her directness with an uncomfortable laugh. She was too curious to withdraw the question, though, and waited him out.

He shrugged. "Sure. You and Maggie both. But I don't interest either of *you,* because neither of you has got your pelt."

Maggie had mentioned something about her missing pelt. Ellie was far more focused at the moment on the news that Torran was attracted to her. And Maggie! Who was almost old enough to be his mother! But how convenient, that she could make this conversation about Maggie instead of herself.

"So…" She started to collect little bits of eggshell that had fallen on the blanket, an unnecessary task. "How does this work? If Maggie had her pelt, would you and she be…dating now or something?" It occurred to her suddenly that he and Maggie could be lovers already. They'd obviously talked a lot when she wasn't around, to have planned this whole selkie demonstration.

She hoped not. She didn't like the idea of Maggie meaning more to him than she did. Which was ridiculous, but there it was.

"Um…probably not dating."

She laughed, reassured by his obvious discomfort. "Just fucking, then?"

He was actually a little pink around the edges, she thought. His golden skin didn't show a blush easily. "Not fucking, present tense. Fucked, singular, past tense. Selkies practically invented hookup culture."

Hookup culture. She'd read articles lamenting it in the campus paper, bemused and curious to learn that her classmates sometimes hooked up at parties and ghosted one another by morning, intimate strangers parting without so much as an exchange of phone numbers. She'd found the information perversely comforting. Maybe she wasn't missing so much, after all.

If she'd had her pelt, would she and Torran have done that?

She said, "So that would have happened, and now you and Maggie would be avoiding each other?"

Torran sighed. "Christ, this is an awkward conversation." He spoke deliberately. "In my limited experience, yes, we'd be avoiding each other now. Seals don't really do romance, you know. I think it's the same for selkies. There's a powerful procreational urge, and then we move on."

She considered that, a little skeptically. "But...Maggie's husband was a selkie, right? So they had some kind of romance—to get married, and stay together long enough to have two kids."

"Yeah, but notice he didn't stay. Sticking around once the kids come along is a human virtue, and some selkies have more of it than others. Maggie's husband took off. My mum did the same."

And maybe her own mom, too. Did it help, to imagine it was just the selkie way, and not a personal betrayal? "So falling in love is the human part, and running away is the seal part?"

"I suppose that's how I think of it. Maggie's pretty human for a selkie. So's my da. My mum was born a seal, so it's no surprise she didn't stick around."

Ellie was fascinated. "Born a seal! What was *that* marriage like?"

"Short." He smiled when Ellie laughed. "I don't remember—and they weren't actually married, of course. She only stayed a couple of years."

Ellie's mom didn't have the excuse of being born a seal. Ellie was very fond of her mother's parents, Grandma Sandra and Grandpa Rick, who came to the beach every summer to visit Ellie and her dad. Grandpa Rick always took Ellie fishing, and Grandma Sandra liked to sketch her while they lay on the beach and talked. Ellie's mom had not been born a seal, and she'd had a really nice family—nice parents, a nice husband, and a daughter who couldn't have been worse than any other baby, at that age. And Alise had up and left, and made them all grieve for her all these years? They were *still* grieving, Ellie's father and grandparents. Was the seal in her mother really that strong, and that willing to leave them all behind? Or was Maggie wrong, and had Alise really died in that car crash after all?

There was no point asking Torran, who'd never met any of these people. "Which are you?" she asked instead. "More human or more seal?"

"Oh, more human, I expect. My da made sure of that. And my gram."

"What's your da—your dad like? Does he ever turn into a seal?"

Torran smiled. "Like clockwork every summer, and back in the autumn. He's out there now. He teaches school, so he'll be back at the end of the summer holidays."

"How does he get back?" Ellie asked. "Do you have to cry seven tears to get him home?" Maggie had described to her this method of retrieving a selkie loved one from the sea. Of all the facts about selkies she had absorbed yesterday, this one seemed the oddest to her—the most magical and fanciful, the least likely to yield to some underlying scientific explanation.

Torran shook his head, smiling. "If he had to rely on me getting teary for him, no telling when he'd be home. I know he's having the time of his life out there. He does what I did to get back this morning. You choose a cue, something you'll notice as a seal—"

"Sunrise," Ellie filled in.

"Yes. The full moon is good, too. Of course Dad stays more than a month, so he has to use something else. There's a certain type of fish that always shoals around the first week of August. So he holds the image of those fish shoaling in mind as he puts his sealskin on, and as he changes, that cue gets associated with the act of changing. Then, when he encounters that cue as a seal, it triggers the impulse to return. He's always come home in time so far."

"And you could call him back if anything went wrong," Ellie said.

"Aye. I've never had to, though. Dad takes his human responsibilities seriously."

"Do you?" Ellic asked, curiously.

"I suppose I do… At least, that's why I work summers and spend the winters out in the sea. So I can look after things while Dad's gone, make sure he gets back all right."

"So you probably have enough human in you to be capable of romance," Ellie teased.

"Well…" He gave her a challenging look. "So do you."

Ellie protested, "But is it possible to have romance without desire?"

He gave a brief laugh, without much humor in it. "I wouldn't know. Desire always gets in my way."

Unexpectedly, his deep brown eyes met hers. Something hung in the air between them, until Ellie banished it with a nervous laugh. "Well, that's a conundrum."

For a moment it had almost been as if they were—what? Daring each other to fall in love?

"Did you get enough to eat?" Ellie asked, making a point of looking around—anywhere but at him. All the fish and the eggs were gone, and most of the bread and cheese. The sun was well up, the mist had cleared, and the dawn chatter of birds had largely given way to the whir of sun-warmed, summer insects. Also, the tide was coming in. "We're going to get wet in a minute."

He answered with a swiftness that spoke of gratitude for the change of subject. "True. I'm full for now."

Together, they packed up the leftovers. When he handed her the chutney, his hand brushed hers, and though he gave no sign of noticing, it happened again as he helped her fold the picnic blanket. She wondered about the attraction he'd admitted feeling for her. How strong was it? Could he mostly ignore it, or was it an ongoing concern?

He seemed preoccupied, which gave her more freedom to study him. It was strange to be so conscious of his body, to be wondering about her effect on him. Strange too, to wonder how she would feel, if he did whatever he wanted with her. He was so pretty, and she honestly liked him. She imagined being naked, his hands on her. She couldn't really concentrate on the idea—her mind slipped away from it. But she didn't think she'd mind.

Unless he avoided her afterward. That, she would mind.

When everything was packed, he broke the silence. "I suppose you'll be flying home soon to look for your pelt, but what are you doing today?"

"Nothing," Ellie answered, too quickly. "I mean, nothing important. Why?"

"Did Maggie tell you her husband hid her pelt? I thought we could look for it a bit today. If you're up for it. It'd be good practice for you."

"Sure," Ellie agreed. She didn't care what they did as long as she was invited. "She…said something about it. I didn't understand what happened. Why can't she look for it herself? I mean—" she hurried to explain, "not that I don't want to help. I'm glad to. But I thought selkies don't like anyone else messing with their pelts?"

"She's enthralled," Torran said.

The hushed way he spoke told her this was a tragedy. As though he'd said, *She has cancer.* "Enthralled?" she repeated, cautiously, shouldering the now much lighter pack and moving her feet back from the water that kept nudging closer. They were almost out of shore, but this didn't seem like the kind of discussion to have casually, while walking back to the car.

Torran hefted the duffle containing his sealskin. "When someone else possesses your pelt, he can control you absolutely. Tell you how to act, how to feel, what to remember, what to forget." He held her gaze with a bleak seriousness that held no sensationalism or possibility of humor. "He could make you commit suicide, forget your own name. All he has to do is touch your pelt and will it."

"*Jesus*." She shivered. "But…" The implications of this were so awful she could hardly bear to take them in. "Maggie seems *fine*."

"I know. And I think she is, mostly. She did *ask* her husband to hide her pelt—"

"*Why?*"

"Because she was afraid she might abandon her kids. The way my mother did. I admire her for that, to be honest."

Ellie frowned. "Maggie's more human than seal, though?"

He nodded. "Oh, aye. A selkie who wasn't would never think of taking the precaution. But I suppose she didn't trust herself."

Ellie sighed. Torran had not accused her of wanting to abandon her *own* children and swim off to be a seal, but she couldn't help feeling defensive. It was stupid, though. She was probably going to die young, without ever doing that thing that led to children, anyway.

Torran went on, "So the worst of Maggie's enthrallment is that she can't call her husband back. That's the part that he did without her consent."

She said, "Logan the Missing. Do you think she wants to call him back? It sounds like she's better off without him."

He shook his head. "I have no idea. And that part doesn't matter. If we find her sealskin and return it to her, she won't be enthralled anymore. Then, she can call him back or not, just as she pleases."

"Do you have any idea where to start looking?"

"I think I do!"

Ellie liked how his face brightened with enthusiasm. "Tell me," she said.

"I need to fetch something from the place I'm staying," he said. "Let's head back and I'll tell you on the way."

They climbed the bluff. At the top, she turned for a look at the loch, where cat's paws of light reflected off its shimmering surface, and at the empty dome of Seal Rock. She wondered if the seals were out there waiting for them to leave. How long would it take them to repossess their rock, once she and Torran were gone?

Chapter 17: Torran & Ellie

June 2014 - Isle of Skye, Scotland

Torran forced himself to concentrate on explaining his plan for tracking down Maggie's pelt. The slim, cool lass who had walked beside him through the shrubs and bracken and handed him the keys so he could drive the van was making him half mad with distraction, ever since he'd realized he was going to take her to the cheap hotel where the tour company had put him up. She was going to be in his bedroom. With his bed. In every expectation of privacy. And he wanted her so badly he could barely think. It was useless to remind himself that none of this was real—it was only pure, dumb, biochemistry. He couldn't look at her without a cascade of pornographic images tumbling before his mind's eye. He was practically hallucinating, and he feared no observant party could overlook the evidence of his general state bulging beside his fly.

Fortunately, Ellie gave no sign of being an observant party.

Oh, bloody hell. That wasn't *fortunate*. That was the entire problem!

As they had talked on the shore, the logistical challenge of managing Maggie's elaborate meal and his hunger had been useful distractions. But the moment they stood and began moving around each other, packing up, coming into glancing contact as they handed off jars and folded the blanket, he'd kicked into some state of arousal overdrive. The discussion of enthrallment had put a slight damper on things, but now, in the van, her body so close beside him and a sweet, grassy scent that had to be hers teasing his nostrils, he felt close to losing it.

He couldn't endure a whole day like this. And he couldn't take her to his room—that was madness. He'd ask her to stay in the van, and he'd go get the map and take half a minute, tops, to deal with this infernal hard-on, and then... Maybe he could find a tactful way to leave her behind with Maggie. It would be better that way. She just drove him fucking crazy and he couldn't *function*.

*   *   *

Ellie glanced over at Torran as he drove. He seemed distant and distracted, and she was still confused about his plan for finding Maggie's pelt. He'd trailed off in his explanation on the walk back to the van, and for the last few minutes they'd been driving in silence. He seemed uncomfortable, shifting in his seat.

"Are you okay?" she asked.

He glanced over briefly. "Sure. Why?"

"You're just quiet. And I wondered—if it felt weird being human again. I mean, you were a seal an hour ago."

He smiled a little, keeping his eyes on the road. "It really doesn't. Except for the hunger, it's actually rejuvenating. You make your body new again when you change. I think a lot of stuff gets—fixed? Burned off? If you're injured, you heal in the change. Or if you're ill, you get better. Selkies who change often tend to live a long time."

"That's cool," she said. But then it struck her that the opposite was true, too. Selkies who didn't change didn't live long at all.

She looked out the window at the rocks and the heather and the land sloping up to the sky—all the early morning beauty—and suppressed a sigh. She didn't want him following that line of thought, or feeling he had to watch what he said around her. She didn't want to talk about death now.

He didn't break the silence, and she puzzled again over his shift in mood. Had she offended him somehow? Maybe that conversation about Maggie's enthrallment had troubled him. It was a troubling topic.

What *was* his plan for finding Maggie's pelt? He'd said something about some cliffs and a lighthouse.

She broke the silence. "You said that yesterday morning, you wanted to go out from the cliffs by the lighthouse because it's less exposed. And Maggie insisted the other place was better. But *why* does that mean that her pelt is by the cliffs?"

He said, "Neist Point is infinitely better than Snizort Beag. The cliffs are full of nooks and crannies and hidden spots where a selkie can change with no chance of anyone seeing. And you can park nearby so it isn't far to carry a heavy pelt. Snizort Beag was an easy walk to the water but it's barely better than Portree Harbor, exposed on every side and enough tourists around to make it really dicey changing during the day. At first I was furious with Maggie for insisting it's a better spot, when any sane person can see it isn't. But then I thought—Maggie *isn't* sane where her enthrallment's concerned. What if that's why she couldn't consider Neist Point? The more I thought, the stranger it seemed that she didn't even give a reason for shunning it. Just 'No,' and that was that."

"Huh." She mulled over the logic and didn't see anything wrong with it. "Clever! But we're not going to Neist Point now?"

"No. It's miles of cliff face and beach, and if Maggie's husband has some hidey hole there, it's not likely we'll just waltz up to it. There's one main trail to the lighthouse and the point, but it's possible to get down to the bottom of the cliffs at the base of the peninsula if you know the way. Tourists hardly ever go there. I'm hoping if I sit Maggie down with a map and ask her to help us plan a walking tour of the area, I can get a better sense of where she doesn't want us to look."

"And then we'll look there!" Ellie said. "Brilliant!"

Torran gave a short nod, not seeming as pleased as Ellie thought he should. "We're going by my place first, though. I've a big, topographic map of the island—really detailed—that I want to show her."

He lapsed into silence again. Ellie slipped off her sneakers without untying them and put her sock feet on the dashboard, arms around her knees. She hoped Torran would talk more, but he didn't, and as the miles slipped past she felt her own mood dipping low.

She couldn't blame him for retreating from her. She would probably do the same in his place. She was a disaster, and he'd done so much for her already. He probably couldn't wait to get away from her.

It wasn't his fault that she felt so much better when he was close and warm and meeting her eyes and telling her his thoughts and asking to know hers. And it wasn't his fault that she was desolate with him beside her in body but seemingly a million miles away in spirit. Her feelings didn't mean he owed her anything.

Why did he affect her so strongly? Was it the distraction? Did she just like him filling the silence so she didn't have to contemplate her depressing fate?

No. She hadn't liked the way Maggie filled the silence. She had wanted Maggie to leave her alone to contemplate her depressing state.

With Torran it was something else. With Torran she wanted *in*. He was like some enchanted cottage. She had peeked through the shutters and now she was desperate with curiosity to see the whole place, all its nooks and crannies and secrets and cunning details. Like Goldilocks, she wanted to taste the porridge and sit in all the chairs and lie in all the beds.

Unlike Goldilocks, she wanted the bear to invite her inside.

The bear in question was driving with a preoccupied concentration that made her despair of invitations. She watched him out of the corner of her eye. There was something so *right* about the way he looked—the strong lines of his body, his shining dark hair, the thoughtfulness that moved behind his deep, brown eyes. Maybe he would strike any other girl the same way. He was gorgeous on the order of a fashion model or a movie star. But she'd never cared about fashion models or movie stars. They belonged to everyone and so to no one. She wanted Torran to be *hers*. More than he was anyone else's.

Good lord. Was this a crush? Was this what a crush felt like, without the sex? Bears and cottages and Goldilocks and movie stars?

She was completely absurd.

She felt herself heating, flushing with embarrassment and turned subtly away from Torran, afraid suddenly that he would read her thoughts on her body.

That's when it struck her. Her body. His body. He wanted *in* with her, too—literally and not metaphorically. He had said so. And maybe for him it was just chemicals, selkie biology trying to have its way, but did that matter, really? On a basic level, he wanted closer to her, and she wanted closer to him. And she didn't think she'd mind his kind of closeness, even if she didn't crave it the way people were supposed to.

She would like to be able to give him something he wanted. She would like to *be* something he wanted.

She snuck another glance at him, trying to imagine how to broach the subject. He still seemed just as brooding, just as distant. Just as—tense? Eyes out the windshield, jaw tight, hands gripping the wheel more firmly than seemed strictly necessary. Was he angry?

If she asked him, would he turn her *down*?

She couldn't stop her gaze from dropping to his crotch, thinking about how he'd looked naked, wondering what it would be like…if it would hurt…if he…?

She could see the outline of his penis.

She averted her eyes and shifted in her seat, hoping that both her looking and her looking away again had gone unnoticed. The ridiculous thing was that she wasn't completely sure if it meant anything. She didn't look at guys' crotches, really. For all she knew, she might be able to see the outline of any guy's penis, if his pants were tight and she were looking.

But—it was *possible* that he had an erection. And even though she'd read that guys—young guys especially—got them randomly, and maybe it was just the road vibrations having a mindless effect, it was *possible* to imagine it had something to do with her.

Possible.

She put her feet on the edge of her seat and hugged her knees closely, taking courage from the thought.

Chapter 18: Torran & Ellie

June 2014 - Isle of Skye, Scotland

Torran felt deeply relieved to reach the hotel that served as his temporary home. "You can wait here," he told Ellie, pulling up by the side entrance closest to his room. "I'll only be a moment."

Startled, Ellie failed to reply before he'd gotten out and shut his door, and for a moment she struggled with a mixture of relief and disappointment. She could wait here. It wasn't too late to procrastinate, or ditch this plan completely. But as he collected his sealskin from the back, she regained her courage.

She got out and joined him behind the van. "Can I come in for the bathroom?"

"Right," he agreed, thinking, *Bloody hell.* And then, *No, it's all right. She won't have to come into the room.*

Her voice had sounded odd, though. He glanced over at her as he closed the van door, having decided against removing the duffle bag. She looked flushed, flustered.

"Feeling all right?" he asked. If she were ill, that would make it easier to leave her behind with Maggie. Not that he wanted her to feel poorly.

"Yes! Fine. Just—all that tea." *Damnit.* Her voice had been squeezed by nervousness, and she'd hoped he wouldn't notice. Her face, already warm, grew hotter.

"Aren't you going to take your bag in?" she asked, as he locked the van with the key fob and headed for the hotel.

"Changed my mind. I'm better keeping it with me. I'm not the only one with a key to my room, here."

"Oh…" She wondered where he usually kept his sealskin, when he wasn't living at a hotel, but something—instinct?—stopped her from asking. It had to be terrible manners to ask a selkie where he kept his pelt.

She followed him into the hotel corridor, self-consciousness crawling over her. Walking normally, not hugging herself with shivery nerves, not crowding him too closely or trailing too far behind, were suddenly matters requiring concentration.

"The loo's there." He pointed down the hall.

She stopped, dismayed. "Not in your room?"

He couldn't help smiling. Americans never seemed to expect the toilet to be down the hall. "These are the cheap seats. No ensuite washrooms on my boss's dime."

"Well, which room is yours?" she asked, suddenly afraid she was going to miss her chance. Despite what she'd told him, she'd only drunk a few sips of tea and didn't need the bathroom.

"There." He pointed to a door. "I'll just meet you out here, though."

Ellie wondered why he was making this so hard. "Can I see your room?"

Christ! If he had to look at her standing by his bed, it'd be all he could do not to topple her onto the mattress. He could remember far too viscerally how it felt to be a great bull seal with a smaller female pinned and wriggling beneath him. But those females were wriggling *closer*, in season and in on the game, just like the selkie lasses he'd met as a human. Ellie would not be.

He said, "It's completely and utterly ordinary. It's not even tidy because we don't get maid service."

"I'm just curious," she pressed. "Please?" She felt the indignity of having to beg, but she had come this far and hated to give up now.

Heaven help him. He unlocked the door. "See for yourself." He moved aside so she could stand in the doorway, remaining in the hall so she wouldn't go in.

Ellie silently agreed that the room was small, and ordinary. Despite Torran's claim of untidiness, the bed was made, though not with professional neatness. She was impressed, but somehow not surprised, that Torran was a bed-maker. She herself was not one. The room had a small sink, where his toothbrush lay, and a table with a chair rolled beneath it that held some books and mail and a laptop computer. The curtain of the ground floor window hung closed, so she couldn't assess his view. A wardrobe stood in the corner of the room, its drawers and doors closed. That was it.

She wanted to tease him that he'd left nothing shameful out, no underwear on the floor even, so why mind her looking? But she was too nervous for decorative flourishes. She stepped inside but he didn't follow. She looked back at him, stuck holding the door that would slam shut and leave him in the hall if she let go. His expression wasn't good.

Was he *angry* at her? Was she making a terrible mistake?

Torran was at his limit. So help him, he was going to have to *tell* her why she wasn't safe here with him. And to do that, he was going to have to go *in* with her and shut the bloody door! He wanted to pray—he didn't know to whom—but all he could see in his mind's eye was Ellie falling back on the bed, her legs apart, reaching for him. His dick led the way into the room.

"Ellie, you can't be alone with me here!" he burst out, the moment the door shut behind him.

In the same moment Ellie said, hugging herself, "I was thinking we should have sex."

Their words crossed in the space between them.

"Why?" Ellie suddenly hoped he hadn't heard what she'd said, guiltily imagining some point of selkie protocol that her instincts had failed to warn her about.

Torran's breath rushed out of him, becoming incredulous laughter. He was sure he'd misheard her. "Should?" he repeated weakly. "I'm sorry, I thought you said we should have sex."

"Maybe *should* is the wrong word." Ellie hugged herself more tightly, rushing to explain. "If I don't find my pelt I might not get another chance. And you said you…wanted to?"

He put his forehead against the door, needing something to bear against. "Well, of course I want to! I'm an animal in rut right now! The point is, *you* don't want to."

Ellie sat nervously on the edge of the bed. "I do want to. I want to know what it's like."

Torran groaned, thudding his forehead not very gently against the door. "I'm not the one to show you what it's like, though! I'm not a good lover. I've never had to be. I've only ever been with girls who want it as much as I do, and it's over and done in no time. It's selfish, right? I won't be able to make it nice for you."

Ellie was touched—and brave again—now that she understood the problem. "Torran, I don't want some generic person who will make it nice for me. You want me to rent a gigolo? I want it to be with you because I like you. I'm more worried I don't know how to make it nice for *you*."

Torran couldn't really follow her thinking. "Rent a gigolo?" he repeated, turning around. He knew it was funny, but at the sight of her the ache in his trousers became a silent imperative that wiped his mind clean of everything but need. She sat on his bed, all rose and gold and soft as petals, her big eyes full of anxious invitation.

She said, "I'd rather not." She thought he looked pained, tension down all the lines of his body, his face blank except for his eyes, which begged her for something. She reached out, offering whatever she could give, and he walked to her hands.

The bulge in his pants was right in front of her now, and she touched it experimentally. He leaned immediately into her hand, so she knew it was okay. She was a little startled by its firmness, and the way it twitched against her palm. It was sort of like its own creature.

He sighed and fingered his belt, and she took the hint and unbuckled it for him. His stomach was firm against the backs of her fingers as she unbuttoned his pants and unzipped his fly.

His penis stood through the opening of his boxers. She only caught a glimpse of the sculpted, elegant shape before he shucked both jeans and underwear and stepped out of them. She studied him freely, the shocking veined stalk, the delicate red tip like some kind of fleshy jungle flower. A drop of nectar welled from its tip. Impulsively, she leaned forward and tasted it.

The drop was slippery on her tongue, and faintly salty.

She wasn't sure how it happened, but the next moment he was in her mouth. Of course she'd invited him without realizing. It seemed important not to embarrass him by admitting the mistake. Instead, she closed her lips politely and made every effort to get her teeth out of his way.

Torran knew, in some distant corner of his mind, that he should stop before he utterly disgusted her. But her mouth was too soft and wet and perfect and he had no will. Instead he tangled his hands in the impossible richness of her hair, rocking, helpless against the glow gathering and building in his pelvis.

Ellie was afraid for a moment that she would gag when he began to thrust, but she changed her angle and steadied herself with one hand against the springy hair at his base. With her other hand, she gripped his hip. Then she could adjust to meet him, and keep him from going too deep. She thought, from the way he was groaning and burying his hands in her hair, that she must be doing okay. It was just a little tricky not scraping him with her teeth, keeping her lips tight around him as he moved, figuring out what to do with her tongue.

She wondered if he was going to come in her mouth, and if she would mind. But if she took him out he'd come on her instead, probably, and she wasn't sure how big a mess that would be. Maybe he had a plan for this. She would have to trust him.

Her mouth was full of frothy spit and plunging Torran. She needed a pause so she could swallow, but she lifted her eyes for a glimpse of his face and found him gone from her, his head thrown back and his mouth open, his breath labored and catching on itself. He arched and stiffened and gave a loud groan, and her mouth filled with the mildest taste in the world, as if her own spit had taken on the faintest, salty hint of sea. He rocked a few more times, convulsively, and slowed until she was able to slip him from between her lips and swallow. There was no aftertaste. She smiled, relieved, triumphant, and looked up at him. Should she put him back in?

Torran glimpsed her bright, warm eyes smiling up, and a dart of mingled relief and remorse penetrated his bliss. He dropped to his knees, deprived of grace by muscles that felt like overcooked spaghetti, and cupped her cheek with his hand. "I'm such a pig, Ellie! Are you all right?"

She laughed, her eyes sparkling. "*I'm* all right. Are you?"

"Oh, Christ. I'm grand. I'm grander than grand. How are you so good at that?"

Her smile grew delighted and a little smug. She shook her head against his palm. "I've never done it before."

He stroked her cheekbone with his thumb. "I haven't either. I think that's the nicest thing anyone's ever done for me."

Ellie did not let herself think. She leaned forward and kissed him.

Torran experienced a moment of startled doubt. He'd never gone in much for kissing, never seen the point. But after what she'd just done for him—she was an amazing sport—he was determined to be kind. Though he worried a bit about tasting himself in her mouth.

Torran's lips were wonderful against hers, soft and firm at the same time. She felt that she'd startled him, though, and drew back sooner than she wanted to.

Torran couldn't for the life of him think what he'd ever had against kissing. When her lips retreated from his he pursued them, leaning against her legs and supporting himself on the mattress with a hand on either side of her hips. She came back to him then, opening her knees so he fit between them, her lips parting under his, her tongue meeting his shyly, then less shyly. He moved his hands to her waist and up her sides, and felt her arms circle him, her hands stroking his back. He kissed her harder, and she kissed him harder back.

Ellie had never imagined kissing would be so easy, or so nice. He was delicious, like cold water when she was terribly thirsty, but she would never grow full of kissing. She could spend the rest of the day tasting his lips, his tongue, his smooth teeth, nibbling and pulling and teasing and letting go and coming right back for more. His hands were on her waist, her sides, her stomach, and she slid her own hands under his shirt. At first she only touched the smooth planes of his back, the dip of his spine, but then she explored the twin mounds of his butt and slid around to his hard, smooth stomach.

He leaned back briefly and pulled his shirt over his head. She looked at him, fully naked, and thought again how beautiful he was, his long lines and smooth muscles, his golden skin. His cock was standing up again—or still? She checked his face and she could tell from his smile that he'd seen her looking. "I can't get enough of you," he said, and reached for the hem of her shirt.

She raised arms for him like a trusting child as he peeled off her T-shirt. Her bra was pretty, white with lacey edges, but he lost no time taking that off, too. He'd never really concentrated on a woman's breasts before, but hers were such beautiful twin handfuls, her nipples pink and tight. He kissed those, each of them, taking them in his mouth and sucking on them, gently at first and harder when she didn't seem to mind.

Her face was enigmatic as the Mona Lisa's, wearing only a faint smile, but she seemed lit from within. He fully wanted her again, though he knew he probably couldn't come again so soon. What did *she* feel, though, her passion muted by her missing pelt? She kissed him eagerly and touched him without shyness. But did it *drive* her the way it did him?

"How do you feel?" he whispered.

She drew in her breath and sighed deeply. "Lovely," she said dreamily.

He was glad, but that didn't really answer his question. "Is there anything you want me to do?" he asked.

Ellie was drifting in a fog of bliss, and she couldn't be bothered to talk much. "Do everything," she said. "Anything you like."

Torran laughed a little. He had no idea what to make of her, but he was very happy.

"Keep touching me," Ellie urged, stroking his chest, sliding her fingers across his stomach, trailing them over his dick and making him gasp.

"Let's get you out of these," he said, and she helped him shuck her jeans, and then her panties. Naked, she was an exquisite shape. "Did you know you have a perfect body?" he demanded, feeling slightly aggrieved that she kept all this beauty hidden beneath her clothes. She deserved to be painted into masterpieces and hung in the Louvre. Except he suddenly didn't care much for the thought of some lecherous painter ogling her form. He'd rather keep the secret to himself.

She shook her head, her smile pleased but dismissing his flattery.

"Truly," he said. "Look at you." He touched each part as he named it. "Perfect ankles. Perfect legs. Perfect stomach. Perfect breasts. Perfect arms. Perfect fingers. Perfect face."

"Stop," she said. "You should talk. You're like some kind of movie star."

"You think so?" He usually gave very little thought to how he looked, except he sometimes suspected people were nicer to him because of it. Her words filled him with unexpected warmth. He was surprised by how much he wanted her to admire him.

"Yes. Now come here." She made room for him on the bed and he lay beside her, drunk as a lord on her warm curves and soft skin, the feel of her all down his wanting body, her intoxicating kisses.

Ellie was in some beautiful, dreamy place. Her eyes kept drifting shut because she could feel more that way, and against Torran's solid warmth she relaxed until she felt on the edge of sleep. But she didn't let go because she didn't want the kissing to stop.

She protested faintly when he sat away from her, but then she felt his hands gently parting her thighs. She opened her eyes, not wanting to miss the sex part. She should ask him about condoms but what if he didn't have one? She couldn't stand for him to stop.

He checked her face, but she only smiled that Mona Lisa smile at him. *Do everything*, she'd said. As if he had any more idea what that meant than she did! *Everything.* He'd never done anything but stick his dick into a willing girl and have at it. In every other way, he was as much a virgin as she.

He looked for a long time at her secret place, whorled and glistening. He'd never looked at this part of a woman before, except in porn, and the sight of her excited him almost more than he could believe. She smelled incredible, and he knew he'd have no trouble coming now. He wanted her badly, and that was as novel as anything else that was happening. He'd never wanted a girl again, after the first time. They were always so fierce and closed, taking and leaving, the same as him. Ellie was something entirely new, as though she'd made herself a gift to him and put her body in his hands.

He ducked his head between her thighs and kissed her, tasting the salt of her, breathing her dizzying smell, finding his way inside her with his tongue. She gently touched his hair, stroking his sides with her feet, so he knew she liked it. His dick attempted to bore a hole through the mattress, but he wanted to wait for as long as he could. Another new impulse.

Her voice sounded sleepy when she spoke. "Do you have a condom?"

She watched his face appear above the plane of her belly. He wiped his mouth and chin, looking for all the world like a boy emerging from a slice of watermelon. He sat up fully and studied her. She smiled up at him quizzically.

"I do," he said. "Do you want that now?"

"Don't you?" she asked.

"Of course I do. I'm a simple creature. But what do *you* want?"

Now she studied him, as if the answer to his question was written on his skin. "What does it feel like to you? Wanting—that. Wanting…me?"

He laughed. "Well, there's a very particular sort of urgency right about—here." He ran his finger gently up the length of his cock, trying not to shiver as he reached the sensitive spot at the glans.

Ellie sat up to face him. "What sort of urgency, though? If you'd never felt it before, would you know what to do? Would you want something particular?"

He laughed again. What an odd set of questions! "I want it touched. Stroked. If there's no one else around, I'd do it myself. And yeah, I'd definitely know what to do."

She frowned thoughtfully.

"Isn't there anyplace like that for you?" he asked. He touched her nipple gently with his index finger. "Here?"

She nodded.

He brushed her lips. "Here?"

She caught his hand and kissed his thumb. "Yes."

He drew his fingers up the inside of her thigh. "Somewhere around here?"

"Yes."

"Can you show me?" he whispered. "Show me where you want me to touch you?"

She smiled. "Yes." She put her hands on top of her head, and stroked them down her hair. "Here." She drew them down the sides of her neck, over her collarbones, across her breasts, "And here," over her stomach, around her hip, under her bottom and back up, dipping between her legs, stroking down her thighs. "I want you to touch me everywhere. It's like a drug. I never want you to stop."

"Does any of it ache?" he asked, puzzled.

"No? Only if you stop, I start to feel sad." She sighed. "But I'm probably not normal. Maybe other girls ache."

"I don't know," he answered honestly. "I've never asked. The selkie lasses seem to have an ache like mine, but they haven't said as much."

"What *do* they say?" She was curious—not jealous, quite, but wistful. She didn't care too much about the ones in his past. It was the thought of the ones in his future that she minded.

He snorted. "Not much. Some heavy breathing and a bit of moaning, maybe."

She smiled wickedly. "Like you a little while ago."

"Uh—yeah." He was embarrassed, suddenly. "I must have looked ridiculous."

"No." She touched his arm. "You looked..." She stared thoughtfully into space, trying to find the words. "When I watched you change to a seal and back again, it was miraculous, when I think about it. But while I was watching, it just seemed normal. Like, *This is what it looks like. Now I know.* Watching you just now was like that, too. You weren't ridiculous at all."

She met his eyes. It was much easier now than it had been before—easier than it had ever been with anyone. He was open to her now. He'd invited her in.

"Why aren't you kissing me?" she asked, smiling into his eyes.

Deliberately, he stood and walked to the dresser. She admired him, even as she hated the distance between them. But she wasn't worried. She'd seen in his eyes that he was with her. He rummaged in the top drawer and returned with something he placed in her hands. A wrapped condom.

She tilted her face to him, her eyelids at half-mast and her lips parted, and it was too much for him. He bowled her backwards with hands on her shoulders and lost himself in her lips, her mouth, her tongue, her body yielding and seeking beneath him. He craved her with the desperation of the long-deprived, as if his need only grew with having.

Ellie felt his hunger, felt the length of his body yearning against hers, felt him hard and pressing her thigh, and gloried in it. She didn't mind that nothing like it swelled in her. She wanted his wanting as badly as he wanted her.

When he sat away from her and put on the condom, she couldn't watch too closely. She knew that loose bit at the top was supposed to be there, but it looked wrong, like a piece of trash scarring the face of the wilderness. She watched him as he held himself above her, expecting him to disappear from her as he'd done before, getting lost in the rush. But this time his eyes stayed intent on her face. "I don't want to hurt you," he whispered, sliding against her until they almost fit.

"I'll be fine, don't worry." She didn't know how to explain how she felt with him—a state of peacefulness and trust so perfect she thought an earthquake could shake down the room around them and she wouldn't care. They'd be safe inside this bubble that held nothing in the world but him and her. She couldn't feel pain right now. Not with him here.

"Tell me if you want me to stop."

"I will," she said. "I won't." She gave an impatient wiggle of her hips.

He smiled, and sank himself very slowly, watching her. He stopped when her eyes widened slightly. "Does it hurt?"

"No. Go *on*! Don't you want to move faster?" It wasn't pain. Only a sort of stretchy feeling. She was glad of it in a way, not sure how much she'd feel of him without it. This was easier than taking him in her mouth, and she liked being able to see him, if only he'd stop being so careful.

He stopped worrying about her. "You feel amazing," he told her, and gave himself over to his motion.

She watched him go a little hazy behind his eyes before they fluttered shut. His lashes were long and dark and thick against his cheeks. His teeth were lovely and straight between his parted lips. His hair grew damp and glistening at its edges and the strain grew on his face. She wanted to hold him, but she didn't want to distract him. She stroked his back gently and he said, "Oh, Ellie," without opening his eyes.

"Torran," she whispered back.

"Oh Ellie, oh Christ, oh *fuck*!" The sounds he made after that weren't words, but she could almost imagine what he felt from the shape of them, though she wasn't sure if he was chasing something or trying to hold it back. She braced herself, almost laughing at the onslaught of him and how loudly he groaned her name at the end. He seemed to want everyone down the hall to know who he called for this particular good time, and she liked that thought very much.

He'd never come shouting a name before. He'd never imagined wanting to. But this time, for the very first time, he was not alone, and he wanted Ellie—wanted the whole world—to know he was with her.

He collapsed gently over her, moving his weight to the side. She felt him doing something about the condom and didn't watch, and then he wrapped his arms around her and pressed his face into her neck, kissing her there. She stroked his damp hair, closing her eyes, so perfectly at peace that her sleepless night caught up to her all at once and rendered her unconscious like the flip of a switch.

Chapter 19: Ellie

June 2014 - Isle of Skye, Scotland

Ellie woke to Torran kissing her forehead, her cheeks. She turned her lips to meet his without opening her eyes. She'd been very deeply asleep, but she was happy waking to him.

"I let you sleep as long as I could," he whispered. "I went over the map with Maggie. I know where to look."

With an effort, she opened her eyes and tried to take stock. She couldn't tell what time of day it was through the still-closed curtains—only that it *was* still day. She was still naked, but the covers were over her. She couldn't believe Torran had covered her up and left and come back again, all without waking her.

"What time is it?" she asked groggily, sitting up. He sat beside her on the edge of the bed and she leaned forward and put her head against his shoulder. He stroked her hair.

"Just after two. You've been asleep for a couple of hours. I left a note in case you woke while I was gone but I guess you didn't. You must have been tired."

"Mmhm," she agreed. She was waking up enough to remember that she didn't want to talk about her sleepless night or the reasons for it. She didn't want to remind Torran, or think herself, about how tragic she was. She was happy now, and that was enough.

"Do we have to go right away?" She turned her face against his neck and kissed him there, and felt his hands stroking down her naked back.

"Yes. You have to get dressed or I'll be terminally distracted. I'm not sure how long it will take, and we need to go before it gets any later."

"Okay," she said agreeably, and fell back onto the mattress. She felt drugged and bleary from daytime sleep and only wanted to lie here with Torran. She didn't care about the rest of the world right now, even Maggie's sealskin.

Immediately his hands were on her, stroking over her breasts and stomach. "Oh, no," he said. "If you do this, we'll never go, and I don't have another day off for more than a week." She closed her eyes and felt his mouth on her nipple. He groaned. "Ellie, I don't even understand what you do to me. The more I get, the more I want of you. It's like an addiction."

"Take me, then," she said, smiling, perfectly content. "It doesn't take long. It'll wake me up."

"Last time it put you to sleep," he reminded her skeptically.

"Hair of the dog that bit," she said, and he laughed.

She kept her eyes closed, still smiling. He got up, and she waited to look until she heard the wardrobe drawer and the rustle of condom wrapper, and knew she'd won. He was shucking his clothes beside the bed. She reached out to stroke his cock, which was standing at firm attention once again. "Does this thing ever go down?" she teased.

"No so much today," he said ruefully.

In an instant she remembered Maggie. And she thought she shouldn't ask, but she had to know. "Is it the same for you, being around Maggie as it is being around me?"

There was a pause. He sat on the bed, and said thoughtfully, "No, it isn't."

"But you want her, too?" Ellie knew it was completely unfair of her to be bothered. He couldn't help how he was.

"I *want* every selkie woman I've ever met," he said. "But it's different with you. I *like* you."

Like was a mild, unsatisfying word, never mind that it's the one she would use to describe her feelings for him if anyone asked. "But you like Maggie, too. You're helping her…"

"It's different," he insisted. "I do like Maggie, but if it weren't for the damned selkie pheromones, I'd like her like she was my aunt, too. As it is, I'd shag her on the kitchen table, it'd be over in —no time—and that would be that. And I'd just hope she'd still be willing to feed me the next day. With you…" He began to run his fingers up and down her leg—over her hip and down, back up the inside of her thigh, then over and down again. "I don't know what it is with you. I just want you more and more. I've never felt that about anyone before."

Ellie sat up so she could look into his eyes. He met her gaze fearlessly, and she liked what she saw there—honesty and need. She couldn't help asking, "You *didn't* shag her on the kitchen table, did you?"

"No!" He actually seemed offended, and she kissed him swiftly in apology. When his lips were free he added a little sulkily, "She doesn't want to. And her enthrallment puts me off her a bit, to be completely honest."

"I want you," Ellie whispered, and it was true, even though she knew it wasn't the same kind of wanting he meant.

"Thank god," he said, bearing her down on the mattress, and for a while they didn't talk any more, except with their bodies.

*　　*　　*

"That is completely insane," Ellie said. Torran had spread his map over the end of the bed and was showing her the path Maggie had sketched with pencil along the coastline at Neist Point. The line began a bit inland near a marked road and went straight to the coast, then followed along the shore for a while. Except there was a gap, a missing piece, right in the middle. No dip, no curve, no detour, just an inch of map where the line didn't exist.

"What happened?" Ellie asked. "How did you get her to do that?"

Torran shook his head. "It was wild. I started asking her about Neist Point and she didn't want to talk to me. She didn't get angry —she just seemed to forget we were talking and got up to putter in the kitchen. But I kept asking her specific questions, which trail she would recommend and the like, and she finally did point me to the lighthouse trail. It goes along the top of the cliffs, mostly, but there are steps for getting down to the shore. I asked her about those, and she got really vague. Finally I handed her a pencil and said, 'Isn't there a trail along the shore? Will you sketch me where it is?' And she could hardly sit long enough to do it, but in the end that was it."

"Amazing," Ellie said. "So we look there, obviously. How much distance is that?"

"About a quarter mile. Not nothing, but a hell of a lot better than trying to search the whole point!"

He folded the map, and Ellie slipped on her shoes, the last step in getting dressed to go. "What are we looking for, then? A cave?"

"Most likely… I doubt it'll be easy to find, though. That's a popular tourist spot and there *is* a walking trail there. A cave would get plenty of traffic if people could stumble on it easily, and that's the last thing a selkie would want. Also, it can't be at shore level or it would flood."

In the parking lot, Maggie's van was parked in a slightly different place. "Here, she sent these for you," Torran said, handing her a packet of sandwiches wrapped in wax paper as she got in on the passenger side. "Tuna, I think."

"Yum." She was hungry again, now that she was awake. "Did you tell her where I was?"

Torran gave her a humorous side glance as he pulled out of the parking lot. "I said you were awfully tired and I'd left you to have a nap at my place. I didn't specifically say you were exhausted by all the fucking."

"Ha." Ellie bit into her sandwich, grinning.

"She might have suspected," Torran added. "She's worried about you."

"Doesn't she trust me with you?" Ellie teased, avoiding the point.

"She'd be a fool. But I didn't mean because of me."

Ellie sighed. "I know. She thinks I'm going to go all to pieces at some point. But I won't."

"Why not?" Torran asked gently. "I think I would."

Ellie felt the kindness acutely but couldn't let it in, afraid she'd break. "What's the use? All I can do is go home and look for my pelt. I'll do that until I find it or until I…can't look any more. It's simple, really. But today I'm having fun with you, and I don't want to think about it."

"I'm having fun with you, too," he said, and then was quiet for a while as she ate.

Neist Point, Ellie knew from the map, was on the far side of the island from Portree, all the way back to Snizort Beag, where they'd been that morning, and some distance beyond. Torran had said it was about an hour's drive.

"I know you said you didn't want to talk about it," he said after a while, "but I've been thinking about your pelt, how I'd go about looking for it…"

"Tell me," she said. "If it's practical advice I'm all for it."

"I don't know if it will help. It's just where I'd start if it were me. Did Maggie tell you there's a chance your mum's still alive?"

"Yeah. She said as a last resort maybe my dad could call her back. Drop seven tears of true love in the sea and call her name? But the thing is, I'm not sure Dad will feel true love anymore, if it turns out she faked her death and left him to grieve for her all these years. She wouldn't really be the person he loved, if she'd done that."

"Yeah," Torran said. "And there's something a bit off about it, in my mind. You see, my mum, when she went back to the sea, tried to take me with her. The only reason she didn't is because Gram caught her smuggling me and my sealskin out of the house in the middle of the night. Gram told her to be on her own way and good riddance, but she'd take me over her—Gram's—dead body."

"So what are you saying? Your mom loved you better than mine loved me?" Ellie was teasing but she felt a little stung.

"Don't talk rubbish. I'm saying if your mum left to be a seal and never meant to return, why wouldn't she take you, too? It's the natural thing, she being a selkie, you being a selkie, she being your mum."

"Ah." Ellie thought for a bit. "So you're saying, maybe she did die in that accident after all? I was already thinking that. My dad and my grandparents are really good people who loved her a lot. I don't see why she would have left them in such a cruel way."

"Right," Torran said. "And if she'd died in an accident, unexpectedly, she wouldn't have left your sealskin somewhere for you to find."

"No," Ellie said slowly, following the thought. "She would have hidden it wherever she hid hers. Right?"

"That's what I'm thinking," he agreed.

They drove in silence for a while. Ellie had been on this road so many times in the last twenty-four hours, she was starting to recognize landmarks. The farmhouse with the oddly luminous white paint, the peculiar rock formation. She watched the scenery and let her thoughts drift through what she knew about her mother's life.

"I just had another crazy thought," she said after a while. "We assume my mom was a selkie because Dad isn't one, and one of my parents had to be." Maggie had explained this to her yesterday. "But no one actually knows for sure. I came along really soon after they met. I always figured Mom must have gotten knocked up on their first date. But what if she was already pregnant?"

"You mean, what if your *dad*, and not your mum, was the selkie?" Torran asked.

"Yeah…though if that's the case, my chances of finding my pelt would be…pretty much non-existent." Given what she understood about selkie attraction, her father could be some utterly random dude her mom had met and fucked at a filling station and never seen again.

"If that were the case," Torran said, "he'd likely have been there for your birth."

Ellie couldn't make any sense of that. "What do you mean?"

"Selkie dads are drawn to the birth of their children. If the mum's not a selkie, it's the only way someone will be there to save the pelt. But it's a powerful instinct for any selkie father. My da says he'll never forget the night I was born, how he was down at the pub with the lads and something told him as loud as he'd ever heard any silent thing in his life that he'd better get home. He arrived just in time to catch me when I popped out. He'd only been gone an hour and Mum hadn't even been in labor when he left."

"That's so weird!" Ellie said. "So I should find out from Dad if there were any strange men hanging around when I was born?"

"It's worth asking," Torran said.

After a brief silence, Ellie hugged herself and shuddered. "It's a horrible idea. My dad is the only parent who's been there for me. I'm not sure I could bear it if he wasn't really my dad."

Torran glanced over at her. "Yeah. That would suck."

Ellie was oddly grateful to him for admitting it straight like that, not trying to put a good spin on something that didn't have one.

A mile or so later he said, "If you haven't found your pelt by the end of the summer when I'm done with this job, I'll come help you look. I'm not sure how, but I'll find a way."

"Thanks," Ellie said softly, her heart brimming. She reached over and touched his knee, and he picked up her hand and kissed her fingers. She didn't know quite what was happening between them—it seemed much too new to name—but whatever it was, it made her very happy, and filled her with a kind of hope she wasn't afraid to feel.

He said, "There's another part to it." She sensed reluctance in his tone. "You should look for another selkie to breathe on you when you get home. You'll be ill, otherwise."

She said, "Yeah...but how am I going to find one?"

"I have some ideas, but I don't care for them." He beat his thumbs restlessly on the wheel.

"Visit known selkie hangouts and wait for one to pick me up?" Ellie guessed wryly.

"Basically," he said.

She protested, "But I don't know of any selkie hangouts. North Carolina doesn't get many seals."

"Being someplace with seals would help. And pubs, places that serve good, cheap seafood. You wouldn't have to stay any one place long. Any selkie—any male selkie—there will sniff you out in moments and try to slip you one."

Ellie took interested note of his scowl. "You didn't," she reminded him. "Try to slip me one." The crass phrase amused her.

"Only because you didn't want me. I worry that not every bloke would be sensitive to the distinction. Especially since you'll need him close enough to breathe on you. Even worse if he's been drinking."

"Hm." She saw his point. It was much easier to discourage a randy drunk guy *before* you invited him close enough to breathe on you. "You realize I'm not old enough to drink at home? So I won't be searching bars with a lot of drunk dudes."

"Still," Torran said. "He's going to want you bad, and when he breathes on you and you go all blissful on him…That might be too much even for a sober man."

Ellie sighed. This was all very distasteful and complicated.

They drove in silence for a while, Ellie watching cloud shadows playing on the stark hillsides.

"If I had my pelt," she asked, "and I wanted these hypothetical selkie guys as much as they wanted me, would it bother you if I fucked them?"

Torran thought before he answered. "I'd be a hypocrite if it did. I guess it wouldn't. As long as it was only shagging and you went your separate ways, after."

"So you're fine if I shag them as long as I don't like them?" Ellie asked, bemused.

"I guess, yeah."

She thought some more, then said, "With you, I'd worry that you'd like the shagging better."

"With some random selkie bird?" He sounded shocked. "Why on earth would I?"

She didn't think the answer was all that mysterious. "Well, she'd want you in a way I can't, and…you might like that better."

"I wouldn't," he said soberly. "I like you better than any lass I've ever met. And that includes the shagging."

Ellie leaned to kiss him, aiming for his cheek, but he turned swiftly and kissed her lips, keeping the wheel steady.

"Does that mean you wouldn't shag them?" she asked quietly, a moment later.

He smiled. "It means shagging is just shagging. For both of us. You'll see when you get your pelt. Do whatever you want. Just keep liking me better."

"You too." Then she added, a little fiercely, "Don't you *dare* like anyone better than me."

Chapter 20: Torran

June 2014 – Isle of Skye, Scotland

Neist Point was a spectacular headland, the westernmost point of Skye, and Torran's favorite part of the island. The lighthouse itself was nothing special—closed to the public and only about a hundred years old—but the view from the cliffs was grand and there might be no better place on earth to watch a sunset. He'd driven several tour groups out here in the last week, and was familiar with the concrete path that led down the point to the lighthouse. The spot of map Maggie had left blank was not along the lighthouse path, though. He led Ellie through a segment of pasture with no marked trail and they climbed to the shore down the steep bluff, precursor to the sheer cliffs farther along the point. The beaches were sandy coves divided by ridges of jutting rock, and the gap in Maggie's line coincided almost perfectly with the second of these coves. As they went, Torran imagined shouldering his pelt, and felt it was not too far for a fit man to carry one. These coves were perfect spots for seals, too. He'd seen a few the first time he'd been out this way.

"If you were a cave, where would you be?" Ellie asked, as they surveyed the cove. She was out of breath from their last scramble over the rocks, but she hadn't complained.

"There." He pointed out the only possible spot, a mounded dome of rock some distance back from the water, high enough to conceal a hiding place that the highest spring tides and storm surges couldn't reach. Of course, no cave could be seen. It was only an ordinary-looking mound of rock—steeper on the seaward side and maybe three times Torran's height, but not too steep to scramble around on, and accessible from the landward side. They approached it, wary of the low, spiny gorse that sprouted as the sand of the cove gave way to higher ground. Without discussion, they separated, he circling the base to do a thorough survey from below, and Ellie clambering up right away. The cove was loud with the lonely sounds of the surf crashing in and seabirds calling. Afternoon light slanted in from the sea.

Torran had started to lose hope at the obvious shortage of cracks or crevices nearly large enough fit a human into—or a seal—when Ellie called doubtfully, "Here's something…"

He scrambled up to join her.

On the inland side of the rock, about halfway up, she'd found an indentation about the size of a human torso. "There's a crack here," she said, and moved so he could see. He put his face into the indentation where hers had been, and only then saw the crack. It was surprisingly wide, twenty centimeters or more, concealed by a bulge in the rock, and he couldn't tell how far back it went or where it led to. It was the kind of crevice that no one thinking of spiders or creepy crawlies or nesting birds with sharp beaks would feel sanguine about sticking a hand into.

"Do you have any poisonous snakes here?" Ellie asked anxiously.

"Adders. They're not terribly venomous, but it wouldn't be any fun being bitten…" After a moment's thought, he stripped off his T-shirt.

"Ooh," Ellie said, eying his chest. "Really?"

He grinned at her. "If I survive this," he said, and wrapped the shirt around his hand as a makeshift glove.

"Good idea," Ellie said. "Maybe the adder fangs won't go quite so far in."

"That's my hope," he said drily.

He hoped Ellie couldn't detect quite how much courage he needed to reach into the blackness. He put a hand in gingerly, and found that the crack seemed to widen as he reached the depth of his elbow and then, with the last of his will, his shoulder. Ellie watched his face, grimacing anxiously. He was losing the world's best opportunity for the gag where he pretended something had seized him and was yanking him into the rock. But he was frankly too scared to spare the breath for it. When his hand brushed something yielding, he screeched like a lass—he couldn't help it—and snatched his arm back, scraping his elbow on the way out.

Ellie screamed, too, in sympathy. "What was it, what was it?" she jittered.

Gripping his scraped elbow against the sting, he analyzed the sound he'd heard as he'd touched the—whatever. A crumpling, sort of crackly sound. The sound made by a plastic tarp.

"Christ," he said. "This might really be it!" He reached in again with slightly more confidence, though he couldn't help thinking anything he'd startled the first time would be ready for him now.

There. The yielding surface, the crackle. He couldn't feel much through the shirt, but whatever it was seemed big. He couldn't find the edges of it. He tried, and managed briefly, to get a grip.

"I want to help you pull," Ellie said. "Like that story about the turnip."

"I hope this doesn't take the whole barnyard," he said, remembering the story she meant—the little old man and the little old woman and a host of animals down to a mouse. The thing was heavy, and kept getting stuck. But it was coming. And he thought—he was nearly certain it must be—a bundled sealskin.

Part of the tarp was now visible at the opening—blue, and not faded. Soon, Ellie could get a grip on it, too, and after that it was a matter of wiggling and pulling and working at it to finally get all of it around the bend in the rock. At last, the whole thing cleared. It was heavy, and he said, "Let it go, let it go," as he swayed for balance and grabbed Ellie as she almost lost her footing. They steadied each other and watched the bundle— which bore a marked resemblance to a beanbag chair—slither down the rock.

Ellie shrieked. "Oh my god, did you see that spider?"

"Wolf spider." He tried to sound unconcerned, though the spider that had dashed clear had looked nearly as big as a golf ball.

"We have those at home," Ellie quavered. "They're just so startling!"

"Come on!" He bounded to the ground. "I think we found it!"

He glanced around carefully for anyone in sight, but they were in a low place, hidden by the rock and some bushes, out of view of the concrete path that wound through the pasture above them.

The tarp was the large, round kind used for collecting leaves, with a drawstring around its edges. The drawstring had been pulled tight and wrapped many times around the bag's opening to make a kind of stem. Torran worked at the knot and finally loosened it, and unwound the cord. Ellie helped him as he released the drawstring. "Be careful not to touch," he warned, and she gave him an exasperated blink to let him know she was well aware.

Three sealskins, small, medium and large, in similar shades of speckled beige, shone in the afternoon sun.

"It's them!" Ellie gasped. "I can't believe we found them!"

Torran stared for a moment, then moved, swiftly and superstitiously, to tie them back up and hide them from view. "I can't either. I really can't. That should have been impossible, but we went straight to them."

"Bless Maggie's enthrallment," Ellie said.

He shook his head in disbelief. "Bless Maggie's enthrallment," he agreed.

He thought, and didn't say, *If only yours will be this easy to find!* He was afraid the chances of her finding it, after all this time, were terribly slim. But every hour he spent in her company made him less willing to acknowledge it.

Getting the pelts back to the van was no joy. He went up the slope with the bundle slung over his shoulder by its stem, and Ellie came behind him, clinging to his belt, supporting part of the weight with her head. He wasn't sure she was helping much, but he didn't have the heart to say so. And he liked having her close.

By the time they finally reached the van they were both gasping for breath and dripping sweat. The car park was packed. Some folks were finishing up their hikes and heading off in search of supper, and others were arriving for the sunset.

"My goodness, you two are working hard," said a friendly American voice as they dumped their burden into the back of the van.

Torran caught a glimpse of Ellie's stricken expression, but he turned to face the lady—gray-haired but fit, decked out with clothes from L.L. Bean and hiking sticks. "Live and learn," he said. "That's a bloody awful way to pack the camping gear."

"Oh dear." She laughed, and went away.

"You're good!" Ellie said, with more admiration than he thought he deserved. "I hadn't thought of what to tell people!"

"It's just habit. Mine is always camping gear if anyone asks."

"Still," she said. With that admiring expression in her eyes and sweat pouring off her, she was unbelievably sexy. He couldn't help imagining how slippery she'd be if he undressed her now. He settled for pressing her up against the side of the van and kissing her until he couldn't anymore without humping her and coming in his trousers.

A few wolf-whistles and some clapping erupted as they got into the van.

Ellie's face was pink. "I think we were a spectacle."

He grinned at her. "Lucky them. We make a fine spectacle. Almost as good as the sunset."

"I wish we could stay for it," she said. "But we shouldn't make Maggie wait for her pelt."

"I don't know," he said. "She might not want us bringing them by when the kids are awake and the guests are still coming and going. I'll give her a bell."

He rummaged for his phone, couldn't find it, then realized he'd left it in the door pocket of the van. He'd missed five calls from Maggie in the last half-hour, and a text from her saying, YOU FOUND IT!!!???!!!!

"How on earth did she know?" Ellie asked, when he showed her.

He shook his head, as mystified as she, and called Maggie back. "How do you know?" he repeated, when she answered by singing into the phone, "Torran, you're my hero forever!"

He put her on speakerphone so Ellie could hear the answer.

"It was the oddest thing! I was sitting at the table, doing the accounts, and feeling sorry for myself. There are all these bills from the handyman I never had to have in when Logan was here, and Logan used to do the bookkeeping, too, and I was thinking how much harder it's all been since he's been gone, and how I hadn't been out in the sea since Cait was born, and feeling just worn down to a nubbin. And the next thing I knew, tears were pouring down my face. And then I knew you'd done it, because I wasn't enthralled to him anymore! I was afraid the tears would stop right then because I was so happy, but I seemed to have such a backlog they kept coming and coming. So I caught seven of them in my hands—or maybe seventeen in case they weren't all for Logan—and rushed out and rinsed them in the bay. He might even be home tonight, if he's happened to stay close by."

Ellie and Torran exchanged increasingly confused looks as this narrative went on.

"I'm a bit surprised you want him back," Torran said, when Maggie paused for breath.

"Oh!" Maggie laughed. "Well, you see, true love gets to be a different sort of thing when you have kids together and your lives are all tangled up. I'm not sure if I miss *him* or if I only need him back so badly to look after the kids so I can get some time in the sea. But it's all love, and it's plenty true. I'm sure it will work."

Ellie looked offended. "Aunt Maggie," she said, "by that standard you could cry seven tears of true love for the babysitter!"

"Hello, dear." Maggie sounded completely unruffled, either by Ellie's indignation or her unexpected presence in the conversation. "I'm not a bit sure I couldn't, at that. It's not quite what I meant, though. I only meant—love for the kids, and love for Logan, and love for our life together all become part of the same thing, and you can't untangle them one from another after a while. It's not at all the way you think when you're young and love is only never wanting to wear clothes when you're around each other."

Ellie clapped her hands over her mouth so stifle her laughter, and Torran couldn't suppress his own grin, particularly because Ellie seemed to be avoiding his eyes. "Well, speaking of that," he said, "would you like us to bring your pelt now, or hold off 'til a bit later on?"

"Later would be much better," Maggie said firmly. "Nine or nine thirty after the kids are in bed. No need to dress yourselves for several more hours."

"Very good," Torran said, and ended the call abruptly as he and Ellie exploded into laughter.

Ellie wiped tears of mirth from the corners of her eyes. "Well, I guess it's official: We're in love."

"Good," Torran said. "Now that that's settled, shall we move to the back and take off our clothes?"

Ellie looked doubtfully at the double row of back seats. "Are the windows tinted enough?"

He said, "If you did that amazing thing with your mouth again, there would be less to see."

Ellie smiled her Mona Lisa smile at him, and climbed past him into the back.

*   *   *

They figured out how to flatten the back seat, piling all the sealskins forward and making a nest back there. Ellie did the amazing thing with her mouth, and then he took off her clothes and touched her everywhere the way she liked, and after that they lay naked in each other's arms and talked, and kissed, and ate the leftovers from the morning's picnic, and kissed, and talked some more. They had fully intended to watch the sunset through the back window of the van, but somehow they got distracted and missed it, only noticing the time when it got dark. By then it was already nine-thirty, and they had an hour's drive ahead of them.

On the drive back, Ellie said, "Torran," in a way that told him something was bothering her.

"Yes, love?" he said, to reassure her. It was odd how easily the word fell off his tongue.

"When you give Maggie her sealskin back, she'll want you as much as you want her."

"I doubt that will be very much," he said lightly. "I've had a *very* busy day. Not much wanting left in me, I guess."

"But what about tomorrow? It doesn't really go away if you don't do anything about it, right?"

"It would go right away if I did do something," he pointed out, still hoping to tease her out of her worry. "That's by far the fastest way to deal with it."

"Torran." Her voice had a warning in it. "I'm not calling it love. That was Maggie. I'm not calling it anything or saying I have a claim on you. But for some reason it really bothers me to think of you spending all day fucking me and then fucking my aunt!"

He knew better than to answer her lightly now. "Ellie. I will not fuck your aunt."

She drew a trembling breath. "Oh, you can. If you have to, to get it over with, you *can*." Her voice rose unmistakably into tears. "Just wait until I'm gone. Wait until I'm *dead*. I just don't ever want to *know* about it, okay?"

The sound of her sobbing in the dark hurt his heart. He wanted to pull over and hold her, but he couldn't find a spot, and it was already late, and they had sealskins to deliver. Instead, he lifted the armrests between them and tugged her awkwardly across the console between their seats to lay her head in his lap. He drove one-handed and stroked her hair, and felt her tears soaking hot, then cold, through his trousers.

He felt wiser than usual, knowing that she wasn't really crying about Maggie. She was crying because she was exhausted, and scared of dying, and because whatever was happening between them now was bigger than either of them could have imagined just that morning as they'd picnicked by the loch, barely more than strangers to each other. He had no idea how to handle it, and he supposed she didn't either. That's why she was crying.

After a while, she stopped. He kept stroking her hair, and he worried that she couldn't be comfortable, but she didn't move. "Are you asleep?" he whispered.

She shook her head.

"Well then, I want you to know that I am never going to fuck your aunt. Ever. No matter what. And also that…I think I do love you."

She nuzzled her cheek against his lap, and he felt her hand slip around the front of his knee.

"I think I love you, too," she said.

*   *   *

By the time Torran pulled up at the Skye View Inn, Ellie was sound asleep—leaning against her door now, rather than his lap. He was glad. He could run in, deliver Maggie's sealskin, and come right back before any pheromones could kick in. And Ellie could spend the night with him. In fact, Ellie could spend all the rest of her nights with him. He'd breathe on her all night and keep her feeling fine, and he'd wake every morning to her perfect, soft skin and glorious body and that Mona Lisa smile. He couldn't think of anything better. He'd get his first paycheck in a few days, and with any luck it would be enough to pay for his ticket so he could go home with her. Then he'd never have to risk her to the breath of some American selkie arsehole. And he would turn over every single stone until they found her sealskin, because not finding it was not an acceptable alternative. He couldn't think why this plan hadn't occurred to him before.

He hauled the tarp with the sealskins in it around to the inn's back entrance, the family side, out of sight of any guests. The time was nearly eleven and the place was all dark except for a light in the kitchen. He knocked very quietly. Almost before he'd moved his hand away he heard the turn of the lock. Maggie flung the door open.

He had just time to notice that she was in her dressing gown before she flung herself on him. He let go of the tarp full of sealskins and let it drop behind him in order to free his hands to catch her. Or fend her off, more like it, though by the time he'd registered the need she was already plastered over him too tightly for him to escape without violence. Her bare legs clamped around his hips and her mouth covered his and her arms clung to his neck. For a moment it felt like a greeting by an over-exuberant Saint Bernard, and his only thought was to pry her loose and get back to Ellie.

Then, regrettably, the pheromones kicked in, leaving him in no doubt that he was being positively humped by a wildly attractive woman who was not wearing any knickers. He turned his head to free his mouth—his usual lack of interest in kissing back in full effect—but Maggie only used the space he'd won to slide down him and reach for his fly.

He was ready for her. The whole thing was that automatic. He wouldn't fuck her. He'd simply stand here and she'd fuck him, and it wouldn't even be his fault. Likely Ellie'd never have to know.

His dick was standing in the open air. There was nothing he could do.

But he had *promised*.

He seized Maggie by the hips, not to drag her closer but to push her away. He got her far enough so he could see her face in the dim light from the doorway, her puzzled look shifting to something behind him and morphing to sudden alarm. "Logan, *no!*" she shouted.

Something smashed with terrible force against the back of his head, and everything went black.

Chapter 21: Ellie

June 2014 – Isle of Skye, Scotland

Ellie woke to the van being opened at the back, the lights coming on, and Maggie's voice saying "Praise the bloody saints, it's still here!" The door slammed shut and the lights went out again before she could shake off her sleep enough to open her eyes, recognize the Skye View Inn in the dim yard lights, and wonder where Torran had gone. She turned her head just in time to see a bathrobe-clad Maggie and a large, naked man disappear around the corner of the inn. The naked man was carrying something. Not the tarp with Maggie's sealskins.

Torran's duffle!

Ellie slammed out of the car in an instant and chased after them, unsure whether to shout for Maggie or find out what the hell was going on, first. She found them by the back door, in a pool of light from the open doorway. The blue tarp full of sealskins lay on the doorstep. Torran sprawled on the ground as though he'd fallen backward over it, horribly still. Maggie and the naked man crouched over him. The bag containing Torran's sealskin lay on the ground beside the naked man.

"*Torran!*" she wailed, and rushed to crouch by his head.

She knelt on broken pottery and soil. One of the heavy planters from the back wall had shattered. Torran's eyes were closed, and now she saw the puddle of blood beneath his hair.

"*What happened?*" she screamed. It was a protest from the depths of her soul.

"Shut up!" the naked man said fiercely.

"Hush!" Maggie said at the same time. "He's not dead. Help us get him into his pelt."

Ellie detected an unspoken *yet* after the word "dead," and spiraled toward hysteria.

"Now, Logan!" Maggie said. "Ellie, help me sit him up."

Ellie remembered Torran saying, *If you're injured, you heal in the change.* Understanding dawned, and steadied her to action. She took one arm and Maggie took the other, and they propped Torran up to sitting. He was warm. He was breathing. She clung to these facts, and tried not to look too closely at the bloody place on his head.

Logan—*so Maggie's idea of love had worked*—knelt and drew Torran over his shoulder, staggering under his weight as he stood again.

"Quickly!" Maggie seized the duffle bag, and Ellie took the other handle. Logan carried Torran through the parking area and along the short path by a hedge down to the shore.

"Help me," Maggie panted, setting the bag down and unzipping it. Ellie forced herself to seize a handful of the fur inside. It felt all wrong, but she didn't know if her nausea was the wrongness of touching Torran's fur, or the wrongness of everything else.

Maggie helped her spread it on the pebbled beach with the opening in the belly facing up. Logan knelt, and Ellie and Maggie helped ease Torran down. He was still warm, Ellie tried to comfort herself. He was still breathing. *Oh, god, let this work.*

Maggie was tugging at Torran's shirt, lifting it. Of course, they'd have to undress him so he could change. Ellie helped her wrestle it gently off and over his head.

"Get his trousers," Maggie urged. "Hurry."

Ellie rushed to his feet, frantically removing his shoes, his socks. Unbuckling his belt. She noticed with some corner of her mind that his fly was open. Maggie helped her drag his pants down, the naked man tugging the cuffs.

When Torran was fully naked, Maggie helped Ellie work the sides of the opening around him, tucking him in. It was like trying to fit a sleeping infant into a bunny suit, Ellie thought hysterically. Except horrible, not cute. *Please, god.*

She bent and swiftly kissed Torran's lips. It was terrible the way they didn't kiss back. She watched his face so hard, so desperately, it was as though she would drag him back to consciousness with the force of her gaze. His face was so still. But then, she thought his eyelids fluttered. His lips parted. She kissed him again and this time he kissed her back, ever so slightly. "Torran!" she whispered.

"Now, love," Maggie said, "let him heal," and drew the pelt over his face.

For a long, awful moment, nothing seemed to happen. The three of them knelt around the fur-wrapped bundle. A chill wind blew off the water, and in the dim, reflected light, nothing moved at all. An infinite coldness began to gather in Ellie's chest.

Something shifted. She peered more closely at the edges of the slit in Torran's fur and couldn't find them. The opening had knitted closed. Now the shadows shifted over the pelt. It swelled, grew, filled out, flanks rounding where before had been loose folds of fur. A large bull seal took form, and in the corner of her sight, Ellie saw Maggie and Logan move backwards. Still, she knelt. The bull moved his head and gave a sudden sinuous twist, flipping from his back onto his belly. He lifted his huge head with a snuffle of breath, only the faintest liquid gleam of his eyes visible in the shadows. Ellie crouched, transfixed. She was much too close, and Torran was wild now—no longer hers. He turned his head and gave her a long look, his eyes unfathomable dark pools.

A scrape of pebbles on the beach drew his attention—Maggie and Logan stepping still further back. Suddenly, he gave a loud grunt and lunged at Logan, teeth snapping as Logan leaped, then turned and ran through the opening in the hedge, away from the shore. When Logan was out of sight, the seal swung his heavy body around, humped vigorously across the pebbly shore, and plunged unerringly into the bay. He splashed a long, noisy way through the shallows, then dipped beneath the surface and was gone.

"Oh," Maggie said faintly. "Oh my."

Tears prickled in Ellie's eyes, a surge of strong emotions too mixed to sort out. Relief that Torran was okay. Grief that he was so suddenly gone. "When will he be back?" she asked Maggie shakily.

Maggie said, "Well…" Ellie didn't care for the silence that extended. "We should get in touch with his da, most likely. Unless you…?"

Ellie caught Maggie's speculative glance, and understood. Torran hadn't been conscious, so hadn't been able to choose his own time to return. Someone would have to call him back by dropping seven tears of true love into the sea.

Torran had *said* he loved her. She had said it back. But…it was so new! Maybe too new to be *true* love? How awful to have their sincerity put to the test the first moment the words were out of their mouths!

Maggie went on while Ellie was thinking. "But he mustn't come back too soon. He'll be dangerously depleted, changing yesterday and twice today, and that's not even taking into account the injury… No, he should stay out for several weeks, at least, to get his strength back fully."

"What would happen?" Ellie asked, her chest tightening with new fear for Torran. "Is he okay right now?"

"Oh, yes. You saw him—he's all right now. A bit hungry and skinny, I'll be bound, but it's summer and he'll feed up easily. But if he were to come back too soon, he'd be peaked, as if he'd had a long illness. He'll take weeks to get his strength back." Maggie looked around. "Now where did Logan get to?"

"Aunt Maggie," Ellie said accusingly. "What *happened*?"

Maggie stepped through the opening in the hedge. Ellie followed her without stopping to gather Torran's clothes. Was Maggie avoiding her question? "What happened?" she demanded again, catching up to her.

Maggie said, "Logan came back as I was thanking Torran for returning my pelt. He got a bit hasty with a planter." Her tone was a little too matter-of-fact.

Ellie felt sick, remembering Torran's open fly. He had promised. *Promised.*

She had more questions but she couldn't bear to ask them—couldn't bear to reveal her feelings to Maggie. At the moment, she nearly hated Maggie. Maggie knew! She'd made that comment about not having to put on their clothes! She'd guessed that Ellie might be able to call Torran home! How *could* she?

But much worse, how could Torran?

The pieces of broken planter still littered the back walkway. The tarp-wrapped bundle of sealskins still lay on the doorstep. The back door of the house was shut, now, but there was no other sign of Logan.

"Help me carry this in," Maggie said, bending to heft the tarp.

Automatically, Ellie grabbed the opposite side and helped Maggie maneuver it through the door, the entry, the hallway into the kitchen. They set it down on the floor near the fridge. Maggie said, "Thanks, love. Now will you go collect Torran's clothes from outside?"

Ellie might have resisted doing as Maggie asked out of sheer fury, except that she knew Maggie didn't want her watching when she hid the sealskins, and she herself felt a strong impulse toward discretion. It was as if Maggie were about to type her password, or had announced that she was going to change clothes. Ellie left the kitchen without a word.

Down at the shore, she had to hunt around in the uncertain light reflected off the water to find Torran's clothes. She buried her face in them, inhaling not just Torran's wonderful, spicy smell, but the unmistakable musky scent of sex.

How could he be gone? She'd only just found him!

She wasn't sure she could bear herself right now. Too much had happened today. She'd slept far too little. She couldn't process or react to anything else and she couldn't stand the thought of speaking to Maggie. She was in no mood to meet Logan. Logan was a brute.

She stood for a while, hugging the clothes to her chest and staring out over the glinting water. Torran was out there right now, swimming in the dark. He was only a seal, now. He couldn't think of her. She could not imagine what he was seeing, feeling, doing right now. Not being able to imagine his experience made her infinitely more lonely. He was probably right out there, maybe close enough for her to see him if he surfaced, but he might as well be on the moon, as far as he felt from her.

The shards of ceramic on the walkway had been over a quarter of an inch thick, and she quailed at the thought of his head being the surface which it had shattered that pot. What if Logan had cracked Torran's skull, damaged his brain? Would changing heal *that*?

Torran had seemed fine, as a seal. He'd attacked Logan—that demonstrated a reassuring presence of mind. And he had not attacked her.

Goddamnit. Why couldn't he have kept his promise about Maggie? Didn't any of it mean anything to him?

Tears prickling, she headed back to the inn. She would avoid Maggie and Logan and go straight up to bed. Even if she couldn't sleep, at least she'd be alone.

As she set Torran's shoes on top of the shelf in the entry and put the pile of his clothes on top of them, she heard footsteps coming down the stairs, too heavy to be Maggie's. She drew back against the door, hoping Logan would go by without seeing her.

When the footsteps had passed and she heard a murmur of voices from the kitchen, she started to creep up the stairs. But then she heard a loud gasp—Logan—and Maggie's voice saying firmly and clearly, "Don't come near me." Ellie froze, listening.

Logan croaked, "Maggie, please—"

Maggie spoke over him. "I'm sorry, pet, but you've been gone much too long, and I need some time of my own before I can welcome you back."

Ellie tiptoed very quietly toward the kitchen. The fear in Logan's voice chilled her and made her desperately curious at the same time.

Maggie's voice continued, "I'm going out in the sea. It's been *eight years*, Logan, and you haven't been here to breathe on me. So I'll be going now. You'll need—"

Logan interrupted, "Maggie, wait—I haven't even seen the kids —"

"Don't speak to me."

Ellie could peek through the kitchen doorway now. Neither Maggie nor Logan noticed her. A tall cabinet beside the refrigerator was swung away from the wall on one side, as if on hinges. Ellie glimpsed the blue tarp in the space behind it. This must be where they kept the pelts. Maggie stood in front of the cabinet with a sealskin overflowing her arms. Unlike any of the light-colored sealskins from the tarp, the one she held was large and very dark.

She's enthralling Logan! Ellie realized.

Logan, dressed now, stood a short distance into the kitchen, his back to Ellie. He looked hunched and miserable from behind.

"Take good care of the kids," Maggie said. "And the guests. You may call me back in two weeks, though if I were you, I'd leave me to come back in my own good time. Don't try to stop me going, and forget about this hiding spot and the pelts until I get back."

She paused, staring thoughtfully into space. "What else? Make explanations to Liam at Skye Tours, so he doesn't come looking for Torran. Make sure Ellie gets home to her da. Tell the kids I love them very much, and will be back soon."

She stood quietly for another moment, then sighed, "That'll do." She tucked Logan's pelt into the hiding spot and wrestled with the tarp until she got the rope untied. Logan stood silent and unmoving, watching her. So did Ellie.

Finally, Maggie freed her sealskin. Hoisting it awkwardly over her shoulder, she closed the hiding spot by shoving the cabinet back against the wall until Ellie heard the slight click of a latch catching. Maggie came to stand in front of Logan.

"I'm sorry about this," she said quietly. "Apparently, I truly love you, or you wouldn't be here. Maybe when I get back, I'll be able to feel it properly."

Ellie swiftly ducked into the den so Maggie wouldn't see her on the way to the back door. From her hiding place, she listened to Maggie going into the entry, and opening and shutting the back door. From the kitchen came the sound of vomiting.

Ellie fled up the stairs.

Locking herself in her room, which she remembered now was Logan's office, she packed swiftly, uneasy that he might try to enter. She was suddenly full of revulsion for this place, for Maggie leaving the kids without a word of explanation, and—worse— leaving Ellie here with Logan. If he was enthralled, did that mean he *wouldn't* be attracted to her? She didn't know, and had no intention of waiting around to find out. The thought of Torran was too painful to dwell on right now. She was much too disturbed to sleep. When she was packed, she sat on her bed and used her phone to research bus schedules between Portree and Edinburgh until she heard Logan come upstairs and shut the door to his and Maggie's bedroom.

She waited a while longer, until she was sure from the sound of snoring issuing down the hall that Logan was asleep. Then she snuck down the stairs and let herself quietly out the back door. The walk to the bus stop was a mile and a half, but fortunately, her suitcase was the kind with wheels. She called her dad, who was still wide awake on U.S. time, and told him Maggie had left unexpectedly and she needed to come home. She had rarely been more grateful for a parent who handled every emergency with swift and quiet practicality. Douglas asked only the questions that were relevant to getting her home, and emailed her the ticket before she reached the bus stop.

On the sheltered bench, which she felt lucky to have to herself, she wrapped up in her jacket, pulled the hood down to conceal her face, and draped herself over her suitcase for whatever sleep she could manage before 6 a.m. when the bus was due. Only the rest of the night, four buses, and three flights separated her from home. She had thirty-six hours to decide what to tell her dad— and what to ask him.

Chapter 22: Ellie

June 2014 - New Bern, North Carolina

When Ellie's dad met her at the airport, her hunger was the only thing stronger than her desire to sleep for a very long time in her own bed. She and Douglas stopped at a Chinese place in New Bern, near the airport. Chinese was a staple of their diet—always seafood for Ellie, always something else for Douglas, and the vegetables Douglas insisted were his duty as a parent for both.

As soon as they had ordered, Douglas returned to the subject they'd been discussing in the car. "Maggie didn't even wait to say goodbye to the kids, or reintroduce them to Logan?"

"No…" Ellie's conscience had been troubling her all the way home. "But Dad—I didn't either. Maybe it would have helped if one person they knew had been there when they woke up the next morning, but I just couldn't stand how awkward it was. *I didn't know Logan, and what I did know of him, I didn't like!*"

She couldn't voice her other concern—that Maggie had proved herself a typical faithless selkie mother the moment she got her pelt back. And Ellie hadn't filled in for her, which probably meant she was just as bad. And maybe Ellie's own mother had been the same. Maybe that really was how all selkies were, and Ellie was stuck with it.

Douglas reassured her. "He's their father. I expect they'll find their way. People rarely give fathers much credit where their kids are concerned, but we often do all right in a pinch."

"*You* do a wonderful job," Ellie rushed to say. "If Logan's a quarter as good, they'll be fine."

Note to self, she thought: *Only have kids with a safe, steady human, not another flighty selkie. Not Torran. Not someone who would fuck any old passing selkie after he promised not to.*

She couldn't think of Torran or she'd start dripping tears into her wonton soup.

Douglas ducked over his own soup, but Ellie could see him smiling with pleasure at the compliment. He said, "*You* seem to be feeling better, still?"

"I think so," Ellie said cautiously. "Right now, I'm so tired it's hard to tell." For the last three days she'd been sleeping like a fugitive, on benches and bus seats and planes. She hadn't had a shower since the morning she'd retrieved Torran from Loch Snizort Beag. She undoubtedly still had Torran's sweat on her skin, though by now her own had overpowered it. Her exhaustion had a frantic edge, a fear of the undertow of illness that she knew was coming, even though it hadn't reached her yet. She'd been looking everywhere—on every bus, at every passerby at the airport, around this restaurant as they'd arrived, at every new person who came in the door—scanning fruitlessly for anyone with golden skin and shiny hair and dark eyes who might be noticing her back. Looking for a selkie to breathe on her had become an obsession, never mind that the idea of even a pheromone-drunk selkie finding her attractive in her current greasy and disheveled state defied the imagination.

She had so little time.

She said, "Dad. What would you do if you were in Maggie's place? What if Mom showed up and said, 'Just kidding, I wasn't dead. Ta-da!' Would you be glad to see her? Or would you feel like Maggie, that you'd need some time to think about it first?"

"But no one ever thought Logan was dead!" Douglas protested. "It's not the same at all."

"Still," Ellie pressed. "Would you still love her?"

She'd chafed against this problem all the way home. Even if Alise were still alive, and even if her father still loved her enough to call her back, what was the point in telling Douglas about selkies, trying to persuade her practical, scientist father of a truth she had no way to demonstrate, if persuading him would only destroy his love? The thought that Alise had deliberately left them to grieve for her would wreck every understanding that shaped his world, and in the end, Ellie still wouldn't get her mother back to ask about her missing pelt.

"I can't imagine it," Douglas said quietly. "If you could remember her, and how much she loved you, you couldn't, either. Nothing short of death could have made her leave either one of us."

Their food arrived, her Kung Pao shrimp and his chicken with curried vegetables. Douglas laughed quietly as the waitress left, resuming his thought. "You should have seen the battle she had with her parents after we met. I've lived in fear your whole life of a fight like that with you. Your mum insisted on staying with me at the holidays, and then she dropped out of university after only one semester to come with me when I took the job at the marine lab. You were on the way by then, or I'd have tried harder to convince her to stay at school. I wouldn't have succeeded, though. No one on earth was as single-minded as your mother in love."

Ellie was truly frantic for seafood after the diet of cold-cut sandwiches on which she'd subsisted the last few days. She bent over her shrimp and ate with a silent concentration that was only partly feigned, as a cover for her thoughts. She didn't know if her dad was right that her mom had been fierce and steady in love. Maybe he was, and maybe that meant Alise had not been a selkie after all. But even if Douglas were wrong, if Alise had managed to hide her selfish, irresponsible seal nature from him in their short and passionate marriage, Ellie would never convince her dad of this and she wasn't going to try. She couldn't ask him to call her mother home. She would have to find her pelt another way.

"Tell me about when I was born," she said, when her plate was half empty. She still hated everything about the possibility that her father had been some random selkie instead of Douglas. And she was pretty sure she would have heard if a strange man had appeared at her birth. But at least it was an easy item to cross off her list. "I was born at home, right?" In fact, this was the only fact about her birth that she remembered having been told.

"Right." Douglas sipped his tea. After a while he said, with obvious reluctance, "I wasn't there. I've always regretted that. I can't tell you much."

Ellie put down her fork in surprise. "You weren't? Who was?" She'd always assumed it was one of those hippie home births, with a tub of water and a midwife, and her father instructing her mother to breathe.

"No one," Douglas said. "Your mother was all alone."

Futility gathered like a weight in Ellie's chest. If a mysterious selkie father *had* shown up for her birth, no one but Alise would know! She couldn't cross this possibility off her list at all. It would just dangle, an unsolvable mystery, with no witness except a dead woman. "Tell me what you know," she said, hopelessly.

He frowned. "It's an uncomfortable story. I've never told it to you for a reason. I don't like to think of it myself."

Ellie's attention sharpened. "Tell me," she demanded.

Douglas sighed. "It's no reflection on you. Your mother and I were both as happy to see you as any parents could have been."

Ellie was beyond imagining where he was headed. She widened her eyes in impatient suspense.

He said, "You were born very quickly and unexpectedly. Your mum was asleep, and woke up so far into labor that she couldn't get downstairs to the telephone to call me. She just stayed where she was, and you were born right there in our bed. In the room that's your bedroom now, in fact."

Ellie knew her dad had moved to the other bedroom after her mother died. Too many memories, she suspected, though he always claimed Ellie had needed the bigger room for all the toys her grandparents gave her.

"What's so bad about that?" Ellie asked, disappointment looming. "You're just uncomfortable because you weren't there?"

"No." Douglas sounded uncharacteristically testy. "I'm getting to it. Your mum was lying in bed with you, having just given birth and still wondering how to get to the phone to get some help, when someone came into the house."

Ellie held her breath.

"She had a creepy ex-boyfriend with a penchant for stalking. When I first met your mum, she was hiding from him. When you were born, he was supposed to be a hundred miles away, but instead he was lurking outside the house and heard your mum yelling."

"Oh my god," Ellie whispered.

"He called the rescue squad, at least. And he disappeared once they arrived. But your mum was terribly upset. The two of you were fine as fine, by the way. By the time I met up with you at the hospital, everyone was amazed how well you both were doing. But your mum…he came into the house, you see, when you were so new and she was so helpless. There was nothing she could do to stop him, and it shook her badly, even though he didn't *do* anything in the end. It's my biggest regret, knowing she never needed me more than she did that day, giving birth alone, and dealing with him, and I wasn't there to protect her."

"Dad." Ellie felt strangled. She saw that he was near tears, but she couldn't hold back the question or think how to help him. "Do you remember his name?"

Douglas shuddered, but seemed to collect himself. "I'll never forget it. Elliot Thorne."

She heard him say her name, and couldn't make sense of the syllables that came after it. Misreading her confusion, Douglas said, "I know. But she said Ellie had always been her favorite name. She refused to let him ruin it for her."

Elliot Thorne! A thousand mixed feelings hung suspended. The one closest to landing was a hope so thin and razor sharp it cut at her. She didn't know if she could find him. He might be a seal. He might be dead. He might know nothing about her sealskin. But at least he had a name, and that was a place to start.

That name, though. Was there any chance her mother hadn't *named her after the man? Her biological father?*

"Do you know what happened to him?" she asked, feeling almost sick with mingled hope and pain.

Douglas gave her a strange look. "I've no idea. I was just glad the bastard didn't show up to the memorial service. If he had, I'd have put a fist through his face."

*   *   *

The drive home took an hour, and it felt like the longest of Ellie's life. She wanted desperately to use her phone to search the web for Elliot Thorne, but with her dad right beside her, she couldn't. Disloyalty festered in her chest. Bad enough by far that she wasn't genetically her dad's kid. So much worse that her father was a man Douglas hated. She was a cuckoo's child—a seal's daughter.

She could never, never tell him.

Home at last, she fled to her room, pleading the need for immediate sleep, and typed *Elliot Thorne* into her laptop's browser with hands that shook so badly she needed three tries to get rid of the typos.

She stared at the thumbnail images heading the search results, their significance registering in her stomach before her mind could make sense of them. Clicking them larger, one after another, she saw that they were paintings. The meticulous details, the quality of light, the scenes that might have been abstract renderings of galaxies or alien starscapes and had titles like *Abstract XII*, to her eyes were plainly delicate anemones; bright, floating shrimp; a stray, refracted sun beam making fish scales blaze out of the dark. The scenes were painted in a thousand shades of blue.

Elliot Thorne was an artist. He painted underwater scenes from a seal's point of view. And the shop that advertised his work was in Bar Harbor, Maine.

*   *   *

By the time Ellie had showered and slept—fitfully and troubled by anxious dreams despite her exhaustion—the following day was half over, and her dad was at work. She ate two cans of tuna straight from their tins, pacing the kitchen as she did so. She felt desperate, frantic, her anxiety to track down Elliot Thorne and find her missing sealskin driven by the dullness she had sensed the moment she woke up—not bleariness from jet lag and too much sleep after far too little, but unmistakably, the first sign of Torran's breath wearing off. The leading edge of death.

Everything she'd said to Torran that morning on the shore of Snizort Beag had changed inside her. All her hard-won detachment, the letting go, all measure of acceptance she had managed to gather around the thought of her own death, had evaporated without a trace. She didn't know if Torran really loved her or if he'd just gotten carried away in the moment. She didn't know what had happened between him and Maggie. But she couldn't die without seeing him again and trying to find out. She *had* to live, she *had* to find her pelt, and now she knew exactly where to look. Before, the dullness that meant death was closer every day had been a refuge—an unconsciousness where fear and grief couldn't hurt her. Now its encroachment filled her with terror. She couldn't let it win. She had too much to do.

Before going to sleep she had coaxed Google every way she knew, but had found no website, no studio address, no phone number or email address for Elliot Thorne. Nothing at all, except a two sentence description on the Bar Harbor art gallery website describing Thorne as a local artist. He was not in the news. He was not featured on any other gallery website. Images of his paintings were linked here and there, mostly in the social media or blog posts of people who had bought them. Except for the paintings, she could find no trace of the man.

She had saved the gallery's number on her phone and now she called. She braced herself for the voice on the other end to be remote and snooty, because she somehow expected that from an art gallery, but the woman who answered said, "Bar Harbor Fine Arts!" in such a sunny tone of voice that Ellie relaxed immediately. She'd rehearsed this conversation all night long between fitful periods of sleep.

"I wonder if you can help me? My aunt gave me a painting she bought from you all, by Elliot Thorne? And I love it. It's my absolute favorite—I just get lost in it all the time—and I want to write Mr. Thorne a letter to tell him. Would you be able to give me his address?"

"Oh dear," the friendly voice said. "I certainly understand what you mean about the paintings. I feel that way myself. Let me see. I know I don't have an email address for him. I'd be shocked if he *has* email, frankly."

Ellie had anticipated the offer of an email address. "I was really hoping to send him the old-fashioned kind of letter. I thought that might be better."

"I'm sure it would be… The trouble is, I flat don't have one for him. I know I don't, because I went all around with the man about how to pay him for the paintings we sell. He wanted direct deposit and we just aren't set up for that. He wouldn't give me so much as a phone number. He's a real character. Lovely paintings, *difficult* personality. It happens with artists."

"How do you pay him?" Ellie asked, her hopes sinking dismally.

"Hand him a check when he comes in with new paintings. It was the only thing he'd agree to."

"When do you expect him?" Ellie was grasping at straws. Maybe she could just *go* there, and lie in wait.

"Oh goodness. I don't! That man shows up when he shows up, and if we sell out and have nothing for three months, well, that's our problem, not his. I'm sorry. I think my feelings are showing. The paintings are worth it, though, they really are. The best thing I can tell you is, send a letter here and I'll give it to him when I see him. Do you need the address?"

"I'll get it from the web site," Ellie said. "Thank you…"

"Not at all. It's a sweet impulse. I will warn you, though. I doubt very much you'll get a reply."

After she hung up, Ellie slumped at the kitchen table, the edge of its battered wooden surface digging into her forearms. It made sense, didn't it? Elliot Thorne was a selkie. He was probably off being a seal a lot, and didn't want to have to explain the absences.

But now what?

If neither the Internet nor the gallery could help her, she was out of ideas, and the ominous vagueness looming behind her thoughts made her despair of constructing a new plan.

Sea air. It helped the sickness.

She texted her dad: *I'm taking the boat out.*

He answered swiftly: *It's going to rain.*

She hadn't noticed the weather. The dim light and heavy air matched her mood so well she hadn't registered a distinction between inside and out. She checked the weather and texted back, *Just rain. I'll come back if it storms.*

Her dad replied with a worried emoji, but she'd already grabbed her cap and the boat key. She knew as well as anyone that afternoon rain in the summer was hardly ever just rain, no matter what the forecast said, but she needed the wind in her face, and the freshness it would bring, too badly to care. Ocean air was not as effective a medicine as selkie breath, but it was what she had.

The boat was a small speedboat she and her dad used for fishing, for getting out on the water, for navigating the intersection of wind and sea and sky. Douglas had taught her to pilot the boat years before she could drive. In the summers, he kept it tied up at a spot he rented along one of the waterfront docks—expensive, but well worth the convenience, only three blocks from their house.

She stowed the cover and the floating bumpers and puttered straight across the channel, threading her way through the marshy shallows in the estuarine reserve around Horse Island. The rain held off, though the wind tugged at the visor of her cap and blew the grasses and the wax myrtle leaves in fitful gusts so their silver undersides lifted to the sky.

What to do? What to do?

She needed to find Elliot Thorne. But first, she was going to need a selkie to breathe on her, and soon.

Go where there are seals, Torran had said, and there were seals in Maine. There were a lot of miles of coast between here and there, too; a lot of crab shacks and oyster bars and boardwalks and public beaches where a selkie might pick her out of the crowd if she showed up and lingered.

She could tell her dad she was visiting a college friend. He'd humor her, as long as she was *doing* something, not driving him mad with worry sitting on the beach staring out to sea without a thought in her head. Not dying before his eyes. She could drive to Maine and look for selkies all along the way.

She didn't know how many days of clear thinking she had left. Not many, she feared, before she began losing time, drifting off into the dullness where hours leaked away without her noticing. She couldn't drive in that state.

But what could she do? She had to try. She had to hope she found a selkie in time. Once she got to Maine… Maybe she could get a job at the gallery so she'd be there when Elliot showed up?

A single dose of selkie breath wouldn't be enough for that. For that, she'd need a selkie boyfriend.

She came out the other side of the estuarine reserve, and the water opened up. The rounded cape end of Shackleford Banks loomed a few miles ahead, the inlet between it and Fort Macon opening to the wide Atlantic beyond. She aimed the boat's nose toward the horizon line where water met sky, and opened the throttle.

Goddamn everything. She didn't want a selkie boyfriend—not some random one she'd only be stringing along for his breath.

She wanted Torran.

What did it matter if he'd fucked Maggie? He'd said himself it wouldn't mean anything. Yes, he'd promised, but if he'd failed, it only meant his selkie nature was too strong for him. Or Maggie's was. He'd meant his promise when he made it. He had said he loved her.

She believed him, because she loved him, too.

And not only because she was dying without him.

She barely noticed the rain mixing with the spray flung by the boat's nose speeding through the choppy waves. The water driven over her cheeks by the wind, shattering on the breeze in her wake, was an inextricable mingling of sea and rain and tears. Lighting flashed across the sky, and into the crack and rumble of the thunder that swiftly followed, she screamed into a world too loud and empty for anyone to hear.

"Torran!"

Chapter 23: Ellie

July 2014 - Lewes, Delaware

The sleek shape wedging through the moon-stained surf and wriggling across the sand toward the dune was the first thing to catch Ellie's attention in hours. The fireworks had been over for a long time, and the night-shrouded beach, which had earlier swarmed with July 4th revelers, accessorized by beach chairs and coolers, was deserted. The air was sticky with salt, with heat, with the long-lingering hint of fireworks smoke that hung on the humidity.

Still mired in the trancelike state that had stalled her on the sand, like a wind-up toy run out of wind, Ellie didn't move. She remained with her knees drawn up and her arms wrapped around them and tracked the seal with her eyes. It thudded by quite close to her and came to rest at the foot of the dunes, half-obscured by the shadows the dune grasses cast in the light of the full moon, and by the lights from the ferry terminal half a mile or so down the shore.

He—the seal was too large to be anything but a bull—began to tremble and subside, and shortly a man pushed aside the covering and sat up on his knees. In the shadows and the dim light, his features weren't clear, but his shape was young—lean and tall and wiry and not yet fully thickened through the chest and shoulders. Ellie's consciousness, which had reached such a low ebb that until now she had only watched the selkie with a camera-like detachment, flickered as he studied her across the yards of beach that separated them. She lifted her head a little, returning his attention, aware now on some very dim level that she needed something from him.

He stood and, after a slight hesitation, crossed the sand to her. She was not surprised or even struck by his nakedness, or by the way his dick stood at stiff attention. She needed—what? Her thoughts were like hardening concrete.

He reached her and knelt, his eyes scanning her face, his hands hovering just shy of reaching for her. She had it, now.

"Breathe on me." She hadn't meant to whisper, but her voice was only a ghost.

"What?" He leaned closer to her.

She tilted her face to him and closed her eyes. "Breathe across my face." The words were better than a whisper, but still a rusty creak.

Uncertainly, he put his hands on her shoulders and did as she asked, opening his mouth and exhaling a warm gust that stuttered some in the middle.

The effect was instantaneous—like sunrise blooming and driving out the night. "Oh!" Ellie sighed, shivering with swift violence at the relief of coming back to herself. "Oh, thank god."

Her euphoria was tempered by a competing horror at the realization that she had come to a complete standstill, all alone on this beach in Delaware. If this selkie boy had not happened along…

He was still holding her shoulders and watching her face with mingled desperation and confusion. He was strikingly handsome in the shadowy light, with full lips and a straight, bold nose and serious eyebrows, and a short but unruly mane of hair.

She uncurled her arms from her knees and straightened. She'd meant to demonstrate that she was okay now, he could let go, but quickly realized her mistake. He was in no state to interpret her movement as anything but an opening. His expression shifting to muddled relief, he buried his face in her neck and tumbled her over backward, his body pressing hers against the sand.

She was too relieved herself, and grateful, to be anything but amused. Torran had been right. The boy, ablaze with selkie hormones, had misread her bliss, and was now fumbling with the waistband of her shorts, trying to get them off without making any room between their bodies. He smelled like the sea, and his hands, even in his clumsy urgency, were gentle. But she felt no corresponding desire for him, and the memory of Torran moving inside her had an intimacy and importance she hated to diminish with this stranger, no matter how much she owed him.

She took hold of his wrists and said gently, "Hey."

He went still. His face was still pressed against her neck. "Oh, god," he said. "I'm so sorry."

Surprised by this sudden about-face in attitude, Ellie let go of his wrists, and he pushed himself away from her.

"I don't know what the fuck I was thinking. *Fuck*. I meant fudge. I'm so sorry!" He was practically babbling, sitting up and showing her the palms of his hands. She couldn't help noticing that he was no longer remotely aroused.

"You're fine," Ellie said, sitting up herself, and brushing away sand. "Really, it's all right." She was relieved he had been so easy to dissuade, but she felt bad that he seemed so mortified. "It's completely understandable."

"I'm glad *you* think so." The kid was looking up and down the beach as if checking to see if anyone else was nearby. Or maybe he was just avoiding looking at her. "I should…go."

Nonplussed, Ellie looked around, too. The beach was completely deserted. Even the ferry terminal looked closed. It seemed to be very late at night. The moon hung high and bright over everything. And the kid was stark naked, of course. "Go where?"

He shrugged unhappily.

"Look," Ellie said. "You can't change again until you've at least had something to eat. I have some food in the car. And probably something you could wear." He was quite a lot bigger than she was, but she slept in an oversized T-shirt and some stretchy athletic shorts she thought he might be able to squeeze into, if he wasn't too fashion-conscious.

"Change?" He seemed alarmed.

"Back into a seal," Ellie said, deliberately. "As selkies do."

She had intended to reassure him, but if possible, his expression filled with even more dismay. "How do you know about selkies?"

Ellie was starting to lose her footing in this conversation. She'd assumed the fact that he'd tried to have sex with her meant he'd instinctively recognized her for another selkie. Clearly not. A treacherous insecurity whispered that he had stopped wanting her very quickly after he got close. Maybe being without her pelt had begun to make her—smell bad, or something. Not like a selkie.

"I *am* one," she told him.

"Oh…" He seemed to deflate a little. "Then how come—"

Ellie waited, but he didn't go on. "How come what?"

He shook his head. "Never mind." He shifted on the sand, clearly wishing he were less naked.

She felt there was no way he was going to settle into this conversation until he was covered up, and feared if she left him alone while she went to her car, he might bolt. She held out her hand. "I'm Ellie Murdoch. Do you want—"

He dropped his head back and faced the sky with a wide open mouth, clearly in the grip of some massive revelation. "Ohhhh… *fuck*! Ellie Murdoch. That explains everything."

She froze, furiously studying his appearance all over again. Even in the uncertain light, she was *sure* she'd never seen him before. She echoed him deliberately. "I'm glad *you* think so. Have we met?"

"No." Unexpectedly, he grinned. "But I'm your long-lost selkie uncle. Well, half-uncle. Patrick Fisher." He reached belatedly to shake her hand.

His grip was warm and firm. Ellie's mind spun and utterly failed to find traction.

"But you're younger than me," were the first words to fall uselessly from her mouth, followed by, "*How* are you my uncle? And how do you *know*?"

His assurance seemed to take shape magically from the ruins of hers. "We should talk. But could we get those clothes from your car? And the food?"

"Um. Yeah." Ellie stood up, becoming aware from her stiff muscles that she had been sitting on the ground for a very long time. A wave of dread came over her as she realized all over again how stalled she had been. She'd been out of her mind to make this trip alone. No one even knew she was here! What would have happened to her? Would she have wasted away on the spot? Would strangers eventually have come to cart her away? Would someone have called her dad?

She located the beach access walkway over low dunes, and beyond it her blue Subaru wagon parked in a pool of light cast by a solitary security lamp. It was the only car left in the lot. She pointed it out to Patrick.

He hesitated, glancing toward his sealskin. It made a shadowed mound among the dune grasses, indistinguishable from the sand to anyone who hadn't seen it arrive.

"Do you want to bring it with you?" Ellie asked.

"Nah," Patrick said after a moment. "I'll be able to keep an eye on it from over there."

He didn't trust her, Ellie thought, slightly offended. Then, with horror, she realized how right he was. *He was a selkie. There was his pelt. And here* she *was, needing his breath for her very survival. Why* wouldn't *she enthrall him and take him away with her?*

But she wouldn't. She knew this in her bones, by the way her skin crawled and her stomach sickened and her arms felt weak at the mere thought. *How had Maggie and Logan done this to each other?* She could no more steal his pelt than she could stab him in the heart with a dagger.

They began walking toward her car, and she shuddered off the grisly thoughts and asked again, "*How* are you my uncle? That means you're brother to one of my parents?" An electrifying possibility sizzled through her. "Are you *Elliot Thorne's* brother?"

He shook his head. "Who's Elliot Thorne? I'm your mom's brother." He corrected himself. "Half brother."

"My mom's," Ellie repeated, deflated now, and totally at sea. Alise had been an only child. And Grandma Sandra and Grandpa Rick were still very much together. Impossible to imagine either of them—well, it would have to be Grandpa Rick, wouldn't it?—sneaking off to father a kid younger than his grandchild.

"Her name's Alise, right?" Patrick said.

Ellie stopped walking and glared at him. She had been on the verge of deciding that he had her confused with some other Ellie Murdoch and the whole thing was a crazy mistake. "Explain," she demanded. "Who are *your* parents?"

"My dad's name is Silas McNally. He's your mother's father, too, but she never met him."

"No way," Ellie said, once she'd had a few seconds to understand him. "You haven't met my Grandma Sandra, or you would know there is no way in hell she ever cheated on my Grandpa Rick. She adores him, for one thing. And for another, she's never done the wrong thing in her life. She could write etiquette books. She is always perfectly behaved."

Patrick smirked and started walking again toward her car, leaving her to trail behind him so she could hear him over the surf noise. "It's not her fault her selkie hormones got the better of her."

Ellie walked in silence, thinking. It did make sense. Grandpa Rick was definitely not a selkie, with his freckled, pale skin and light blue eyes. Grandma Sandra had more of the look. And her family was the one with the New England sea captains in it, so a selkie could have snuck in. But the whole thing made Ellie's head hurt, because hadn't she decided that Elliot Thorne was her selkie parent, not her mom? Had Alise and Elliot *both* been selkies?

She caught up to Patrick at the car, which she unlocked with the fob in her pocket.

He peered inside. "Are you living in this thing?" The back seats were laid flat and covered with her camping mattress and a tangle of blankets and clothes.

"I'm on a road trip," she said. "And on a budget. The car's a lot cheaper than a hotel." She opened the hatchback and rummaged inside, emerging eventually with the pajamas she had envisioned might fit him. She was glad she hadn't worn them yet on this trip. "See if these work."

Patrick examined them a little dubiously before putting them on. The shorts were inoffensively plain and black, and went on easily over his skinny hips. Once on, however, they were skin tight and left very little of him to the imagination—not that Ellie needed her imagination by now, to know what he looked like naked. The T-shirt was one a classmate had made and distributed. *Marine Biologists Do It Underwater*, it read in curly white script on a royal purple background, *and analyze the data all night long.*

"Sorry," she said, as Patrick looked down at it, a little grimly. "I don't wear it in public either. But at least you're covered."

"An improvement," he agreed. "Thanks."

She found a couple of tins of sardines in the front passenger seat, which was doubling as her pantry, and a plastic fork. "How hungry are you?" she asked.

"Starved!"

Ellie was hungry, too, but figured she needed the food less urgently than he did. "Eat these," she said, handing him both tins. "We can go get something else in a bit."

She and Patrick settled side by side on the back bumper, beneath the raised hatchback door. She noticed him glancing toward the beach again. It was still completely deserted, clearly-lit and yet mysterious in the silvery moonlight, and though she couldn't pick out his sealskin from here, they had a clear line of sight to the place where it lay. The surf curled in lazily, the foam at the edges of the waves faintly luminous in the otherworldly light.

"I still don't understand how you know who I am," Ellie said. "And why it explains everything."

"Okay," Patrick said around bites. "So my mom did a bunch of research on your mom, because Silas wanted to know what happened to her after he gave her her sealskin. He always felt bad that he never got to talk to her or tell her anything about being a selkie. He thought maybe she'd just stayed a seal. But Mom looked up all these old newspaper articles, and found out that your mom came right back after only, like, two days. But then, she died a couple of years later. And that's how Mom found out about you, because your name was in the obituary."

"But why would she even tell you any of this?" Ellie asked. "And why would you remember? I can't even remember the names of relatives I've actually met!"

"Well…" Patrick sheepishly stuffed his mouth full of sardines and took his time about answering. "Because of the selkie hormones. Because even if you weren't a selkie, you have it in your family, and selkies usually hook up first and ask questions later—or not. But Mom is an obstetrics nurse, and she worries about things like incest. So she made a really specific point of making sure I knew that if I ever met an Ellie Murdoch, I wasn't supposed to fuck you."

"Geez," Ellie said. "Okay."

"Yeah." Patrick opened the second tin. She thought he was avoiding looking at her.

"You didn't ask my name," Ellie pointed out.

"My powers of rational thought were totally fucked," he admitted.

Ellie considered this. "They recovered quickly." Torran's attraction to her had not worn off as he spent time with her. But Patrick's appeared to have died a swift and sudden death the moment he touched her. She wished she were less sure, but he'd been too naked to leave her in much doubt.

Patrick sighed. "This is going to sound weird, so don't get offended, okay?"

She didn't think she should make any promises, but luckily he went on without waiting for her response. "So my parents say it can happen, when you're out being a seal, that you'll get really attracted to some human on the shore—either another selkie or someone with selkie in them. And you'll come ashore and change and—yeah."

"Okay," Ellie said. Neither Maggie nor Torran had covered this particular point, but it sounded plausible to her.

"I'm sure that's what happened with you," Patrick said. "That's sure how it felt, anyway. But—you didn't smell right."

"Oh god," Ellie said, shame prickling all over with this confirmation of her fears. "I mean, I haven't been showering enough, sleeping in the car—"

"I don't mean you stink," Patrick said. "You smelled fine. But you smelled the opposite of sexy. You smelled like my mother or something. And you weren't into it either, so I thought I'd made a mistake, that you weren't the reason I was here. That's why I thought you weren't a selkie. But then, when you said your name, I realized, we're related! So maybe that's why you weren't sexy, once I was human."

"Maybe…" Ellie was dubious. "But why would you be here at all? I mean, why would your seal instincts have brought you here?"

Patrick gave her an embarrassed grin. "Seals don't care about that stuff. That's why Mom was worried about it. She says seals don't have any problems mating with their relatives, so selkies might not have any instincts against it."

"That's true," Ellie said, heroically attempting to sound clinical. "I've studied them. Both the males and the females return to the same breeding territories every year—to the same place where they were born. So the females do end up mating with their fathers or their brothers sometimes."

"Well, good thing we didn't meet while we were seals, then!" Patrick said.

"Yeah." Ellie sighed, depression suddenly crowding out embarrassment. "There's no immediate danger of that."

"Why is that?" He asked idly, more focused on fishing the last sardine out of the back of the tin than on the question.

"Because I don't have my pelt."

That snapped his attention to her very quickly. "What happened to it?"

"I've never had it. I don't know what happened to it. That's why I'm on this road trip right now—to look for it."

Patrick dropped the tin on the ground. "Whoa. I'm so fucking confused. If you've never had it and you don't know what happened to it, how do you know you're a selkie?"

Ellie suffered a moment of pure vertigo, wondering for one, crazy-making moment whether she could offer any proof that she *was* a selkie.

Patrick went on, "Because that's really bad, you know, if you're a selkie but you've lost your pelt. You'll die of it. That's what happened to Silas's mom."

She was instantly infuriated. Did he think she would take it *back*, if he pointed out how bad it was? Her confusion cleared. "That's *how* I know. Because I'm dying of it. Because the only thing that helps is selkie breath, which is what you did for me when you showed up. Thank you. I was in very bad shape. I also know because two Scottish selkies, one of whom is my aunt, recognized me and told me what I was." *And I feel it*, she wanted to add; *I knew it was true the moment I saw Torran change. I felt it in the deepest part of me.* But she didn't know how to say that without sounding foolish.

"Fuck, I'm sorry," Patrick said. "I live with both feet in my mouth. That totally sucks."

"Yeah." Ellie was slightly mollified.

After an uncomfortable pause, Patrick asked, "How are you looking for it? Where are you going?"

Ellie told him briefly about Elliot Thorne, her birth, and the selkie's-view paintings at the gallery in Bar Harbor.

"Shut up!" Patrick said.

Ellie did, briefly, and looked at him, half-curious and half-annoyed.

"I live right next door to Bar Harbor!" Patrick was nearly shouting. "You've got to come home with me. Silas will lose his shit when he meets you. My mom can help you find this Elliot dude—she can track down anyone! I'll breathe on you whenever you like. Fuck, this is perfect!"

Ellie stared at him, momentarily speechless. Overwhelm and gratitude swelled her throat and prickled her eyes.

"I'll get my sealskin," Patrick said. "We can eat more on the way. Your treat."

Chapter 24: Silas

July 2014 - Camden, Maine

At the sound of the back door opening, Silas dropped the bolt he was screwing into the nearly completed swing-set and spun around in alarm. Heidi was napping in her crib upstairs—the baby monitor receiver lay on the grass nearby—and Nora wasn't due home for hours. No one should have been in the house.

"Patrick!" He felt a rush of liquifying relief to see his son emerge onto the back steps, but stared at him in confusion. Patrick was supposed to be a seal right now, and neither Silas nor Nora had called him. Also, his clothes were very odd.

Patrick grinned at the expression on Silas's face. "I had to borrow this girl's pajamas."

Silas's eyebrows went up. A girl with attractive selkie pheromones would explain why Patrick was back so soon. Girl's pajamas were not an improvement, fashion-wise, over the assortment of stolen and borrowed swim trunks that checkered Silas's past, but they did indicate a certain lasting friendliness on the part of the girl. The idea worried Silas, since Patrick was only seventeen.

He worried more as Patrick held the door for a young woman who came out and stood on the deck, smiling at Silas a little shyly, but with a curious intensity in her face.

Silas was expecting the girl to have some selkie in her, but had not expected the trait to be visible in her appearance. He was startled by the resemblance she bore to everyone else in his family. In fact, she and Patrick seemed oddly matching. She was much smaller than tall, gangly Patrick, but with skin the same warm shade as his, and hair similarly dark and shiny, rippling with improbable blonde streaks. Their features were similar, too, their dark eyes similarly spaced above straight, elegant noses. They were absurdly beautiful, both of them.

Nevertheless, Silas didn't feel the least flicker of lust for the lovely girl. Maybe that particular selkie instinct wasn't as reliable as Nora thought. Or maybe he was too old. Or maybe human inhibitions simply had the upper hand with him these days. Whatever the case, he was grateful not to be lit with arousal by his son's girlfriend, who was, after all, young enough to be his granddaughter.

He took a moment to put on the shirt he'd stripped off in the sun. Heidi's nap time, his only opportunity to work on projects, invariably took place during the hottest part of the day.

Patrick stayed on the deck and the girl came down the steps into the yard as Silas crossed to greet her.

"Guess who?" Patrick said, watching his face with disconcerting intentness.

Silas took a closer look. The girl watched him back, humor in her bright brown eyes, and curiosity, but a hint of something else, too. She was *so* familiar. She had his mother's eyes. Not just their sunlit brown color, but their expression, happy and sad at the same time. And he remembered another girl—uncannily similar—laughing with a group of children on a riverbank at a girl's camp, and coming out of the darkness, shy as a doe, to claim the sealskin he'd left for her on the dock.

Not Patrick's girlfriend, he realized.

"I'm Ellie Murdoch," the girl said, shaking his hand.

Alise's daughter.

"*Ellie,*" he whispered, awed.

He'd thought about her so often, had driven himself crazy wondering about her. He and Nora had hoped, when they read about Alise's death, her car discovered underwater in the sound, her body missing, that she wasn't really dead but had simply made a permanent choice to be a seal. Silas had tried calling her back—not in any hope that he could persuade her to change her mind about her human life, but because he felt that even one conversation with her would settle questions that ate at him, even if the answers were painful. Many of those questions had to do with Ellie. Was she a selkie? If so, what had Alise done about her pelt?

But Alise had not come. He'd tried several times, wiping seven tears from his eyelids and rinsing them into the surf, calling her name against the crash of the waves. But she hadn't come. He tried to hope the problem was simply that he didn't love her enough for the spell to work. But his heart knew this wasn't true. She didn't come because she couldn't. She wasn't out there.

"But what about Ellie?" he had asked Nora. "What if she's a selkie? Shouldn't we check on her?"

The question had troubled them both. If Ellie was a selkie, how would they know? Short of finding her pelt, seeing her change, or asking her directly, what other ways were there of identifying a selkie? And what if she didn't know? "She could be dying without her pelt," Silas had fretted.

"And what if she is?" Nora had answered, pained. "There would be nothing we could do for her. It could have been destroyed at her birth. Alise could have hidden it anywhere."

Neither of them had been satisfied that doing nothing was the right thing, but Heidi had been born a year ago, not long after Silas's first attempt to call Alise and before they'd given up on her. Life had not been conducive to long road trips and spying on unsuspecting relatives since then.

Silas squeezed Ellie's hand tightly in his own, feeling he was too sweaty to hug her as he wanted to. Instead he kissed her cheek. The scent of her skin came over him unexpectedly—less smell than emotion, a familiar echo of what he felt inhaling Heidi or Patrick.

Mine.

He should not have worried that he wouldn't know if she was a selkie. He didn't know if her looks, her scent, or some other instinctive awareness told him, but the answer was as plain as speaking, as certain as gravity.

"I'm so glad," he told her. "So glad you're here."

*   *   *

In the kitchen, demolishing the emergency snack supply of canned salmon, Ellie and Patrick—now less of an eyesore in his own jeans and T-shirt—talked over each other with all the rude comfort of people who'd been related for years. In fact, they had met less than twenty-four hours ago, having taken turns driving all night from Delaware.

Silas had a clear idea of the forces likely to have brought about an introduction between two selkies of the opposite sex, one a seal and the other a human on the shore, but since Patrick seemed no more attracted to Ellie than Silas was himself, he felt no need to ask for details. Patrick didn't offer any. "Ellie was just sitting there in a trance. Her sealskin is missing and she gets really sick when she doesn't have a selkie to breathe on her—"

Silas, who was standing against the kitchen counter as the other two sat at the bar, turned away in agony at this confirmation of his worst fears. *Had Ellie appeared in his life just in time to fade away like his mother? This was all his fault. He'd told Alise* nothing *about being a selkie. Had she even known to save Ellie's sealskin?*

"Are you okay?" Ellie asked Silas.

He bent his head, focusing on mundane details to fight the tears. His feet were bare. The kitchen floor needed sweeping. "I'm just—"

Patrick said, with the perceptiveness that sometimes flashed out unexpectedly from amidst his usual tumble of high spirits and profanity, "Ellie has a plan. And she'll be okay with me to breathe on her. We just need to find this selkie dude in Bar Harbor that we think is her dad."

"My biological father," Ellie corrected. "I *have* a dad."

Silas inhaled slowly, breathing in hope. A selkie father might well know what had happened to Ellie's sealskin. Though old as Ellie was, a selkie father should have brought it back to her long since.

"What do you know about him?" he asked, but a querulous blast from the baby monitor at his elbow—he always kept the volume turned up too high, paranoid that he'd miss Heidi's waking—interrupted Ellie's answer.

Patrick ran up the stairs, and Silas turned down the baby monitor just in time to mute Heidi's shriek of happiness when she saw him. Silas laughed with Ellie as Patrick came back down carrying his beaming sister, brown curls tousled and cheeks rosy from her nap. Heidi announced, "Pa! Pa!" to Silas, as pleased as if she had invented Patrick herself.

With Heidi awake, the conversation got more fragmented. Silas moved through the afternoon in a blur of emotion—feeding Heidi fish sticks in her high chair, cleaning up as Ellie and Patrick bickered about who should get the first shower, starting for dinner a seafood casserole he'd developed as one of his specialties. He learned more about Ellie in bits and snatches—that the man Alise had married was a good father, the strange story of Ellie's trip to Scotland. He was both grateful and guilty hearing of the selkie aunt from the other side of the family who had provided the help that Silas had not. He was keenly aware of being surrounded by all his living offspring—irrepressible Patrick and happy, strong-willed Heidi, and now lovely Ellie, who reminded him in vivid flashes of his mother—her smile, the side-long humor with which she parried Patrick's goofiness, her calm kindness. His heart hurt for missing Alise, whom he had never had a chance to know.

Heidi seemed to recognize Ellie as one of her own and courted her shamelessly by bringing her all of her books. "Wee!" she insisted.

"Read?" Ellie asked, and for answer Heidi plunked herself into Ellie's lap.

Silas laughed. "She's a bit of a tyrant."

Ellie kissed Heidi's head and opened the book she'd been given. "You are a very charming tyrant," she told Heidi.

Nora walked in the front door just before six, already unsnapping her scrub top for Heidi, who was famously impatient around this ritual of reunion. "We have company," Silas warned her, and Nora looked up and paused, shocked, in the doorway. Ellie sat on the floor with Heidi and a book in her lap. Patrick grinned his mischievous smile from a bar stool. Silas set the casserole that he'd just retrieved from the oven on the top of the stove to cool. Clutching her shirt back together, Nora went to hug Patrick one-armed, exclaiming "What are you doing back, pup?" Heidi screeched with outrage at this infidelity, and Silas, who was already at Ellie's side, having anticipated the upset, scooped Heidi up and handed her to Nora as she turned, laughing, "Sorry, little pup." Silas kissed Nora, trying somehow to communicate a world of gratitude that she was home—along with a warning to brace herself—in the very brief contact of their lips over Heidi's head as she burrowed imperiously into her mother's shirt.

Patrick said, "Mom, this is my niece, Ellie Murdoch!"

Nora, who had just hooked a chair out from the table with her foot, sat down hard with Heidi, who was making indecent smacking noises, determined to pursue her nursing despite her mother's changing positions. Nora sought Silas's face, wide-eyed, knowing just what this would mean to him, and after this swift touch of gazes turned an amazed smile to Ellie. "My goodness! Ellie! How did this happen?"

Ellie said, "I was driving to Maine from North Carolina, and got stalled on a beach in Delaware. Patrick found me and—"

"I saved her life, Mom, and then I brought her home because she needs help," Patrick interrupted.

Nora asked, "*How* did you find her?"

Patrick rolled his eyes. "Good news, Mom. Nieces aren't sexy, even if you bump into them naked on a beach in the dead of night."

"Neither are uncles," Ellie said, making a face.

Nora laughed, and shot Silas a relieved glance. Silas, who had always been a bit disturbed by Nora's concerns about selkie incest, hoped this meant they could now stop discussing it forever.

Patrick likely shared this hope. He forged on, "Ellie's a selkie, too, but she's missing her skin. And we think there's a guy in Bar Harbor who's a selkie, who might be her dad, who might know where it is. I told her you could help track him down."

Nora shook her head, as if to settle all this new information into place. "*I* could help? I don't know any selkies in Bar Harbor, do I?"

"With your magic librarian skills," Patrick said.

"I see," Nora said. Nora's mother had been the librarian, but Nora had learned a few things growing up in the reference section, which is how she described her childhood.

Nora again caught Silas's eye. A great deal flashed between them—perhaps lovemaking between their sealskins had made them psychic at other times, too. Or maybe Patrick's tendency to gag loudly at much of what they said to each other had turned them into adept silent communicators. Silas saw that Nora understood how desperate he felt about Ellie because her face softened. It was only a flash, an expression in her eyes, a blink, but to Silas she had said, *Oh, my love. Of course I'll help.*

He sighed with relief.

"Tell me what you know about him," Nora said, and listened carefully as Ellie, with Silas and Patrick interjecting details from previous tellings, explained about Elliot Thorne's appearance at Ellie's birth, the paintings from a seal's perspective, the Bar Harbor gallery that didn't know his address.

Heidi detached and sat up with the vague, milk-dazed expression that always touched Silas and amused him in equal measure. The sight of his wife nursing his child moved him in a complicated way, the two of them so complete without him, a universe unto themselves, but also a small tableau of everything he held dearest in the world.

Nora said, "If he owns property, I might be able to find the address in the county records. But let's have dinner. It could take some looking."

Dinner was, for Silas, more of the wife-nursing-child feeling, except bigger and more chaotic and from an inside perspective. *He* was doing the feeding this time, and his whole family was eating—even Heidi, who no longer considered her evening nursing session a substitute for dinner in her high chair. Ellie took one bite of the casserole, which was made with shrimp and scallops and grouper and crab, white wine and breadcrumbs and plenty of cream, and moaned with happiness. "You know what makes it even better?" she said, looking a bit guiltily around at everyone. "No vegetables!"

Nora and Patrick exchanged a glance and both burst out laughing. "Grandma always made us eat our veggies!" Patrick said, aggrieved.

"We skipped it whenever she wasn't around," Nora added.

"We're obligate carnivores," Silas said. "Seals are, anyway. Nora researched it because none of us can stand vegetables. Heidi throws them across the room. We wanted to make sure we wouldn't stunt her growth."

Heidi, aware that she had become the center of attention, put a messy handful of the fish Silas had cooked especially for her, without the wine, into her hair, and then looked around at all of them with a slightly defiant smile.

After dinner, Nora gave Heidi a bath while the others cleaned up the kitchen. Neither Ellie nor Patrick had slept the previous night except a few hours in the car, and they began yawning uncontrollably as they loaded the dishwasher, setting each other off until Patrick complained that Ellie was making his jaw ache. She was too busy yawning herself to respond with anything other than an inarticulate groan. They went to bed at the same time as Heidi—Ellie in Patrick's downstairs bedroom, Patrick on the living room couch, and Heidi in her own room, which was Patrick's old one upstairs.

Much as Silas had loved having all his family gathered around him, he was terribly relieved to retreat with Nora to their bedroom and finally have her to himself. As soon as he shut the door she found her place in his arms, hugging him tightly. "How are you doing?" she whispered.

"What happens if Ellie doesn't find her sealskin?" He'd been swallowing this fear all day, but now it spilled out of him. "If I lose her like I lost my mother, if I have to watch it happen knowing this time what's coming... I can't stand that, Nora! I think I'd rather die."

"I know..." Nora just held him. "I know you can't stand it."

Silas shook in her arms, not quite in tears, but full of a nearly unbearable tension. "Why does it hurt so much? I just met Ellie. I never knew Alise at all! Why does losing something you never had hurt just as badly—maybe worse—than losing something you did?"

Nora didn't answer right away, resting her cheek in that spot against his chest where she perfectly fit. "Oh, Silas," she said finally. "Because that's you. That's your oldest, deepest wound—the father you never had, the missing sealskin that killed your mother. All your life, the things and people you've never had have hurt you most. Your whole life has been spent trying to fill those empty places."

Now his tears did spill. It was exquisitely painful, and yet a profound relief, the way Nora saw straight to the center of him, as if he were made of glass.

He remembered the feeling from earlier, the joy and the ache of having all his family around him at the dinner table. Nora was the center of it all, mother to his children, but more than that, his home. Without her, he would have no place to stand, no place from which to know and love—anyone at all.

"What would I do without you?" he asked.

She smiled up at him for answer, so he kissed her.

His desire for Nora never flowed far from the surface, but tonight she felt like half his soul—the most important half. He needed her the way a broken thing needs to be whole. His intensity burning against her ignited her, too, and in an instant the kiss went from a taste to a devouring.

The need to merge far exceeded any impulse toward completion. Their intercourse was a near-silent communion of interlocking gazes and joining mouths and bodies bearing hard against each other, and though their urgency was extreme, their pace was slow. They almost couldn't bear the space between them necessary for removing clothes, and though Silas needed to be inside her as critically as he needed to breathe, he held back, knowing that to continue was to end. Nora was the one who dragged him to the bed, her eyes holding deeply to his gaze as she joined them, sharing with him every unspeakable nuance of sensation and emotion.

The ecstatic grief of finishing was eased somewhat by a compensation Silas had never imagined before Heidi's birth—the sight of Nora arching over him, head tipped back and lips parted, viewed through a confusion of fine, white filaments. Her milk released, a manifestation of her pleasure, a lacy echo of his own, and arched in a dozen directions, falling as warm rain and beading in his chest hairs.

He was nearly asleep when Nora slipped out of his arms. Through drowsy lids he watched her pull on pajamas and return to bed with her laptop. He roused. "What are you doing?"

"Looking for Elliot Thorne," she said. "Go to sleep, love. I'll wake you if I find anything."

Silas had no intention of sleeping. He sat up and watched quietly as she found the website for Hancock County's Register of Deeds and searched for the last names Thorne, then Thorn. At least thirty names came up for each spelling, none of them Elliot.

"Now what?" Silas asked.

"I'm going to check all the surrounding counties, too."

He tried to stay awake, but as each search yielded Thorne after Thorn, but no Elliot, his eyelids started to flag along with his hopes. He'd been asleep long enough to grow stiff and cramped, slumped against the headboard, when Nora's excited gasp woke him.

"Did you find him?"

Nora pointed to the screen and he blearily read: *Robert Thorne and Anne Elliot Thorne, December 11, 1994.* He was looking at a news article, not a database record—a list of names and dates, fatal accidents that had occurred on a bridge that was being rebuilt. Nora said, "His parents! They have to be. They lived in Asheville, North Carolina—that's where Alise grew up. They still own property in Penobscot County." She clicked to another window, a Register of Deeds property record. "And here's the address!"

Chapter 25: Ellie

July 2014 - Penobscot County, Maine

Cell reception died miles short of the destination. Ellie, who was navigating while Patrick drove his family's aging Ford Explorer, glanced nervously at the turn-by-turn instructions on her phone. "I guess it's still working? I don't understand how." Ten minutes ago they had turned onto a county road that didn't even have a name, just some numbers attached to the stop sign. Since then, they hadn't passed another car or even a driveway, just unrelieved pine forest—the trees were some kind of needled evergreen, anyway—on both sides. At least the road was paved, but Ellie half expected the asphalt to end at any moment.

"I think it uses GPS satellites or something," Patrick said. "Just don't drop the route, because it can't recalculate without a signal."

Ellie sighed. Getting there was only the first thing to be nervous about. Then there was everything else. "That lady at the gallery made it sound like Elliot is not the nicest guy."

"But you're his fuckin' long-lost selkie daughter," Patrick pointed out. "He'll be glad to see *you*."

Ellie appreciated the reassurance, but she wasn't sure it was justified. If Elliot Thorne didn't have her sealskin after all, she couldn't imagine he'd enjoy having to tell her. If he didn't have it, or know anything about it…

She couldn't think about that now. One thing at a time.

But if Elliot *did* have her sealskin, why wouldn't he have brought it to her, the way Silas had been compelled to bring Alise's pelt to her at that camp? Ellie lived in the same house where she'd been born—in the very same bedroom, even. And unlike Alise, who'd lived too far from the ocean for Silas to sense when he was a seal, Ellie lived practically within spitting distance of the Beaufort waterfront. Elliot could have found her easily if he'd tried.

Nora had already left for work by the time Ellie and Patrick got up. Silas had given them the address, and been dismayed when they proposed to set out immediately after breakfast. "Do you have any sort of plan?" he had demanded.

"Sure," Patrick had told him. "Knock on the door and ask him where Ellie's sealskin is!"

Ellie had smiled apologetically at her newfound grandfather. She liked him very much, with his appealing mix of innocence and age. "That's my plan, too. Subject to adjustment as circumstances unfold."

Now Ellie glanced over at Patrick, whose lazy, one-handed grasp of the steering wheel stood in contrast to the frown of concentration with which he watched the road. He worried about moose, he had said. She still couldn't believe fate had brought him to her—her Little Uncle, she had decided to call him, because he was seventeen to her twenty, and because he towered over her.

Patrick, Silas, Nora, and baby Heidi: How amazing that she had this whole, secret, selkie family; that she'd found them, that they *felt* like family, far more than Maggie's family did—as if she belonged to their set. But she struggled with a painful, superstitious feeling that the amazing luck that had brought her to them, with their ability to prolong her life, must surely be fate's version of a consolation prize. *Sorry Ellie, no sealskin for you, but here is some good company and a few extra years.*

She could not possibly be lucky enough to get this family *and* her sealskin.

Not that I'm not grateful, Ellie thought guiltily, in case fate was listening. *This helps a lot.*

"Was it strange getting a dad when you were already in high school?" she asked Patrick, mentally shifting subjects. Listening to the stories last night at dinner, she had wondered how she would have felt if her mom had suddenly come back from being a seal when she was fifteen.

"Well, sure," he said. "But my life *is* strange, so that's normal. And Silas is really shy, so most of my friends never even noticed when I suddenly got a dad. He just stays home and cooks really good food and keeps the house nice—and looks after Heidi, now. When we lived with Grandma, Mom was super stressed out all the time and now she's really happy. And also—I know guys who got stepdads when their moms remarried, and that's shitty because it doesn't have to do with the kid, you know? But Silas really is my dad, and he thinks I'm great. So that's pretty cool."

"That's very cool," Ellie agreed. "And he doesn't seem like a *strict* parent…"

Patrick made a humorous noise in the back of his throat. "No. Mom's got all these fuckin' rules, and Silas and I are both looking at her like, *Why?* And half the time she doesn't even know—she's just doing what moms are supposed to do. Silas doesn't know what the fuck people are supposed to do. I think that's why he's happiest at home."

"Can't blame him for that," Ellie said. She was amused by the way the cheerful stream of Patrick's profanity had gone underground around his parents and had now returned.

The pine forest on either side continued uninterrupted by houses or side roads. Her phone had shown Elliot's address as forty miles from Patrick's house, on a route that led almost directly inland.

"Is it weird that a selkie would live this far from the ocean?" she asked.

Patrick said, "I was just thinking that."

Her phone spoke suddenly. "In two miles, the destination is on your right."

After that, Ellie was too nervous to speak until she spotted the mailbox—incongruous in this wilderness. She pointed doubtfully. "There?"

Patrick came to a stop in the road as they looked. The grass in the center of the driveway, which led through dense trees and vanished around a bend, was tall enough to leave some doubt as to whether anyone had driven on it recently. Ellie could see no sign of a house.

Belatedly, her phone announced, "The destination is on your right."

Patrick turned in. "Wish we'd brought some pamphlets we could wave," he said. "No one actually shoots Jehovah's Witnesses, do they?"

"I wouldn't count on that. It's so isolated, he could probably get away with murder." Ellie wrapped both arms around her stomach, trying to contain her butterflies.

"Shit," Patrick said. "That's helpful."

They drove for several minutes through looming woods, broken occasionally by bright yellow "Trespassers Will Be Prosecuted" signs. Several rabbits hopped ahead of them, zigzagging before bolting into weeds beside the driveway. "I might like to see a moose," Ellie said, just to break the silence.

Patrick said, "No, you wouldn't. We'd just have to sit on our asses. There is not one fucking thing you can do to hurry a moose."

With no warning, the driveway turned a corner, emerged from the trees, and ended at a clearing and a cabin. The cabin was small, with small windows. Once it had been white, but now the paint was cracked and flaking, revealing the weathered wooden siding beneath. The porch, and the three steps leading up to it, looked as if they might soon rot away from the house, though some newer boards had been clumsily nailed in place to shore them up. The grass in the small lawn grew knee high.

"No one's here," Ellie said, her heart sinking. "No cars." The driveway ended in a patch of gravel and a turnaround in front of the house. There was no place for another car to hide. "He's probably off being a seal."

Patrick drummed his fingers on the steering wheel of the Explorer. "We'll just have to keep coming back until we find him, then. But might as well look around while we're here."

"Don't try to go in," Ellie said. "We really could get shot for that. And if we hear anyone coming down the driveway, we're back in the car before they see us, like we never *dreamed* of getting out."

"Yeah. This feels like a shoot first, ask questions later kind of place." Patrick opened his door.

Ellie emerged slowly. Her chest was tight with anxiety, and she drew a deep breath to steady herself. Why was she so nervous? Elliot Thorne was an artist. And a seal. And probably her father. She shouldn't fear him. Especially if he wasn't here.

But she did. Because if he couldn't help her, that was the end.

Patrick skipped the rickety steps with his long legs and stood on the porch. He knocked gently on the glass of the storm door, then peered through the grungy window beside it.

"What do you see?" Ellie asked nervously, when he'd been looking a while.

"Kitchen," Patrick said briefly. "Dirty dishes that might be recent. And a fucking army of booze bottles lined up on the counter. Like he ran out of room in the recycling."

"Great," Ellie said, anxiety knotting even tighter in her chest.

She looked more carefully around the yard for signs that someone was here after all, ears sharpened for a car coming down the driveway. The woods seemed to crowd in from all directions. A tumbledown, open-fronted shed at the corner of the yard held a rusty lawnmower and some neglected-looking long-handled tools. The sun heated her skin to stickiness. Biting gnats swarmed her face. A path—the grass worn away to dirt, no paving stones or gravel—led around the corner of the house. Ellie followed it, and heard Patrick jump down from the porch to accompany her.

The house was somewhat bigger than it appeared from the front, and, judging by some segments of newer siding, had been repaired haphazardly over the years. The path led purposefully to the back of the house, where a screened-in porch had been clumsily enclosed. It had many more windows than the rest of the house, but they were all of mismatched sizes, as if they'd been salvaged from multiple sources. A small, concrete stoop marked the entrance.

Ellie froze, suppressing a gasp: The door stood open except for a screen, and someone was inside.

She whirled to warn Patrick to silence, but he was frozen huge-eyed, having already seen. He stepped beside her and they stared together.

A woman wearing a faded t-shirt and shapeless jeans, her hair in a long, dark braid, stood at an easel, her back to them. She feathered a series of fine, indigo strokes over a background of bluish-gray.

Elliot Thorne had an assistant? His wife?

But the woman was not assisting. Ellie was no artist, but she could see that what the woman was doing was not peripheral—it was the process itself.

Elliot Thorne was a woman?

But no, of course not—he'd been her mother's boyfriend, and the gallery woman had definitely said *he*.

The woman didn't seem to have heard them, which was strange. The car hadn't been quiet. Was she deaf?

A woman painter was infinitely preferable to a drunk man with a gun. Giving Patrick's arm a quick squeeze, Ellie went forward. The room was large, and light poured in through the odd-sized windows. A heavy table stood beside the easel, covered in paints and jars with brushes in them and messy rags. A daybed stood against the wall, and a stack of painted canvases leaned beneath a window. The floor was light-colored linoleum, liberally streaked with paint in many shades of blue.

She knocked on the wooden frame of the screen door. The woman startled visibly and whirled around in swift irritation. She held a brush in one hand and a palette in the other. When she saw Ellie, her face went blank with shock.

Ellie's own face might have mirrored the expression. Literally mirrored. Ellie seemed to be peering at her own reflection—aged a couple of decades and wearing different clothes and a streak of pale blue paint across one cheek, but otherwise identical. She and her reflection stood gaping at each other until Patrick broke the spell. "Holy shit," he whispered.

The woman beckoned for them to come in. Ellie opened the screen door and stepped inside, Patrick on her heels.

"I thought you were Elliot," the woman said, a little breathlessly. "He knows not to bother me."

Ellie's heart pounded in her chest. She understood something with her body that her mind had not yet accepted. Beside her, Patrick glanced incredulously from the woman to Ellie and back to the woman again. He said, almost stuttering, "You're—you two are—you must be—"

"*My mother?*" Ellie breathed.

The woman shook her head. "I don't have any children." The words sounded uncertain. "Who are you?"

Ellie took a deep breath. "I'm Ellie Murdoch."

"I'm Alice Thorne," the woman said faintly. Without watching what she was doing, she set the palette down on the table beside her, on top of some paint tubes.

Alice, not Alise. But the names were close.

Patrick turned his head and whispered very quietly in the direction of Ellie's ear, "Someone has her pelt?"

Ellie grabbed Patrick's arm to steady herself. If this was Alise, and she was enthralled...did that mean...*dear god, don't let it mean*...that Elliot Thorne had stolen her, and kept her here against her will for *Ellie's whole life?*

Beside her, Patrick introduced himself, but the roar of shock and horror in Ellie's mind was so loud she barely heard him.

The woman—Alice? Alise?—nodded vaguely at Patrick and said to Ellie, "You're very pale. Are you all right?"

Ellie shook her head.

Patrick said, "You're white as a sheet. I didn't know that really happened."

Alice—it was easier to think of her as Alice, since that's who she believed she was—pointed to the daybed against the wall, made up with a blue bedspread and only one pillow. It was clearly a bed and not a couch. Automatically, Ellie followed the suggestion to sit down.

Alice came and sat beside her on the edge of the daybed. Ellie looked at her face. There were little lines at the corners of her eyes. Her skin was delicate—thinner, somehow, than Ellie's. But otherwise...

Alice said quietly, "Ellie is my favorite name. It always was, even before I met Elliot. Sometimes I tease him that I only like him for his name. I always thought I'd have a daughter, and name her Ellie."

Ellie grasped for something to say, wondering what this woman believed her story was. Her thoughts felt like wisps of smoke. "How did you meet Elliot?" she asked, finally. Vaguely, she was aware of Patrick dragging a wooden chair over and sitting down.

"We were high school sweethearts," Alice said. "He followed me to college but we dropped out and got married..." She trailed off. Her mind clearly wasn't on the story. "Tell me about your mother," she said. "What happened to her?"

Ellie tried to collect herself. If Alice were really Alise, enthralled to forget, was there anything Ellie could say to make her remember? With Maggie, the things she *couldn't* say had been the important things. But Ellie didn't know what to ask.

She began almost at random. "Her name was Alise Miller. She was from Asheville, North Carolina—"

"So—" Alice interrupted, then stopped, shaking her head. "So are Elliot and I. Go on." She fixed Ellie with wide, brown eyes.

Ellie said, "Elliot was her boyfriend."

Alice frowned. "Elliot was *my* boyfriend. He's never been with anyone else."

Ellie shrugged and went on. "Her parents, my grandparents, are named Sandra and Rick. She went to college at UNC-Wilmington."

Alice took a quick breath as if to interrupt again, but then changed her mind, motioning with her hand for Ellie to keep talking.

"She met my dad, there. Douglas Murdoch. He's Scottish."

Ellie looked for some reaction, but Alice only nodded for her to go on.

"He was much older than my mom. He was a post-doc, and she was a freshman. He says they were crazy in love."

Alice's expression didn't change, but Ellie had a sense that shutters had come down behind her eyes, as if she were listening politely to a story she didn't believe.

Ellie struggled on. "She got pregnant with me and left school to be with my dad when he got a job in Beaufort. I think her parents were really mad about it."

A shadow crossed Alice's face. "My parents disapproved of Elliot. I haven't spoken to them since we came here."

Ellie nodded. At least Elliot hadn't made her believe her parents were dead. She continued, "I was born at home, very suddenly. My mom didn't have time to call anyone for help. Luckily, Elliot stopped by. He was the one who called the paramedics."

Alice frowned. "Not *my* Elliot?"

Ellie nodded, afraid to press the issue.

Alice's dismissive smile indicated that she had remembered she didn't believe this story.

It wasn't working. Ellie rushed to the end, ready to be done. "Anyway, when I was eight months old, my mom was in an accident. Her car went off the road into the sound and she… died."

"But it was Elliot's parents who were in a car accident," Alice protested. "*They're* the ones who crashed into water and died."

Ellie exchanged another glance with Patrick. Silas had told them how Nora had identified Elliot's parents. "Yes. In Asheville, right? They went off a bridge."

Alice had been watching them. "You know, the two of you look a bit alike," she said suddenly.

"*We* look alike?" Patrick demanded, incredulous. "The two of you look like…look like the *same person*, only time-traveled."

Alice said, "But you have the same hair as we do," as if the resemblance between her and Ellie were an established fact, not the elephant in the room. She reached over and lifted a handful of Ellie's hair where it lay loose against her shoulder. "I keep mine back so it doesn't get in the paint."

Ellie opened her mouth to ask why the paintings were sold under Elliot's name if she was the painter, but stopped. A very strange expression had come across Alice's face, and she lifted Ellie's hair to her nose.

The unexpected intimacy reminded her of Torran breathing across her face. *Torran.* The thought of him snagged somewhere in her chest. It always did.

Patrick should breathe on her, Ellie thought fleetingly. Then the thought vanished utterly, because Alice dropped her face into the handful of Ellie's hair, inhaling long and deeply, with an unsteadiness that Ellie realized was from tears. She froze, sucking in her own breath with surprise and discomfort, and as she did, she caught a hint of something, underneath the smells of paint and turpentine that pervaded the room. She leaned closer to Alice, seeking, drawn by that familiar thread.

"Oh god," Alise whispered. "Oh god, Ellie. *You're mine.*"

A sense of absolute belonging stole through Ellie—peace, a loosening of every tension-tightened muscle. *Home.*

Tears welled in her eyes.

"*Mom,*" she choked. The knowledge was as visceral as gravity telling her which way was down.

"Wow," she heard Patrick remark with a corner of her mind. "I should have thought of that—pups and mothers knowing each other by smell."

The sound of an engine and the crunch of tires on gravel made them all sit up straight and listen.

Alise hissed in alarm. "Elliot's home! You have to hide!"

Chapter 26: Alise

July 2014 - Penobscot County, Maine

There was no time. Through the house, Alice heard Elliot slam through the front door, shouting her name. He was frantic over the strange car in the driveway, of course.

"Back here!" she called, making sure her voice sounded normal.

Swiftly, she gestured Ellie and Patrick out the door they'd come in. "Crouch down and stay out of sight!" They hurried to obey, and she watched them duck down beneath the level of the windows.

Inside her was a roar of fierce, consuming possessiveness for the girl who'd just left her side—a hunger that felt like a need to take her back inside her body, where she could keep her safe and never lose her. And inside her equally was a tearing, wailing cry of grief that seemed to go on and on, because she had already lost this child who was no longer a child, this woman she knew with her body but not with her mind.

Alice had no understanding of why and how. But the beautiful girl had nothing, not a solitary trace, of brooding, lonely Elliot in her. She belonged to another world entirely. A world that should have been Alice's.

She met Elliot at the other door, the one that led to the rest of the house. Instinctively, she blocked his way. She didn't like him coming into her studio.

"Who's here?" he demanded.

He had not aged well. His face had thickened but still looked boyish and soft, and he'd developed a paunch while keeping his gangly limbs. His hair had thinned, and because haircuts meant going out in public, he rarely got them. His hair was too long, and stringy.

Elliot was the most familiar person on earth to her. She knew him as well as she knew herself.

She had no idea who either of them was right now.

Her pounding heart forced her to speak in breathless bursts. "It's interesting. My daughter Ellie dropped by for a visit."

He gaped at her, his mouth opening and shutting again.

She waited.

"How do you know it's her?" he croaked at last.

Alice had been holding open a tiny possibility in her mind that Elliot was not to blame. She had listened to Ellie's story, and it was a story she knew now—but only because she had been told it. She couldn't fill in any details. She didn't remember Douglas— meeting him, or loving him, or what he looked like. She didn't remember giving birth to Ellie. But the idea of being crazy in love (her love for Elliot had never been crazy), the idea of carrying a child inside her body, felt familiar somehow—felt likely. They felt like stories told by older relatives about things she had done when she was too young to remember.

A part of Alice was willing to be convinced, not that this life had never been hers, but that Elliot was not the one who had taken it. He might have said, *Who?* He might have said, *What daughter? You don't have a daughter.* He might have been a victim along with her of some terrible, unfathomable mistake.

His pale eyes reflected none of her own bafflement. Instead, she watched them fill to drowning depth with terror. She had never seen it take him over like this. And yet, his fear was always present, always driving him: fear of strangers, of going into public, of taking her anywhere people might see her, of ever letting anyone—even the UPS man or someone to help enclose the studio—come to the house. It was the demon he subdued daily with alcohol, and this early in the day he was not drunk enough to beat it back.

She understood in a flash: Elliot's worst nightmare was coming true. The world had reached out to claim her from him.

No wonder that in nineteen years she'd never managed to reassure away his fear of losing her. He'd known, as she had not, that she did not belong to him.

"Where is she?" he demanded. She saw his intention to shove her out of the way and wedged herself in the doorway. He had never hit her. She didn't fear him.

"Not in here," she said quickly. "I sent them to walk the loop trail so I could talk to you." The woods were full of trails. Walking was what she did when she wasn't painting—blazed trails, or followed the ones made by deer or other creatures, hiking for miles and finding her way back by luck and instinct. The loop trail was only a mile, though—and marked.

"There's nothing to talk about." Elliot yanked her out of the doorway by her shoulders and shoved her roughly, so she fell against the pile of leaning canvases. She felt something tear as she caught herself, and knew she'd put a hand through at least one of them. She didn't care about the paintings, except the one she was working on. Once they were done, they died for her. It was Elliot who cared, Elliot who stopped her from painting new ones over the old, Elliot who needed the money from selling them in order to buy liquor.

She jumped up immediately, too bent on stopping him to notice or care if she was hurt, sure he would make a beeline for the outside door. She hoped to god that Ellie and Patrick had had the sense to crawl around the corner, fully out of sight. If Elliot laid a finger on Ellie, she would *kill* him.

Instead he charged across the room, seized the wooden dining chair that Patrick had been sitting in, and smashed it into the wall behind her bed. It was the odd section of outer wall where Elliot had refused to put a window. He'd said he couldn't find one the right size, and had built the wall up there instead, for reasons that had never made sense to her. He smashed a second time, and a third.

Alice turned and ran through the house, true fear chasing her for the first time.

Elliot was after something inside the wall. He must have hidden something there, where the wall was strangely thick. He held some power over her that she did not understand, and she was certain he intended to use it now.

She had to stop him.

Elliot himself had been the one to teach her how. He kept his gun—his father's Colt pistol—in the kitchen drawer near the front door. He'd insisted on teaching her to shoot it, in case anyone bothered her during one of his occasional trips out for liquor and groceries and art supplies, or to cart her paintings to the gallery. Now that she knew what strangers he'd truly feared all these years, the thought flashed through her head: *Had he hoped she would shoot her own daughter? Or her daughter's father?*

Elliot always kept the gun ready to fire in an instant. She checked the full magazine, the chambered round.

She was back in the studio less than thirty seconds after she'd left, but an entirely new scene greeted her. Elliot was hauling a torn, green suitcase out of the crater in the wall. The suitcase snagged, though, and he snatched at the sleek and shining fur that was spilling out of it.

Ellie and Patrick materialized in the doorway. Patrick gasped and Ellie cried out softly.

Elliot whirled to face Alice, his arms full of fur and a wild light flaring in his eyes as he saw the gun in her hand. "Shoot them!" he shouted. "Do it now!"

Alice stared at him. She couldn't believe she'd been right. He wanted her to kill her own child.

For a pregnant moment, no one moved. The look of tense expectation on Elliot's face changed, and he dropped the sealskin in his hand, beginning to turn back to the hole in the wall.

Patrick roared and hurtled across the room, tackling Elliot and knocking him to the floor. Ellie was right behind him.

In the smashed wall, another glimmer of fur shone from inside the torn suitcase. Alice sidestepped the tangle of brawling bodies on the floor, drawn as if by the only truth in a universe of lies. She plunged her hand into the wall and drew out a second pelt.

Hers. Her sealskin.

Alise enfolded it in her arms. A seismic event rolled through her consciousness. She remembered the first ecstasy of wriggling into her pelt on the dock, but almost instantly that memory was overcome by that of fighting Elliot in a car in the pouring rain, the green suitcase, the fainting, dying moment when she knew he had her pelt as well as Ellie's, stomping down on the accelerator to end herself in the canal.

It was happening all over again.

Alise only faintly registered the sight of Ellie picking up her pelt and fleeing with it through the screen door as Patrick pummeled Elliot with his fists. Patrick struggled up from the floor a moment afterwards, directed one last kick at Elliot's ribs, and ran after Ellie, shouting her name.

All Alise saw was Elliot, his nose bloody, staggering to his feet. She saw the murder in his eyes when he realized she held her sealskin. He didn't say a word, or even glance at the gun she still held ready. He simply lunged at her.

She didn't think at all. She raised the Colt and fired.

Chapter 27: Ellie

July 2014 - Penobscot County, Maine

Ellie reached the Explorer, the glorious softness of her very own pelt weighing in her arms, and realized she didn't have the keys, just as Patrick came running up behind her. "We have to go now," she told him. "I have to get to the sea." She knew he was going to object to this, for reasons she couldn't be bothered to evaluate, but it was the only thing in life to her.

"Ellie, believe me when I tell you I understand how you feel right now."

She shook her head stubbornly, refusing to listen. A white truck that hadn't been there before was in the drive, half-blocking the Explorer. "Nevermind, I can take this."

"No!" Patrick shouted but she was already yanking open the driver's side door. Patrick ran around to the passenger side and jumped in beside her. Their hands collided as they jointly made the discovery that the keys were not in the ignition.

Patrick grabbed her wrist and held it tightly. "Ellie, listen to me. We have to—"

The sound of a gunshot interrupted him.

It was the only thing that could have gotten through to her. "My mom," she gasped, at the same moment Patrick said, "Your mom!"

"What if he shot her?" Patrick said. His face had gone tight and stark, which set off the swelling lump on his cheekbone. Ellie thought she remembered Elliot's skull connecting with Patrick's face at some point in the struggle for her sealskin.

"Come on," she said, sliding out of the truck, making sure to keep a firm grip on her pelt. She felt half-frozen inside but they had to find out. She couldn't go to the sea until she knew what had happened. "We'll stay out of sight."

They got to the corner of the house. Patrick kept a tight hold on her arm that was either for reassurance or to keep her from running away.

"Oh god," she begged or prayed, and peeked around the corner.

She was blocking Patrick's view, but when she didn't jerk back into hiding, he peered around her. She couldn't see Elliot. She could see Alise moving around, and let out a shaky breath that she seemed to be unharmed.

"Where's Elliot?" Patrick whispered.

She saw just as he asked, and pointed to the unmoving heap on the floor. She could see Elliot's leg, and his shoe, through the doorway. Something told her she didn't want to see anything more.

Alise came to the doorway then, her sealskin in her arms, and walked slowly down the steps. "Let's go," she said as she came up to them.

Ellie was frightened of the stillness in Alise's face. "What happened?"

Alise didn't answer, just continued walking and disappeared around the corner of the house.

Ellie and Patrick exchanged tense glances and together went a little closer to the doorway, Patrick still gripping Ellie's arm. The smell of turpentine reached her just ahead of the smell of smoke, the realization that flames, almost invisible in the sunlight, were flaring up and dancing over Elliot's still form.

"Holy fucking shit," Patrick whispered. "He's dead."

"Good," Ellie said. It was really all she could think. Alise was okay and Elliot wasn't in the way. She could go to the sea now. "Let's go."

Alise was already seated in the back seat of the Explorer, sealskin in her lap, when they got to the car. Ellie and Patrick got in and Patrick managed, with some awkward maneuvering, to get out of the driveway without hitting the truck.

The tug of the sea from forty miles away, an unbearable eternity away, was the only thing Ellie could care about, but Patrick asked, "Will anyone come looking, do you think?"

"That place will burn to the ground before anyone notices," Alise said. Her voice was so calm. She might have been discussing the weather. "He was a drunk and a painter. Oily rags catch fire all the time."

"You were the painter, though?" Patrick asked tentatively.

"I don't exist," Alise said. "I died twenty years ago."

A silent mile or two of deserted road unwound beneath them before she added quietly, "Elliot killed me."

* * *

The sea glinted at the end of the street as Patrick turned into his neighborhood. Obsession welled up in Ellie at the first glimpse of the ocean, a storm of desire so intense that her body could barely contain it. Her palms ached. She felt swollen and heavy with need.

Patrick said, "Go through the house. There's a path behind the house that goes to the beach. A more hidden spot."

Ellie was consumed by the thought of her sealskin, by the thought of Torran, by the memory of kissing him with his body pressing her hard against Maggie's van. That day, she had been under a spell of drowsy, sweet contentment. Now, remembering, she felt on the verge of an explosion.

"Ellie. Did you hear me?" Patrick was speaking slowly and loudly to her. "Take your sealskin and go through the house."

She managed a nod. *Through the house.*

She had her door open before Patrick had fully stopped in the driveway. Sleek fur filled her arms, the dense weight settling her as if she'd finally found her true, correct relation to gravity.

She stumbled blindly and righted herself against the Explorer, her feet carrying her without instruction through a door that opened for her, past a glimpse of Silas's face gaping at her in amazement, though dream-like rooms and into grass and sunlight again, through a corridor of green, dirt beneath her feet turning to sand, then rock, then air as she flew off a bank she didn't even see because—before her, foamy, churning, shining on forever and roaring its welcome, was the sea.

A charge built and built beneath Ellie's skin. A wild promise hovered now within reach. She dropped her pelt onto the rocks at her feet and shed her clothes, exchanging them in a process like alchemy for the soft, enfolding darkness of her sealskin. Her whole being gathered to an exquisite peak.

Torran! She was tumbling, dissolving, pulsing and golden, all her edges blurring and giving way. She inhaled the salt air and bounced across the stones and splashed at last into the sea—*the sea!*

Chapter 28: Alise

July 2014 - Camden, Maine

Alise emerged at the end of the path and watched from the top of the bank as the beige, speckled seal that was her daughter rippled into the waves and disappeared, leaving only a tangle of clothes behind on the rocks. Alise slid down the bank a bit awkwardly, her arms full of her own pelt and Ellie's sandals, which she had collected along the path. She found herself in a channel between two hummocks of rock, hidden from the other people—families with children playing further down the shore— whom she'd glimpsed from the top of the bank.

Watching Ellie, she well remembered the obsessive need that had compelled her into her sealskin that first time. But herself, as wonderful as her pelt felt in her arms right now—its weight, its dense softness—and as much as she yearned for the freedom and oblivion of being a seal, she was in control.

And she was not quite ready.

She set her sealskin on the ground and collected Ellie's clothes, automatically turning them right side out and folding them, stacking them in a neat pile on top of her sandals. It was habit—the same thing she would have done with any clothes left lying around, but she couldn't help wondering if it was a mother's impulse, too.

Those short, short months of Ellie's infancy had been overshadowed by her desperation to get Ellie's pelt back from Elliot, but she was pierced by the memory of their sweetness, too—the soft weight of her baby sleeping in her arms, the incomparable, fierce tenderness she had felt gazing down at that little face. She remembered the sharp pull of Ellie nursing at her breasts.

And, oh god, she remembered Douglas. Ellie had been her heart and Douglas had been her home. He'd been her rock, her safe place, her greatest consolation and her most exquisite pleasure. She remembered how he'd watched over her shoulder as the pink cross announcing Ellie's presence formed on the white stick, how he hadn't shown the least fear, but only said, *Marry me.* She could not remember saying yes to him, only surging to meet him, making love right there on the bathroom counter because, in that moment, they only seemed to have one body and one soul between them.

That had been twenty years ago.

Since then, she had lived in her paintings. All her energy, passion, enthusiasm. Her soul had been kept alive—if it had—in the motion of her brushes, the application of paint, the images that came to her only in dreams.

She crouched on the shore with her sealskin gleaming by her side like the one unbroken promise left to her. The ocean lunged toward her and retreated, vast and restless, leaving traces of foam a few feet from the toes of the very battered black clogs Elliot had picked up for her at Goodwill. Gulls shrieked and the breeze tugged tendrils from her braid and tossed them about her face. She inhaled the incredible, fresh smell of the air, tasted the tinge of salt on her lips. The sea stretched before her all the way to the sky. She clenched a handful of pebbly sand, hard enough so the little rocks bit into the palm of her hand. She wanted to impress the landscape fully on her senses.

Everything was sharp-edged, vivid, more *real* here by the ocean's edge. She was more alive with the sea filling her senses than she ever was anywhere else. This was not a new discovery. Her whole life, she had longed for the beach whenever she was away from it. She'd felt truly wronged by parents who insisted on a home in the mountains instead. But all those years with Elliot, though that longing had expressed itself through her paintings, she had not felt it.

Had she *forgotten* the sea? Had Elliot taken even that from her?

Not quite. She had not forgotten its existence. She had recognized the subjects of her paintings, as little as she consciously chose them. Elliot had not stolen her memory of the sea itself, but he had stolen her love for it. He had stolen all her loves. The ocean. Her parents. Douglas. Ellie. He had taken everything that mattered and replaced it with himself.

And now, she had killed him.

She searched, and couldn't locate within herself the feeling she knew as guilt—the ache of regret and protest, the longing to make what had happened *not true*. She was not glad Elliot was dead. She had not enjoyed watching him die and felt the horror of the details—the way he'd crumpled, and the blood, and the thought of flames consuming to a carbonized husk the body she had known so closely and so well. She was shocked by the way he had been fully there one moment and then utterly gone, how he'd been Elliot, then not, driven out of his body and his life by the bullet she had fired at him.

But she could not find guilt. Long ago, it seemed to her, Elliot had told her, *You will not live without me*. And she had not. She had been dead for nineteen years while Elliot lived a parasitic half-life feeding off her corpse. In the end she had killed him back. A life for a life.

There was no guilt in that.

Now, she felt a vast emptiness. Not like the sea, which teemed with life beneath its deceptively blank surface. Not like the sky, which was full of clouds, and birds, and the movement of air. She was empty like the great, black, emptiness of space, hidden beyond the sky. No one looking into that blithe blue would suspect the freezing vacuum behind it. No one looking at the small woman kneeling on the shore would suspect the void within her.

She heard a noise behind her, someone sliding down the bank, and turned in swift alarm, reaching for her pelt. The man with the young face and silver hair, like one of Tolkien's elves, who had held the door for her as she'd rushed after Ellie, came slowly towards her. He had the air of someone approaching a wild animal—reassuring, willing to stop if she showed signs of bolting.

She wasn't scared. She felt no impulse to snatch her sealskin from sight or run away. Instinct told her this man was a selkie, too. Patrick's father, he must be.

"May I sit with you?" he asked.

"I won't be here much longer," Alise said, but made room for him to join her on the side away from her pelt.

"I'm surprised you're still here." He sat with an ease that struck her as unusual for someone so gray. His body must be as young as his face. "Ellie's long gone?"

"Yes…"

"What's stopping you?" His voice was so kind. She turned to him instinctively, something unfolding within her.

Trust.

How strange.

He looked at her as if he'd always known her. He had remarkable eyes. Deep, chocolate brown, infinitely deep.

"When I leave, I'm never coming back," she said. "So I'm just trying to get things straight before I go."

"What sort of things?" he asked.

His curiosity was the kind that made her want to answer.

She found she was still holding the handful of pebbly sand. Now she threw it into the foamy remains of a breaker as it swished to its limit and began to retreat again.

"My mother told me I could say no," she said.

He laughed, a brief noise of humor and surprise. "That sounds like her."

She turned more fully toward him, surprised herself. "You know her?"

"A little, a long time ago," he said, watching her steadily, but with a new carefulness in his eyes. "She told *me* no. Which was hard, because *my* mother told me to stay with her and look after you."

Her mind ruffled up around his words, around what they seemed to imply. But it was too strange to guess at fully and speak aloud. He would have to be the one to say it. "Who are you?" she asked.

"I'm Silas. I'm…your father." He grimaced self-consciously. "Biologically speaking."

"Aren't you Patrick's father?" Irrationally, she felt that one should preclude the other.

He nodded. "Patrick is your half-brother."

She laughed. "He's so *young!*" She seemed to have very little control over the words coming from her mouth. Her mind was in free fall.

Silas's smile didn't quite reach the anxiousness in his eyes.

Understanding snagged and held.

"Apparently my mother didn't say "no" to you *all* the time," she said. She remembered, as if from another lifetime, her mother saying, *I haven't always said no when I should have.* Silas struck her as far too—*considerate,* somehow, to be a rapist. But then, she herself had never said *no* to Elliot. A lot could happen in the space between *yes* and *no.*

Silas was wry. "She said *yes,* very definitely, just the once. But even then, it was probably some recessive selkie genes that said yes—not her, exactly."

Alise, remembering an irresistible man approaching her camellia bush, experienced a revelation. *Recessive selkie genes.* Maybe *that's* what it had been about Douglas. The first thing about him, anyway.

"Were my parents already together?" she asked.

Silas nodded. "They weren't married yet, but…"

She felt a burst of sympathy for her mother. She doubted any moral argument on earth could have stopped her from intercepting Douglas on that sidewalk. If that's how Sandra had felt about Silas… "She really loved my dad," she told Silas. The echo of her own past tense stabbed her belatedly.

"Loves," Silas said firmly. "Ellie says they're both alive and well."

Alise sighed. *Alive and well.* She wouldn't see them again. They'd never know the same was true for her. But she was very glad to know they were still here.

"How did you find Ellie?" she asked.

He shook his head, a trace of amazement in his smile. "She found me."

"Me, too," Alise said faintly, realizing for the first time how remarkable it was, that a daughter she did not remember, and who did not remember her, had somehow discovered her in the wilds of Maine and returned her to herself.

Silas said, "We're very lucky to have her."

Alise's eyes filled suddenly with tears. "I don't have her, though. Elliot took her from me. He took everything." That was the void inside her. It was the emptiness left behind by everything Elliot had stolen from her, that she could never, never get back.

Silas watched her quietly, not speaking. She ducked her head against her knees and closed her eyes.

"I want to go," she told him wearily, not looking up. "I just want to disappear and never have to remember anything, ever again."

"You can," he said softly.

Her tears ran more swiftly. "I'm afraid," she sobbed. She understood suddenly what was stopping her, why she hadn't followed Ellie into the surf but was still crouched here, paralyzed.

"Why?" he asked.

"I don't want anyone to call me back! And someone always does! My mother, the first time. And I could never be a seal again because Elliot knew how it worked. He would have just cried seven tears and dragged me right back again."

"Did you love Elliot?" Silas asked.

"No, never." This seemed very clear to her now.

"You wouldn't have come back for him, then," Silas said. "What Elliot did to you wasn't love. That was an infinite selfishness disguised as love. You might have come back for him anyway if you had loved him, but you didn't. Seals are very simple. They come back for sex, and they come back for the people they love. And even then, they usually just turn around and leave again."

His words were like a silent explosion in her mind. They kept combusting and combusting. *You wouldn't have come back for him.*

If she had known, she could have escaped from Elliot. She would have been gone in a flash, never to meet Douglas, never to become Ellie's mother, never to spend half her life so far as Elliot's slave.

A loud silence, full of surf crash and screaming gulls and children shrieking out of sight down the shore, stretched between them. The void yawned again inside her, the bright world only the thinnest membrane over it—too thin to be real, too thin to hold against the darkness.

She could have said no to Elliot. She had been free to say it all along.

She was free to say it now. No to Elliot. No to guilt. No even to remembering him. No to her human life. And no to the void.

"Seals know how to say no," she said, almost without meaning to speak out loud.

Silas took a while to respond. "I think seals always say *yes*. Yes to life, yes to food, yes to a mate. But they say yes all the way, and every all-the-way *yes* is an all-the-way *no*. No to death, no to hunger, no to going without a mate. Your mother was kind of like a seal that way. She said yes all the way to your dad. So that meant no to me."

"But you said yes to her?" Alise was curious despite herself.

Silas nodded. "I did. But that didn't make it true love. For true love, both people have to ask. And both people have to say yes."

She thought for a while before she spoke. "Elliot said yes to me, even though I didn't ask. And I didn't say it back. But I didn't say no to him, either. So when I said yes to Douglas, I couldn't say it all the way, even though I thought I had, because I hadn't said no all the way to Elliot. That's how I lost…everything."

Silas said softly, "I see."

She felt impossibly tired. But also at peace. She put her hand on Silas's arm. "I think I've got everything straight, now," she said. "Thank you. I'm going to go."

Silas's deep brown eyes looked almost as sad as she felt herself. "I wish I could have done more for you. I never wanted to leave you alone."

Alise leaned to kiss his cheek. The scent of his skin came over her, not as powerfully as Ellie's had, but recognizable all the same. *Mine.*

"You've been here at critical moments," she said. He had set her life in motion, after all. And he had made her a selkie, which was the only aspect of that life that she still valued.

A new thought came to her. "My sealskin. Were you the one who brought it to me? At camp?"

He nodded. "I was under the dock when you put it on. I wanted to speak to you, but I would have scared you."

She smiled, unexpectedly glad to have this old mystery cleared up. "Thank you."

He gave her a crooked smile in return. "You're welcome."

He stood, again with that unexpected grace—his gray body moving with a young man's vigor. "I hope I see you again."

She only smiled up at him, as he stood dark against the bright sky, because she hoped never to return and couldn't say it back. "Goodbye, Silas."

"Goodbye, Alise." With one last nod, he turned and climbed the bank and vanished up the path.

When he was out of sight, Alise stripped off her clothes and never thought of folding them. The sea could have them. She lifted her heavy fur, glorying in its sun-warmed heat against her naked skin. *Oh*, this was right, this was good, this was the only answer. She was finally coming home. She slung the pelt around her shoulders, the golden electricity of it building, building in her body. She stepped inside, drew the sealskin over her head and dissolved in ecstasy.

This.

This.

In three rippling bounds she was in the water. In three more, the cool, heavy envelope embraced her completely. The limitless sea extended before her.

She was free.

Chapter 29: Torran & Ellie

Late July 2014 - Off the Coast of Maine

*T**he black bull came out of the sea like an arrow and bounced up the rocky shingle with a blind disregard for the other seals who had been peacefully sunning, and now, rudely awoken, bit out and hooted their disapproval in his wake. He reached a little beige female and began nosing her furiously, almost flipping her over in his enthusiasm. Woken abruptly, she didn't react as the others had. Instead, she lay very briefly still, as if stunned by the bull's enthusiastic onslaught, then became electrified and began nosing him back, joyfully burrowing into his flanks and rolling over and under him as he did his best to surround her on all sides at once with his wriggling body.*

The other seals gave them a wide berth. Several, radiating affront, left the shingle in search of better-behaved companions.

Soon the little female began edging toward the water, returning to nip at the bull's sides when he didn't instantly follow. Once he grasped the invitation, he came along willingly. Together, they slipped through the surf that pounded the small, rocky island—

visited by no one except seals and gulls—and beyond the breakers, headed south. The little female was certain of the way, and the black bull kept tandem with her, the water that separated their flanks no more than a thin ribbon, formed and flowing between them as they swam.

A couple of hours of steady swimming brought them to a different shore, this one dotted with humans and their houses. The little female was unafraid, and the bull followed her into a v-shaped divot in the shore, where two sloping shoulders of rock formed a hidden valley between them. Just beyond the surf, she lay still and fine tremors began running over her body. The bull sniffed her curiously, then began to tremble, too.

*   *   *

Ellie flung her sealskin aside, shrieking *"Torran!"*

Torran, emerging from beneath his own pelt a moment later, sat up in time to catch her as she hurtled into his arms. A frenzy of kissing prevented either of them from asking any questions.

"It's really you!" he exclaimed as their lips came apart in their struggle to get more of their bodies in contact.

"It's me," she gasped. "It's you. Oh, god, Torran—" Her mouth joined his again, and her speech subsided into whimpers in the back of her throat. His body's hunger for her was the strongest thing he'd ever known. The storm of her desire, a force beyond anything she'd ever known or imagined, swept every level of his consciousness. Nothing stood between them. She surrounded him and he joined her, a union that was everything she longed for and instantly not enough. They crashed together over and over, determined to break themselves against each other. At last, she cracked and spilled, her ecstasy billowing to repeated peaks that launched him too, to pulse and soar and cry out with her until, together, they slid down a long, sweet slope and came to rest.

They lay gasping with exertion and amazement, a tangle of limbs and still-joined bodies. "So that's what it's like," she whispered.

He made gradual sense of her astonished sense of accomplishment. "That was your first orgasm?"

She murmured into his neck, "No wonder people like them…"

"It was extraordinary," he assured her, rocking his hips against hers gently and savoring the little rippling aftershocks that went through her. She was some kind of miracle. She lay replete against him and yet he felt—in the nerve endings he unaccountably shared with her—that she'd soar like a kite on a gale again the instant he lifted her. Was it because she had her pelt, now, that with his cock inside her he could read her mind? Or at least, her feelings? He resolved to stay very still, so as not to leave her and break the spell that joined them.

"You found your pelt!" he said, realizing.

At the same moment she jolted away to look at his face, exclaiming, "Torran, how the *hell* did you get to *Maine*?"

"Swam," he answered briefly, grabbing at her hips, but it was too late. She'd parted them.

His dismay could not compete with the shock he felt coursing through her, practically ringing in her ears.

He was still in her mind, hearing not her thoughts but her emotions. *What was happening?*

"Can you hear what I'm thinking?" he asked her.

She shook her head, too bewildered and impatient to register his question. "Seals don't swim across the Atlantic, Torran. There are seals in the west, and there are seals in the east. The populations have been genetically separate for *one million years*."

She stared accusingly at him, as if waiting for him to retract his story. When he didn't, she went on, "Do you understand what that means? Not once, in the last *million years*, has a seal swum from Scotland to Maine and gotten laid. What you've done is impossible."

"To be fair, a ship helped me out," he said. "Probably wouldn't have made it otherwise."

"What happened?" she demanded. He felt an undertow of foreboding beneath her question.

She was still propped over him, her eyes fixed on his face. She was heart-meltingly beautiful. He wanted to feast his eyes on her. But he could feel that the rock was uncomfortable under her arms, so he drew her down and settled her against him, her head tucked into the hollow of his shoulder, his arm around her, her thigh thrown over his.

That's when he realized they were lying on his pelt. How had it taken him so long to notice, when every instinct in him should have rung alarm bells?

The telepathy! This must be why.

Her pelt lay in a heap only a few feet away. Experimentally, he reached the leg that was not under her toward it, and let his toes brush against her fur. He expected her to startle or stiffen against him, but he felt no change in her body.

Ellie, savoring how perfectly she fit in this spot beneath his arm, became aware that Torran was waiting for some reaction from her. "What?" she said. "I'm waiting to hear the story."

"Ellie. Can you feel what I'm feeling right now?"

It was an odd question, but she felt so perfectly close to him right now—almost as if they were the same person. Was that because of the sex? She had loved sex with Torran before, but this time, with her pelt, it had blasted her so wide open it didn't even seem strange that now she could feel his thoughts. "Yeah…you're really, really happy—not just your mood but your whole body—and…you've just figured out something amazing." She stroked the neat patch of fur on his chest. "What? And why do I know that?"

He was doing something with his feet. She looked. He was dragging her sealskin closer to them with a foot hooked under it. It was strange that she didn't mind him touching it at all. But then, now that she noticed, she was lying on his.

Suddenly, she understood, and her excitement flared to match his. "We're touching each other's pelts? And we can feel each other's feelings?"

Their eyes met, amazement radiating between them. She said, "Can we have sex again so I can feel what it's like for you?" And then she laughed, because his instantaneous surge of enthusiasm for this idea was as apparent to her as to him.

"I felt you," he said, desire already swelling between them at the shared memory.

"Tell me about the ship, first," she insisted, though she pressed her hips against his thigh with new hunger.

He sighed. "That's not a sexy story."

"Tell me," she said. "Start at the beginning. When you gave Maggie her pelt."

He felt a little sting of hurt beneath her words, and understood it perfectly.

"I didn't fuck her," he said. "She was all over me, but I was keeping my promise. I was pushing her off me when…"

"Logan smashed your head with a planter," she supplied. "One of those really thick ones by the back door."

"And they put me in my sealskin to heal?"

She nodded. "It was so scary. You were—I was afraid you were dead."

"I thought you were there," he said. "It's blurry. But you *were* there, when I changed?"

"Yeah."

"You must have been the last thing I thought of. You were the trigger for my return…."

She was horrified. "So you swam across the ocean to me? That's—suicide!"

"It doesn't make sense, though," he said. "If you were my trigger, I'd change if I happened to stumble across you while I was a seal. Which…I *did*, I guess. But we don't seek out our triggers. I wouldn't have swum across an ocean to you unless you called me."

He felt her bewilderment. "I didn't, though! I never would! I mean, I missed you horribly. I thought I might—literally—die without you. But I *know* seals can't cross oceans! I would never have tried to kill you that way!"

She fell silent, thinking. "I think *you* were the last thing I thought of as I changed, too."

"That would explain why you came back here to change when you found me," he said. "This is the spot you left from?"

She didn't answer. A terrible consciousness was taking shape in her. Torran felt it building toward awful realization, and stroked her hair, her back, already trying to comfort her.

"Oh, god, Torran. *I did.* I did call you. I took the boat out in a storm, and I was crying and it was pouring rain and the sea was blowing in my face and I screamed your name… I didn't mean to! It never occurred to me!" She began to cry. "I could have killed you!"

Her guilt and horror hurt him. He gathered her close and kissed her head, "Don't, Ellie. Don't, love. It's all right. I didn't die. I found you."

"*Why* didn't you die?" she asked brokenly.

He didn't want to tell her how close he'd come. But, of course, she felt his reluctance and understood it fine. She shook with sobs.

"Hush," he pleaded, desperate to get the story over and move past it. "I swam out to sea. And you're right—it didn't go well. I couldn't rest, so I swam until I was exhausted, and then I got caught in a fishing net. One of those big factory ships. I'll never hate them the same way again, even if they are overfishing… Anyway, I got really lucky and they pulled the net up before I drowned. And there was this one bloke—I didn't understand at the time, but I think he argued for me. He realized, maybe, that a seal didn't belong where they'd found me and I'd die if they threw me back. So they made a pen for me on the deck and fed me fish and dropped me off when they came into port. I don't know where. North of here, I think. Probably they were Canadian. And when I hit the water—that was only a couple of days ago, I think —the same instinct was still pulling on me, and I followed it straight to you."

"I can't believe you found me," she said. Her tears ran down his chest. They tickled.

She felt the tickle and wiped at them with her hands.

"I must really love you," he said, and knew it was the truth by the way he wanted to wrap himself around her and keep her with him always.

She pressed her body close against him, even closer than she'd been. "No more oceans between us. *Ever.* Because I obviously can't be trusted."

"Come here," he said, as if she could be closer than she was, and began kissing her tears, then licking them, until she couldn't help beginning to smile. He ran his hands along the lines of her body, feeling the miracle of her soft skin and swelling curves, the way her heart almost hurt, it was so full. She filled her senses with him, too, exploring all his textures. They lost themselves in kissing, and in time, their wanting so exquisite that they drew back and back from it until it towered too high to stand. It toppled and curled down over them, tumbling them until they lost all sense of up or down or him or her or anything but the perfection of being one with one another.

Chapter 30: Alise

November 2014 - Cape Lookout, North Carolina

*S*he hung in the shallow waters just beyond the breakers, watching the shore furtively, only her eyes and nose and whiskers breaking the surface. All afternoon and into the evening she waited, anxiously observing the white expanse of sand, empty except for flocking sea birds and the man. She'd been swimming for many days and nights, drawn further and further into these warm, southern waters, compelled by an instinct too insistent to ignore. Here, the impulse told her now, but she could not obey. The beach extended in a vast, unbroken sweep in either direction. Anywhere she came ashore, the man would see her.

The wind blew unceasingly from sea to land, bearing the man's scent away from her. She waited for him to leave, but he did not.

She had no choice but to haul out here. The instinct insisted.

But she could delay until dark.

The man lit a fire. The steady wind carried the smoke away from her, too, but the flickering brightness of the flames increased her unease.

Gradually, the sun sank behind the land. Even more gradually, light leached from the sky, until all that remained was a profligate spill of stars and a thin sliver of new moon trailing the sun beyond the horizon.

All around was enveloping darkness and the crash and hiss of surf to hide her as she came ashore. But she was compelled to the very edge of the circle of firelight, the one place every other instinct warned her from. She could wait no longer. Very quietly, she nosed her way through the surf, over the firm sand at the waterline and across the broad beach until it became dry and sinking beneath her. She was much too close to the fire, to the man moving around it.

She had no choice.

*   *   *

Alise shivered loose from her sealskin onto dry sand. The chill in the air bit her skin—her human skin.

No! she felt in furious despair. *I won't!* She drew her pelt tightly around her, tucking her head far inside of it, determined to make it take her back. Her sealskin refused, remaining stubbornly separate and inert.

It had refused the last time, too.

The last time, on the riverbank at camp. That must have been a thousand years ago.

She wasn't sure how long she had been a seal. Casting back through her memories, she could count only a couple of seasons since she had swum joyfully away from that Maine beach. Where she had met Silas. The memory of Ellie was there, too. And Elliot crumpling as she shot him, but she shuddered away from that.

She'd left Maine in summer, which had faded now to winter. Only half a year, when she'd meant to stay a seal forever.

Why was she here? A seal did not belong on this soft, wide, southern beach, even in winter.

A naked human did not belong here in winter, either. Even as tightly as she could wrap herself inside her sealskin, the chill air reached fingers through the opening that gaped in her pelt.

She wanted to shout with frustration, but she had to stay quiet because of the man.

Who had a fire.

Stealthily pushing her skin away from her face, she peeked out. The man was moving around his fire about ten yards away, his back to her, his shape only a dark silhouette against its steady, orange flicker. He seemed unaware of her. She watched, studying his economical grace as he knelt, the shape of his shoulders, his height, the angle of his head as he bent in concentration over a cooking pan.

Her heart lurched and soared in her chest and landed again with a jolt, knowing before her mind caught up.

Douglas.

She couldn't seem to breathe. She couldn't name or separate the emotions storming in her—joy, grief, and terror swirling like cyclone winds. She stood and took a step toward him, and then another, her pelt wrapped around her shoulders.

She wanted to run to him.

She needed to hide.

Before she could do either, he stood up from where he knelt and turned slowly to face her. His features were only darkness against the fire.

"Alise?" His voice reached out to her, uncertain but *his*. She would have known it anywhere. All those long years with Elliot, his voice had spoken to her in dreams.

He'd known she was there. He had turned his back to give her time. He'd moved slowly so as not to scare her—a man trained to observe wild creatures. Had he watched her change?

She couldn't move.

"Alise?" he called again. "Is it you?"

She thought she heard his voice tremble, and it gave her courage. "It's me," she replied softly, going toward him. The sinking sand underfoot, her shaky knees, made the distance seem farther than it was.

Part of her wanted to fling herself into his arms, but too much time and too many questions stood between them. Her pelt around her shoulders, and her nakedness, made a wary bubble around her.

She stopped a few yards from him, and he made no move to close the distance. But she still couldn't see his face in the shadows, and she circled the campfire by a few steps. He turned to face her until the flickering light illuminated his expression.

She couldn't read it, but she guessed that behind its stillness was a storm similar to hers. Her heart pounded in her chest as though it wanted to escape. He didn't look the same. His face had new lines and shadows, and his hair, though still thick, began a bit further back on his forehead and was threaded with gray. But he looked like himself, and his rightness sang all through her, the way it always, always had.

"How did you know I was here?" she asked, her voice unsteady. She tried to catch her breath, but her lungs felt squeezed.

"I called you," he said, his loved, familiar voice sending shivers through her. "I thought I saw you out there, earlier today. I've been waiting for you."

"How did you…" her question trailed off in confusion. *How had he known to call her? How had he seen her? Had he recognized her, even as a seal?*

"Ellie told me," he said. "She told me…everything."

"Everything?" she asked faintly. She was trembling, in long shivers that seemed to shake her from head to toe.

"You're freezing," he said. "You should get dressed before we talk."

She shrugged helplessly. She had nothing to put on. The sealskin covered her top half but the wind was turning her bare legs to blocks of ice. Douglas wore jeans and boots and a thick, windproof jacket.

He said, "I brought some things of Ellie's. She said they would fit. They're in the tent, in the blue bag. There's a lantern by the door." He pointed behind her.

She remembered seeing the tent earlier, when she was a seal.

"Thank you," she said, trying to imagine what Ellie had told him. That she was a selkie. How to call her back. And, almost certainly, where she had been.

He must know about Elliot.

"I'll finish getting dinner ready," he said. "You're hungry?"

"Very." She couldn't tell from his face what he thought of—whatever he knew about Elliot.

He still looked like Douglas. He still looked like *hers*.

She found it difficult to look away from him. And he made no move to break whatever it was that held them facing each other. Finally, she made a conscious effort, and turned in the direction he had pointed.

The tent was tucked into a hollow at the base of the dunes, a short distance from the fire. She fumbled with the zipper at the doorway and got it open, brushing the sand off her feet before she stepped inside. She hadn't been inside a tent since she was a child. The cabin where she and Elliot had lived, so far back in the woods, so old and drafty in the freezing winters, had been close enough to camping as it was.

Winters there had been *so* cold. The power would go out in storms and not come back on for days. Too cold to paint, the oils stiff in their tubes, she could do nothing but sit right up against the stove with all the quilts around her. As Elliot warmed himself from a bottle and eventually passed out, she had escaped the misery and boredom by drifting into dreams, the ones she painted, the ones that were always blue…

Suddenly, with her seal memories fresh in her, she knew for the first time why her paintings were blue. She loved blue and always had, but that was only partly why. The world had no color when she was a seal. Her seal's eyes saw vividly in a thousand increments of gray. Her human longing must have turned her seal dreams blue.

Inside the tent and out of the wind, the scent of sleeping Douglas, the wonderful smell of his sheets, his bed, his dreaming breath, came over her. She didn't reach for the lantern at first, but let her sealskin fall from her shoulders as she felt for his sleeping bag and lay down, pulling its warming folds around her, burying her face in his pillow, inhaling his scent deep into her body. It was like breathing in peace and belonging.

She wanted to be in his arms.

He was waiting for her outside.

She sat up again and felt for the lantern.

When she'd switched it on, the hazy light revealed Douglas's camping mattress and sleeping bag which must have been lying neatly before she rumpled it. Various bags and bundles ranged along the other half of the two-person tent. A large green backpack. A blue canvas duffle bag. Another sleeping bag in a green stuff sack.

She opened the blue bag and went through its contents. The years with Elliot might as well have been a time warp as far as style was concerned. Elliot had bought all her clothes at Goodwill —men's jeans and flannel shirts and t-shirts, the wardrobe of his college days. He'd liked it when she wore his clothes. Two decades of fashion had passed her by without a trace. Ellie's jeans were a degree of skin tight that Alise had only dreamed of achieving in middle school, when plastered-on Jordache denim with zippers at the ankles had been all the rage and well beyond her budget, but these were stretchy in some miraculous way, and went on easily. The sweater seemed to be made of a warm cloud, thick as wool but infinitely softer and without the itch. The socks and boots and coat seemed normal enough.

After some hesitation, she stuffed her sealskin into the now-empty bag. She could leave it here in the tent.

Douglas was waiting.

She wanted to hurry back to him. She wanted to stall.

Seals are very simple, Silas had said. *They come back for sex, and they come back for the people they love.*

Here she was in Douglas's bed, putting clothes on, rather than taking them off. The thought of sex with Douglas caused an inner lurch and a shiver that had nothing to do with cold. But sex hadn't called her back. *Douglas* had.

And she had come because she loved him.

She eased the tent's zipper down. Douglas was busy at the fire, his back to her again. God, how the sight of him went through her. He had been the most delicious thing in life, against her skin, all down her body. Would he still…even now that they were *old*… feel the same? Would he even want her now?

Douglas didn't know what she was like. Why would he? She had been someone different with him. She had burned with passion and stubborn will and she had gorged herself on the beauty of life, taking what she wanted without fear or apology. Who was that girl? The other Alise—the one she'd been her whole life without Douglas, without her sealskin—was a pointless creature without will or desire. She had been only what was asked of her.

That's why Elliot had taken away her sealskin. To get back the pliant, passive girl she'd been without it.

Only Douglas had known her whole, and loved her for it.

She zipped the tent door closed behind her and went toward him.

He turned from the fire and offered her a plate. A heavenly smell rose from it. Flounder, fried in butter, and very, very fresh. She gasped. Douglas didn't even like fish. "You *did* know I was coming!"

He smiled. He had the most beautiful smile. It almost hurt her, it was so lovely. "Not much to do out here. Thought I'd keep busy while I waited."

She began picking at the fish with her fingers, little nibbles, trying not to burn herself. She was *so* hungry. "This is delicious!"

"Here." He handed her a fork.

She selected a spot out of the campfire's smoke and settled cross-legged, already busy with the fork before she sat down. The fire was hot on her face, the wind frigid at her back. "How long have you been waiting?" she asked, between bites.

He filled his own plate and settled beside her before he answered.

"You're having fish, too?" she asked, surprised.

"It's Ellie's fault," he said, smiling at her sideways. "It was either learn to eat it, or make two meals every night. I even sort of like it, now."

All those years. All those meals, just him and Ellie. She'd only had either of them for a few months. They'd had each other for nineteen years.

She wanted to cry. She wanted to scream.

She put a bite of flounder in her mouth and stayed silent.

"I—called—you about a month ago," Douglas said, answering her earlier question. "I thought of going to Maine, but Ellie said you wouldn't mind the swim, and…this is home."

Home. She thought of the little Beaufort bungalow, with the blue and white curtains and the downstairs phone and the breeze off the estuary blowing in the windows. It was the only place that had ever truly felt like home to her. "Where are we?" she asked.

"Cape Lookout."

She was startled she hadn't recognized it. Twenty years of storms must have altered its shape. Cape Lookout National Seashore extended the length of the barrier isle directly across the sound from Beaufort. She and Douglas had come here when they were first married, taking one of the marine lab boats across the sound and hiking through the live oaks and wax myrtle and tangling vines to the wide, white beach on the Atlantic side. *This* beach. They'd come in April, when she was five months pregnant, and spent all day walking in the surf and hunting for shells and… Like now, they'd had the place to themselves. They'd made love on a blanket on the sand, right out in the wide open, where anyone could have seen, and lain naked in the sun afterward with the breeze blowing over them. She had been as happy then as she had ever been in her life.

"Do you still live in Beaufort?" she asked him. As if they were old classmates, catching up at a reunion. As if she hadn't just been remembering how he'd felt inside her.

The beach of her memory was a sun-drenched paradise, but around them now was bleak winter darkness. The Douglas of her memory had been as close as her own body, her own heart. Now they didn't even touch.

"The same house," he said. "The same job."

All of it going on without her as if she had never been.

Suddenly she was lost and aching, swamped by loneliness.

"I haven't been out here the whole time," he went on. "I knew it would take a while for you to get here. Just the last week, I've been spending nights out here. And today…I don't know. I had a feeling."

"Douglas," she said, looking down at her plate to hide how close she was to tears. She had taken the first edge off her hunger, but now her throat felt too swollen with sorrow to eat any more. "Why did you call me back?"

He was silent.

A terrible fear surged up in her. What if, now that he'd seen her, he realized he didn't want her after all? What if he saw how empty she had become, and knew he'd made a terrible mistake? Was that why he wasn't answering?

She began to cry. She hoped he wouldn't see, but a tear dripped onto her plate, the firelight making it shine like a falling star.

Tears.

As suddenly as it had risen, her fear subsided again.

Seven tears of true love. This is what it meant that he had called her. He'd had nineteen years to forget her, but he still loved her enough to cry for her. He hadn't forgotten her at all.

Finally, he spoke. "I've thought for so long about what I would say to you. I've made such eloquent speeches in my mind. I've lain awake nights, going over everything. And now—Christ, Alise. Do you know how beautiful you are? I see your face, and I just... don't even want to speak. I just want to drink you in."

Relief sang through her. He hadn't changed his mind!

A moment later, spirits sinking again, she realized it didn't matter. She knew what she was now, whether he saw or not. She said, "Douglas—" She should warn him. If he truly looked, he would not see beauty. Not now.

"Wait," he said. "I know we only knew each other for a brief time. And now that Ellie's told me—now that I've seen you with my own eyes come out of the surf in a seal's body—I realize that in some ways I didn't know you at all."

Despair pierced her. "I know I should have told you. I can see that, now. I just—didn't know how."

"How did Elliot know?" he asked quietly.

Her heart broke. He didn't trust her. How could he?

She said, "Oh, Douglas—I didn't tell him. I would never have told him and not you. He guessed, and he spied on me, and…I could never get away from him. He was like some horrible curse that I could never escape."

Douglas said, "Why didn't you ask me for help? Didn't you trust me?"

She was frantic to explain. "I *did* trust you…" She floundered, trying to reach the answer. "I was an idiot. I was a child. I didn't know what Elliot could do, and I was afraid…" Her voice broke on sobs. "I loved you so much, and I needed you so much, and I was so afraid if you knew I was…maybe not even human…you wouldn't believe me, or you'd be so angry I hadn't told you, or you wouldn't love me anymore, and…I didn't even *want* it to be true. I didn't want to be a selkie. I only wanted you, and Ellie, and our life. I guess I thought if I ignored it, it would go away. I thought if I ignored *Elliot*, he'd go away."

Douglas reached out and took her hand. It was the first he'd touched her. The warmth of his palm and the strength in his fingers felt like rope to a drowning person. She gripped him back, hard.

"I hope he rots in hell," he said quietly.

Oh, she wanted to savor this moment—savor Douglas and his touch and the way they were ever so slowly closing the distance between them. But her stomach congealed into a frozen lump at his words. She saw all at once that Elliot still stood between them —more immovably now than ever. If Elliot rotted in hell, she was going to rot there with him. She could never escape him now. By killing him, she'd become corrupt. His death, his murder, could never be undone or changed. She would always carry the ugly stain of him.

She suspected Douglas already knew, but she had to make it plain. She owed him that. Fate always snatched her away from him, but at least this time she would not keep secrets from him. Secrets had never kept either of them safe. She said, "I killed him. I shot him. I did it on purpose, right to his face, and I'm not sorry about it. I'm a murderer, Douglas."

He stroked the top of her hand with the one he wasn't already using to hold it. "I know," he said. "Ellie told me. She told me how he threatened her. I've had such nightmares—"

About her. She was the nightmare. She tried to pull her hand away, but he held tight with both of his and wouldn't let her.

He said, "Listen—I've had nightmares every night about killing him myself. You can't imagine all the ways I've murdered that man. I have shot him, stabbed him, strangled him, buried him alive, burned him alive. I have beheaded him with swords, run over him with tanks, drawn and quartered him. I don't think there is any way I haven't killed that bastard by now. You know why these are nightmares? Not because I don't enjoy them. I enjoy the hell out of them. They're nightmares because every time, I have to wake up and realize that it's just a dream. I haven't killed him, and I never will, because he's already dead."

She met his eyes. He looked back at her defiantly.

A very small part of her wanted to laugh. She couldn't. It was all too horrible. She *had* killed Elliot, and she would never laugh about it.

"I want to kiss you right now," she said instead.

She saw the leap in his face, the transformation to pure delight. She started to lean to him.

He frowned—only slightly, a quick flash of reservation.

She froze.

She was an idiot. Of course he didn't want her. *God*, why was she here? The sea was right there waiting for her. She'd go the moment her pelt would have her, and she would never, *never* come back.

She tried to pull her hand away, but again, he held on tight. "Wait, Alise. I want that, too, more than anything, but I have to finish. It's too important."

She looked down, still freezing with despair.

He shook her hand a little. "Just listen, all right? I love you. I always have, and by now I'm very sure I'll never stop. There have been other women. I thought you were dead, and I'm not made of stone, and—oh Christ, I was lonely without you. But I've never found anyone who didn't make me lonelier in the end. Because there's no replacing who you are to me. And eventually I realized that and didn't want to try."

She couldn't look at him. Her heart swelled with so much love, and so much grief, she thought she might burst.

"You asked why I called you back," he said. "I called you because I love you, and I want you to come home and be my wife again. I want to start all over. We might not be too old to have another child. I want it all with you, Alise—every blessed thing that we can wring out of the time we have left.”

Tears streamed down her face. Oh, how she wanted that, too. She wanted to come home to Douglas and live with him and love him every day. She wanted to see her parents again and put her arms around them. She wanted to know Ellie and love her and take pride in seeing her become the woman Alise had not had a chance to be. She wanted to talk with Silas again—her mysterious, unexpected selkie father. She wanted to sleep with Douglas beside her and wake to him every morning. She wanted to make love with him, feeling that golden flower that had once bloomed within her open more and more each time he reached her center. She wanted to be pregnant with his child. She wanted him to hold her firm, round belly and feel the baby stretch and move inside her. She wanted a soft, heavy infant to nurse at her breasts. She wanted to be a mother across all the days and years and stages she had missed before. She wanted it *all*.

But it was impossible.

“I’m a murderer, Douglas,” she reminded him in anguish. “Even if I don’t feel guilty, and even if you forgive me, I can’t just— there’s nothing I can do to make it go away. And I’m not brave enough to pay for it! I couldn’t stand to go to jail. I’d rather die a thousand deaths. I’ve lost too much of my life already—”

“That will never happen,” he said firmly. “I doubt you’d go to jail in any case, but Ellie and I went over every bit of the news, and so did Silas and Patrick and Nora, and there was nothing. The place burned to the ground. Nothing was left. A drunk painter died in a house fire. No one questioned it for a moment.”

“But where would I say I’ve been?”

"Alise," he said desperately, "That's not the problem."

What *was* the problem, then? Of course there *was* one—that went without saying. She never fully reached the happiness she could imagine. The world always stood in her way.

"What is it?" she asked, hopelessly.

He still held her hand, but she couldn't find the sprit to return his grasp. Her fingers lay like limp scraps in his grip.

He said, "You've lived in hell for nineteen years. And now you have the option to forget it all, and live out the rest of your days as a seal, which Ellie tells me is one of the nicest things there is. Being human again, having to live every day with the knowledge of what was taken from you, and the memories of what you've been through—I can't ask that of you, Alise. No one could. It's the most selfish thing I can imagine, asking you to come back for my sake and endure that. Not when you have another choice."

"Then why did you call me back?" Her voice was small. She didn't understand. If he thought they could never be happy together, that their whole future was already broken by the past… what was the use in any of it?

"Because…Elliot took away all your choices. He took what he wanted and he never asked what you wanted. And…I know you chose being a seal. And I know that might be the best thing for you now. But then I thought—at least you should *know*. You should know you have a home, and people who want you back, and a place you still belong.

"If you'd rather be a seal, you'll never even have to remember that you made a choice. And I will be all right, because I'll know you have the life you want, and that's the most important thing to me. But Alise—I can't live out the rest of my days wondering what you would have said if I'd asked you to come back to me—and never knowing, because I didn't have the courage to ask."

His voice had broken a few times toward the end. Now he simply looked down at their joined hands.

He was waiting for her answer.

"Oh, Douglas." She didn't hesitate. Her answer was not words but action.

She tumbled their long-forgotten plates aside and climbed into his lap. She put her arms around his shoulders and felt his hands at her waist. Eyes closed, she breathed the wonderful scent of his hair and his skin, and kissed his forehead while he held her, his arms tight bands of longing.

As if no time had passed, as if she were once more the girl stumbling from beneath a bush of passionate red blooms into her lover's arms, desire claimed her. She inhaled his scent and pressed her body to his and knew that nothing short of the taste of his mouth and all his skin on hers and the demanding motion of him deep inside her would ever meet this wanting. The breath she drew shuddered with need and she felt it coursing through him, too, all his muscles taut and yearning toward her.

She sought his mouth with hers.

His fingers pressed against her lips.

She opened her eyes, astonished.

His expression in the flickering campfire light was both haunted and determined.

"I want you to kiss me," he said. "And I want everything that comes after. I want that with you, no matter what. But I need to know your answer. I need to know, when I make love to you, if it's the beginning or the end."

God. She had almost done it again, letting her body answer, her body decide. Her body wanted Douglas and it always would. But wanting him was not enough. This time she had to choose.

And, having chosen, she had to speak her choice loud and clear so there could be no misunderstanding.

"I choose you," she said. "I choose you for the rest of my life. I want to be your wife and have your children and be their mother and live with you until we're very, very old. And maybe I will want to be a seal sometimes, but not for long without you. I want to love you. And I want you to love me. Have I left anything out?"

He drew a breath to answer, but she went on before he could.

"Yes, I have. I want to kiss you. I want to do it right now. And then I want to go into that tent and make love with you, and sleep in your arms and wake up and do it again. And in the morning I want you to take me home."

His eyes glowed with joy too fierce for smiling. Firelight streaked his face, reflected in the tracks of tears.

"Okay?" she asked him.

For answer, he cupped her face and drew her mouth to his.

She stalled his kiss with her fingers, smiling, though she was crying, too. "Yes?" she said.

He tipped his face to the sky and shouted over the crash of the surf, up to the infinite stars, so loud she felt the vibration as she leaned against his chest.

"Yes!"

Acknowledgements

The longer and thornier the path to publication, the more daunting the acknowledgements are to remember and write. *Seven Tears in the Sea* has been eight different books and took a dozen years to launch, and so many people helped in so many different ways an exhaustive list would be impossible.

A thousand thanks to Arlene Cox for tireless beta reading and precious companionship in the cold, dark trenches of the trying-to-get-published. She's a shining light and I thank my lucky stars for her. Marina DelVecchio for rescuing me from a paper towel predicament in a writer's conference ladies room and going on to become my writing hero and dear friend. And Jane Buehler for being an insightful reader, an inspiration, a kind and practical advisor, and a valued walking companion. Thanks also to P. R. Brewer and Nathan Kotecki for honest and insightful beta reading.

Many, many thanks to Russell Galen for being my friend even when he couldn't be my literary agent, for encouragement and mentorship and employment and insight into the ways of traditional publishing, however blocked they remained to me. Also for the spiffy shorthand moniker 7T, which is vastly better than the more obvious abbreviation, 7TITS. So much gratitude to Katherine Boyle, too, for vast patience, kindness, and encouragement on the first half of this journey.

Blessings and gratitude to Erica Hill for being my dream reader, and to Lynn Swain for reviving my lost hopes, both in very different ways providing bolstering and encouragement when I'd all but given up.

Many thanks to Susan Sewell for publishing the first edition of this story on her office copy machine, and to the ladies of Bookish Wimmin for being my first book club readers, so long ago they will likely not recognize the *Seastruck* they read in the book 7T has become!

So much gratitude to Aileen Macdonald-Haak and Jackie Methven, strangers of infinite generosity who read multiple early drafts to correct the phrasing of my Scottish characters. The story has changed so much since their efforts they likely wouldn't recognize it, and they must be held fully blameless of any mistakes in the published edition!

Deep gratitude to my grandmother, Ella Murdoch Miller Moore, who died years before I sat down to write this book, but whose presence I have sensed at every step, in the financial means to commit to my writing, in the passed down love of Scottish ballads through which I first learned of selkies, in her empathy for all wild creatures, in the names of my characters.

Thanks to Barry Wilson, for encouraging me to dedicate myself to this path when I believed it was impossible, for checking out all the books about seals for me from Duke's Perkins Library, and for all the drafts he let me read aloud to him so I could hear how they sounded. Thanks to my daughters, Clara and Helen, for all the years they've blithely told people I was a writer when tangible proof was sadly lacking. And to Michael Perry, for encouraging my dreams and being my indie publishing hero.

Infinite thanks to my parents, Joyce and Allen Moore, for all the years of emotional and material support and endless reading of drafts, for filling my childhood with magical songs and stories and for bringing me up in a bookstore and for believing in me and for far too many other things to name.

About the Author

Adrienne Moore is a writer, tarot reader, crystal and mineral enthusiast, amateur astrologer, and internationally recognized snail pornographer. She lives in Hillsborough, North Carolina, with an assortment of teens and animals, both domesticated and otherwise.